Victor yanked a mask from the tree rack.

"Victor, no!" Alias shouted. "It could be a trap!"

"Oh, yes," Mist said. "Did I fail to mention the masks must be removed in a particular order?"

With a shocked look, Victor set the mask back on the tree rack, but it was too late. The floor began to shake as all around the cavern hidden gears of massive proportions began to turn.

Mist laughed. "Oh, dear. It doesn't look as if we shall be able to complete our little transaction after all. Die well, Alias of the Inner Sea. And fond good-byes to you, Lord Victor." The dragon skull sank back into the pool.

The level of water in the pool began to rise until it poured over the edge, splashing to the floor. The sound of gears grinding stopped, and there was a moment of relative silence. Then they heard it: the sound of rushing water, as loud as the ocean itself. . . .

## THE HARPERS

A semi-secret organization for Good, the Harpers fight for freedom and justice in a world populated by tyrants, evil mages, and dread concerns beyond imagination.

Each novel in the Harpers Series is a complete story in itself, detailing some of the most unusual and compelling tales in the magical world known as the Forgotten Realms.

# THE HARPERS

**THE PARCHED SEA**
Troy Denning

**ELFSHADOW**
Elaine Cunningham

**RED MAGIC**
Jean Rabe

**THE NIGHT PARADE**
Scott Ciencin

**THE RING OF WINTER**
James Lowder

**CRYPT OF THE SHADOWKING**
Mark Anthony

**SOLDIERS OF ICE**
David Cook

**ELFSONG**
Elaine Cunningham

**CROWN OF FIRE**
Ed Greenwood

FANTASY ADVENTURE

# Masquerades

## Kate Novak
## and Jeff Grubb

# MASQUERADES

First Printing: July 1995
Printed in the United States of America.
Library of Congress Catalog Card Number: 94-68145

9 8 7 6 5 4 3 2 1

ISBN: 0-7869-0152-7

TSR, Inc.                                          TSR Ltd.
201 Sheridan Springs Road         120 Church End, Cherry Hinton
Lake Geneva, WI 53147                   Cambridge CB1 3LB
U.S.A.                                             United Kingdom

**To Judith Weddell—
science fiction teacher extraordinaire**

# THE PLAYERS

## THE HEROES

ALIAS—Swordswoman of the Realms, created by FINDER WYVERNSPUR; a cheap heroine.

DRAGONBAIT—Companion to Alias, called CHAMPION in his native tongue; a saurial.

OLIVE RUSKETTLE—Rogue Harper, self-proclaimed bard and role model to halflings everywhere.

## THE NOBLES

LUER DHOSTAR—Patriarch of House Dhostar, Croamarkh of Westgate. His only son is VICTOR.

NETTEL THALAVAR—Matriarch of House Thalavar, employer of halflings. Her granddaughter is THISTLE.

SSENTAR URDO—Bad-tempered Patriarch of House Urdo and would-be smuggler. His sons are MARDON and HAZTOR.

OTHER NOBLES—Other noble merchant houses in Westgate include ATHAGDAL, GULDAR, MALAVHAN, SSEMM, THORSAR, and VHAMMOS.

## THE SERVANTS

KIMBEL—Personal servant to House Dhostar, a geased assassin.

KANE—Butler to House Dhostar.

BRUNNER—Servant to House Dhostar; a harbor worker.

DREW—A halfling in the employ of House Thalavar; a shipping clerk.

MISS WINTERHART—A halfling adventuress hired by House Thalavar.

MAXWELL BERRYBUCK—A halfling in the employ of House Thalavar.

MERCY—A half-elven servant girl at Blais House.

## THE LAW

DURGAR THE JUST—Priest of Tyr, chief justice and master of the watch.
RIZZI and RODNEY—Members of the watch.

## THE NIGHT MASKS

THE FACELESS—Leader of the Night Masks.
THE NIGHT MASTERS—A ten-person secret cabal that serves the Faceless. Seven hold regional offices: HARBORSIDE, THUNNSIDE, GATESIDE, PARKSIDE, CENTRAL, OUTSIDE, and EXTERNAL REVENUE; and three have executive positions: ENFORCEMENT, FINANCE MANAGEMENT, and NOBLE RELATIONS.
MISTINARPERADNACLES—Advisor to the Faceless, a dead red dragon.
MELMAN, KEL, BANDILEGS, TIMMY THE GHAST, LITTLEBOY, TWIG, SAL, JOJO, KNOST, MARCUS, and ONE-EYE—Various underling Night Masks. There are others who run off or die before we learn their names.

## THE TOWNSPEOPLE

JAMAL—Street performer and social critic.
MINTASSAN—Young sage of Westgate and traveler of the planes.
BIG EDNA—Keeper of a tavern in a tough part of town.
DAWN—An elven dressmaker.

## AND INTRODUCING ...

THE QUELZARN—Legendary monster inhabiting the sewers of Westgate.

# One
# The Night Masks

Alias watched the young couple seated at the edge of the plaza fountain. They appeared as stark silhouettes backlit by a golden sunset. The swordswoman shielded her eyes from the glare and picked out more detail. The boy's tender face and oversized jerkin were both blackened by soot, and the young woman's face and apron were dusted with flour. Apprentice smith and baker's daughter, Alias guessed. Oblivious to the presence of others, the pair sat side by side, staring wordlessly into one another's eyes. The boy leaned forward; the girl leaned forward; their lips hovered inches apart. . . .

Then the girl turned her head and giggled. The boy scowled and frowned, certain that she was laughing at him, at something he'd done. Then the girl looked back at him; the light danced in her eyes, and she smiled. The boy's face twisted into a lopsided grin. He leaned toward the girl, and they began the courtship dance again.

Alias smiled, too, until her reverie was broken by the sharp cough of her reptilian companion, a sound akin to a sword being unsheathed.

"Fur-gathering about courtship?" teased Dragonbait. The saurial swiveled on his hips so that he stood upright, his heavy upper body balanced by a prodigious tail that now twitched back and forth impatiently. Although he stood at his full height, he had to look up at the swordswoman. Even the top of the flared fin erupting from between his eyes and cresting over his skull reached only to Alias's shoulder. Beneath his hooded cloak the

saurial's face was more dragonlike than human, and his
hide was made up of smooth, pebbly scales. He wore a
soft leather tunic cinched at his waist with a broad belt of
interlocking metal plates. In one clawed hand he carried
an ornate staff of ash decorated with mouse skulls and
orange feathers. He was trying to make it appear as if he
actually needed the staff to walk, so would-be thieves
would not be so quick to assume the staff was some powerful piece of magic, which in fact it was. To complete the
illusion of being a lame beast, he had even gone so far as
to give his enchanted blade to Alias to wear on her
weapon's belt.

Alias's hand slid down beneath her cape to her own
scabbard, reassuring herself that her sword and Dragonbait's weapon were both within reach. She wore chain
mail over her tunic, plate protectors over her leggings,
arms and shoulders, and an iron collar about her throat.
Even without the armor, though, there was no mistaking
she was anything but a swordswoman. Her attractive figure was muscled from years of drilling for combat,
trekking about in heavy armor, and battling monstrous
foes. She wore her bright red hair cropped short, and her
green eyes were constantly shifting about, alert to any
and all possible dangers. "The word is woolgathering,"
she corrected her companion.

Two passing pedestrians turned their heads to see if
she was talking to herself, for Dragonbait had spoken in
Saurial, a tongue too high-pitched for the normal human
ear, while Alias had replied in the ordinary Common language of the Realms. A magic spell gave her the ability to
hear and understand the saurial's "voice," and even
speak it, but only a decade of comradeship allowed her to
pick up the nuances of the accessory scents, clicks, and
postures that conveyed his mood and tone. Other reptilian creatures, such as dragons and lizard men, still often
understood him more swiftly and completely than she
did.

Conversely, the more subtle nuances of her language
often eluded the saurial. "Isn't wool the fur of sheep?" he
asked.

"Yes, but you have to say woolgathering," she replied.

"Why?"

Alias shrugged. "Maybe something to do with counting sheep before you go to sleep."

Dragonbait nodded at the wisdom of tallying a herd before resting, but still couldn't understand what that had to do with daydreaming.

"Actually," Alias countered before her companion could distract her further, "I was not woolgathering about courtship. I was thinking about how foolish those youngsters are. Look at them, oblivious to the world."

"Their eyes are for each other," Dragonbait whistled, and Alias caught a whiff of rose and honeysuckle—sort of a saurial sigh. He was thinking, she realized, of CopperBloom, his mate who had remained behind in the Lost Vale with their children. Alias also knew that the paladin had agreed to adventure so far south with her only because their mission was for the good of the saurial tribe.

"For each other, yes," Alias grumbled, "not for the world around them, or for their change-purses. They're oblivious to how long I or anyone else may have been staring at them. Splashing water in the fountain would drown out any sound of approaching footsteps. They're sitting ducks for any purse-snatcher, pickpocket, or grifter that happens by."

"They should be fairly safe," Dragonbait argued, puzzled by her assessment of the dangers. "They are in the middle of a city with lots of people around. And surely they have friends nearby."

Alias gave a derisive grin and snort, "We are in the middle of Westgate, my friend. Crime is this town's hobby, vocation, and major export. Didn't you read the sign at the port entrance—'Welcome to Westgate, Home of the Deadly Night Masks'?"

"I saw no such welcome sign," Dragonbait stated.

"I'm joking, Dragonbait. Remember humor?"

"I do not understand the humor. Maybe because I'm saurial."

Alias shook her head. She switched to the Saurial

tongue, "Or maybe because you're a paladin," she suggested. "Haven't met the paladin yet who could catch a joke on the first bounce."

"How many paladins have you met besides me?" the saurial asked.

Evading the question, Alias declared, "We should get going. The sooner we find this sage Mintassan, the sooner we can unload that staff and escape this wretched city."

Dragonbait nodded in agreement. The saurial wizard Grypht had arranged for them to meet the sage Mintassan and exchange the staff for a scrying device to help protect the saurials from attack. If not for the importance of the mission, the paladin never would have agreed to travel to Westgate. His two previous trips to this city had been fraught with peril, and he did not harbor any fondness for the merchant town.

Alias surveyed the six streets leading away from the plaza. "This way," she instructed, pointing down the least grand of the thoroughfares.

The two adventurers left the plaza and the young couple behind in the gathering shadows. The westward sky had turned the crimson of dragon's blood, coloring pink the mounting clouds over the bay to the east. As if in response to the dangers of the darkening city, the clouds were fleeing southward, leaving only starlight to shine over the city below.

The buildings surrounding the plaza, homes to merchants and taverns catering to traders, while not of the most recent or expensive designs, were neat and well scrubbed, and the roads immediately adjacent were spacious and relatively uncluttered. As the two adventurers probed farther into the city, the quarters became more tightly packed, the alleyways narrower and strewn with the debris of civilization. Alias, taking one shortcut after another, dragged her companion off the main flagstone roads and down alleys of hard-packed earth until the saurial paladin had seen more backsides of buildings than front.

As they stepped onto another main artery of the city,

Dragonbait noted that the merchants were pulling down the great overhanging wooden shutters that provided shade from the sun during the day and protection from criminals at night. Lanterns were already alight outside the bars and slophouses, though their weakly flickering flames served more for advertisement than to chase away the gathering shadows.

Dragonbait mewled once with consternation and pulled from his belt a folded piece of paper. He grasped the edges, and the sheet unfolded like a delicate Turmish paper sculpture. Dragonbait paused beneath a lantern pole, squinted at the human letters and lines scrawled in octopus ink, looked around for a landmark, then squinted again at the map. He growled.

Alias had already crossed the street and was about to plunge into a wide alley before she sensed that her companion was no longer in tow. With a huff, she stomped back across the street and tugged on the paladin's cloak. "Will you come on?" she demanded. "I'd like to make this exchange and find decent quarters before midnight."

Dragonbait did not look up from the map. "I do not recognize this area," he said flatly.

"Don't worry," Alias reassured him breezily. "We're on Silverpiece Way, north of the market. We cut down this alley, cross Naga Way, go left on Southgate Market Street to where Fishman's old place was before the fire, go right, and we're there."

"This alley is not on the map," he countered.

"Of course not," replied Alias, "You think an ink-stained mapmaker is going to risk his hide in this neighborhood? Anything you see sketched in the poorer sections of town—it comes from a cartographer's imagination—it's just doodles. The poor don't buy maps, and the wealthy never come this way. Come on. I know where we're going. I grew up here, remember?"

"You did not. You were born—" Dragonbait began arguing, but stopped when he realized he was addressing Alias's back as she headed for the alley.

He refolded the map hastily, shoved it into his belt, and chased after his companion, emitting clicks—the saurial version of grumbling.

Alias had not grown up in Westgate. She had not grown up anywhere. She was a magical creation designed by an alliance of evil beings who tricked the great bard Finder Wyvernspur into building her. Their intent had been to use her as their personal assassin, but she had found the strength of will to turn on them and destroy them. A swirling azure tattoo graced her right arm from elbow to wrist, a constant reminder of her previous enslavement, and of her quest for freedom.

Nonetheless, in order to complete the illusion of a real human, Finder had invested Alias with memories of growing up in Westgate. Although the memories were total fiction, they provided her with an intimate knowledge of the city—a knowledge that, so far, seemed infallible.

The shortcut Alias took now plunged through an even more decaying quarter of the city. The alley was wider, as if the buildings on each side did not want to get too close to the greenish sewage that flowed down the center of the lane. The walls had been blackened by decades of grime and colored with graffiti. Any windows or doors that had once opened to the alley at the ground level were walled over with mismatched stone only slightly less dirt-encrusted than the surrounding stone.

Dragonbait ambled after Alias with a growing feeling of anxiety. He concentrated on his *shen* sight, the ability to perceive good and evil, a gift from his gods to aid him in his duties. Although he could see nothing in the darkness, he could sense trouble up ahead on the right, two souls pricked by constant greed and rotted by a disgusting pleasure in the pain and humiliation of other creatures.

First one, then the other—hulking brutes, human, but a head taller than even Alias—stepped from the shadows. They were dressed in dark leather jerkins and trousers. The satin capes that hung over their shoulders fit so poorly that Alias suspected the capes had been acquired from much smaller and no doubt weaker persons. They had kohl-marked eyes and a broad swipe of soot running from temple to temple. They reminded

Dragonbait of raccoons—with unsheathed swords.

The leader held up a gloved hand and thundered, "Hold, trav'lers. You need to answer a few questions."

Dragonbait growled, and Alias gave a short, almost imperceptible nod. She didn't need *shen* sight to realize the pair meant trouble. "Who's doing the asking?" the swordswoman inquired politely.

"We are humble customs agents," said the lead raccoon, and his companion stifled a grin. "It is our duty to make sure trav'lers have the proper paperwork for items they bring in t' sale in Westgate, transactions they revoke here, and material for exportating—ah—taking out."

Alias, who could hardly check her own amusement, wondered who had taught this thief his patter. She heard the scrape of boots on hard earth behind her, and guessed there were more "agents" blocking escape from the mouth of the alley. Dragonbait would be aware of them with his *shen* sight.

"Ah," said Alias, throwing back her cloak in a gesture to show that her hands were empty, and incidentally giving her easy access to her scabbard, "but as you can see, we have no such paperwork. Your fellow customs agents at the watch dock determined that we carried nothing of sufficient value to warrant any fees. As you can see, we carry only personal property. So you need waste no more of your time on us." She smiled sweetly.

The second raccoon edged forward and whispered something in the leader's ear. The lead raccoon waved him back in annoyance. "Well, y'know those boys at the dock are so overwarked, they get careless," the leader said. "For instance, your pet—"

"He is not a pet," Alias snapped, her smile becoming brittle. "He's my companion."

"—carries an interesting staff," continued the raccoon leader.

"My companion uses the staff because he is lame," Alias argued, her tone now more severe.

"Nonetheless, we'll have t'zamine it, prob'ly take it back to our superiors for—um—" The thief fumbled for the word. No doubt he was new to the shakedown trade, more accustomed and suited to the mindless violence of muggings.

"Proper evaluation?" suggested Alias.

The thief nodded. "Prop'revaluation," he agreed and flashed a gap-toothed smile.

"I see," said Alias. "Dragonbait, show the nice man your staff."

The saurial limped forward, looking like a tired, lost, wounded puppy. He held his arms out with his palms upward, the staff resting across them. The raccoon leader towered over him and reached out to snare his prize with a free hand.

Dragonbait arched his tail around and slapped the ornamented end of the staff. The thick ash of the lower portion of the staff swung upward and smashed the thief square in the face. The thief dropped his sword and grasped his nose and mouth with both hands. Sputtering blood and bits of teeth, he fell to his knees.

Alias tensed, listening to the shuffle of heavy boots behind her and, without looking back, swung an elbow upward sharply. There was a cracking sound as her elbow guard connected with something solid. A rear-guard raccoon gasped and groaned, having discovered that grabbing the swordswoman from behind was not as simple as it looked.

Alias spun about, launching a kick in the direction of the groan. She struck her assailant in the hip, and he crashed to the ground. From behind him came a fourth raccoon, wielding a blade.

The swordswoman retreated a step, pressing her back briefly against the saurial's as she drew her slender sword. Dragonbait's hand slid back and patted her hip, indicating that, although he'd dropped the staff, he had no intention of drawing his own enchanted blade from the swordswoman's second scabbard. For such dishonorable opponents he preferred to go hand to hand.

The paladin hopped onto the kneeling raccoon leader's shoulders, driving the thief into the ground, then used him as a springboard to leap, snarling and clawing, toward the leader's companion. A trained fighter might have had the presence of mind to meet the charge with his sword, but the companion reacted instinctively, raising both arms to protect his face from what appeared to be a raging beast. Dragonbait landed hard on his foe, sending him sprawling back into the brackish green sewage flowing through the center of the alley, knocking the wind out of the thief. The last thing the human saw was the saurial's gleaming, sharp white teeth, then Dragonbait snapped his jaw shut and head-butted him in the face. The human remained motionless as the water dammed up behind him and finally flowed around him. Dragonbait rose, pawing and sniffing with distaste at the evil-smelling, oily liquid splattered on his tunic.

The last assailant, the one facing Alias, had the wisdom to hang on to his weapon, but not much experience in its use. He led with his sword, lunging at Alias, who neatly sidestepped the thrust and brought the heavy pommel of her own blade down hard on the back of his neck. The raccoon-faced man sprawled forward and did not rise.

The entire battle took only thirty seconds.

"No fatalities," Dragonbait observed as he kicked away their felled opponents' weapons.

"We can find the local watch and send them in to—" He hesitated, noting how Alias stood stock-still, scanning the rooflines of the buildings surrounding them. "Problem?" he asked.

Keeping her eyes on the rooftops and switching once again to the Saurial tongue, Alias explained, "The Night Masks guild is the strongest criminal organization in the west; some say it's the real power in Westgate. They didn't get there without more cunning than our humbled 'customs agents' here possess. The guild assigns watchers to spy on their thugs—to make sure they don't skimp on reporting their loot and to provide backup in case of emergencies. I'm looking for this group's nanny. . . . There!" Alias declared, pointing up at a roof to the north.

Dragonbait snapped his head upward, but caught sight of only a fluttering cape disappearing beyond the roofline.

"He'll go for reinforcements. Let's get moving," Alias suggested.

Dragonbait picked up the staff, inspecting it hastily to be sure its sudden impact with the Night Mask's face hadn't damaged it. Then he hurried down the alley after Alias.

A second alley crossed the one they traveled in, and they hurried through the intersection with all their senses on the alert. From ahead came the sound of music, singing, and shouting.

Dragonbait and Alias exchanged glances and headed toward the sound. Their ears led them to a small paved street that opened into a plaza dominated by a fountain just like the one where the lovers had sat. Probably both had been built by the same works project to bring more water to the commoners, Alias guessed.

A local street fair was just getting started all about the fountain. Paper lanterns swayed in the trees. A bonfire crackled on a patch of flagstone before the fountain. An old woman with a yarting and little boy with a drum were playing reels for girls who whirled about in the street and taunted boys on the sides to come dance with them. Tavern owners were setting up chairs and makeshift bars of sawhorses and planks. Dwarves rolled great barrels of ale and mead through the street to supply the bars. A couple of halflings were already halfway through one of their never-ending drinking songs. The air was full of laughter, shouts, mild curses, and the smell of spit-roasted fish.

Alias and Dragonbait hung at the fringes of the growing crowd. With so many witnesses, the Night Masks were unlikely to try an ambush, but Alias fidgeted with impatience and anxiety. Hanging around a celebration, while amusing ordinarily, was not getting them closer to their destination, and the Night Masks could employ more subtle methods of reprisal. With so many people about, an assassin could stand right behind her, and she might not notice until she felt a dagger between her ribs.

Fortunately, Dragonbait had other senses available. The saurial paladin scanned the crowd, squinting his eyes in the manner of a buyer trying to discern the fine print of a merchant's bill of sale.

"Well?" Alias prompted.

Dragonbait snarled testily. Elminster had once told him that human paladins detected the presence or absence of only evil, a less elegant and simpler sense, but certainly better suited to crowds. When the saurial paladin used his *shen* sight in a random gathering of humans like this, he was bombarded with more information than he could analyze. So many individuals, so many colors of souls and spirits and intentions, cascaded past him, around him, and through him.

Alias held her breath. An eternity seemed to pass before Dragonbait motioned with his muzzle toward the timbers being assembled into a makeshift stage. "That skinny human in the leather leggings and vest," the paladin said.

Alias locked glances with the lanky man lounging against the piled timbers, and the man quickly looked away.

"There and there," Dragonbait added with another jerk of his muzzle. "Beneath that apple tree. They may or may not be Night Masks, but they have the darkest readings of any among this rainbow of souls, and they definitely don't like our presence."

"They're Night Masks, all right," Alias said. "A reprisal squad, by the look of them. They'll be packing poisoned knives. Standard guild operating procedure requires they teach us a lesson for hanging on to our own property. They intend to corner us somewhere, poison and gut us, and leave a calling card on our corpses."

"Calling card?" Dragonbait queried.

"A domino mask," Alias replied. "To remind the populace that they really rule here, not the noble merchant families. The Night Masks do not like people standing up to them. It's bad for business. Makes it harder to intimidate the next mark."

"Shouldn't we alert the watch?" the paladin suggested.

"We are not in Suzail or Shadowdale. This is Westgate. The watch is safe inside at this hour. What we should do is a little reprisal work of our own. Come on."

Dragonbait followed after the swordswoman, though he was certain he did not like the glint in her eye. Alias weaved her way through the crowded plaza, stopping to admire the roasting fish, the musicians, the dancers, buying a loaf of bread from a baker and a bag of produce at a fruit and vegetable stand, and chattering in the dwarvish tongue of the south with an old dwarven brewer who was doing a brisk business among the crowd from his wagon of beer kegs. She pressed some platinum coins into the brewer's gnarled paw. The dwarf smiled broadly and turned to shout at his workers.

Dragonbait furrowed his brow in confusion; he knew how much Alias hated ale. No doubt she was enlisting the dwarf's aid, but the saurial couldn't imagine what the brewer could do to help them battle assassins. He turned his concentration back onto his *shen* sight to fix the positions of the three supposed Night Masks. The thieves circled around their quarry, following them through the crowd, stopping when they stopped, looking the other way whenever Dragonbait looked at them.

Once Alias reached the far edge of the plaza she nudged the saurial and, free of all human interference, the pair broke into a run. The three stalkers, no longer worried about remaining undetected, hurtled after them.

The chase was short, less than half a block, to a passage so narrow that Alias had to turn sideways to slip along it. By the light of the bonfire in the plaza, Dragonbait could see that their pursuers now had their knives out, and, as Alias had predicted, the weapons dripped with green ichor. The saurial dodged after Alias, annoyed that she had not shared with him whatever plan she had, no doubt because she knew he might not approve of it.

It was dark in the passage. The only light came from the entrance where they'd come in. In a moment, that too was in shadow as the Night Masks slid in after them. The thieves were laughing now, certain that they were about to make their kills. With his *shen* sight, the paladin noted that their evil was stronger when they were together than when they stood apart.

Alias stopped in front of him. In Saurial she ordered, "Hand me the staff and take your own sword. Stay low and give me a light on my signal."

Dragonbait passed the ashen staff and took his own enchanted blade into his hand. Behind him he heard one of the assailants curse as he realized his night vision was no better than his prey's.

"Now," Alias commanded.

The thieves heard a deep growl in the passage before them. They halted, and a moment later cried out as the saurial's sword burst with a great roaring noise into a brilliant blue-white flame that temporarily blinded them. When they finally adjusted their vision to the now lighted passage, they were much less certain of their victory. Dragonbait crouched before them holding out his fiery blade. The passage was already warming from the energy the weapon gave off. Behind the saurial, Alias stood with her cloak thrown back and her sword at the ready. Dragonbait could smell the green ichor that dripped from Alias's blade, and he gave a low chuckle, which sounded quite ominous to their opponents.

"Come on, boys," Alias taunted. "Are we going to fight or not?"

While the Night Mask enforcers were not unused to resistance, their opponents were not usually equipped with such deadly weaponry. Raw steel did not frighten them, but they had no desire for a taste of their own poison, and the fiery sword made them cringe instinctively. There was also something unnerving about the fey tone in the swordswoman's voice. They were assassins, not warriors, and they'd come to kill, not be killed. They began backpedaling down the passageway.

They found their way blocked by a larger-than-man-sized ale keg seated upright. It became clear to the paladin what Alias had purchased from the dwarven brewer. With a grin, Dragonbait closed in on the assassins. Alias followed just behind him.

"Surrender now, and I'll let you leave with your lives," Alias said.

The Night Masks looked back at Alias and Dragonbait,

then at the keg, then back at their would-be victims.

Dragonbait rotated his wrist so the point of his weapon traced little looping circles of light in the air.

The lead Night Mask dropped his poisonous weapon, and the other two followed suit.

"I don't think you have the paperwork for any of those weapons, boys," Alias said. "Better leave them all with me so I can evaluate them."

The Night Masks hesitated. Dragonbait growled and ran his fiery blade down the side of the building to his right so they could see the scorch marks left on the stone. Soon there was a pile of Night Mask weaponry lying at the saurial's feet.

"Keep stripping, boys," Alias ordered. "I'll tell you when to stop."

Out in the street the dwarven brewmaster had set up a second bar to handle the spreading crush of party-goers. The red-headed swordswoman had paid him to block the alley with the large keg once he saw the Night Masks follow her in. Then, as per the swordswoman's additional instructions, he announced that he would be giving out free samples from the great barrel of Chondath Dark Ale. He waited until he had a sizeable crowd about him, then tipped over the great keg standing across the passageway and knocked a tap into the end.

From the passageway beyond, the old dwarf heard the redhead say, "You'd better get moving, boys. I may not give you a second chance."

The dwarf moved back from his tap as three men came rushing toward him and clambered over the keg of ale. The crowd howled with laugher, for all three men were naked save for their domino masks. These they clutched in a desperate effort to conceal what modesty they had left. The trio bolted through the crowd as fast as they could and disappeared into the dark streets. No doubt they stopped eventually to steal some new clothing, but they were not seen in Westgate again.

As Dragonbait and Alias climbed over the keg, the brewmaster offered them both a mug of ale from the barrel Alias had purchased. Alias declined, but insisted that

Dragonbait enjoy a pint.

While the saurial sipped his beverage, Alias drew out the loaf of bread she'd bought and began using it to wipe green goo off her sword. She offered the paladin a bite first.

"You know I hate avocado," he replied.

Alias shrugged. "I've gotten quite fond of it. It has that rich, buttery flavor. The flavor of revenge." She popped into her mouth a chunk of the bread spread with green fruit.

"Was there a point to all of that, other than to amuse the crowd?" Dragonbait asked.

"A point?" Alias repeated. "We don't need a point. They tried to rob us, and we got even. It was a good joke. Humor, remember humor?" She finished polishing her sword and sheathed it next to the saurial's enchanted blade.

Dragonbait sipped his ale, looking at her over the top of his mug with a sad, paternal stare.

"All right," Alias snapped. "There was a point. Those three may actually reconsider their lives of crime. At the very least, they won't be leaving their masks behind tonight."

Dragonbait blew the air out of his cheeks with a harrumph. "Three tiny leaves plucked off the tree of evil."

"The axe hasn't been forged that's big enough to cut down the Night Mask tree in Westgate," Alias argued. She took another bite of avocado and bread.

"Then one must dig out the roots," the paladin replied.

"Dig out the roots. What's that supposed to mean? We came here to make a deal with Mintassan the Sage, not go into the tree-pruning business."

"I thought you might want to help the people of Westgate, free them from the shadow of the Night Masks."

"Why would I want to do that?"

"You grew up here, after all," the saurial said with a sly grin.

Alias glared at her companion, uncertain if he was trying to get her to renounce her false memories or really hoped to get her entangled in the web of treachery that made up

Westgate's power structure. "I did grow up here," she insisted. She looked up at the buildings around her. The memories felt so real, so fresh. She'd been on this street before, when she was just a little girl, chasing a cat she'd hoped to keep as a pet. "As a matter of fact," she declared, "our house was just around the corner. I can show you." She slid off the keg of ale and headed down the street.

"Alias, please, don't—" Dragonbait called. Now he wished he had not teased her. When her memory betrayed her like this, it often ended in pain for her.

But Alias was now in another world, one of nostalgia for a past she didn't really own. "Come on," she called back over her shoulder. "It shouldn't take us too far off our route."

"Boogers," Dragonbait muttered. It was one of the foulest curses Olive Ruskettle had ever taught him. He shouldered the ashen staff and loped after his companion.

"Around the corner" turned out to be one corner, three blocks, a second corner, an alley, and another corner. The part of the city they traveled through had seen better days. The cobblestones were intermixed with potholes and bald patches where locals had quarried the street to patch up their chimneys and walls. The paint on every door was peeling. Trees and shrubs in the gardens were all overgrown. Still, there was the occasional streetlamp made of a utilitarian post of iron with dimly glowing, smoking oil in a small bowl at the top.

All of the shops on the ground floor were shuttered and locked tight, but there were a number of small lights in the upper stories—constellations of candles, lanterns, and the occasional magical light stone.

"There," Alias announced in an awestruck tone, as if she had discovered the lost city of Shandaular.

She pointed to a small, two-story building sandwiched between a stable and a dressmaker's establishment. According to a weathered old sign over the door, the shop on the first floor specialized in second-hand clothing. The original proprietor's name had been painted over, but no new moniker had been posted to take its place.

"Very nice," Dragonbait said, as gently as he could

muster, "We'd better be going, though."

Alias scowled, "You don't understand. I was born here. I grew up here. I have memories of this place."

Dragonbait sighed, "I know, but they're memories sung into you by Finder. You were never here, really here, before tonight. If you'd like, we can come back tomorrow when its light and ask if anyone here knew Finder. I think for now, though, we'd better—"

Dragonbait's words were cut short as the front door of the shop smashed open and three humans barged out of the building—a man and a woman both with slight frames and close-cropped hair and a second man large enough to be a bouncer at a very rough bar. All three wore domino masks and were dressed in velvet dyed a black so deep that it absorbed light, as if they were chunks of the Abyss loose in the Realms. The big man carried a blazing torch. The smaller man banged a nail into the doorjamb. The woman hung a black domino mask on the nail, then nodded curtly at the big man. The big man flung his torch through the doorway, back into the building.

The black-garbed woman shouted up at the houses all around, "Jamal is marked!" then all three figures dashed down the street.

Alias raced forward and started to shout, "Fire! Bring water!" but her words were lost to the boom of a great explosion. The entire front of the store bulged outward, then tore loose in a gout of flame, knocking Alias and Dragonbait to the ground and covering them with burning rags.

## Two
# Victims of the Fire

Alias staggered to her feet. The smell of burning cloth, mingled with a complicated mixture of odors from Dragonbait, stung her nostrils. The saurial stood beside her, apparently unscathed, emitting the scents of brimstone and violets, then baked bread and ham, as his confusion and fear gave way to anger and worry. He stood before her, holding his hands on her shoulders, but it was several moments before she realized by the occasional clicking of his tongue that he was speaking to her. She'd been partially deafened by the blast.

Uncertain whether the saurial's hearing was any better than her own, the swordswoman signed with her hands, *I'll be all right. We have to help the people inside.*

She lurched toward the flame, then took a second step. By the third stride she had shaken off most of the bone-jarring effects of the blast, and by the fourth she was running into the blazing shop, Dragonbait hot on her heels.

Most of the planking that made up the front wall of the shop and the shutter that had covered the shop's front window lay smoldering in the street, while the frame that remained standing blazed ferociously. Alias plunged though the wreath of flame about the doorway and paused a moment in the foyer. The entrance matched her "memory." The door on the right led to the clothing shop, now an inferno of burning cloth. A few feet beyond the shop door was the staircase to the apartments above; the staircase handrail was draped with fiery clothing, and the steps gleamed with burning oil.

Dragonbait stood in the doorway on the right, peering into the shop. Alias signed, *Don't go in there, it's too dangerous,* but the paladin signed back, *Someone's in there.*

Alias grabbed her friend's arm to hold him back. She remembered Old Mendle, who ran the shop long ago, when she was a child. He used to let her play dress-up among the bins of garments he had gathered from the better homes, and which Mrs. Mendle had then sewn or knitted back into serviceable shape. He lived in the back of the shop now, alone since Mrs. Mendle had died. Alias released her hold on the saurial warrior and gave him a nod to proceed.

As she hurried up the stairs, using her cloak as a shield against the smoke and heat, she realized there probably was no Old Mendle. He was an invention Finder had put in her memory—unless he had drawn the indulgent clothier from some other, real, little girl's life.

Whether the fire's victims were those she remembered or not made no difference to the swordswoman. She was angry that her remembered home was burning. The stairway rail, from which she remembered having led imaginary attacks on invisible dragons, collapsed into the hallway below, and her craw knotted in fury. She paused on the landing where she had—no, where she remembered having had scribbled pictures with a charcoal stick. By the light of the fire, she could see there were scrawls on the wall still, but she hadn't time to examine them.

She turned on the landing and dashed up the second flight of stairs; the steps had begun to list inward from structural damage. The smoke was thicker up here, and she bent down to stay beneath its lethal embrace. She turned again and peered down the hall at the doors leading to the three apartments. The arsonists had piled rags before each door and lit them.

Alias pulled her sword and used it to thrust aside the pile of burning cloth in front of the door nearest to her. The door led to the apartment overlooking the streets, the apartment Old Mendle used to rent to transients with money to waste on the view. The Company of the Swanmays, an all-female band of adventurers, had once rented it, or so she remembered. Alias put her hands against the door. It was cool to the touch. She touched the knob. It, too, was cool, but it would not turn. The swordswoman stepped back, drew a lungful of smoky air, and gave the door a hard, sharp kick.

The doorjamb, already weakened by the fire, splintered, and the door swung inward. Alias peered into the darkness. She grabbed up a burning rag on the end of her sword to use as a torch. The room held four beds with straw tick mattresses, all empty. As she stood there, reassuring herself that the room was vacant, Alias heard a grumbling noise, and a section of the room's floor near the front wall collapsed into the shop below.

Alias leaped backward just as a serpent of flame swept up the wall and kissed the room's ceiling. The swordswoman thought of Dragonbait. His scales gave him some protection from the fire, but not from a floor falling on him. Hopefully, with the aid of his *shen* sight, he'd already found his quarry and had pulled him out.

She could hear shouts below—the locals had not been so far gone in their sleep that they could ignore the explosion. If they started a bucket brigade to the nearest water trough quickly, they might keep the structure from collapsing, though their main concern would be to keep the fire from spreading to their own homes.

The sound of something heavy falling farther down the hall brought Alias's attention back to her task. The door to the second apartment was opened, and someone had unfurled a rolled-up carpet over the pile of burning rags. A human shape, dressed in a flowing house robe, lurched out of the apartment, clutching a box the size of a wizard's tome. A woman, Alias guessed, as the figure collapsed over the carpet, seized by a racking cough.

Alias rushed forward and bent over the woman, noting the gray and red curly locks that escaped from beneath her garish silk head scarf. There was something familiar about that scarf, those curls. Alias pulled on the woman's arms until she had risen. The swordswoman was just about to ask if there was anyone else in the building, when the robed woman turned around. The words caught in Alias's throat as she caught sight of the face of the other woman.

"Mama?" Alias gasped. Immediately she realized how foolish she was to think such a thing, yet she could not stop the squeezing ache in her heart caused by all the false memories Finder had given her of this stranger.

The stranger's eyes widened, and she gasped, "Gods!" as if she recognized Alias in return. Her reaction, though, took Alias completely by surprise. With a sudden, panic-induced energy, the older woman slammed the heavy wooden box she carried into Alias's chin, smashing the swordswoman's jaw back and sending her sprawling down the hall.

Alias could taste blood in her mouth and realized that the floor was uncomfortably warm. It took her several moments to shake off the stunning effect of the blow. As her attacker dashed past her, the swordswoman grabbed at the other woman's leg, but came away with nothing but a leather slipper. She pulled herself back up to her feet and caught a last glimpse of the woman crashing down the charred and broken staircase. Her hand flung upward to toss the slipper after its owner, her mind insisting, "She's not your mother," but her fingers did not let go of the slipper.

From down the hallway Alias heard someone cry out. She shoved the slipper into her belt and retrieved her sword from the floor. The cry had come from the third room, the one at the back of the building. Once again Alias used her weapon as a pole and brushed aside the pile of burning rags planted in front of this apartment door. The heat from the hall behind her was now unbearable; the flames shooting up the stairwell were more white than red. Alias was sure her cloak would burst into flame at any moment, but still she felt the apartment door to be sure it was cool. From within she could hear high-pitched squabbling. The swordswoman steeled herself against what she was certain she would find and rushed into the room, slamming the door behind her.

Alias, breathing the slightly cooler, slightly less smoky air, was suddenly bent over with a coughing fit. When she recovered a minute later she looked up at the room's inhabitants—a family of halflings. They'd gone silent at her arrival, but once she stopped coughing, they ignored her and returned to squabbling and rushing about.

There were seven of them—no, eight, Alias corrected, trying to count them as they dashed about like fish in a pond. They were dressed in their nightshirts and engaged in packing all their worldly belongings into a trunk so large that even a hill giant might think twice before lifting it. Mama Halfling was overseeing everything that went in, rejecting things she did not consider worthy of the limited space—pipe collections, mug collections, rock collections, bottle collections. This resulted in the squabbling, since Papa Halfling and the Junior Halflings insisted their contributions were invaluable.

Alias felt the door warming at her back and saw the smoke winding up her legs as it crept beneath the door and between the floorboards. She staggered forward, pushing Mama Halfling and most of her brood away from the chest, toward the window.

"Have you gone nuts?" Alias cried. "This isn't moving day! You haven't got time to pack! You're going to be troll meat any minute now!" She scooped up the closest halfling child, a girl no higher than her knee, and slammed open the window shutters.

The room overlooked an alley, where a crowd had already gathered. In the center of the crowd Dragonbait knelt over a prone human. Alias gave a shout and caught the saurial's attention. On her signal he strode to the window, set down the staff, and waited. One by one, Alias dropped halfling children into the paladin's arms. Dragonbait caught them easily, as if he fielded plummeting children every day of his life, and handed them off to others in the crowd. The children shrieked with delight, and the crowd applauded each catch.

There was a brief argument between Mama and Papa Halfling over who would go down last. Alias eyed the door anxiously. It's shellac veneer was bubbling and steaming as the wood on the opposite side was consumed in the hallway. Alias picked up Mama and, with not a little pleasure, tossed her out the window to Dragonbait below.

As she reached down for Papa Halfling, who clutched his pipe collection to his chest, the door broke off its hinges and fell to the floor. A monster of yellow and white fire leaped into the room, making for the fresh air coming from the window and the last victims it could claim.

Alias half jumped, half fell out the window, dragging Papa Halfling with her. She managed to twist enough so that she broke the halfling's fall with her own body, but nothing broke her fall. She landed seat first on the hard-packed dirt, and the pain that sliced up her spine brought tears to her eyes.

Papa Halfling rolled off the swordswoman with a wink and a tip of an imaginary hat and proceeded to help Mama Halfling gather their brood. A bucket brigade had formed, but the workers were concentrating on wetting down the roofs and walls of adjacent buildings. The used clothing shop had been abandoned to its fate. Alias suspected that the brigade did not want to be seen putting out a fire started by the Night Masks.

Mama Halfling took a last look up at the window where the family's possessions were now being devoured by the beast fire. She sighed. Then, without so much as a good-bye, the family disappeared down the street and into the darkness. Alias wondered idly where they would go, but since she'd also noted that both Mama and Papa had bulging money belts strapped around their night-shirts, she didn't feel obliged to worry about their future.

She was seized with another coughing fit, and every hack sent a jarring stab of pain down her lower back. When the fit subsided, she was aware of Dragonbait kneeling beside her. "Are you going to be all right?" the paladin asked.

"Took too much smoke," Alias replied, unclasping her cape, hoping the cool night air on her back would relieve her sense of suffocating. "And I *really* hurt my tail when I landed."

"I think you *lost* your tail when you landed," the saurial teased, pretending to look around for a detached appendage.

"If I lost it, it couldn't hurt this bad," Alias complained.

Dragonbait laid his hands on her back and began whispering a prayer to his god for the gift of healing. Alias remained politely silent. Praying generally left her uncomfortable, as did anything to do with the gods. After ten years in the paladin's company, though, his healing prayer felt to her more like a lullaby, summoning in her spirit a sense of being cherished.

The paladin's hands began to glow gently with a blue light, which slid down along her body. The tenseness in her lungs eased, and the pain in her posterior region subsided. She still felt as sore as a landshark tunneling through the walls of Waterdeep, but now at least she could stand without agony.

Dragonbait helped her slowly to her feet. He made a face as he caught sight of her jaw, which had turned purple and swollen. "What happened to your face?" he asked with concern.

Alias tried to explain, but with the paladin's hands pressing about her chin, her words came out, "Ikoddajoorybuck." She paused and waited as more blue light flowed from the saurial's hands, this time to her face. In a moment, the swelling had subsided, and she repeated her words more clearly, "I caught a jewelry box under the chin. Did you see an old woman come out. Housecoat, scarf, one slipper?"

Dragonbait shook his head, "I had to come out the back door. The fire was too strong. They'd set pine tar torches in the clothing and oil on the floor." He bent over and retrieved the staff.

"With a touch of smoke powder for a big bang to make sure everyone knows it wasn't an accident," the swordswoman added.

"I take it this old woman wears the mate to the slipper tucked in your belt?" the saurial asked.

Alias looked down in surprise; she'd forgotten she'd hung on to it. "For some reason she was frightened of me," the swordswoman explained. "She attacked me and ran. I hope she got out alive."

"This is the one I sensed," Dragonbait said, nodding curtly at the human form sprawled in the alleyway. "He died before I could help him."

Alias forced herself to look down at the man Dragonbait had tried to rescue. To her relief, it was not Old Mendle. From the gaudy clothing the man wore she guessed he had been the current shop owner. The fire had barely touched him, and he hadn't died from breathing the smoke. There were great splotches of red on his yellow silk shirt and in one of his gashed hands he clutched a domino mask with a torn string.

"Stabbed," Alias said. "He must have come in on them while they were setting the fire."

"I do not like these Night Masks at all," Dragonbait declared.

"No one does, but they're too afraid to do anything. You can see what happens to their enemies." Alias looked around at the crowd. They were watching for the clothing shop to collapse. No one came forward to collect the body of the shopkeeper. Now that the heroics were through, no one wanted to be seen talking to the heroes. And of course there was no sign of the City Watch. "A typical Westgate evening," Alias muttered.

"The Night Mask agents shouted that Jamal was marked," the paladin reminded her. "Do you think he is Jamal? Or the old woman is?"

"Well, it's hard to imagine they had it in for the halflings. The old woman—" Alias hesitated. She switched to the Saurial tongue. "She's my mother. Finder left me a memory that she's my mother, but I don't know her name. She must have thought I was nuts, calling her mama." Alias kicked furiously at a hunk of smoking timber that had fallen from the shop, spraying sparks through the alley.

Dragonbait plucked her cape from the ground. It was scorched and smoke-drenched, but he hoped she would take comfort in the feel of its weight on her shoulders. "We should leave this ghost home. There is nothing for you here."

The roof of the shop crashed through the second story to the ground. Now that it was down, the bucket brigade turned its attention to the ruined shop.

"Why did Finder choose this place as my home?" Alias wondered aloud.

"He didn't need a reason, Alias," the paladin said. "It was just a game to him, giving you memories. It never occurred to him that your feelings would be hurt when you learned those memories were false." It never occurred to Finder to worry about anyone's feelings, he added to himself.

Alias shook her head. "No. There was a reason. He had to have a reason."

Dragonbait remained silent as Alias stood staring into the flames of her memory home. Just as he was beginning to worry how long she would dwell on the unreasonable, she suddenly returned to the original task at hand. "Let's find this Mintassan and get him the staff," she said. "Then we need a room in an inn—preferably one made of stone."

Dragonbait nodded in agreement. "I hope you know where we are," he said, "because I lost my map in the flames."

Alias smiled grimly. "Yeah," she said. "It should be right around the corner here."

# Three
# The Actress and the Sage

This time it was around four corners and about a half-mile away, through empty streets and past bustling bars, past groups of young toughs who gave the smoky warriors a few catcalls and older, more grizzled veterans who gave them a wide berth.

At the last corner, the appearance of the neighborhood improved markedly. The pavement stone was uniform and unvandalized. The buildings were constructed from more brick and stone than wood. The oil in the steetlamps burned more brightly and smoked less. The streets and thresholds of every building had been swept within the last week. There was no visible sewage.

Mintassan's townhouse was constructed of brick in the Sembian style—the first story was half underground, its door at the bottom of a narrow, descending stairway surrounded by a brick retaining wall, and the second story was raised several feet, its door atop a broad stone staircase. The lower quarters, usually reserved for servants, were where Mintassan had set up his shop. A sign mounted over the lower door displayed the sage's sigil, the Beastlands symbol topped by a waxing crescent moon and surrounded by a circle. The sign read, "Mintassan's Mysteries—Curios from *Very* Faraway Places." The door itself was divided horizontally, and the top half stood wide open. They could see there was a light blazing in the shop within.

Just as Alias and Dragonbait approached the stairs, a high-pitched shriek came from the room below. Alias and

Dragonbait exchanged glances. There could be a completely innocuous reason for a scream to be coming from the sage's shop, but after all their other evening adventures, caution did not seem out of place. They crept down the staircase and hovered at the doorway, peering in and listening.

Magically glowing stones in glass globes hung from the ceiling, illuminating the shop. Shelves and tables within were covered with the curios from *very* faraway places. Most of the items were creatures that had once been alive but were now pelts, skeletons or stuffed trophies. Most were creatures Alias had never seen before, but a few she'd heard of in bards' tales. Mixed in among the trophies were a few sculptures of strange creatures and vases and bowls depicting mythic beasts.

In the center of the room, a big man sat on the arm of a red velvet sofa directly beneath a globe. He wore a billowing cotton shirt and baggy pants, both white, and a powder-blue vest embroidered in gold thread. His long chestnut-brown hair was pulled back into a ponytail with a leather thong. His back was turned to the door, so Alias could not see his face. In one large hand he held up the bare, shapely leg of someone lying on the sofa, and was currently rubbing something on the sole of the foot belonging to the leg. The high back of the sofa also blocked Alias's view of whoever was lying there, but whoever it was was no doubt the source of the first shriek, for a moment later a second shriek rose from the sofa, followed by a woman's voice crying "Ow, ow, ow."

"The pain'll be good for you," the man said. "Remind you not to go fire-walking without both your slippers. Personally I prefer heavy boots when I run around burning buildings. Now don't fidget. It takes a moment for the salve to work."

"It *wasn't* my idea to go barefoot," a woman's voice argued from the sofa. "It was that witch. I told you, the slipper came off when she grabbed my leg. She nearly had me. I was lucky to escape with my skin still on."

Even if Alias hadn't recognized the situation described

she would have recognized the voice. It was a little sharper and more nasal than her memory recalled, but it sounded like her mother, the phony mother Finder had given her.

"Jamal, be reasonable," the man requested. "She's dead. She's been dead for years."

"Since when's being dead slowed down a wizard?" the voice on the couch argued. "I'm telling you, Mintassan, Cassana's come after me. The Night Masks set the fire, of course, but she was there, too. She's trying to kill me for that rude skit we did about her and that lich-boytoy of hers."

Mintassan gave a long-suffering sigh and insisted, "Cassana's dead, Jamal."

No, she isn't," Jamal retorted, sitting up straight on the sofa and waving her finger in Mintassan's face.

"Well, actually, yes, she is," Alias said, turning the handle of the lower half of the door and letting herself into the shop. "I cut through her staff of power myself up on the Hill of Fangs ten years ago. I survived the blast that killed her only because I was half standing in another plane. Cassana was burned to ash. And if she came back by some fell sorcery, I'd know immediately, but she hasn't. She's still dead."

Jamal's complexion went as white as an underfed vampire's as she stared wordlessly at the newcomers, one a dead ringer for the sorceress Cassana, the other a lizard creature resembling a monster from a tale of darkest evil.

"Cassana was a *distant* relation," the swordswoman explained as she circled the sofa and stood before Jamal and Mintassan. "Alias the Sell-Sword, at your service," she introduced herself with a sweeping bow, "and this, I believe, is yours," she added, holding out the slipper she'd taken from the woman in the burning building.

Mintassan shook his look of surprise at Alias's self-announced entrance and smiled broadly. "There, Jamal, see. There was a perfectly rational explanation. Pleased to meet you, Alias. I'm Mintassan the Magnificent, though my friends call me Mintassan the Mad." Mintassan offered his hand, and Alias accepted it in her own.

Mintassan was tall with broad shoulders, but somewhat overweight—his gut parted the center of his vest.
Nothing, Alias thought, that a few laps around the Sea of
Fallen Stars couldn't take care of. Perched on the sage's
nose was a pair of gold-rimmed spectacles made with
glass as thin as soap bubbles. Alias wondered if the spectacles were magical or if Mintassan wore them to give
himself a look of erudition. In his baggy white pants, billowing shirt, and bright-colored vest, he really looked
more like a merchant than a sage. Aside from the glasses,
the only other clues to his scholarly interests came from
the sigils embroidered in his vest and a tiny ornament
fastened to the vest's lapel—what appeared to be the
skull of a tiny mammal.

As Alias shook hands with the sage she realized his
eyes lingered over the azure tattoo emblazoned on her
right arm. Alias pulled her hand away self-consciously
and turned her attention back to Jamal.

Jamal remained frozen, staring at the swordswoman,
trying, as she fought off her obvious terror of a long-dead
sorceress, to take in all of Alias's and Mintassan's words.

Alias set the slipper down on the floor in front of the
sofa and stared back at the other woman. Jamal was
older than the "memory" that Finder had given the
swordswoman, with wrinkles etched about her eyes and
her neck, but she looked almost regal with her posture
straighter than a schoolgirl's and her flowery housecoat
draped dramatically over the sofa. She remained
unbowed by the pressures of Westgate life or the sordid
attacks of its underworld. Yet there remained something
comic about her appearance, the frayed sleeve of the
housecoat, the singed hem, the scarf half falling off, the
missing slipper. Alias was reminded of meeting an
artist's model once. The painting looked just like the
woman, but the woman was nothing like the painting;
without the brush strokes, she was less romanticized, but
much more real.

"I'm nobody, also at your service," Dragonbait whispered in Saurial.

Alias shook herself from her reverie. "Oh, and this is my companion, Dragonbait," she said, indicating the saurial with a wave of her hand.

"Yes, of course," Mintassan said, nodding and offering the paladin his hand as well. "Dragonbait the Saurial Paladin. Companion to Alias of the Magic Arm. We've heard a halfling bard tell of your exploits down at the Empty Fish. Haven't we, Jamal?" the sage asked, nudging the older woman.

Alias fidgeted slightly, but kept her agitation in check. The only thing she disliked more than strangers knowing details of her life was when the strangers were spellcasting sages like Mintassan.

Jamal finally overcame the shock of Alias's resemblance to the sorceress Cassana and was able to concentrate on Mintassan's words. "Ruskettle," Jamal said. "Milil's Mouth, can that woman ramble."

"Exactly," Mintassan agreed. He turned back to Alias. "The tales, however, do not do justice to your loveliness."

Alias fidgeted again under Mintassan's appraising eyes. He had a bold gaze that she found rather forward.

Jamal sighed and slapped the mage's leg. "Mind your manners," she reprimanded.

Mintassan grinned and asked, "Please, allow me to present to you my current charge, a patient singularly lacking in patience, that talented and fearless righter of wrongs, Jamal the Thespian, Jamal the Lady of Cheap Heroes and Cheaper Theatrics—"

"Jamal the Slightly Parboiled," Jamal finished, as she picked up her recovered slipper and slid it gingerly over her wounded foot. "So what were you doing in my burning house?" the woman asked, her distrust obviously not completely allayed by the fact that the swordswoman was a character in the halfling Ruskettle's tales.

"Um—We just happened to be passing by when we saw the Night Masks run out of the building and toss a torch back in," Alias explained.

"And then you followed me here just to return my slipper?" Jamal asked suspiciously.

"Well, no. We have business with Mintassan," Alias

said defensively.

"What business?" Jamal insisted.

"Grypht's business," the sage replied with a theatrical grimness. "And for such dark work we should retire to the back room." Mintassan strode off behind the shop's counter and through a doorway hung with a curtain of glass beads. "You might as well join us, Jamal," the sage called back over his shoulder. "I'll make tea. You can be mother and pour. You can serve as a witness to our transaction, too."

Jamal rose slowly and motioned for Alias and Dragonbait to go before her. Alias suspected she did so more out of caution than courtesy. Jamal did not want them at her back.

Alias moved cautiously through the curtain, into an extraplanar graveyard. While the trophies in the front of the shop had an air of respectability by virtue of their mounted settings, the remains of the dead in the back room gave the place a grisly appearance.

Fur and hide pelts of every color hung from the ceiling. Work tables all along one long wall were covered with boxes of bones and skeletons in various stages of being pieced together with pins and wires. Pickled internal organs filled jars on the shelves over the work tables. The ceiling was covered with strange insects stuck there with pins in their thoraxes. A box at Alias's elbow contained red eggshells and the remains of three baby birds. Snake skins and feathers lay out on the writing table beside a sketchbook. There were piles of boxes and crates beneath all the tables and all around the perimeters of the room. Alias did not want to know what was inside any of them.

"Wonderful what he's done with the place, isn't it?" Jamal said with sarcasm as she noted Alias's discomfort. "Early Abattoir—a Sembian style you don't see displayed much in the finer homes of Westgate."

"Grypht gave us to understand that your specialty was transmutation, which, if I recall, excludes the necromantic arts," Alias said, treading as politely as she could into what Mintassan's business was with so many dead things.

The sage looked back at the swordswoman with a gleam of curiosity in his eye. "My, my. Heroism, sword skill, beauty, and brains all in one. Where, I wonder, did you learn about the art?"

Alias flushed, but did not reply. Finder had filled his creation with everything he'd known, and she could forget none of it. It wasn't the first time she'd embarrassed herself with a demonstration of more knowledge than she ought to have.

"Yes," Mintassan replied to the swordswoman's comment when he realized she wasn't going to reply to his query, "you're quite right. Specializing in transmutation does exclude necromantic studies. But while other transmuters choose to study the more mundane and commercially lucrative transmutations, straw to gold, salt water to fresh, sow's ears to silk purses, and so on, I prefer investigating the mutation of nature itself—or herself, as your religion requires."

Mintassan stood beside a massive table, which dominated the center of the room. The table, some castoff from a Westgate festhall, judging by its thick legs and velvet-covered sides, was littered with various scholarly debris: maps of the inner and outer planes, tomes with mildewing leather covers, diagrams and sketches of creatures, calipers, rulers, magnifying lenses. The sage picked up a hunk of amber larger than his fist and held it out for Alias to see.

"I am seeking the secret," Mintassan said, "of how the descendants of a creature like this—"

Alias peered into the amber and could see an animal that resembled a bat embedded within.

"—become a creature like this." With a flourish the sage yanked a black cloth cover off a second specimen—the mounted, mummified head of a tanar'ri, a powerful denizen of the Abyss.

Alias and Dragonbait drew back, startled. The next moment, though, Alias's eyes squinted in disbelief. Mintassan was teasing them, or testing them somehow. "And whose ancestor is that little fellow?" she asked, pointing to the tiny mammal skull Mintassan displayed on his vest lapel.

Mintassan stroked the tiny skull almost reverently. "My own," he declared, but a moment later he looked just a little doubtful, "I think," he amended. The sage picked up the tanar'ri head, looked around with a frown for another empty flat space, and finally set the grisly trophy in an empty crate labeled, "Spell keys and other darks." From Finder, who had traveled in other planes, Alias knew those were planar slang for magic components and mysteries.

"Please, have a seat," the sage said as he pushed all the remaining junk on the table to one side. "Excuse me while I get the tea things together." He disappeared into a side alcove, leaving Alias and Dragonbait alone with Jamal.

"Planar travel has scrambled his wits, but he's really sweet and harmless," Jamal said matter-of-factly. There were eight completely mismatched chairs set about the table. The actress flopped into an overstuffed chair of worn and tattered brocade and put her feet up on a rocker of woven cane.

Alias settled into a wooden chair with a wolf skull mounted atop its straight, high back. Dragonbait's choice was limited by his massive tail, so he perched on a three-legged stool carved from ruby quartz.

From the alcove came the sound of rattling pots, the squeak of a hand pump, and a magical cantrip, followed by the *whoosh* of an enchanted flame igniting. Mintassan was singing a bawdy version of "Lie Down, Ye Ladies" in a passable baritone.

An uneasy silence had settled over the occupants at the table. Jamal watched Alias with the attention of a fox watching a wolf. Alias held her smile until it felt like a brittle, dried leaf.

Jamal tilted her head from side to side, studying Alias. Finally, she said, "I remember you now."

Alias felt her chest tighten. "You do?"

"According to Ruskettle's tale, you're the one who popped in over Westgate with the mad god Moander, chased by your friends, riding a red dragon."

Alias felt her heartbeat slow to its normal rhythm.

"I saw that battle," Jamal declared. "Moander puffed up like an overproofed loaf of bread. The dragon spat flame at it. Boooom! Fried dragon and chunks of rotting god rained on the city. Took out a piece of the city wall, the Dhostar warehouses, and a lot of the northwestern slums."

Alias felt the heat return to her face. "It was an accident. If there was something we could have done to avoid damaging your fair city, we would have. Cassana and her crew jumped us right afterward, and after we killed Cassana, we ended up in another plane, so we never got a chance to apologize."

Jamal laughed raucously. "Apologize? Whatever for? That crash shook out this town like a dirty rug. The town's merchant nobles thought a new Flight of Dragons had arrived! There was total chaos while they all tried to save themselves and, of course, their merchandise. All of them had egg on their faces when the furor died down, especially Ssentar Urdo. Family Urdo called in a marker with some old Thayan necromancer to protect its docks. The necromancer was inebriated at the time, centered his spell too low, and teleported a squad of skeletons into the dock itself. Little rib cages and arms and skulls waving around, trying to pull the rest of their bodies through the wood. Mintassan collected a specimen as I recall. He really wanted the dragon's skull, but someone else snatched it up before he reached the scene of the crash. He was so disappointed."

Alias shuddered to think what someone in Westgate would want with the skull of the dragon Mist. While the ancient wyrm had been an ally at the time of her fiery demise, the beast had hated Alias. The swordswoman would have preferred to hear Mist's remains had been laid to rest in their entirety.

"Kids were playing 'Dragons and Warriors' in the streets for weeks afterward," Jamal continued, "and everyone talked about what cowardly leeches the merchant nobles were when push came to shove." Jamal sighed. "But, alas, when you did not return with more dragons, the merchants and the Night Masks reestablished their grubby holds on everyone's lives. Ah, well. I got three months worth of material for my street theater even if I had to invent a cheap hero for it."

"So, what were you doing on my street last night?" Jamal demanded, switching the topic suddenly. "It's not on the way to Mintassan's by any stretch of the imagination."

Alias thought fast for an answer that might satisfy the woman. "I was just passing by, reliving old memories. Someone I knew used to live on that street. The Swanmays," she answered, hoping that memory wasn't another of Finder's fictions.

"That band of female adventurers? That was a long time ago." Jamal smiled at some memory. "They were such great troublemakers. Solid cheap hero material." Her look grew less suspicious. As she came out of her reverie, she said, "You knew it was the Night Masks who started the fire. Even so, you rushed in to save what they wanted destroyed. They have watchers. You've made yourselves enemies."

Alias laughed. "We already made them enemies. This was just the salt in the wound." The swordswoman explained how she and the saurial had taken care of the shakedown team and the assassin squad.

Jamal laughed with delight. "Definitely a cheap hero story."

"What does that mean, cheap hero?" Alias asked.

"Cheap hero. An everyday hero," Jamal explained. "Not one of those highfalutin, noble-born, kill-a-dragon-before-breakfast, always-get-the-girl heroes. But your regular type hero. The merchant who doesn't cheat widows and orphans. The neighbors who bring you hot meals when you're sick. The kid who stops the pickpocket who grabbed your purse. The fishermen who paid a protection racketeer with the racketeer's own teeth. The festhall girl who testified at a murder trial and had to leave town. The apprentices and journeymen who helped the farmers guard their fields so no one could start a brush fire to drive up the price of grain and start famine in the outlying regions.

"I'm the Lady of Cheap Heroes. I tell their tales," Jamal said with a flourish of her hand. "Jamal's Street Theater. Four performances daily. Written, directed, and performed by Jamal herself, with the help of some loyal associates. That's why the Night Masks want me dead, and the merchants wouldn't miss me any. I tell everyone that ordinary people can fight their oppressors."

"After tonight, it looks like you may have to make your living in some other city," Alias replied.

"Make my living!" Jamal laughed till her eyes teared. "You don't make a living in the theater, girl. It's a calling. And Westgate is *my* city. They are *not* driving me out."

Mintassan came bustling back into the room carrying a silver tea service laden with a silver teapot, a silver creamer, a silver brandy flask, a tiny parcel wrapped in brown paper, and four mismatched clay mugs.

The sage sunk into a wood-frame-and-canvas chair, which looked about ready to collapse under his weight. With a flick of his finger, he opened the paper parcel on the tea tray, revealing little cubes about the size of dice but without markings. He dropped two into a mug and held the mug out for Jamal to fill.

"Amnite sugar cubes," Mintassan explained upon noting Alias's curious look. "Among the many things the Amnites have stolen from the Mazticans. For years they were a novelty known only to the upper classes, but last year House Dhostar brought in a huge consignment and lowered the price. Now they can't keep up with the demand. They're all the rage."

Alias picked up a grainy cube, then dropped it tentatively into the mug of tea Jamal handed her. The sugar cube bubbled and dissolved. She blew over the tea's steamy surface while Mintassan added a dollop of cream to his mug. When the sage had taken a sip of his own beverage, Alias hazarded a taste of her own. "It's good," she declared with surprise. "Sweet, like honey."

Jamal snorted. "Sweet, but no kick," the actress said, pouring a more-than-healthy dose of brandy into her own tea.

"So what's your poison, Dragonbait?" Mintassan asked

as he handed the last mug to Jamal to fill.

"I would like it plain, please," the saurial replied.

Alias translated, "He'll have it straight up."

"Please," Dragonbait repeated.

Alias sighed. "Please," she translated.

Mintassan smiled as he handed the paladin the mug of tea. "So it's true what Grypht wrote—Alias does understand Saurial. I always wondered if a human could ever master it."

"I can hardly claim to have mastered it even though I've lived with the saurials for eight years," Alias protested. "Their language is a mixture of sounds, scents, and postures. A *tongues* spell with a *permanency* cast on it enables me to hear the sounds and understand them, and I can smell their scents even better and interpret the emotions they convey, but I'm not very good with the postures. I can speak the sound part as well, but I can't put out the scents, and since I can't do the postures, Dragonbait says, I'm sort of a monotone speaker, and there are levels of subtlety I just don't get. Fortunately, Dragonbait understands my tongue better than I do his. I think other saurials still find it easier to speak with other dragonish and lizardish creatures than with me."

"Perhaps their tongue is related to Auld Wyrmish, or the ancestral dragon languages. Saurials and dragons could share the same ancestors," Mintassan suggested.

"I think not," Dragonbait retorted, emitting a fishy smell that just hinted at how insulting he found the suggestion. Alias translated the words and the emotion.

Mintassan chuckled. "That's the same reaction I got from Grypht."

"Who is this Grypht?" asked Jamal, tearing her attention away from her spiked tea.

"A fellow blood," Mintassan replied.

"A what?" Alias asked.

"Blood," Jamal said. "That's plane-hopper slang for professional traveler."

"Grypht sent Alias and Dragonbait down to Westgate to make an exchange of magic," Mintassan explained. "He and his people are exiles from their own plane and live up north now. He's a saurial like Dragonbait here."

"Except he's ten feet tall and has horns all over his head," Alias corrected.

"He'll always be little Grypht to me," Mintassan said, with a chuckle. "Now, down to business," the sage said rubbing his hands together. "Show me, please, what you've brought for me."

Dragonbait set the staff down on the table before the sage.

Mintassan ran his fingertips along the staff. He sighted down its length. Peered into the little mouse skulls dangling from the top. Sniffed at the orange feather. Rapped it sharply against the floor. Squinted at the runes that spiraled down from the top to the bottom. "Definitely Netheril," he declared. "Beautiful workmanship. A staff of the undead. What can you tell me of its provenance and pedigree? Did it come from the Great Desert?"

"From Anauroch, yes," Alias answered. "A saurial exploration party came across the slaughtered bodies of a Zhentarim patrol decaying in the dunes. The staff was among the corpses.

"That fits, too," the sage said, nodding. "The Black Network has stooped to tomb-robbing ever since their precious city was smashed. Well, I am quite satisfied." He pulled a small box out from under the table and set it down in front of Alias. He turned the handle on the top and the sides fell away.

A perfect blue crystal sphere glowed before Alias, bathing her in a blue light. The sphere floated and spun ever so slightly an inch above a base of white jade carved in the shape of a twisting dragon.

Alias shot a glance at Jamal, but the woman did not seem interested in the magic crystal sphere. The swordswoman looked over at Dragonbait, who squinted at the magic ball with his *shen* sight. "Nothing malefic," the paladin reported.

"I think that Grypht will be happy with this crystal ball," Mintassan said. "It can find anyone in the Realms."

With no magical abilities of her own, Alias was unable

to test the sphere's reputed ability, but since Grypht had said all his dealings with Mintassan had been honorable ones and Dragonbait confirmed the magic was not evil, she gave a short nod. "We accept the trade," she said evenly.

Mintassan smiled and flipped up the sides of the box and twisted the lid back on. He looked up slyly at the swordswoman, noting, "There is, of course, one exception to the sphere's abilities."

"I have a permanent misdirection shield cast on me," Alias explained.

"Grypht mentioned it, and of course I had to test it," the sage said. "I struggled for hours trying to get the sphere to reveal you—without success. You didn't even set off the alarms at my door when you entered the shop. Now that we've finally met, I suppose you'll head right back to the Lost Vale." Mintassan sighed and leaned forward to stare into Alias's eyes. "Protected from magical scrying so only the lucky saurials have the pleasure of gazing on you."

"He must realize we don't find you as attractive as he does," Dragonbait said in Saurial.

"He knows," Alias said in Saurial. "He's flirting with me."

"Really?" Dragonbait asked. "Do you think he'd make a good mate?"

Alias ignored the paladin's question and replied to the sage, "That's our plan. As soon as there's a ship going that way," Alias said. "We may be stuck here a few days, though, according to the harbor master."

"Good," Jamal said to Alias. "Now, if you'll excuse me, I'm going to retire to one of the *spare* bedrooms."

Alias wondered if Jamal was explaining her sleeping arrangements to protect her reputation or to let Alias know the field was clear.

Jamal rose and began limping over to a staircase in the back of the workroom. She turned at the stairway and said, "Since you'll be around a few days, you'll have a chance to catch one of our performances. You'll see what a great cheap hero you make.

"I don't want to be a cheap hero," Alias called after her.

"Too late," Jamal called back as she pulled herself up the stairs by the railing. "I've already written the first act."

"I don't want to be a hero, cheap or otherwise," Alias insisted to Mintassan.

"I don't think you get a say in it," the sage replied. "Anyway, there's really nothing I can do about it. Jamal has total creative control over her theater. At least this time she's picked someone easy on the eyes," Mintassan noted with a grin.

Dragonbait chuckled. Alias glared up at him and said, in Saurial, "I am not going to take on the Night Masks, the merchants of Westgate, or whatever cheap villains Jamal has in mind," the swordswoman insisted.

"Don't worry. I'm sure you'll be a very good cheap hero," the paladin reassured her.

# Four
# The Faceless

Within the city walls of Westgate, but some distance from the neighborhood where Mintassan the Sage lived, a far larger gathering of people would soon be discussing the topics of Jamal, the fire, and the two newcomers.

The room where they met was hidden deep beneath Westgate's well-traveled streets. Long ago it had been protected from magical inquiries and priestly divinations, and over the years its entrances had been regularly relocated, the construction crews that performed these feats quietly slain to ensure secrecy. No long-lost crypt in the Fields of the Dead, nor dark-hearted shrine beneath the wreckage of Zhentil Keep had been as diligently protected. In time, the very secret nature of the place became its own protection. A place no one has seen, which cannot be detected supernaturally, must be a myth, so enforcers of the law, fortune hunters, and revenge seekers had long since ceased to search for the lair of the Night Masters, alleged leaders of the Night Masks, and the Night Masters' lord—the Faceless.

Yet myths and allegations are often true, and the Night Masters and the Faceless met in their secret lair to plan the activities of the Night Masks and to evaluate their successes and failures.

These secret masters of their city were average-looking men and women. Most tended to the sprawling girth that marked success in those fields where the younger and less experienced can be convinced to do the physical labor. The Night Masters did not choose nervous fidgets or careless drunkards to join their number. On the surface above, they were shopkeepers, craftsmen, and lesser merchants, the sort of respectable citizens to whom no one gives a second thought. They cultivated this anonymity carefully, avoiding any flamboyance or ostentation.

In their secret lair, they hid their surface identities. Before they entered the inner chambers, each Night Master donned a mask that covered his or her face from forehead to upper lip. The masks were made of white porcelain, with a black domino mask painted about the eye slits, and each was distinguished from all the others with a different golden glyph painted on the forehead. The glyphs designated the speaker's portfolio within the organization.

Since the masks did not cover the lips or jaws or hair or any part of the torso, the experienced eye could compare a beard or a mole or a head of hair or a physical shape or a certain article of clothing with that of some person in the outer world and have a fair idea of the identities of their fellow masters. Of course, the certainty of such knowledge was not absolute; a fake beard, a wig, make-up, magical enchantments, and other disguises could easily mislead. It hardly mattered, though, whether they knew each other or not. They were the ultimate brethren among their brotherhood of thieves and would never willingly reveal another's identity. For one thing, to betray a member to an outsider would be an admission of the betrayer's complicity. There were also other more horrible costs to betrayal, of which the Faceless made sure they remained aware.

Their numbers varied according to the needs and whims of their lord, and at this time in Westgate's history there were ten Night Masters. The glyphs on their masks identified three of them as general managers—Enforcement, Finance, and Noble Relations—and the remaining seven as regional managers—External Revenue, Harborside, Thunnside, Gateside, Parkside, Central, and Outside.

All were now gathered around a great table hewn from

a single block of obsidian, veined with gold. In the center
of the table a small brazier crackled, giving off not only
light, but also a welcome warmth, for the meeting place,
now, even in the height of summer, was cool and damp.
At the head of the table, on a dais as high as the table,
was a throne of the same ebon material as the table.
There sat the Faceless.

The Faceless dressed like a judge, in billowing black
robes with a thin strip of white silk draped over his shoulders. On his feet he wore black clodders, high-topped boots
worn commonly by Westgate's fishermen, and on his
hands, white silk gloves, like a gentleman. He sported a
wide-rimmed hat of dark black velvet. While all this was
enough to give him a forbidding appearance, it was the
Faceless's mask that unnerved his followers the most.

When the mask lay on a table it looked like a helmet of
mesh chain covered in platinum coins struck with the
glyph of Leira, the deceased goddess of illusion. No one
but the Faceless ever saw the mask's appearance, though,
since once the Faceless donned it, the mask seemed to
disappear, disguising the wearer at the same time. The
disguise was of an astonishing and odd variety caused by
a magical illusion.

Everything between the Faceless's hat and his robe
blurred like a chalk painting at the very beginning of a
rain shower. Anyone who glanced in the Faceless's direction would conclude there was a face to be seen, but one
saw nothing but a shifting pattern of colors, like a swarm
of bees. The harder one concentrated on trying to discern
a face, the harder it became to see anything at all. Stubborn observers found that their eyes began to water and
their heads began to pound with the effort.

Most of the Night Masters believed the mask also
altered the Faceless's voice, for the sound of his speech
was grating and metallic, though still able to convey
emotions as subtle as annoyance or displeasure.

None of the assembled Night Masters knew the Faceless's identity. They could tell he was tall and male
(unless other magic disguised his physical appearance
further), and they suspected he was human. Anything

else concerning their lord's identity was pure speculation. The rewards for serving as a Night Master were great, and the members chose not to risk their positions by angering the Faceless with curiosity. If they suspected who their master was, they did not share it with each other. None of them knew the extent or nature of the Faceless's networks of informants. They did know that those who lied in this chamber rarely made it out again.

One of the more portly Night Masters, the glyph on his mask identifying him as the manager of the Gateside district, stood before his fellows and his lord, prompting himself from a list on a sheet of yellow paper. "The insurance money paid by the Gateside festhalls has increased to ninety percent, up from seventy-two percent, no doubt owing to the recent fires that have plagued nonpaying elements in the Outside district."

The Gateside manager's tone was flat and emotionless, like the singsong of a sergeant-at-arms reading the charges of the hundredth petty pickpocket of the day. "The Ssemm supplies discussed two nights ago have been acquired and moved through a third party to Elturel, where the Vhammos family will purchase it in the name of the Free Traders. The indoctrination of young Haztor Urdo continues. He believes it's all an exciting game, and doesn't suspect we know his identity. We continue to experience difficulties from halfling agents throughout Gateside (similar to those experienced and reported by Harborside), most of which can be traced back to Lady Nettel's employment of inordinate numbers of these vermin." Gateside halted, double-checked his list, then offered the paper to the brazier, which greedily consumed it.

Throughout the report, the Faceless sat in repose, white-gloved hands resting comfortably on the sides of his throne. After the portly Night Master finished, there was a short silence, as there always was. Then the Faceless's metallic voice rasped across the table. "Are all these reports accurate?"

Ten masks bobbed around the table, and ten voices replied in varying tones, "Yes, milord."

The Faceless drummed his fingers on the slick obsidian

of his throne's armrest. "What of the matter of Jamal the Thespian?" he growled.

"Still . . ." Gateside hesitated, as if his words had caught on something, "under review," he finished. It was apparent that he'd been hoping this matter would not come up. "Her home was set afire," he reported, "and the clothing merchant who not only rented her a room but refused our protection was killed as a warning. We have yet to discover if she survived the blaze."

"She survived," the Faceless intoned.

Gateside held hands out, protesting, "We are as yet unaware—"

"I said, 'She survived,' " the Faceless repeated, raising his voice just a fraction, silencing Gateside. "She was rescued by a red-haired swordswoman, who was aided by a lizardlike creature with a staff. Jamal fled the burning building for the quarters of an ally, the sage Mintassan, whom we are unwilling to directly confront. The red-haired woman and the lizardman joined Jamal at Mintassan's."

Gateside tried to interrupt, saying, "We had no knowledge of—"

"If you had followed procedure," the Faceless reprimanded, "and confirmed both the burning and casualties by posting eyes, you would have known. Instead you waited for the watch's report to be smuggled to you, as you have done in the past. Had you posted eyes, your man might have been able to finish off the woman as she fled. I requested her tongue be silenced. As it stands, the wretched banshee is still loose, unharmed, as is her tongue and her annoying troupe of ragtag performers."

Gateside, his eyes now fixed on the tabletop, replied, "I apologize for my carelessness."

"On a related matter," the Faceless continued, turning to face the Night Master in charge of Enforcement, "What news is there of our naked assassins?" Gateside exhaled slowly in relief while Enforcement pursed his lips until they nearly disappeared.

The other nine Night Masters looked puzzled. The Faceless nodded in Enforcement's direction to indicate he should explain.

"External Revenue's people requested the elimination of two out-of-towners," Enforcement reported. "External Revenue's people failed to inform my people that these out-of-towners were heavily armed. Consequently the team who took the assignment was overpowered. The targets stripped my agents naked and forced them to run through a street fair."

There was an uneasy shifting of the other Night Masters. None were amused by the embarrassment suffered by the agents; the cost to the brethren's reputation was too high.

"And these targets," the Faceless prompted, "which gave External Revenue's people trouble and then gave you such trouble . . . describe them."

"Well," Enforcement replied, "one was a red-haired woman, the other was a—" Enforcement paused as he realized his description was about to match the one given of the pair who'd interfered with Gateside's hit on Jamal, "—um, it was a lizardman, carrying a staff."

"I see," said the Faceless calmly. "And you did not think this was an important enough matter to bring to our attention?"

"I hesitated to broach the matter, since External Revenue did not include the pair in her report," Enforcement explained.

The Night Master who managed External Revenue spun in her seat and gave Enforcement a hard glare. Despite her mask, it was clear that she gave her companion a warning.

"External Revenue," the Faceless said, "Enforcement chose not to mention this pair in deference to your silence. Why didn't *you* bring them to our attention?"

External Revenue rose to her feet, "It is not uncommon for out-of-towners, especially of the adventuring sort, to resist the import agents. Once an elimination is called for, the victims' revenue becomes the purview of Enforcement. I left it for him to report the pair. I was unaware that the Enforcement people had mishandled the contract." Here she shot a stern glance at her comrade.

"That Enforcement's people did not succeed seems to indicate they were more cocky than competent."

The Faceless motioned for External Revenue to be seated. He sat back and addressed the whole assembly. "Well, there are a number of swordswomen in Westgate, some with red hair, but not, I think, more than one who travels in the company of a lizardman. Here we have a pair of adventurers making trouble for three separate departments, yet not one department reported on the pair, even though they cost us revenue, shamed us, and interfered with our plans. Just coincidence, you may think. Well, such coincidences interfere with the smooth working of our operation. We live by fear and intimidation, by making individuals perform our bidding out of consideration of the consequences. When an operation fails, when it *publicly* fails, then we lose our effectiveness, and we pay the price in revenue. Enforcement, I trust you have plans to avenge this humiliation. Where are the swordswoman and lizardman now?"

"We, uh, don't know," Enforcement said, visibly nervous. "She seems to elude all our eyes."

"Even the magical ones?" the Faceless pressed.

"Even the magical ones." Enforcement took a deep breath. "*Especially* the magical ones. We think she may have fled the city."

"That's highly unlikely," the Faceless countered. "Since they've outmaneuvered us three out of three times, they can hardly feel threatened by us. I fear we must make an example of them."

"But if my men cannot find them," Enforcement argued, "how can we—"

"I said *we* out of courtesy," the Faceless interrupted. "This is a matter for my own personal agents, not lesser merchants who play at the games of their betters." There was silence around the table, and a few faces reddened with embarrassment. "I'll determine what is to be done about the out-of-towners by our next meeting. As for the quality or lack thereof of certain reports this evening—"

Gateside, External Revenue, and Enforcement all held their breaths.

"Should there be any more glaring omissions in future reports, there will have to be changes in the ranks," the Faceless threatened. "As for the failure to subdue two unknown outsiders, that could happen to anyone. You, though, Gateside, were assigned to take care of Jamal the Thespian, a simple, little actress with no extraordinary strengths. You announce she is marked, then fail to confirm her demise, and finally simply presume she's expired according to your wishes. Now that she is forewarned, I will have to assign my own agents to handle her. Because of your carelessness and the subsequent inconvenience to me, you will sacrifice half your share of income this month."

Gateside opened his mouth to protest, but caught himself. After a long, brittle moment, he nodded his head in compliance.

"The meeting is adjourned," the Faceless snapped.

The Night Masters rose and filed toward the exit. External Revenue and Enforcement smiled menacingly at one another. Gateside glowered, but the others were careful to avoid making eye contact with him.

The Faceless remained seated as his agents departed. Each Night Master took a smoky torch from a sconce in the wall and traveled down the tunnel leading away from the meeting chamber. No one spoke, even in the tunnel, for fear that the Faceless would overhear.

The Faceless rose and paced across the dais. When the sound of footfalls ceased from down the tunnel, the Night Mask lord pushed a panel in the rear of his throne. Behind the throne a section of stone slid back silently, revealing a secret passageway carved through the bedrock.

The Faceless picked up a torch and strode down the passage as the secret door slid closed behind him. He stopped after fifty paces, just before the passage opened into a great underground sewer. Dark water swirled below, and something just beneath the surface made a wake, which splashed up the sides of the sewer. The Faceless drew out a small ivory ball intricately carved with the twisting form of a sea serpent. A gleaming ruby

represented the creature's eye. The Faceless pressed on
the ruby and stepped out onto the narrow span that
crossed the upper regions of the sewer.

On the opposite side of the span, a second, shorter passageway led to a cavern more vast than the meeting room
of the Night Masters. Here were stored the Night Masks'
treasury and arsenal. The Faceless strode by the piles of
riches and weaponry without a glance.

At the far end of the cavern, the Faceless halted before
a large pool of water. A fountain identical to those in the
squares in the city above splashed on the surface. Stones
enchanted with magical light spells had been tossed into
the bottom of the pool so the water shone with an eerie
green radiance and the light played on the wall with
every ripple of the water.

The Faceless bent over the pool and peered within its
depths. Something large and shadowed floated suspended between the bottom and the surface. "Mistinarperadnacles Hai Draco," the Faceless whispered.

The large, shadowy thing rose, breaking the water like
an island rising from some primordial sea. Water slid
down its gleaming white surfaces, dripped from the tips
of its horns, poured from two empty eye sockets, then two
nasal chambers and finally streamed from between the
huge fangs of the great, gaping jawbone. The disembodied skull of the dragon Mistinarperadnacles Hai Draco
hovered over the surface of the water. A sickly yellow
light spun about in its eye sockets, a light that sprang
from the necromantic powers animating the dead monster's remains.

A voice seemed to whisper in the air above the fountain, "What is your will, milord?" The dead dragon's
words did not emanate from her remains, but seemed to
drift about the room.

"When I first summoned you from your eternal sleep
and bound you to my service," the Faceless said, "you told
me something of a pair you held responsible for your
demise, a lizardman and a red-headed swordswoman."

"It was a saurial, not a lizardman," the dead dragon's
voice whispered.

"Do not play games with me, Mistinarperadnacles. Tell me what you know of this swordswoman and her companion."

There was a slight pause, and the glow in the dead creature's eye sockets strengthened.

"The woman called herself Alias of the Inner Sea, Alias of Westgate, and Alias the Sell-Sword. She travels in the company of a noble saurial warrior she quaintly calls Dragonbait. His name among his own people could roughly be translated as Champion of Justice. He and Alias share some magical bond."

"Just how good are they?" the Faceless asked.

"They were each able to defeat me in combat, albeit not without some minor help. That's why I died in their service. Champion's skills are unsurpassed among his own people. This Alias, though, is the luckiest sell-sword I've ever witnessed in battle. Lady Luck, the goddess Tymora, must keep an eye on her."

"How can they be scried?" the Faceless asked.

"As far as I know, they cannot. Apparently there's some enchantment cast on Alias that hides her from friends and enemies alike. Even King Azoun's wizard Vangerdahast couldn't locate her."

"Do they have any Harper connections?"

"It's possible. Neither Alias nor the saurial wore the Harpers' little pin, but the saurial said Elminster the Sage had given Alias a magical stone, and a bard told me Alias had taught her certain songs, which I recognized as belonging to Finder Wyvernspur."

"Who?"

"Finder Wyvernspur. He was a Harper, one of the founders of the Harper revival in the north three centuries back. Fell into disgrace, I believe."

"So would you say this woman and her companion would be formidable foes?"

"Foes. You don't want them as foes, milord. They are not going to be frightened or defeated by mere thieves. They fight dragons and ancient gods and live."

The Faceless drummed his fingers on the ledge around the pool of water. "If they are as dangerous as you say, then perhaps they would make useful allies," he suggested.

The air all about the cavern rang with laughter.

The Faceless scowled. "I fail to see the humor," he barked.

"I forgot, your language does not carry the subtleties of my own. I'll explain slowly enough for your mammalian brain to comprehend. As I said, the saurial warrior's true name translates roughly as 'Champion of Justice.' In other words, he serves the god Tyr. I called him a noble warrior because he has dedicated himself to Tyr's noble cause."

"Like a paladin?" the Faceless asked in surprise.

"Not like one, is one. Or would be if he were human. Saurials with such dedications have gifts similar to human paladins," Mist explained.

"Including the Sight?" the Faceless queried.

"The near equivalent," said the dragon, "More akin to my own race's ability to detect the unseen. He discerns the roiling mass of an individual's thoughts, feelings, and desires that make up the soul and the spirit, and is able to divine with a certain accuracy the individual's intentions. It is called *shen* sight. I don't imagine he would have remained with Alias all these years unless the *shen* sight of her was pleasing to him. He called her his soul's sister.

"So you see, I do not think they will become allied with you. Here I give you advice unbidden, milord," the dragon's dead spirit offered. "Do not pursue them, as I did, down the path to your own destruction. They are like gale winds or floodwaters. You must stay out of their path and wait them out."

"That may not be possible. They rescued Jamal the Thespian tonight, indicating they must be involved with her somehow. Knowing Jamal, she will use them to encourage the people to interfere with my plans. I must use them to further my plans, and I know just how to bring them to serve me."

"The Night Masks who serve you are all motivated by their greed, their cruelty, their sloth, and their arrogance. These two have none of these traits," the dragon's skull argued. "What can you possibly offer them?"

"The chance to serve the cause of justice."

The dragon skull remained silent. Mist had long ago learned not to argue with the Faceless's mad-sounding schemes.

The Faceless slammed his fist into the palm of his hand. "A powerful force this Alias may be, but I know now how to bring her to rein. And when the time comes, I will destroy her."

## Five
# House Dhostar

Mintassan offered Alias and Dragonbait quarters in his own home, but
Alias, uncomfortable with accepting
the flirtatious mage's hospitality,
declined and remained firm against
the sage's insistence. Finally they
reached a compromise. Mintassan
surrendered their company when Alias
agreed to stay at an inn two blocks away, which the
sage recommended.

Blais House did not advertise as an inn, but when they
walked in the front door, as Mintassan had told them to
do, they were greeted politely, albeit with some surprise
at their appearance, by the night manager. The inn was
as elegant as any Alias had ever seen. In the foyer, the
inlaid tile floor gleamed in the light of a great crystal
chandelier. Alias suspected that Blais House did not ordinarily cater to adventurers, but at the mention of Mintassan's name the night manager became instantly cordial.

The price of a room was surprisingly reasonable, causing the swordswoman to wonder what it might have cost
had they not used Mintassan's name. Alias slid four gold
coins across the front desk.

The night manager, a slight man dressed in a red-and-
white silk tabard and black hose, bid them to follow him
as he picked up a gold-plated candelabra. He led them up
a white marble staircase and down a corridor made
soundproof by its plush red carpeting. At the end of the
corridor he produced a key, unlocked the door on the
right, and led them in. Setting the candelabra down on a
table, he assured them that should they want anything

at all, they had only to pull the bell cord gently. The bath, he informed them as he stepped out of the room, was at the end of the hall. Then he pulled the door shut and left them alone.

The room was spacious; the expanse of white plaster walls broken only by idealized watercolors of the city. The ceiling timbers were whitewashed and decorated with painted garlands of flowers. The fireplace was lined with local ceramic tile. The beds had thick, comfortable mattresses with heavy down filling and soft sheets tightly woven of Mulhorand cotton. The great windows were made of green-stained splinter-glass set in the patterns of trees and opened out over the entrance of the inn. The armoire was Sembian, the pair of comfortable reading chairs Waterdhavian, and beneath the beds were Cormyrian-forged copper chamber pots with porcelain lining. A small bookshelf held several well-thumbed popular reads, including *Aurora's Catalogue* and a complete set of *Volo's Guides*.

All the luxury was lost on Alias, who sat down on the edge of her bed, shucked off her boots by stepping on the heels, let her sword belt slide to the floor, fell back on the bed, and was softly snoring, still wearing her chain mail, in under three minutes.

Dragonbait locked the door and windows, ascertained that there were no secret passages in the walls or assassins in the armoire, and tucked the case with the crystal ball under the bed. He flipped a corner of the coverlet over Alias's shoulder and blew out the candelabra. Lying in the dark on his bed, he prayed that if they could not be delivered soon from this city, at least they be delivered safely.

The saurial always slept lightly, so it was he who awakened at the sound of someone knocking. It was a soft, hesitant rapping, not on the door, but on the door frame—as if the knocker did not really want to be responsible for waking up a skilled swordswoman and her sharp-clawed companion.

Alias muttered a curse and turned over, pulling a pillow over her head in an attempt to rescue a few more

minutes of sleep. The sun was shining outside, but Dragonbait was still cautious. When he rose, he picked up his
sword before shuffling to the door. He then concentrated
his *shen* sight on what lay beyond the door. Feeling
rather foolish, he set his sword aside, slid back the bolt,
and opened the door halfway.

"Murk?" he said. Alias had tried to get him to pro-
nounce some basic Realms words, but "what," had been
impossible, and the saurial's "yes," came out a sibilant
hiss that sounded like a dissolving vampire caught in an
open field at dawn. In the end, he answered everything
with meaningless sounds like "murk," relying on inflec-
tion to convey his meaning.

A half-elf girl not yet twelve winters old stood outside
the door. She wore a miniature version of the uniform the
night manager had sported, a red-and-white tabard with
black hose. The paladin wondered if she'd been orphaned
or abandoned, as he knew children who worked as servants often were. Her *shen*-signature was the purest he
had seen in Westgate, and he hoped it stayed that way.

The girl's eyes were at the same level as the saurial's,
but while his were encrusted with sleep, hers were wide-
eyed with astonishment. Dragonbait repeated, "Murk?"
and cocked his head in a manner that humans often
found amusing.

The girl remained speechless, but had the wits to hold
out a small serving tray bearing two letters. Her hands
shook as the saurial reached for the letters. Dragonbait
was tempted to smile and pat her on the head to calm
her, but realized that might have the opposite effect.

Dragonbait picked up the letters and turned away to
fetch a gratuity, but when he turned back with a few
coins, the child was gone, the hallway empty. Dragonbait
shrugged and shut the door.

Alias had risen after all and was peeling off her chain
mail. "I cannot believe you let me sleep in my armor," she
said testily.

Dragonbait shrugged again. "You went out like a candle.
I doubt I could have awakened you if I tried."

Alias snorted, "The best bed I've seen along the Inner

Sea Coast, and you let me sleep in a steel nighty. Ouch!"
She stretched out the kinks in her back. "I wonder what
a hot bath runs in a place like this."

Dragonbait held up the two letters.

"What's that?" Alias asked.

"I think you can afford a hot bath," said the saurial,
throwing the heavier of the two letters on the bed. It
landed with a satisfying thump and jingle. Alias snatched
up the letter and ripped it open. A few magical sparks
danced from the paper, and belatedly Alias saw that it
bore Mintassan's sigil set into the blue sealing wax.

Four gold coins slid out from the letter's folds onto the bed.
Alias leaned against a bedpost and read the letter aloud.

" 'Lovely Alias and stout-hearted Dragonbait,' " she
began, then looked up at the saurial. "How come I never
get to be stout-hearted?"

"How come I never get to be lovely?" Dragonbait parried.

"Hmpph," she said, and continued reading. " 'In the
press of our business dealings last night, I neglected to
thank you for aiding Jamal. She is an old and dear
friend.' I'll just bet," Alias muttered this last. " 'I would
be heartbroken to see her charred to coal. Thank you. We
are greatly indebted to you. I have arranged with the
hostler of Blais House to turn all your charges over to my
account. Please, accept this hospitality as a token of my
gratitude.

" 'I hope that your stay in Westgate lasts long enough
to afford me the opportunity to speak with both of you at
length in order to broaden my knowledge of saurials.
Thank you once again for your courageous rescue. Yours
sincerely, Mintassan the Sage. P.S. Ask for the pan-fried
prawns for dinner—they are a taste treat.' "

"Sounds like you have a fan," the saurial said.

"Me? It's your brain he wants to pick. Probably trying
to prove your people are related to tree frogs or something. He only wants me as a free translator."

"Alias, he's a spellcaster. He can use magic to speak
with me. If he claimed to need you to translate, he would
only be using it as an excuse to hear you speak."

Alias furrowed her brow, but could think of no solid

argument. "Hand me that other letter," she demanded.

Dragonbait held out the second missive by the edges, as if it were a dead thing he did not want to touch. Alias plucked it from the saurial's grasp. The paper stock was far heavier than Mintassan's stationery, and the watermarks gave it the look of a very thin slice of granite. The purple sealing wax was marked with the coat of arms of the Croamarkh of Westgate, the elected leader of the city's council of noble and wealthy merchants.

Alias sniffed at it. "Smells like money," she joked.

Dragonbait harrumphed. "Smells like corruption."

"In this city, it's usually the same thing." Alias slid her throwing dagger between the wax seal and the paper and unfolded the single sheet. "It says, 'From the Office of the Croamarkh, Lord Luer Dhostar, to the adventurers herein identified as Alias and her lizardman companion. Greetings in the name of the Croamarkh of Westgate.' "

Alias took a deep breath and read on. " 'Your recent activities against the criminal organization known as the Night Masks have come to our attention. We wish to discuss with you the possibility of continued employment in that capacity on our behalf. If you are interested in such, a manservant will escort you to our present location for discussions. Such dealings will undoubtedly be extremely profitable for you, and we strongly recommend you avail yourself of this opportunity. My servant is instructed to await a reply. Yours sincerely, Luer Dhostar, Croamarkh of Westgate.' "

Alias let the missive drape delicately from one hand. "What do you think?"

"Last night you wanted to take the first boat back. You said you didn't want to be a cheap hero," Dragonbait pointed out.

"Ah, but the croamarkh isn't offering us the job of cheap hero. He's giving us the chance to be 'extremely profitable' heroes."

"We don't *need* money."

"But I like to think my services are worth money," Alias pointed out. "Lots of money. You're just hurt that he called you a lizardman," she teased.

Dragonbait sniffed with disdain. "He sounds like the sort of merchant who thinks everything can be solved by throwing money at it. The Night Masks are not a simple problem."

"Could take us more than a few weeks," Alias agreed cockily.

Dragonbait laughed and shook his head.

"Look," Alias cajoled, "Grypht isn't expecting us back immediately, and I know you miss CopperBloom, but it couldn't hurt to hear what the man has to say."

"Maybe not," the paladin replied dourly.

"I'll need a bath if I'm going to be presented to the croamarkh," the swordswoman declared, hopping off the bed.

Dragonbait pulled a guest bathrobe from the armoire and tossed it to her. There was a tiny rap on the door frame. Alias draped the robe over her arm and pulled open the door. A tray of fruit, muffins, and tea sat on the floor.

"Complimentary breakfast," Alias noted, looking down the hallway. "Where's the server?"

"She's shy," the paladin explained, picking up the tray, "but very sweet."

"Is she now?" Alias asked. It was rare that the saurial made that sort of compliment. "Well, you'll have to introduce us when I've finished my bath."

"What about this servant waiting downstairs?" asked Dragonbait.

"Dhostar said he'll wait for our reply. Let him wait."

Alias slipped out of the room, closing the door behind her. Dragonbait could hear her launching into a bawdy folk song involving dryads and paladins, as she went in search of the bath.

Dragonbait picked up the croamarkh's letter and sniffed. He couldn't use his *shen* sight on a soulless object, and while he'd joked about the smell of corruption, the only scents he could detect were paper, ink, and wax. Still, the letter made him uneasy.

* * * * *

"Westgate," Alias explained to Dragonbait, while she stuffed down a breakfast roll and slipped into a clean tunic, "is ruled by a council consisting of representatives of all the major trading families, along with a cluster of minor houses. No one else gets a vote in council, not craftsmen, not shopkeepers, not tavern owners, no one, not even persons like Mintassan. Most of the council's power is invested in the croamarkh. Luer Dhostar was elected by the council to three terms as croamarkh, before he was forced to yield to Lansdal Ssemm for a term. No one had really been happy with Lansdal, and during his term interfamily feuding and Night Mask violence was worse than ever. Last spring Luer Dhostar convinced the other families that only he could organize the chaos left by Lansdal, and he was returned to his former office.

"Besides his duty to the city of Westgate, Luer Dhostar oversees a mercantile empire consisting of twelve ships, twenty-four stockyards and warehouses, nine caravans, fifty representatives in other cities across the Heartlands, seventy-five businesses and craftsmen under his direct control and twice that controlled in all but name, a castle, a host of servants, ten purebred Zakharan horses, three carriages, and one son."

"Something tells me you were briefed by Elminster before we left Shadowdale," the saurial said when Alias had finished her monologue.

"Yeah. You think the old sneak had some premonition I would need to be up on current affairs?" she asked as she pulled on her chain mail and buckled on her sword.

The paladin did not answer as he buckled on his own. He didn't like to think of all the things Elminster must know.

As Alias and Dragonbait strolled down the hall, they spied the half-elven servant girl leaning over the railing, staring down at the lobby. Alias leaned against the railing beside her. The girl backed away in surprise, but her escape was blocked by the saurial. Alias turned back to look at her and smiled. "Are you the child," she asked, "who delivered the letters and breakfast?"

The girl gulped. "Mercy," she said, nodding, then added, "My name is Mercy."

"Well, Mercy, it's customary to wait for a tip," Alias said, pressing, not a copper or silver, but a gold coin into her hand. "Part of this is your tip, but part is also payment for services to be rendered. I want you to keep a lookout on our room. If anyone goes into it who shouldn't, I want you to tell me afterward. Will you?"

Mercy gulped again and nodded, her eyes wide with fright. Alias could tell that the girl was glancing nervously at Dragonbait.

"You look the way I must have the first time I saw Dragonbait," Alias said. "I was so frightened, I threw a dagger at him. Fortunately, I missed."

"What did he do?" Mercy asked.

"Well, he dropped the puppy he'd just rescued, and ran off."

"Do you like puppies?" the girl asked Dragonbait in astonishment.

The saurial nodded solemnly.

"I knew you two would have a lot in common," Alias quipped. She looked back down the railing. "So, is that the servant from House Dhostar?" she asked, jerking her thumb in the direction of the foyer, where a man stood with his back to them.

"His name's Kimbel," Mercy whispered, obviously anxious that the man not overhear her.

"Kimbel what?" Alias asked.

"Just Kimbel," Mercy replied. "He *doesn't* like puppies." With that pronouncement the servant girl slipped around Dragonbait and made off down the corridor, disappearing up a back staircase.

Dragonbait hissed, and Alias turned her attention to her companion. The paladin stood stock-still, with only the very tip of his tail twitching. He was glaring at Kimbel as if he might bore a hole through the servant with his eyes. Alias recognized the signs. His *shen* sight had detected something he did not like.

She studied the servant's back. Kimbel was a slender,

almost spidery man. His hairline receded several inches, and what remained of the graying blond hair was pulled back into a severe bun at the nape of the neck, held in place by two long silver hairpins, which Alias guessed could be used as weapons in a pinch. His shirt, trousers, and vest were simply but expensively tailored, all in black. The vest was decorated with silver studs in a geometric pattern. On another man the outfit might have appeared dashing, but it hung too loosely on Kimbel's spare frame.

"I take it that not liking puppies is not Kimbel's only failing," she said in Saurial, grateful to have words that could not be overheard.

Dragonbait rested his hand on the hilt of his sword. Alias could detect the just-baked bread scent of his anger and a whiff of the violetlike scent that he used to communicate danger.

"What color evil are we talking here?" she asked.

"Purple," the paladin whispered, though he could not be overheard.

Alias felt a knot in her gut. Purple evil was the most disturbing to her. Purple evil took pleasure in the pain of others. Purple evil liked to be the inflicter of that pain.

Just then, Kimbel turned around and looked up at them. He wore pince-nez, with darkened lenses that hid his eyes, giving him an inhuman look.

Dragonbait, Alias realized, would be very uncomfortable with this man as an escort. She wasn't thrilled with the idea either. "We should accompany him anyway," she said, "so you can check out the croamarkh with your *shen* sight."

Dragonbait nodded curtly, steeling himself to the task.

Kimbel stood motionlessly, watching the pair descend the stairs and approach him. Alias spotted the trading badge of the Dhostar household pinned to the lapel of his vest, but it wasn't until they stood directly before him that the servant showed them any recognition. Then he bowed very low at the waist, his back as stiff as iron. Alias sensed no respect in the servant's action. The display was intended to prop up the facade of Kimbel's gentility.

When he stood erect again, Alias worked at suppressing a shudder. His clean-shaven but weak chin, and the flat eyes behind the darkened glasses, gave him a snakelike appearance.

"Alias, I presume," he said, his lip curling upward in an approximation of a smile. "I am Kimbel, servant to House Dhostar. I have been instructed to await your reply."

"We'll speak to your master. Where can he be found?" Alias asked.

"He is at the Watch Docks, overseeing the customs arrangements. I have a carriage waiting outside to take you to him." He spun about and strode from the inn. Alias and Dragonbait followed at a deliberately leisurely pace.

The carriage, pulled by four black horses, was a huge, black monstrosity that, though capable of holding eight comfortably, was unable to negotiate Westgate's smaller streets. The house trading badge, a wagon wheel topped by three stars, was painted on the doors. According to the briefing Elminster had given Alias, the design granted by the Westgate city council to family Dhostar required the wheel color be tawny, but the ones marking the carriage had been gilded. Apparently Luer Dhostar liked to show off his political power.

Dragonbait found the carriage ridiculous and would have preferred to walk or even run, but he wasn't about to leave Alias alone with Kimbel. Before he would climb in, though, he studied the driver for a full minute, assuring himself that at least that servant harbored no evil intentions. He sat beside Alias, facing the front of the carriage.

Kimbel folded himself into a corner facing them. Dragonbait, using ordinary vision, stared at him, trying to gather more information, but the servant sat rigid, making no attempt at conversation, betraying nothing of himself. Alias kept her eyes on the view outside the carriage.

The city in daylight bustled with activity. In order to keep the main thoroughfares clear for carriages, the law required expensive and limited permits to load or unload wagons on those streets. To circumvent the fees, brute force had become the means of transport on the wider avenues, which were consequently crammed with milling legions of porters lugging boxes, urns, wicker baskets, crates, and passengers in riding chairs in an ever-milling dance. Added to the crush were shopkeepers trying to hustle customers into their establishments and vendors pushing carts or toting backpacks and hawking the wares they offered.

The carriage passed Mintassan's, but there was no sign of the sage. At one cross-street Alias caught a glimpse of people gathered around a dancing minotaur. Down another she thought she saw a street theater group performing atop a hay wagon, but the carriage moved too quickly for her to notice if Jamal was among the actors.

They came out to the Market Triangle, and Alias had a momentarily unobstructed view of the bay and the harbor, as the northern sections of the city sloped gently down to the sea.

The harbor was a tapestry of sails attached to ships from all over the Sea of Fallen Stars, cogs from Aglarond and Thesk, red cedar galleys from Thay, caravels from the Living City and the Vilhon Reach, strangely carved crafts from Mulhorand and Chondath, and carracks from nearby Cormyr and Sembia. Westgate was a major port on the Inner Sea. It stood at the entrance to both the Neck, the channel leading to the Lake of Dragons, and the northernmost caravan route to the west. It was also one of the few cities that did not belong to a larger kingdom, so there were no national politics influencing the city's trade with the outside world. Trade was the city's reason for being.

The carriage followed the road down the peninsula that sheltered the western half of the harbor from the bay and pulled to a stop at the end of the Watch Dock. The driver hopped down, unfolded the stairs, and opened the door.

Kimbel hopped over the stairs, displaying a liveliness Alias suspected was meant to impress his master, then offered his hand to his charges. Alias accepted the servant's help without thinking about what she knew of him, but Dragonbait hissed him back and hopped over the stairs unassisted.

A great canopy had been erected before the Watch Dock warehouse, and a pole planted before it displayed the banners of those officials currently engaged in business there: the harbor watch's, the customs inspector's and, at the top, the croamarkh's.

Alias and Dragonbait followed Kimbel into the shade beneath the canopy. Rows of tables were set up beneath to process the paperwork required of anyone coming into or out of the city via the harbor. In one line stood ships' officers with bills of lading, in another, servants of various merchant houses with petitions to release seized goods, and in a third, private passengers with their baggage. Alias and Dragonbait had come through this last line the evening before. This morning there was a noticeable improvement in the efficiency of customs personnel.

Alias could pick out with ease the inspiration of the efficiency—a large, solidly muscled man with a stonily impassive face, who hovered behind the customs officials seated at the tables. Each time the man moved to stand behind some worker, the worker wriggled nervously and concentrated with fervor on the work before him. The reaction was so pronounced that even were the man not wearing the chain of office about his neck, Alias would have guessed he was Croamarkh Luer Dhostar. His mantle of snow-white hair was swept back and held in place with a gold headband. The long, sleeveless robe he wore over his silk shirt and velvet trousers was made of the most elaborate brocade Alias had ever seen. Every finger sported a ring set with a stone worth a princess's ransom.

As Kimbel and the adventurers approached him, the croamarkh was leaning over the table beside one worker who perused a document handed to him by a servant wearing the trading badge of the Urdo family. The croamarkh leaned forward and drummed his fingers on the table beside the worker as he read the document over the

worker's shoulder. One might have thought the servant
would have appreciated the extra attention his paperwork was getting, but instead he shifted uneasily from
one foot to the other and bit his lower lip repeatedly.

Kimbel brought their presence to the croamarkh's
attention with a simple, "Milord," but the older man
motioned him to silence.

Alias noted Kimbel's jaw tighten, and was pleased to
learn the servant did on occasion betray his feelings.

The Croamarkh pulled a document out from beneath
the worker's elbow and chastised him. "If you would keep
abreast of the documents sent from the council, you
would realize that this shipment was cleared last week."
He pointed out the relevant lines to the worker. Flushed
with red, the worker whispered a terrified, "Yes, sir," and
stamped the servant's release papers.

The servant from the house of Urdo reached for the
papers, but Luer Dhostar grabbed his wrist. "You tell
your master," he said to the servant, "that this document
releases only the statuary, not the ten pounds of smoke
powder we found hidden inside. He will also be charged
with the time it took our men to drill out the bottoms of
each statue and empty them of the proscribed sub-
stance." With that, he pushed the servant's hand away.

The servant fled from the scene like a game bird
released from a trap.

Only then did Dhostar turn his attention to the newcomers. "Well?" he addressed Kimbel.

Kimbel smiled pleasantly despite his lord's glare. He
stepped forward and gave the croamarkh a half bow.
"Milord," he said, "may I present Alias and Dragonbait?"

Lord Dhostar stepped out from behind the table and
inspected the adventurers with the appraising look he
might give a shipment of goods. He dispensed with pleas-
antry and preamble and addressed the pair directly. "It's
been brought to my attention that the pair of you interrupted a number of Night Mask activities last night."

Alias could tell by his tone that he did not require an
affirmation on their part, though he made the statement
sound so much like an accusation that she wondered if he

was expecting her to make a denial. Alias remained silent beneath the croamarkh's gaze, but kept her eyes locked on his.

The croamarkh raised his eyebrows in appreciation of the woman's nerve. He continued. "Common tongues are always quick to wag about heroes. Wiser tongues question. So—whom do you serve?"

It was hardly the question Alias expected, so she was for a moment confused by it. She shot a look at Dragonbait, who she could see was studying the croamarkh with his *shen* sight. As the paladin did not seem to be exhibiting the same violent reaction he'd had to Kimbel, the swordswoman relaxed and answered the question simply. "No one." Then she decided she'd better rephrase that. "I sell my sword as I choose," she said. "At the moment, it's available.

"So you are not an agent, representative, or servant of another house?" Lord Dhostar queried sharply.

"I'm not working for anyone in Westgate," the swordswoman responded, her brow knitting in irritation with the cross-examination.

Lord Dhostar frowned, apparently unable to believe that she was truly free of allegiances. He stared hard at her, trying to assess her truthfulness. As he did so, another man wearing the trading badge of the Dhostar family approached. He was dressed less fashionably than Kimbel, in a simple white shirt, dusty brown breeches, and muddy riding boots, but from the way he took a place at the croamarkh's right hand, Alias presumed he was a servant of higher rank. He was tall and handsome, with wavy brown hair and bright blue eyes, and although he looked only thirty-some years old, he was more self-assured in the croamarkh's presence than anyone else Alias had seen. He held a packet of letters up, and, as he stood waiting patiently for Dhostar to finish his business with the swordswoman and take the packet, the younger man grinned and winked at Alias.

Finally, the croamarkh harrumphed and said, "We have a watch in this city. It keeps the common people orderly. The Night Masks, however, are a lawless bunch.

I want someone to deal exclusively with them. I want them knocked down every time they have the arrogance to rise. I want them to start fearing the consequences of crossing me. I'm prepared to pay you a retainer of one thousand gold coins. After a ten-day trial, I'll evaluate what I think your continued service would be worth and we can negotiate your pay."

"I'll need more information and some time to consider your offer," Alias replied.

The croamarkh raised his eyebrows again. No doubt it had been a long time since he'd offered someone that much money and been told he must wait for a reply. "Fine," he replied sharply. "Victor, here," and he jerked his head in the direction of the new arrival who'd winked at Alias, "will be your liaison. You ask him your questions and let him know your answer by this evening."

"So, Your Lordship," Victor asked the croamarkh, "are you going to authorize the hiring of more staff for customs inspection?"

"Only if the inspector fires the staff he has," Dhostar growled as he took the parcel of letters from the younger man. "If my people worked as well as his do, I'd be a poor man. Convince this woman she would do well to accept my offer. I'm returning with Kimbel to our own docks."

"Yes, Your Lordship," Victor replied.

Without even a nod, the croamarkh strode away with Kimbel in his wake.

Alias shot Dragonbait a questioning look about the croamarkh.

"Gray," the paladin said.

"Gray? Just gray?" Alias complained in Saurial, hoping for some other insight into Dhostar's character. Gray was neutral, neither evil nor virtuous.

"Bleak and empty, a cold rain drizzling on an abandoned keep. Strong and very, very proud," Dragonbait replied.

Victor, unable to hear the high-pitched tones of the adventurers' conversation in Saurial, stood before them grinning, waiting for Alias to speak. After a moment, he ran his fingers nervously through his hair, pushing it

back off his forehead, and spoke up. "Well, I have my
orders. Do you mind if we walk while we talk? I have to
look over some ships that have come in for inspection."

"Fine," Alias said, following the man from beneath the
canopy. The three walked along the broad stone quay, in
the direction of the lighthouse that stood at the mouth of
the harbor.

Victor began brightly, "The Night Masks have been a
thorn in Westgate's side for, oh, fifteen years, at least.
Most people consider them part of the price of doing business here, but the croamarkh is a man of law and justice.
He wants the citizens of Westgate freed from the tyranny
of their lawlessness."

"Yes," Alias said, "I can see he's frantic with worry for
them."

"I beg your pardon?" Victor said.

"Luer Dhostar is a merchant. His first concern is that
his books show a healthy balance. Now that that balance
is so obscenely huge, there's no challenge to his work,
and, not content with being the bane of the dance floor or
the dessert table, he takes on the mission of proving his
greatness. He keeps a carriage large enough to house a
halfling family. He hangs over customs workers, demon-
strating he's more competent than they in a job he
couldn't stomach for a week. He tries to hire professionals to do away with a thieves guild he tolerated for his
first three terms because *now* they are an embarrassment. Their continued unchallenged activity proves they
have more power than he. He has no more concern for
the people of Westgate than the Night Masks do."

Victor was stunned into a momentary silence. When he
spoke again, though, his tone was fervent. "You're wrong.
Father cares *very* much for the people of Westgate, as do
I. He just has a hard time showing it."

"Very diplomatic," Dragonbait chided Alias in Saurial.
"You've just insulted your new employer to his son."

Alias closed her eyes and stated the now obvious,
"You're his son."

The young man bowed low. "Victor Dhostar, scion of
House Dhostar, heir to Croamarkh Luer Dhostar, bane-

in-training of the dance floor and the dessert table, at your service."

Alias felt a paralyzing blush climb to her face.

Dragonbait gave her an order in Saurial.

"How do you do, Your Lordship?" Alias said, repeating, like a puppet, the phrases the paladin fed to her. "I'm Alias, and this is my companion, Dragonbait. Dragonbait begs that you forget this swordswoman's foolish gaff."

"What gaff?" Victor asked with a smile. Then he was serious once again. "It is true, some of what you say. We are concerned with our books' balances, and Father does like to show off, but we merchants aren't all heartless. Just as I'm sure there are some compassionate sell-swords."

"Touché," Alias conceded the young merchant the point.

"It is true that the merchant families have tolerated the Night Masks too long," Victor said with an apologetic tone. "Some of the families, or to be more accurate, some members of some families, find organized criminals useful. Sort of a shadow government that keeps the more powerful families in check and allows the lesser merchants a leg up with illegal business dealings. All the families use them to handle business they would rather not sully their hands with, or pay to keep them away from their doors."

"Does that include House Dhostar?" Alias asked.

"Hardly," Victor laughed. "The first time the Night Masks demanded protection money from House Dhostar—that would have been at least fourteen years ago, when Father was serving his first term as croamarkh—well, Father threatened all-out war in the streets. To hear Father tell it, he was prepared to torch his warehouses rather than pay any tribute. They have stayed away from most of House Dhostar's concerns."

"I see," said Alias. "Is no one else in Westgate as brave and virtuous as your father?"

"Well, I doubt Lady Nettel of House Thalavar has any dealings with them," Victor replied. "She keeps a lot of halflings on retainer, though, and some people call them the economy Night Masks. I don't suppose that's any more fair than assuming all merchants are heartless. It's my suspicion that House Urdo and House Ssemm are up to their eyeballs in dealings with the Night Masks. Possibly they even serve as members to the Faceless's inner circle, the Night Masters. The other houses, I suppose, just pay them protection and only hire them on special occasions."

"You mentioned the Faceless? Who's he?" Alias asked.

"The Faceless is the Night Masks' supposed lord. There's a lot of speculation about him. Some say he's a powerful spellcaster, others that he's not even human. A few people insist he does not exist."

"So, without denying that your father may care about the people of Westgate, tell me: Why has he waited until his fourth term of office to hire me to take care of them? And why hire me of all people?"

"Well, as to the first, I suppose during his first three terms he didn't take the Night Masks very seriously. Because he faced them down, he presumed they weren't bothering anyone else. He does tend to be removed from the problems of the common people. When he lost the office of croamarkh to Lansdal Ssemm, the Night Masks' activities got much more aggressive and Father began to reevaluate their threat. I suppose I can take some credit for his new outlook. Since I turned thirty he's begun to take me more seriously, too. And I think something must be done about the Night Masks. I really believe the people should have justice.

"As for why you, well, Father's been looking for the right person since he was reelected this spring, and you appeared. If Westgate were a theocracy, you would be seen as a sign from the gods. To a businessman like my father, you're the knock of opportunity. From what we heard of your exploits of last night, you have the skills and the momentum. Businessmen do not slam the door in the face of opportunity. And speaking of business, please excuse me for a moment, I need to attend to something."

Alias nodded and stood beside Dragonbait as Victor

walked down a pier to speak with another man wearing a family Dhostar trading badge.

"Well, what insights into the Dhostar heir?" Alias asked.

"He is all he appears," the paladin replied with satisfaction, delighted to have found another pure soul of sky blue in this city of vice.

"What, another puppy-lover?" Alias asked.

"Why must you joke about it?" Dragonbait asked. "I do not tease you for your virtue."

Alias flushed again. She was never comfortable when the paladin reminded her that he perceived virtue in her. She harbored a secret fear that he saw what he wanted to see in her, and should the veil ever be lifted from his eyes . . . Alias didn't like to think about that. She diverted the conversation back to Luer Dhostar. "Whatever Victor may say, you aren't convincing me that the croamarkh isn't motivated by his vanity and love of power."

"No," the saurial agreed. "The elder Dhostar is not all his son contends. Victor sees him with the eyes of a loving son, and he defends him as a loyal son would. He reminds me of you, the way you always defended Finder Wyvernspur, despite his many flaws."

Alias, determined not to be drawn into an argument about the man she'd thought of as a father, returned her attention to Victor Dhostar.

The young man appeared to be trying to negotiate an argument between the servant of his own house and a halfling dressed in the green livery of House Thalavar, who stood on top of a stack of crates. Despite Victor's efforts, both servants had gone beyond the stage of arguing rationally and had begun screaming at one another at the top of their lungs, each waving a bill of lading in the other's face.

Behind the halfling servant was a Thalavar ship crewed by halflings, and behind the human servant was a Dhostar vessel crewed by humans. The crews of both ships had also turned their attention to the dispute and had begun to scramble off their ships onto the pier to back up the servant of their respective house.

Alias began moving down the pier, against her better judgment, but knowing she would feel bad if something happened to the young Dhostar. Victor managed to talk his family's servant into walking away from the halfling, and it seemed as if a brawl had just been averted, until the halfling called out, "That tub shouldn't just be hauling garbage, it ought to be hauled away as garbage."

The Dhostar servant whirled around, bellowing with rage, and lunged toward the Thalavar servant. Victor shouted, "Brunner, no!" but it was too late. Drawing back instinctively from the charging human, the Thalavar servant apparently forgot his footing, for he took one step too many off the stack of crates and tumbled from the pier. There was a short, high-pitched shriek and a splash as he hit the water.

Everyone froze, including Victor, for the space of a heartbeat, then, spurred by an anonymous shout of, "Get 'im!" a wall of halflings rushed the Dhostar servant Brunner. Brunner tried to swat them away, but there were far too many, and within moments he'd disappeared beneath a pile of green-liveried halflings.

Victor moved toward the pile, but Alias reached his side and pulled him back. "This could be messy, milord," she said. "Please, leave it to the professionals."

Alias waded into the fray and began plucking biting, scratching halflings off the pile, handing them to the Dhostar crew members to be restrained until they calmed down. More halflings surged from their ship and began brawling with the humans who held their comrades. The swordswoman realized she was in a race to get Brunner on his feet and away from the fray before someone, halfling or human, lost his or her temper and drew a weapon.

Then, just as she caught a glimpse of Brunner's black tabard, Alias heard the whistle and felt the breeze of a blade as it cut the air just inches above her head. Someone had drawn live steel.

Instinct took hold of her. Although she stepped back to avoid skewering anyone at her feet, the swordswoman had her blade drawn in the wink of an eye. She whirled about to meet the challenge she sensed from above. She took a defensive stance, determined that this fiasco should not end in a bloodbath, but equally determined to disarm the fool who'd first brought steel into the fray.

Her attacker's sword swept down again, still too high to catch her, but just low enough for her to block the weapon with her own. She lunged forward, and the two blades slid along their lengths until they were locked at their hilts.

Alias glared up at the armed halfling who now stood on the stack of crates. This halfling was female. She wore a scarlet-and-amber cloak cut in the latest Cormyrian style, with the hood pulled up and shadowing her face. Alias reached up with her free hand, caught the end of the tassel fastened to the back of the hood, and yanked hard. The hood fell back, spilling long red tresses about a grinning face.

Alias's jaw dropped open, and she stood momentarily stunned.

"Well, hello, Alias!" the halfling Olive Ruskettle shouted over the din and their locked blades. "I'd been hoping we'd have a chance to cross swords again."

# Six
# Alliances

As Alias struggled to overcome the surprise of meeting Olive Ruskettle, and the shock of discovering that the halfling had pulled a blade on her, Olive took advantage of her. The halfling bard, with a practiced up-and-down jerk of her wrist, was able to bring her short blade to the outside of the human woman's sword, and with a quick push downward, strengthened by her own weight, was able to smash Alias's hand and blade into the top of the crate. Pain shot down Alias's arm, and she jerked backward.

"Olive! What *do* you think you are doing?" Alias growled as she swung with the flat of her blade, trying to swat the halfling on her legs.

"Same as you, I should think," the halfling replied, parrying Alias's blow and delivering a quick, shallow thrust. "Fighting for the good guys!"

Alias extended her sword and lunged, startling Olive into a step backward. Alias leaped onto the top of the stack of crates. "Have you gone crazy?" she upbraided the halfling. "Suppose someone sees you've pulled out live steel and decides to follow your example? You want the pier bathed in blood?"

"I hadn't thought of that," Olive said, looking momentarily repentant, but then she shrugged. "No. Everyone else is still going at it with fisticuffs. The only person paying any attention to us is that cute Dhostar lackey in the riding boots."

Alias half turned her head and caught a glimpse of Victor, standing back from the fray. With Alias's attention distracted, Olive smacked the swordswoman on the shoulder with the flat of her blade.

"Verily, a touch," the halfling squealed.

Alias whirled around, furious. Her chain mail had absorbed most of the blow, but she was sure to have a bruise. "That is *quite* enough," she snapped. She slid her blade back down along the halfling's until they were once again hilt to hilt. With her left hand she grabbed Olive's wrist and squeezed.

"Hey, that hurts," the halfling complained.

"Release your weapon," Alias demanded.

"Well, since you feel so strongly about it," Olive replied, and she opened the hand that held the hilt of her sword.

Alias grabbed the shorter blade with her left hand and turned the blade's tip on the owner's throat. "Now, you're going to behave," she ordered "until this thing is sorted out."

"Okay," the halfling replied with a meek smile, but a moment later she added, "Oops, too late. Fight's over."

Behind her Alias heard a high-pitched whistle that she recognized as Dragonbait's. Alias turned to find the saurial, his scales glistening with water, standing on the pier beside the halfling who had fallen into the harbor. The small servant was sodden, but uninjured.

The others on the pier had also turned at Dragonbait's bidding, pausing for just a moment from their aggressions.

That pause was all Victor needed. The merchant strode to the wet halfling's side, shouting, "Please, stop fighting. This gentle being has rescued House Thalavar's shipping clerk. Should you continue this pointless brawl, we will have to call out the watch."

The combatants remained frozen, certain that they did not want to be hauled in by the watch, but uncertain that they should abandon the fight just yet. All halfling eyes were on the Thalavar family's shipping clerk.

The wet halfling glared up at the Dhostar heir. "What about my ruined clothes?" he demanded, indicating his soaked velvet tabard and breeches.

"I will be glad to make reparations," Victor replied, "once you've apologized for insulting my family's ship."

"Oh, I didn't realize it was your ship, milord. I can see now it's a bonny little craft," the halfling replied cheerfully. Then he added, "But our ship still beat it into the harbor and was at this pier first."

"Agreed," Victor said.

The Thalavar shipping clerk smiled broadly. Then he turned angrily on his own workers and shouted at them like a drill sergeant. "What do you think you're doing? I didn't hire any of you to brawl on the docks! You're supposed to be hauling crates to the deck!"

The halflings scurried back aboard their ship. Two of Dhostar's men helped Brunner to his feet. The big man was quite disheveled, and his nose was bleeding, but then several of the halflings sported black eyes and bleeding noses.

"They got here first only because they cut our ship off in the channel," Brunner growled.

Victor replied with an insistent patience, "But they did get here first. They have first access to the inspector." There was a hint of warning in his tone.

Brunner scowled and shook off the two men who'd helped him rise.

"Is that understood, Brunner?" Victor asked.

"Yes, milord," the human servant replied grudgingly. He turned and stomped back aboard his ship.

"Is that what this is all about? Who's next in line?" Alias hissed to Olive, astonished at the nonsensical reasons people chose to fight one another.

"Yeah," Olive whispered back. "Thalavar's ship had right of way, but Dhostar wouldn't yield. Thalavar's sails stole Dhostar's wind, though, and went whipping past. Dhostar nearly grounded out on a sandbar. They just can't stand giving up anything to a halfling."

"That doesn't explain why in the Gray Waste you pulled a sword on me," Alias growled.

The halfling took her sword from Alias and sheathed it. "It was all for show. The Dumpster's—excuse me, the Dhostar's—minions have to be shown they can't go around stepping on Thalavar halfling toes whenever they want. I had to draw you off before you kicked the

Thalavar halflings' butts. And now Dhostar's people'll remember there was a Thalavar halfling who took on Alias the Sell-Sword. They won't remember which halfling, since they can't seem to tell us apart, so they'll have to be more cautious around all of us."

Alias continued to glare at Olive as she sheathed her own weapon.

"Honestly, you shouldn't take it so personally," Olive insisted. "I swung high. I used the flat of my blade. You know I could have hit you if I'd been meaning to."

Alias harrumphed, but then, with a grin creeping onto her face, she replied, "It's true, Olive. You never missed a target with its back turned to you." She sat down, slid off the crates to the pier, and turned about to give Olive a hand down. The halfling took her hand and jumped down.

"Thank you," the halfling said as she fussily rearranged her cloak.

"You didn't used to be so gracious about accepting help," Alias recalled.

"The knees are getting old, my dear," the bard replied.

Victor finished making financial arrangements with the Thalavar shipping clerk, then he and Dragonbait joined the two women.

Victor bowed to Olive. "Mistress Ruskettle, I'm Victor Dhostar. Thalavar's shipping clerk just told me who you were. I'm so pleased to meet you. Please, excuse this unpleasantness. Brunner and his people tend to be . . ." Victor searched for the words.

"Less polite to people who aren't like them," Olive supplied.

Victor nodded with a sad smile. "Very provincial, I'm afraid. I hope Lady Nettel will forgive this unfortunate incident."

"I'm sure she wouldn't hold you responsible, Lord Victor," Olive replied with a gracious smile. "And may I say, I'm pleased to meet you as well. It's so refreshing to meet someone whose attitudes are more cosmopolitan."

Victor smiled and said, "I'd appreciate any help in making sure that relationships between the Thalavars and Dhostars and their peoples run smoothly. If you have any other problems, please feel free to contact me." He held out a hand.

Olive shook the merchant's hand briefly.

"Well, now. I'm afraid I must ask you to excuse me. There is some paperwork I must examine aboard my ship." He turned to Alias. "I should only be a few minutes," he explained.

Alias nodded. "We'll wait," she said.

"He's not only cute, he's quite a charmer," Olive said once Victor was out of earshot. "If he could bottle that, he could double his family's fortune."

"Yes, he is charming," Alias agreed. "But enough about him," she snapped. "You still haven't told me what you're doing in Westgate."

"Hello, Dragonbait," the halfling greeted the saurial. "You're looking well. How're CopperBloom and the hatchlings?"

Dragonbait signed in the thieves' hand cant, *Very well, thank you. It's always a surprise to see you. What are you doing in Westgate?*

"I've agreed to help out Lady Nettel of House Thalavar," the halfling replied. "Lady Nettel does a lot of trading with the halflings of the Shining South and hires a lot of them to run her business. She tends to trust halflings since the Night Masks don't accept us in their guild. Lady Nettel won't have anything to do with the Night Masks, and since she refuses to pay protection, her ships and warehouses get robbed or vandalized more than anyone else's, and a lot of her halfling workers are getting hurt in the process."

"So you came here as a hired sword?" Alias asked.

Olive shook her head. "I started out teaching music to Her Ladyship's granddaughter. I've sort of moved into an advisory position, trying to keep security tight enough so no more halflings get hurt, and so the Masks will decide we're too difficult a target and leave us be. Of course, I still keep my sword ready at all times. We'll probably be working together now that you're going after the Masks."

Alias's brow furrowed in puzzlement. "Lord Dhostar

made me a job offer only an hour ago. How did you find out?"

"Picked it up on the street," Olive said.

"Mistress Ruskettle!" the Thalavar shipping clerk called out.

"Just a minute, Drew," she responded. "Look, I have to attend to some things. You can reach me at House Thalavar."

Olive joined the Thalavar shipping clerk, and the pair escorted the customs inspector aboard the Thalavar ship.

Alias gave a mock shudder. "Olive as a respectable member of the community. The Time of Troubles was less confusing."

"Aye," Dragonbait agreed.

"So, what do you think?" Alias asked the paladin.

"About what?"

"Should we accept Dhostar's offer?"

Dragonbait sighed. He ran his fingertips down the tattoo on her right arm, the tattoo that had first bound them together. "Alias, you must make this decision for yourself," he said. "You have many reasons to remain. Although you did not really grow up here, Finder put it in your heart to feel it was home. You still need to try to discover why he choose Jamal's face as that of your memory mother. Olive is here. You could sing together again. And, of course, I know you would thrive on challenging the Night Masks."

Alias bit her lower lip and fought back a wave of sadness. Dragonbait had been her companion from the day she'd been created. He was more a father to her than Finder had been. "But you're leaving Westgate, aren't you?" she asked.

"I wish to return home to CopperBloom and my family. I don't expect you to feel obligated to return with me, and I don't want you to feel you cannot stay without me. You have many friends here already. I will stay with you for ten days, whether you choose to work for the croamarkh or not. But *I* will not work for him."

"Because of Kimbel?" Alias asked.

"Kimbel is part of it, yes. More importantly, I don't

think the croamarkh is worthy of my services. I will
serve you, though, as best I can, while I am still here."

Alias sniffed the air about them. Dragonbait's emotions had perfumed it heavily with the smell of lemons
and roses. "You're both happy and sad," she laughed.

"Parents always feel that way when they kick their
children out of the nest," Dragonbait explained.
"Dhostar's son is returning."

Brushing a tear from her eye, Alias turned about in
time to see Victor running down the gangplank of the
Dhostar ship. His momentum carried him nearly into
Alias. He stopped inches away from her. He stood looking
down at her for a moment before he stepped back with a
flush on his face. Running his fingers through his hair to
brush it off his face, he made an embarrassed apology for
nearly running her down.

"I don't fall down so easily, Lord Victor," Alias replied
with a grin. "Shall we continue our stroll? Dragonbait
and I were both enjoying it."

"Yes," Victor replied. "We should make for the Harbor
Tower. There's a spectacular view of the city from the
top."

Alias nodded, and the three left the pier and set out for
the lighthouse that marked the harbor entrance. Looking
south, across the harbor, the city lay spread out before
them, rising from the water to the high wall. Alias could
not remember seeing any other city with so magnificent a
view of itself as Westgate.

"So," Victor began, "what can I tell you to convince you
to join us in our fight against the Night Masks?"

"You should tell me the truth, whether it convinces me
or not," Alias replied. With an ever so slightly flirtatious
grin, she asked, "If I accept this post, will you continue to
be my liaison to the croamarkh?"

"Oh, yes," Victor said. "I'll be the man to handle any
problems for you. Father would hardly delegate this matter to Kimbel."

"Tell me about Kimbel," Alias said.

"Um, well." Victor flushed. "Kimbel is—not very nice."

"That was our impression," Alias said, not yet prepared

to explain about the saurial paladin's *shen* sight. "Tell me more about him."

"When Kimbel first came to Westgate, he called himself an adventurer. He wasn't the sort that kills monsters in their lairs, though. He was the sort that breaks into castles and tries to kill croamarkhs."

"He tried to kill your father?" Alias asked with astonishment.

"Yes. Poisoned all the watchdogs and got as far as father's bedroom door, but he got unlucky and tripped on a cat. He killed eight men before the rest of the guards managed to bring him down. He claims he was hired by the Night Masks, but he didn't know enough about them to betray them. Father decided he was too useful to waste with an execution. We had a geas cast on him. He's magically compelled to serve our family and constrained from harming anyone with Dhostar blood or in Dhostar employ. Father expects him to complete the terms of service due us by the eight men he killed, such terms to be served consecutively."

Victor scooped up a handful of pebbles and began tossing them in the water. "It sounds awfully creepy, I know. It is awfully creepy. He can't break the geas, but still, he's a killer. And there's nothing in the geas to protect people who aren't part of our trading house. Who knows what he does when he's out of sight? Father says Kimbel serves as a good warning to others, though I suspect Father also keeps him near to show people he's not afraid of assassins. I wish he wouldn't." Victor tossed the rest of the stones in the water all at once.

Dragonbait had been right, Alias realized. Victor was like her. He defended the croamarkh just as she had once defended Finder, defying his reason to quell his heart. She knew exactly how Victor felt, and she found herself sympathizing with the young merchant despite her dislike of his father.

They came to the end of the peninsula, which ended in a knob-shaped quay of stonework. Beneath the harbor lighthouse, guards in Westgate's insignia patrolled the flagstone plaza in rigid geometric formations. The lighthouse was an ancient, conical tower built of mortared stone with an external staircase spiraling up its side. Sailors called it the Westlight, and "seen the Westlight" was used throughout the Inner Sea nations to mean that a person had reached land or safety.

Victor nodded to the captain of the guard, and the three were allowed to approach the lighthouse without challenge. Feeling suddenly lighthearted, Alias dashed up the structure's stairs without stop until she reached the walkway at the top. She looked first out to the sea, letting the breeze ruffle her hair until Victor and Dragonbait finished the climb.

"Are you always so energetic?" the merchant lord asked as he stood clutching his side and gasping for breath.

Alias smiled, but did not reply. She studied the light in the center of the walkway—a polished brass framework surrounding a floating marble sphere, which, even in the daylight, shone brightly enough to be noticed far out to sea. "There's a continual light spell cast on the marble?" the swordswoman asked.

Victor nodded. "There are also protections to keep the magic from being dispelled by accident or to keep others from destroying it. The bronze frame can be used to hold up colored screens so we can send coded messages to ships at sea—fire, plague, send help, and so on."

Alias nodded and turned to look back out across the harbor and the city. Victor moved to stand beside her. "There's no better place to start to get oriented." He pointed leftward, out across the bay at various landmarks. "There's the River Thunn. Between the river's east bank and the city wall is Castle Malavhan. Just across the river from that is Castle Vhammos. It was once the royal castle. Those four clustered due south of us are Castles Guldar, Athagdal, Thorsar and Urdo. They were all built at the same time by rival architects from different nations.

"The building in the center of the market is called the Tower. It serves as the city's registry and headquarters for the watch. The jail is in the dungeon beneath the Tower. Against the western wall is Castle Ssemm. South of that is Castle Thalavar. In the northeast corner, by the sea, is the Temple to Talos, and to the west of the Tower is the Temple to Mask. At the base of the harbor's arm are the temples to Loviatar and Gond, and just west of them is the Temple to Ilmater."

"You've pointed out the castles of all the merchant families but your own," Alias noted.

"Castle Dhostar isn't in the city. We're latecomers to the city, here for only three generations. When Father decided to build our family's castle, he decided it was more important to use the land we owned in the city for our warehouses. So we built out to the west. You can see how the city's starting to expand in that direction beyond the walls."

"Can you see your castle from here?" Alias asked.

Victor put his hands on Alias's shoulders and turned her to face westward. Dragonbait's tail twitched nervously. Alias did not like being touched by strangers. To the paladin's surprise and relief, she did not shake off the young man's hands or growl at him.

Victor stood directly behind her and pointed over her shoulder. Alias looked out with attentive interest. "Follow that line of islands there, to that forested bluff. Just behind that is Castle Dhostar."

"Yes, I can see it," Alias said.

"I often come up here to think," the merchant lord said. "Well, really, to dream."

Alias leaned her head back against Victor's chest to look up at his face. "What do you dream about?" she asked with a smile.

Victor gave a small, self-deprecating laugh. "I dream about what I'll do should I find Verovan's treasure hoard."

"Verovan's treasure?" Alias asked with a teasing laugh.

"Yes. About a hundred twenty years ago, Westgate was a monarchy ruled by an incompetent tyrant, King Verovan. He nearly bankrupted the city with his excesses and destroyed it with his intrigues. He fancied himself a great boatman, and challenged the other rulers of the coastal cities to a race. The city coffers couldn't cover the cost of hiring the boat and team Verovan wanted—a windjammer with blood-red sails, crewed by Turmishmen. So Verovan passed a grain tax, clinching his unpopularity with everyone. On the day of the race—"

"On the day of the race," Alias interrupted, "Verovan's crew set a course for a rocky shoal, then teleported away, leaving Verovan to fend for himself. He couldn't. The boat was wrecked on the shoals, and Verovan was presumed drowned. Some people speculated that the 'Turmishmen' were really Red Wizards of Thay who avenged themselves on the tyrant for his intrigues against their nation. The city's leading merchants led a revolt before Verovan's son could be crowned. A mob stripped the royal castle bare. The patriarch of the merchant house of Vhammos moved his family into the castle, and he and the other merchants took charge of governing the city."

Victor gave the swordswoman a puzzled look.

"I was born in Westgate," Alias explained with a sideways look at Dragonbait. The saurial was enjoying the view, watching a round ship from Sembia, riding low in the water, try to maneuver into a dock across the way. "I know all about Verovan. He was real. His treasure, though, is a fable, like the stories about the liches that live in Westgate's sewers or the sea serpent that lives in its harbor."

"You forget you're dealing with a merchant," Victor said. "The books, you see, do not balance. The sum total of everything removed from the royal castle does not even approach the vast amounts of wealth that ever went in. Verovan skimmed a share of every fee and tax the city ever collected, and he bought valuable pieces of magic and art that disappeared into the castle. He never purchased anything with his own money, but with the city's, and he left scores of debts for things he'd 'purchased.' "

"So, you believe in the magic door?" Alias teased.

"What door?" Dragonbait asked.

Alias turned her attention to the saurial, who had not seemed to be paying attention to the conversation.

"There's supposed to be an invisible bridge leading away from one of the castle's towers," the swordswoman explained to the saurial. "On the other side of the invisible bridge, there's supposed to be to an invisible portal. Verovan's hoard is supposed to be behind that portal." With a darker tone, Alias concluded, "Guarded by fearsome monsters. No sage, mage, or priest has been able to find it, though it's said that the Watch has on occasion found a body lying at the base of one or other of the castle's towers."

"I'll remember, when I find the treasure, that you were a disbeliever," Victor threatened with a grin.

Alias laughed again. "So, in your daydreams, what do you do with this hoard of wealth when you find it?"

Victor turned away and looked back across the city. "I make Westgate the greatest city in the Realms," he answered with vehemence. "Greater even than Waterdeep. Clear out the Night Masks so people can stroll the streets at night. Build a second city wall farther out so people can expand their businesses and households. Build a navy so we can protect our ships from pirates. Build a library so scholars would come here to live, and an opera house to bring in bards and musicians. Run irrigation to the lands south of the city, with water from the River Redden, so we never have to worry about droughts."

"They all sound like good plans," Alias said.

"Yes." Then he looked back at her with a sly smile and said, "Of course, if a certain someone, who was, after all, born in Westgate, would agree to help my father and me, I wouldn't have to discover Verovan's treasure first to get rid of the Night Masks."

Alias chuckled at the smooth way the merchant had shifted the conversation back to his father's offer of employment. "Well, since a certain someone doesn't think you'll be finding that treasure anytime soon," Alias replied, "and does think you should do something about the Night Masks in the meantime, I guess that someone had better agree to help out."

Victor turned about and grasped both of Alias's hands in his own. "You'll help, then? That's wonderful. Father will be so pleased. He won't show it, but he will be pleased."

"And you, Lord Victor?" Alias asked. "Are you pleased?"

"Oh, yes. Of course." The young merchant squeezed her hands to emphasize his point, then released them suddenly, flushing with the realization of the liberty he'd taken. "And Dragonbait?" he asked suddenly, turning to the saurial. "You'll help, too?"

"Tell him what we agreed," the paladin said to Alias.

"Dragonbait must return north soon," Alias explained. "He won't be working for the croamarkh, but he will help me until he goes."

"I see, " Victor replied. "Well, I'm grateful for all the time you can give us," the merchant said to the saurial.

Dragonbait nodded politely.

A shiver ran down Alias's back. Even though, as Dragonbait had pointed out, she had other friends here, in her whole life she had never been long separated from the paladin. She studied Victor's face as he took one last look over the city, and felt slightly reassured. With the earnest, handsome merchant lord as one of those friends, Westgate might not only be less lonely but more exciting. Still, a sense of dread lingered in the pit of her stomach. In her first year of life, she'd defeated many powerful and evil beings, yet Dragonbait had always been there to back her up. Now, she realized, she had just possibly committed herself to battling the Night Masks alone.

# Seven
## Street Theater

The adventurers and their new ally climbed back down the lighthouse. In the plaza stood an open, two-wheeled carriage pulled by two yellow mares. An old man, dressed in the black and tawny parti-colored livery of House Dhostar, held the halter of one of the horses. Although the Dhostar trading insignia emblazoned the side of the small black carriage, the insignia was tawny like the horses, not gilded.

"It's not as showy as my father's," Victor pointed out, "so perhaps you wouldn't mind allowing me to drive you back to your inn?"

"Well, I suppose," Alias agreed with a feigned reluctance. She allowed the merchant to hand her up to the single seat. Victor got in on the other side, and Dragonbait squeezed in beside Alias.

The old man released the horses as Victor snapped the reins. The carriage started down the street at a brisk pace. Although they were crowded and the ride was somewhat bumpier than the one they'd experienced in the croamarkh's carriage, the adventurers felt much more relaxed in Victor's company, and therefore cheerier.

"I have other duties I must return to soon, but perhaps, if you haven't made other plans," Victor said, as cautious as a man creeping up on a sleeping beholder, "we could have dinner together."

"Dinner? What sort of dinner?" Alias asked.

"Nothing formal like a banquet or anything," Victor explained. "Just soup and sandwiches while we discussed strategy. You, me, and Dragonbait if you wish. We can

talk about where to start making your assault on the
Night Masks. I've been keeping track of some of their
crimes, the ones that are reported, anyway. They hardly
ever hit near the market surrounding the Tower, for fear,
I presume, of the watch, but I've noticed of late they've
been preying more heavily on the Gateside district.
Whoa!" Victor pulled the horses up sharply as he turned
the curve onto Westgate Market Street.

A crowd of people jammed the street. People on foot
could negotiate through, but not the carriage. There were
already two closed carriages and a dragon cart loaded
with kegs of ale stopped in the traffic as the high-strung
carriage horses and huge-but-gentle draft horses balked
at pressing further into the mass of people. As Victor
began backing the carriage so that he could take it down
a side street, Alias and Dragonbait peered ahead to discover the reason for the gathering.

The crowd, it turned out, was an audience. In the plaza
in front of the House of the Wheel, the local temple of
Gond, was a street theater troupe performing atop the
temple stairs.

"It's Jamal's troupe," the paladin said.

"Are you sure?" Alias asked. "I don't see her."

Dragonbait nodded.

Alias laid her hand on Victor's arm. "I know you have
to get back to your business, but do you mind very much
if we stay and watch this?"

"There's a novel idea," the young merchant said with
amusement. He eased the horses forward, nudging people
aside until the carriage was only thirty feet from the
stairs. Dragonbait stood on the carriage step and Alias and
Victor made themselves comfortable. Looming over the
heads of the other spectators, the three had an excellent
view of the performance.

The performers included actors and puppeteers and
musicians. At center stage stood an actor in a black cloak
and a floppy black hat with a veil of coins hanging from
the hat's brim. All about the actor puppeteers pushed
and pulled on sticks to manipulate the limbs and heads
of life-sized puppets. In the eastern style of puppeteering,

the puppeteers wore white garbs and hoods and remained on the stage with their charges. A man seated to one side strummed on a yarting. He was accompanied by three youths, two boys and a girl, with a collection of percussion instruments and noisemakers.

A hawk puppet made of black felt, with a droopy beak and sad, bloodshot eyes, fluttered to center stage and perched in a nest mounted on the shoulder of one of the puppeteers. The coin-veiled actor held out a hand in front of the hawk. The puppet coughed, and coins popped out of its mouth into the actor's waiting hand. When the coins stopped coming, the actor rapped the hawk puppet with a wooden stick. The stick was split at one end so it would make a satisfying *whack* without really dealing any damage. The hawk puppet's eyes rolled about in its head to the sound of the yarting being struck on the side. Then the hawk began coughing up more coins. Each time it stopped, the actor rapped it and its eyes rolled and the yarting thrummed. The crowd burst out in laughter and hooting jibes.

"I don't understand," Alias said as Victor chuckled beside her.

"The actor in the coin hat," Victor whispered, "represents the Faceless—"

"The Night Masks' leader," Alias added, remembering their discussion at the Watch Dock.

Victor nodded. "The black hawk is the symbol of House Guldar. Their patriarch, Lord Dathguld, has bloodshot eyes. He's supposed to be paying through the nose for protection."

Two more puppets, guided by their puppeteers, joined the hawk puppet. One puppet was a giant blue hand festooned with mealy corn cobs—representing the trading badge of the merchant family Thorsar. The other puppet was a cyclops head with a yellow eye—like the trading badge of family Urdo. Three black-cloaked actors pushed themselves between the puppets. These actors wore domino masks to signify they were agents of the Night Masks.

The Faceless held his stick up like a baton. The Night Masks and the puppet merchants came to rapt attention. The Faceless waved his stick as if he were conducting a collection of chamber musicians. The first Night Mask plucked a tail feather from the House Guldar hawk, who squawked and rolled his eyes. The giant hand representing House Thorsar grabbed the feather from the Night Mask.

Victor whispered into Alias's ear, "Rumor has it that House Thorsar purchases all the goods the Night Masks steal from family Guldar."

On the stage, the second Night Mask ripped a corn cob off the Thorsar puppet, which squeaked like a mouse. The Night Mask fed the corn to the cyclops head of family Urdo.

"And family Urdo buys everything the Night Masks steal from family Thorsar?" Alias asked.

Victor nodded.

The third Night Mask tore a golden hair from the head of the cyclops, who roared, "Ow, ow, ow!" The Night Mask ran the cyclops's hair back to the beginning of the line and wove it into the hawk's nest—family Guldar buying the stolen goods of family Urdo.

Then the whole cycle began anew. The actions continued so smoothly that Alias was reminded of the figures of the mechanized water clocks made in Neverwinter. Every time a Night Mask plucked or handed over a piece of a puppet, the musicians sounded an amusing percussion noise and the puppets cried out. As the actors began to work faster and faster, the noises almost became a tune and the crowd cheered with delight.

Victor continued chuckling, and Alias could smell the vanilla scent of Dragonbait's amusement. She even caught herself grinning as the precision of the humorous movements and noises grew to a crescendo.

A fourth puppet drifted onto the stage, a ghostlike woman in gauzy white robes and tangled white hair. As it observed the fleecing of the merchants, it wailed and moaned piteously. Its cries grew louder and louder, until the merchant puppets retreated. The Night Masks turned as one on the wailing woman. They pulled out sticks and tried to smack at her, but she managed to stay just out of their reach. Then one of the Night Masks pulled out a torch, actually a stick ending in red, yellow and orange streamers, and set fire to the stage, symbolized by having the puppeteers wave bits of red fabric about the wailing woman.

It finally occurred to Alias who the wailing woman was, and she realized what was going to happen next only moments before the Alias actress appeared on the stage.

The actress portraying Alias was too young—just a teenager, and to suggest a more mature figure she had stuffed something beneath the tunic she wore. The tunic had been painted over with a pattern of chain mail. The girl's hair had been badly hennaed, but the blue makeup on her sword arm, and the red cape left no doubt she was meant to be the swordswoman. As the crowd cheered her doppelganger's appearance, Alias felt an urge to cover herself so she would not be recognized.

The Night Masks tried to block the Alias on the stage from rescuing the wailing woman, but she made short work of them, knocking them out with a series of improbable, stylized kicks. The Night Masks rose and shook themselves off as the crowd applauded the Alias character. Then the Night Masks pulled out sticks and surrounded their opponent, but she kicked them down again. They rose yet again, but this time pantomimed running away. The heroine grabbed the cloak of the nearest Night Mask and gave a sharp tug. The cloak came away, leaving the actor naked but for a codpiece painted with a spider. The crowd howled its approval as all three Night Masks fled the stage.

The last scene played out with the Faceless quaking in fear as Alias strode toward him, but the heroine was distracted by the cries of the wailing woman. As she stomped out the 'flames,' the Faceless made his escape. With the wailing woman puppet on her arm, the actress playing Alias struck a dramatic pose and shouted, "Tyranny shall not prevail!"

The crowd demonstrated its approval with shouts and applause and foot stomping. The puppeteers grabbed tambourines and moved along the fringes of the crowd to solicit donations. Alias noted that the audience was more free with its praise than its pocket change. All the troupers got for their trouble was a double-handful of copper and a few silver pieces. The swordswoman remembered Jamal's remark that one didn't make a living in the theater. Alias wondered exactly how Jamal did make a living.

"You were just wonderful," Victor whispered in Alias's ear, applauding with the rest.

"Thanks," Alias muttered, reddening deeply.

"Yes, *we* were, weren't we," Dragonbait said, with just a hint of sarcasm. "At least, I *remember* being there."

"Dragonbait deserves just as much credit," the swordswoman explained to Victor. "He was with me when all that happened."

Victor gave the saurial a sympathetic look. "A victim of artistic license. Perhaps they just couldn't find an actor to do your role justice," the nobleman suggested.

Alias gave her companion a sheepish grin, but another problem caught her eye. She pointed to the far end of the crowd, which was parting for a flying wedge of the watch, which advanced upon the makeshift stage of the temple stairs. "Is there going to be trouble?" she asked Victor.

"Possibly," the merchant replied, though his tone sounded more resigned than alarmed.

The five members of the watch patrol, armored in long black leather tunics and polished steel helms kept their short swords sheathed, but they were shoving at the crowd with short clubs. About half of the street theater audience began dispersing from the plaza, but many remained, though whether from loyalty to the performers or just curious to see what would happen, Alias could not tell.

On the temple steps, all the performers gathered in a group, behind the stage Faceless. Some looked nervous, others resigned, but the majority had an air of defiance.

The watch patrol stopped at the bottom steps. The patrol's sergeant looked up at the performers and asked in an officious tone, "Who speaks for this group?"

The stage Faceless stepped forward, doffing the coin-veiled hat with a sweeping gesture and bowing. Locks of red and gray spilled out, and Jamal the Thespian straightened and faced the watch sergeant. "Afternoon, Rodney," she said. "Out for a stroll with the boys? My, how they've grown."

From her vantage point Alias could see the watch sergeant's ears redden. "Jamal," Rodney demanded, "do you have a license for this performance?" His tone started out gruff, but his voice cracked, and his last word came out a squeak.

"License?" Jamal parroted loudly with a surprised tone. "Let's see." She slapped her body, causing the robes to billow out like a thundercloud in a crosswind. "Alas, no," she said at last. "I must have left it with my other mask." There was a titter of laughter from a remaining member of the crowd. One of the watchmen, a freckle-faced youth, spun and glared at the source. The tittering died, but others in the crowd chuckled at the youth's display of humorlessness.

"You need a license to perform," Sergeant Rodney said.

"Milil's Mouth, I know that, Rodney!" Jamal huffed. "I've been performing in this town since before you were born. I'll just have to purchase a replacement license." Jamal peered into the tambourines her actors had used for soliciting funds. "I've got about fifty copper here," she said. "Will that cover it?"

Rodney shifted uneasily, and Alias wondered if he had been bought off that cheaply in the past. "The price of a license," the sergeant replied stiffly, "is fifty pieces of gold."

"Fifty pieces of gold?" Jamal shouted in mock astonishment. "If I had fifty pieces of gold, I could rent a hall and charge admission, but then none of these good people here would be able to afford our performances. Is that what the people of Westgate want?" There was an unpleasant muttering among the crowd. Alias hoped Jamal knew what she was doing.

"Performing without a license amounts to a disturbance of the peace," Rodney announced. "You'll have to come with us."

To Alias's horror, Dragonbait appeared beside the watch sergeant, tapped him on the shoulder, and queried, "Murf?"

"Oh, no. Why does he always get involved in these things?" Alias muttered. She sighed. "Excuse me," she said to Victor, stepping down from his carriage. She began elbowing her way through the crowd to reach the paladin's side.

Sergeant Rodney spun about to offer a sharp reprimand to whoever had interrupted his business, but he was so startled by the saurial's appearance that he took a step backward and would have tumbled down the stairs had his men not steadied him.

Dragonbait jingled a pouch of coins in Rodney's face and repeated, "Murf?"

Sergeant Rodney stared goggle-eyed and tongue-tied.

"This is Dragonbait, Rodney. He's a patron of the arts, offering to pay for the new license," Jamal said smoothly, as if help from lizard creatures was a common occurrence in her life. "Right?" she queried, asking the paladin to confirm her guess.

"Murf!" Dragonbait replied, nodding and shaking the pouch of coins at Rodney again.

Sergeant Rodney stammered for a moment, then regained his composure. "Licenses must be applied for before the performance starts," he insisted. "And they can't be issued for daytime performances on any street leading to the market."

"What good is a license if I can't perform somewhere where people will see it?" Jamal argued.

"Jamal," Rodney growled, "I'm going to have to take you in."

Alias, who'd just reached the bottom of the steps, called out, "Why is it that five of Westgate's finest spend their time arguing with street performers while the Night Masks rule every shadow in the city?" She climbed up the steps so that she stood beside Jamal.

There was a scattering of applause in the crowd. The freckle-faced youth in the watch gave the swordswoman a bone-chilling glare while the other members shifted uneasily.

Sergeant Rodney spun to face the new challenger, and Alias saw that a thin film of sweat had formed on his forehead. He wasn't used to being challenged and wasn't sure how to handle it. Perceiving that he was dealing with an unruly mob and would need reinforcements, the sergeant reached for the small silver whistle on the chain about his neck. Before he could raise the whistle to his lips, though, a heavy hand settled on his shoulder.

"I'm sure this isn't so complicated that you can't handle it with a little initiative on your part, Sergeant," Victor Dhostar said calmly, giving the sergeant's shoulder a squeeze.

"Lord Victor!" the sergeant gasped.

"Your devotion to duty is most admirable, Sergeant Rodney," Victor commended the man, "but arguing about licenses in front of the lady's audience is like arguing with a partner in front of a buyer. It's bad form, you know."

Sergeant Rodney's lip stiffened. "With all due respect, Lord Victor, this show has blocked traffic all the way back to the market."

"To be fair, it is the audience, not the performers, blocking traffic. Please, at my behest, take this"—Victor took Dragonbait's pouch of gold and set it in Rodney's hands—"and issue this lady a license to perform here."

"But the traffic—" Sergeant Rodney protested.

Victor waved out to the street. Since some members of the audience had moved on and the others had squeezed closer to the makeshift stage, the plaza had cleared sufficiently for the carriages and carts to move through. "You see, it was only a momentary problem," Victor said.

The sergeant took a few deep breaths, then nodded. "As you wish, Lord Victor," he said. Turning to Jamal, he regained some of his stern demeanor. "This performance may continue, but consider yourself warned. The city cannot have its commerce brought to a standstill for entertainments!"

"I will encourage my people to be less popular in the future," Jamal said with a straight face. To the crowd she announced, "We have been informed by the most illustrious Sergeant Rodney that we may continue our entertainment, with thanks owed to that great patron of the arts, Dragonbait the Paladin, and the glib tongue of Lord Victor Dhostar."

There was a smattering of applause. Dragonbait bowed, and Victor, a little self-consciously, waved at the crowd.

"We dedicate this performance to them," Jamal announced, "and, of course, to Westgate's newest hero, Alias the Sell-Sword!"

Whistles and bellows of approval came from the mob. Alias felt her face reddening.

Alias, Victor, and Dragonbait slipped back into the crowd as the musicians started playing and the false Night Masks took the stage, juggling wooden swords and axes.

"You seem popular," Victor said.

Alias shrugged. "I don't know what I was doing up there. You're the one who deserves the credit for rescuing Jamal's troupe."

"Ahhh, but I wouldn't have bothered to help if you hadn't rushed up there," Victor said. "That's the whole point of heroes, isn't it, to inspire us with their courage?"

"Is that what you were doing? Inspiring him with your courage?" Dragonbait asked with amusement. "I thought you'd only come up to chide me for getting involved."

Alias shot the paladin a warning look.

"Well, I enjoyed that little foray into street justice, brief as it was," Victor said. "Thank you—uh, oh."

"What?" Alias asked, and she looked in the direction Victor now peered.

The croamarkh's carriage stood parked by Victor's curricle. The driver of the larger carriage stood up in his seat, indicating with a wave of his hand that Victor should make his way to the carriage.

"It seems I'm being summoned by Father. Time, I fear, to pay the piper. Excuse me, please."

Victor waded over to the croamarkh's carriage and disappeared inside.

Alias looked back at the stage, where a skit involving two Night Masks stealing a medusa's head was unfolding. "Let's move on," she said to Dragonbait.

The two made for the perimeter of the crowd, then circled

about to Victor's curricle. A boy stood holding the horses' reins. Victor must have pressed him into service, Alias realized. She tipped him a silver piece and told him he could go.

As she rubbed the noses of the two yellow mares, Alias spoke to the paladin in Saurial. "That money you offered could have been perceived as a bribe, you know. You could have been arrested. How would that look, a paladin in the local hoosegow?"

"Wouldn't be the first time," the paladin replied with a chuckle. "I could not sit by and watch the words of the law confused with the spirit of the law."

"What's the spirit behind the law against disturbing the peace?" Alias asked.

"That no one should be injured. No one was. At the worst, a few carriages and carts were inconvenienced."

"I don't imagine the merchant lords in those carriages will take your side in that argument," Alias murmured. "Imagine all that fuss over a puppet show when the Night Masks get away with murder in this city."

"As the croamarkh pointed out, the watch can only ensure that the lawful obey the law, but the Night Masks are lawless," Dragonbait reminded her. "I don't imagine the watch is content that this is so."

"You're saying I shouldn't have insulted them," Alias replied. "You're probably right. Not very politic—"

Alias halted. From the croamarkh's carriage she could hear the croamarkh and Victor arguing. More accurately, she could hear the croamarkh's angry words, but only the slightest hint of Victor's voice. While Lord Luer wasn't exactly yelling, he was one of those people to whom it would never occur to modulate his voice. No doubt he believed it was the only way to make others listen.

Alias realized that since the carriage curtains were closed, Lord Luer probably did not know she stood near enough to hear.

"—and I cannot *understand* what motivated you to support that woman," the croamarkh was saying. For a moment, Alias was concerned that she was the subject of Lord Luer's tirade, but the croamarkh's next words disabused her of that notion. "Not only is she as common as dirt, but she is a rabble-rouser, and her little shows do nothing but breed discontent. I sat here and had to watch you cross an officer of the law, your *father's* law, in front of all these commoners."

Victor responded briefly, but too softly to be understood. Then the croamarkh continued, "It is *not* your place to act as judge. That's what Durgar is here for. Did you think that maybe Jamal's street people would start treating nobles better if they had a noble patron? Did you think they would stop spreading lies about us, about the Night Masks, because you threw some money around? And how does it look to the commoners, that you could buy justice in public? Will they believe that justice is not bought in private as well?"

Victor started to speak, but his father interrupted, "You did *not* think. That is the problem. Now if the watch shuts her down for some future violation, it will appear that the croamarkh's house is weak. If she continues, the other nobles will think we have her in our employ—which means they will think that what she says comes from our mouths. You've made a muddle of this. Have you done any other damage this morning that I should know about?"

There was a long pause as Victor answered too quietly to be overheard. Lord Dhostar was still huffy, but not as irritated as he replied, "Well, that's something. We need someone to clean out the stables, see justice served against those scoundrels."

Victor said something else that undoubtedly angered the croamarkh, for he answered loudly, "You will *not*. We have a dinner and talks with Lord Urlyvl and his people over at Castle Athagdal. I hired that young woman for her sword, not for you to practice your courtly graces. You may return to your duties."

The carriage rocked slightly. Alias handed the horses' halters to Dragonbait and retreated five paces. As the carriage door opened, she walked up toward it, creating the illusion that she had just arrived on the scene.

Victor stepped down the carriage steps, grim-faced and angry, but brightened immediately upon spotting Alias. "Hullo," he greeted her. "I've just told Father about your decision to join us."

Another man exited the carriage behind Victor, a broad-shouldered stranger with close-cropped white hair and a heavy silver mustache covering his mouth. He wore blue-and-purple robes tied loosely with a white sash, a white glove on his left hand, and a black glove on his right—the ceremonial outfit of a priest of Tyr, the blinded, one-handed god of justice. Beneath the robes the man wore a chest plate elaborately engraved with a scale of justice balanced on a war hammer—the god Tyr's symbol.

Once the stranger had closed the carriage door, someone within thumped once on the ceiling. The carriage driver urged his horses forward, and the carriage pulled away from the crowded plaza.

"Your Reverence," Victor addressed the priest who stood at his side, "please allow me to present Alias the Swordswoman and her companion, Dragonbait. Alias will be helping us with our Night Mask problem. Alias, this is Durgar the Just of Tyr, who heads our watch and serves us as judge.

Alias and Dragonbait nodded politely to the elderly priest. Durgar fixed his steely gray eyes on Alias for several moments without speaking, and Alias realized she was being assessed with skillful judgment.

When Durgar finally spoke, his voice was chill and void of emotion. "The croamarkh has informed me of his plans for you. I can't say I'm particularly pleased. While Westgate has a rich history of employed mercenaries, they never seem to last for long. Justice requires constant, unending, organized vigilance. That's why I founded the watch here. For fourteen years my men and I have done all that can be done to blunt the ravages of the Night Masks. I informed Lord Luer that in my considered opinion he was placing too much stock in your abilities, but he went on about fresh eyes, fresh blood, and fresh approaches, as if my experience meant nothing. Take care, young woman. The Night Masks are savage brutes who would spill your blood in the street without a second thought."

Alias might have taken offense at the priest's vote of no confidence, but there was the slightest trace of exhaustion in Durgar's tone, which prompted her to refrain from a heated reply. Westgate's judge, she realized, was a man who continued to struggle at a seemingly hopeless task because he believed in it. Consequently, the swordswoman framed her reply as diplomatically as she could. "Perhaps, Your Reverence, I'll get lucky. If I can throw the Night Masks off balance, the Night Masters and the Faceless might grow careless and give your watch an opportunity to capture them."

Beneath his mustache a trace of a smile flickered across Durgar the Just's face. "That's very gracious of you, but the watch is not about to waste its time on fictional characters of puppet shows."

"His Reverence," Victor explained, "does not believe in the existence of the Night Masters or the Faceless."

"Why not?" Alias asked.

"You aren't the first adventurer hired to uncover them, you know?" Durgar replied. "Yet in fourteen years, no divination by mage or priest or magical item has been able to detect any persons called the Night Masters or the Faceless. No warrior or hired thief has been able to discover their lair. No offer of wealth and power has enticed anyone to betray them. The Faceless and his Night Masters are all myths. The Night Masks foster these myths because they lend to them the illusion of power and authority. The common people believe these myths because they cannot accept the fact that chaotic forces have such control over their lives. They choose to believe people like Jamal—" Durgar waved in the direction of the performers, who were now leading the crowd in a high-spirited song— "who spread this romanticized notion that lawlessness is embodied in one being, a Prince of Night, a Lord of Thieves. Then all they need is a hero to vanquish it once and for all." Durgar's voice took on a passionate tone as he declared, "But lawlessness is not vanquished once and for all. It must be fought every day, without cessation, till the end of time."

Realizing that any argument she might make would be construed as a challenge to the priest's convictions, Alias replied simply, "I see."

Durgar, recognizing that the swordswoman was not

really acquiescing, huffed. He nodded at the performers. "Jamal may spew whatever nonsense she chooses, but if the watch catches her without a permit again, Lord Victor, not even your patronage will keep my men from bringing her in for disturbing the peace. As for you, woman—" Durgar's steely gray eyes rested on Alias once again— "at Lord Luer's request, I have ordered the watch to render you any assistance you need, but you do not have leave to interfere with their official business. Good day to you."

Durgar turned his back on the trio before Alias could return his farewell. He plowed through the crowd, which parted for him more widely than it had for the five members of the watch.

"I wouldn't take Durgar's rejection personally," Victor said. "He's just blowing off steam after having had to listen to Father tell him how to do his job. You just got in the way."

Alias nodded. "You didn't mention Westgate had a church of Tyr," she said.

"It doesn't," Victor replied. "Durgar was a wandering adventurer. He ran with a group called the Invisible Hand. They had some run-ins with the Night Masks, and only Durgar survived. He stayed and convinced the nobles to charter the watch."

"He seems pretty orthodox as priests of Tyr go," Alias noted, "yet he doesn't wear the gauze strip across his eyes to symbolize his deity's blinding."

"He did, immediately after the Time of Troubles, but Father and the other merchants forbade him to continue. It's bad enough to be ridiculed in the street and have the Night Masks steal you blind, but can you imagine the comments when the head of the watch wears a blindfold? I don't think Durgar likes it, but he follows orders."

Behind them, the audience applauded again as the performers took a final curtain call, and the puppeteers huckstered once again for loose change.

"About tonight's dinner—" Victor said, looking down at the ground.

Alias sensed his discomfort and remembered the croa-markh's sharp commands. "I'm afraid we'll have to decline your offer," she interrupted hastily. "Dragonbait reminded me we have a previous engagement. I will keep in mind your suggestions about the Gateside district, though."

Victor looked up at the swordswoman with a sheepish grin. "You heard Father dressing me down, didn't you? That's very gracious of you to provide me with an out. Still, I ought to apologize for extending an invitation I could not honor."

"I'm sure there'll be another chance to honor it," Alias replied, offering Victor her hand.

Victor smiled with delight. "More than one, I hope," he replied, clasping her hand in both of his own.

The swordswoman blushed. "We've kept you from your work too long," she said. "Please, don't feel obliged to see us back to our inn. We need to familiarize ourselves with the streets, and we really do have a previous engagement."

Victor held her hand a moment longer. "In spite of what Durgar says, I have a good feeling about you. You're just the hero this town needs. I know you'll succeed."

"I'll do my best," Alias promised.

The young merchant released her hand and bowed. Without further words, as if he might become over-whelmed with emotion if he spoke again, Lord Victor climbed into his carriage, took up the reins, and drove away.

"So *do* we have another engagement?" Dragonbait queried with amusement. "Or did you only say that so Lord Victor would return your hand?" he teased.

"I guess there's no way around it," Alias said. "I'm going to have to go back to Mintassan's with you and wind up playing 'Ask-me-another' about the saurials."

"So you can grill *him* for information on the Night Masks," Dragonbait guessed.

"You know my methods," Alias replied.

"Then?"

"Then, although they don't know it yet, we have an engagement with the Night Masks. With any luck, more than one engagement."

## Eight
# Engagements

Timmy the Ghast had not earned his appellation from any kinship to the undead or for his revulsion of the clergy, but rather for the simple fact that he smelled as bad as (some said worse than) a ghast. Timmy's unique personal scent was the result of his chosen career and his less-than-fastidious attitude about his personal hygiene. Timmy was a midden man. He broke into townhouses and family quarters through the kitchen waste pits. While the thief occasionally gained access from a wood or coal cellar, the contents of the kitchen refuse never deterred him from making an entry if the midden was his only choice. Unlike other midden men, however, Timmy never felt compelled to bathe after a night's work; the closest he came to washing was being caught in a drenching rainstorm. Consequently, while Timmy the Ghast had many coworkers, he had very few drinking companions.

Tonight Timmy had begun his evening's work on a burglary assigned to him by the Night Masters. He was to steal a certain necklace from a certain courtier's daughter. Although Timmy wasn't given the necklace's history, he assumed it had been a gift from a wealthy merchant who had imagined himself enamored of the gift's recipient. Now, no doubt, the relationship had cooled, and the gift giver wanted to dispose of the gift so that it could not haunt him—or his wife—in the future. Timmy would be paid five hundred gold for the necklace and was free to keep any incidental plunder that came his way.

According to Timmy's sources, the family was at a dinner

engagement, the servants had been given the night off, and the household had no dogs. Timmy slithered through the tunnel he'd dug into the refuse pit and waded his way to the access door, unperturbed by the stench, the bugs, or the rats. Timmy had had two friends who had suffocated trying to sneak into a house through a chimney and one who'd broken his neck climbing into a second-story window. Timmy preferred the safety of the refuse.

Timmy climbed up into the kitchen. There was a low glow from the fireplace, and the thief let his eyes adjust to the dark. Two young children, scullery help, were curled in front of the fire, in an exhausted sleep. As he made his way out of the servant quarters, Timmy's boots squelched along the passageway, leaving filthy tracks on the carpets. The midden man wasted no time finding the young debutante's room and her jewelry box. The necklace, a diamond-and-ruby chain, was concealed rather amateurishly in the box's lining. There was an inscription on the clasp, but Timmy could not read, which he realized was probably his best qualification for being hired to steal the necklace.

Timmy tossed the chain into a sack, then dumped the remaining contents of the jewelry box in with it. He slipped into the master's bedroom and added the contents of the debutante's mother's jewelry box to his sack. Timmy did not bother searching for any other treasure. "Portable property only" was his motto. The bounty on the necklace and his earnings for this job, even with the fence's cut and the tax to the Night Masters, were sufficient to keep him in comfort for weeks.

Timmy headed back for the kitchen. His teacher had gotten nicked once when he bumped into the house's owners coming in the front door. "You won't meet the owner in the midden," was another of Timmy's mottoes.

Timmy snitched a peach from the kitchen larder, wolfed it down, and left the pit on the kitchen table before he slid back into the refuse pit. He peered out of the tunnel. Slick Jack, his lookout, was not standing by the hole, which was odd. Night Masks did not abandon their posts. Timmy popped his head out of the tunnel, like a turtle from his shell, and looked around. He spotted Slick Jack across the alley, resting comfortably, unconscious, his wrists and ankles tethered with leather thongs.

Timmy the Ghast tried to back into the warm, moist darkness of the midden, but his retreat was too late. Clawed fingers grabbed him by the shoulders and pulled him from the tunnel. The thief found himself nose to muzzle with a snarling monster with a lizard's hide and the glowing red eyes of a fiend, or so he told his mates later.

The monster, unprepared for Timmy's overripe odor (freshened by his latest foray), began gasping and gagging and dropped the culprit.

The break-in artist didn't hesitate, but hit the ground running. Unfortunately, he got all of three steps before someone else tripped him with a scabbard between his legs. As he tried to get his feet beneath him again, a hand grabbed him by the collar and slammed him into the wall of the house.

"Phew! This one reeks!" his captor cried. She was a muscular woman with red hair and a blue tattoo along her right arm. Her companion, the lizard monster, snarled something, and she replied, "Hang on, let's do a little cleaning up before we wake the house."

When the watch arrived, summoned by one of the scullery maids, they found Slick Jack tied up in the alley and Timmy the Ghast naked in a rain barrel, muttering about the unfairness of being not only nicked, but forced to wash as well.

\* \* \* \* \*

Bandilegs collected the loot while Sal and Jojo held their dagger tips steady at their prey's throats. It was a moxie pinch, smooth and easy. The swells, foreign traders from Turmish, had obviously assumed from Westgate's size and prosperity that it was an outpost of civilization where they would be immune from attack. They'd been strolling the streets with their airs and their purses and their rings and had been shocked by the three youths who'd popped out of an alleyway and demanded at dagger-point that they hand over their valuables.

Bandilegs ran back down the alley with the purses and what rings could easily be pried from nervous fingers. Even with the cut for the Night Masters, there would be plenty for everyone.

Jojo and Sal backed away a few steps from the terrified merchants. Sal gave the high sign to their lookout, who faded into the darkness at the end of the street. Then she and Jojo spun on their heels and dashed after their companion. They'd traveled half a block before the merchants regained enough of their voices and their spines to begin shouting. No doubt they shouted, "Thieves!" or "Help, watch!" but since they shouted in Turmish it was hard for the thieves or anyone else within earshot to tell.

Bandilegs, with her long legs, was a blur, far ahead of her two mates. Sal was the muscle, and Jojo could pick the marks, but Bandilegs was their runner, the one who ensured the goods made it clear. She was the main reason theirs was the most effective "import" team in the Gateside district.

At least until tonight. As she fled, Bandilegs saw a slender but well-muscled arm jut out in front of her. Then the arm, ending in a wrist bracer and a gloved fist, caught Bandilegs right at her throat. Sal and Jojo heard a *thwack* and saw their runner's legs fly forward and up, as the rest of her body fell backward to land with a solid *smack* on the packed earth. They made a half dozen steps toward their runner before they, too, saw the arm. It came, they realized, from someone standing in one of the innumerable two-foot gaps between buildings that laced Westgate's neighborhoods.

The pair thought at first they'd become prey to a poacher, a thief who robbed other thieves, but when Bandilegs's assailant stepped out of the narrow passageway, Sal, at least, realized they'd come up against something more dangerous. Sal enjoyed Jamal's street theater, so she recognized the red-headed, blue-tattooed swordswoman. Jojo reacted as he would to any lone poacher. He drew his blade and snarled, expecting Sal to back him up. Sal was backing up, all right, backpedaling as she calculated her chances at escape if she were to run back out the alley, past the Turmishmen they'd just robbed, and keep going. She spun around, but immediately abandoned her plan to flee.

Behind him Jojo heard a roaring noise as a light flared brightly enough for the thief to see his own shadow. Sensing that Sal was no longer behind him, Jojo shot a glance over his shoulder, then did a quick double take. Sal was laying her weapon down at the feet of a small, dragonlike man who clutched a flaming sword in his paws. Jojo looked back at the armored swordswoman, then again at the dragon man. He sighed and laid his dagger on the ground. He added his boot knife for good measure.

The Turmish merchants were at their inn, bemoaning their fate and trying to figure out how to recoup their losses, when the innkeeper knocked on their door and handed them their stolen valuables. A woman and lizard-man had dropped them off with the request that the Turmishmen stop at the Tower tomorrow to identify their attackers, who were now in custody.

\* \* \* \* \*

Big Edna wiped tankards with the dry end of her bar rag and rehearsed her lines. "It's been a tough week," she murmured. "What with so many Night Mask muggers in the area, many of me regulars are afraid to go out at night."

No, it's no use, she thought. Littleboy didn't care that her business was slipping. All he cared about was getting his regular cut of what he claimed her profits should be. Littleboy would not listen to reason.

Edna surveyed her little establishment, such as it was—a bar made from a few planks laid across some barrels, a stock of whiskey, brandy, and ale of questionable origin, empty barrels and crates serving as stools and tables, five dozen pewter tankards, and a cracked mirror mounted on the wall so that she could watch the customers. Tonight her only customers were four old fishermen, a one-handed pensioned dockworker, and a pair of cloaked and hooded adventurers. Were Edna one to gossip, she might guess the adventurers were priests of some outcast religion, like Talona or Cyric. Edna, however, did not gossip. That was one of the attractions of her little hole-in-the-wall: You could drink in quiet without being disturbed by the chatter of the owner or the other customers.

The door crashed open, and Littleboy waddled in, flanked by his two toughs. A careless observer might mistake Littleboy for a bald halfling or a shaved dwarf, for the hairless Night Mask was short and barrel-shaped. His round face and apple cheeks gave him a cherubic look, but one that was quickly belied by his unpleasantly cruel attitude. Littleboy dressed in a heavy, open-fronted cloak and a great slouch hat. His supporters were two lantern-jawed lunks who looked as if they had hobgoblin blood sloshing through their veins.

Littleboy climbed onto one of the barrel stools and rested his elbows on the bar. His boys remained standing and silent. "So, Edna," he said.

Edna threw a small pouch of coins on the bar without a reply. Littleboy picked it up, hefted it, and frowned. "You're light," he noted.

"Not a lot of customers," Edna replied, trying a casual shrug.

"Then you don't need a lot of furniture," Littleboy said. He tucked the pouch into his cloak pocket and snapped his fingers. One of his boys moved off. Littleboy heard the satisfying sound of one of the barrels smashing over one of the other barrels. His eyes never left Edna's face. Her eyes widened for a moment, then became slits.

"Let this be a warn—" Littleboy began. He was interrupted by two *thumps* behind him and startled by the ghost of a smile on Edna's face. Littleboy looked up in the mirror behind the bar.

The Night Mask collection agent was once again flanked by two figures, but they weren't his boys. One was an armored woman in a scarlet cape, the other a big lizard. "Kezef's blood and bladder!" Littleboy muttered, recognizing the pair from the stories that had been coursing through the grapevine.

Littleboy did not need to look around to know his own boys were sprawled on the floor. He laid both his hands on the bar, one resting over the ornate ring of the other.

"Is there something I can do to help you?" he asked coolly.

"You can close down your little extortion racket," the swordswoman said. The lizard made a chuffing noise.

"I have no idea what you're talking about," said Littleboy. "I have a business deal with Edna here. My boys do some of her heavy lifting and serve as bodyguards to protect her and her establishment from the city's more unsavory elements. Isn't that right, Edna?"

The swordswoman looked at Edna. The bar owner's face was a study in uncertainty and fear. While everyone's attention was focused on Edna, Littleboy removed the face of his ring, uncovering a small needle, which wept a single greenish drop of venom.

"No," Edna announced, possessed by some wisp of courage. "He's been shaking me down, like you said."

The swordswoman pulled Edna's pouch of money out of Littleboy's cloak pocket and tossed it back to the bar owner. To Littleboy she said, "I suggest you leave this place and not come back."

"You shouldn't interfere in my business," Littleboy said. "I have powerful friends."

"Then you should stay with them for a while," the swordswoman replied.

Littleboy sighed and twisted as if he were about to hop down from the barrel stool. A second later, he thrashed out with his right fist to slash his poison needle across the swordswoman's face. The lizard snarled, and the adventuress reacted with lightning quickness, grasping the extortionist firmly by the wrist and bending his arm backward.

"That hurts," Littleboy gasped. The lizard brought a pewter tankard down on the Night Mask's head, and blackness claimed him.

"Now what?" Edna asked.

"Call the watch," the swordswoman said, as if it were simple.

"It'll only be Littleboy's word against mine," Edna complained. "And, like he said, he has powerful friends."

The adventuress held out the extortionist's ringed hand. "Carrying poison will get him hard labor and banishment from the city, no matter who his friends are," she pointed out.

"So it will," Edna said. She took the tankard back from the lizard and started wiping it clean again, only now she wore a grin. "Fritz," she called to the pensioned dockworker, "fetch Durgar's boys round, will ye?" With an uncommon flash of festive generosity, she added, "There's a free ale in it for ye."

The pair of adventurers followed Fritz from the bar. Edna began going through the unconscious Night Masks pockets, pulling out the money pouches of all the other businesses Littleboy had terrorized tonight. There would be enough, Edna noted, to buy a new bar, maybe even an inn.

Just then, the red-headed warrior woman poked her head back through the door and said, "Edna, my friend wants me to remind you that everyone else Littleboy shook down was hurting like you, and could really use their money back. Since you know the neighborhood businesses, could you please see to getting the money back to the right people?"

Big Edna nodded wordlessly. The adventuress left again. Big Edna stared longingly at the pouches of gold. With a long sigh, she began making a list of the other neighborhood businesses she knew had been paying protection to Littleboy.

\* \* \* \* \*

By the time Alias woke up the next morning, Dragonbait was gone. By nature, the saurial was most active at dawn and dusk, and he never seemed to need much sleep in the warm season. Alias, on the other hand, felt most active after dark and would sleep the morning away

whenever she had an excuse. She wondered which of her
creators had established this pattern in her. Finder, as an
entertainer, would have kept the same sort of hours, but
so would the Fire Knives, who had expected her to
become an assassin like them.

Alias rolled over and sat up. Someone had set breakfast on the table. The swordswoman vaguely recalled
having heard a knock on the door and Mercy's voice earlier in the morning. The young half-elf must have lost her
fear of the saurial. Alias padded over to the table. Once
again breakfast consisted of tea, fresh-baked muffins,
and fruit, but today she had time to admire the details
she'd missed yesterday. The china teapot and teacup
were nearly translucent and gleamed like mother-of-
pearl; the butter was molded into clamshell shapes; deco-
rating the bowl of berries were pieces of melon cut and
shaped like dragonflies. There was a fresh-cut red rose in
a bud vase of frosted glass. Alias could see why this particular inn did not advertise among adventurers; they
generally wolfed down food without looking at it and
were notoriously hard on china and glassware.

Alias sat down to eat, musing over yesterday afternoon's events, starting with the meeting she and Dragonbait had had with Mintassan. The experience had
tested her patience and her conversational skills to their
limits. They'd started with the requested conversation
about saurials. The sage had asked Dragonbait so many
questions, even Alias had learned things about saurials
she hadn't known before. When, after at least an hour,
Mintassan had shifted the topic to Alias's background,
she'd turned the tables and started grilling him about his
theory on the transmutation of creatures into other creatures. Finally, when she felt she'd learned enough about
the beasts of the Prime Material and Outer Planes to
qualify as a sage's apprentice and had Mintassan at ease,
she'd shifted to the topic of the Night Masks.

To her disappointment, it soon became evident that
Mintassan, like most sages, lived in his own little world.
His understanding of the city's problems came to him
secondhand. "Mostly," so he said, "from Jamal." Although

he confirmed Durgar's claim that the Night Masters and the Faceless could not be located with magic, he did not concur with the priest that they did not exist. His reasoning, though, had more to do with Jamal's certainty that they did than with any firsthand experience. Jamal, Alias realized, was the "sage" she needed to consult to learn more about the Night Masks.

Mintassan had walked them back to Blais House for dinner. They'd ordered the recommended pan-fried prawns, which were indeed excellent. Mintassan was also a gourmand, and during their discussion of Westgate eating establishments he revealed one useful piece of information. He'd mentioned the extortionist Littleboy, who was apparently responsible for the decline of one of Mintassan's favorite taverns. The sage had left them with a promise to set up a meeting with Jamal, and after a brief nap Alias and Dragonbait had gone out hunting Night Masks.

Alias began dressing, reflecting on her progress against the Night Masks. They'd come across the midden man and several muggers and purse snatchers, thanks to Dragonbait's *shen* sight. Without the paladin, Littleboy might have been her only coup, and if the extortionist hadn't been such a fool to use a poison ring, the watch might not have arrested him. She needed more informants.

She also needed to start watching her back. So far, she and Dragonbait hadn't challenged anyone with a stomach for fighting, let alone any real skill with a weapon. That was bound to change soon, she realized. Even if it meant bringing in hired help, the Night Masks would find ways to protect their operatives and try to stop the swordswoman and her companion.

Alias was brushing her hair when Dragonbait finally turned up. The vanilla scent of amusement wafted off his body, and he made a strange clicking noise that Alias recognized as chuckling.

"Well?" Alias said, fastening the longer strands of hair at the nape of her neck with a ribbon. "Are you going to let me in on it?"

"I was checking on Jamal's troupe's new play. Come

down and see." Although the paladin tried to sound casual, Alias could tell he was itching for her to come.

Alias sighed. "You always did have this childlike fondness for puppet shows." She buckled on her scabbard. and grabbed the last muffin to munch while she watched the show.

They did not have to go far. Jamal's troupe had set up stage on the foundation of the burned down warehouse only three blocks from Blais House. A large crowd had gathered in the empty lot around the razed building.

A halfling with a gigantic green plume in his hat was juggling eggs. A green feather, Alias recalled, was the trading badge for the Thalavar family. Jamal must have good relations with the halflings of this town, Alias realized. Usually halflings wouldn't participate in human theatrics, and human producers cast children with brushes tied to their feet in the roles of the smaller people.

Behind the stage bobbed the cutout of a ship. The crow's nest, though, was real, and from it the Faceless looked down at the halfling. After a moment, the Faceless tossed an egg at the halfling, which the halfling skillfully added to the three it was juggling. The Faceless added a fifth and then a sixth egg, which the halfling also juggled smoothly. Frustrated by the halfling's dexterity, the Faceless threw a seventh egg stage left. The egg splattered against a great wagon wheel decorated with golden stars—house Dhostar's trading badge. The wheel began spinning and moved toward the juggling halfling with a menacing growl. The halfling alternated between alarmed looks in the wheel's direction and tucking eggs in his pockets even as he juggled them. Before he could dispose of the last three eggs, the wagon wheel rolled into him, forcing him off the stage. The eggs hit the stage, *plop, plop, plop,* and then there was a splash of water up onto the stage.

The actress playing Alias leaped onto the stage. She waggled her finger at the Dhostar wheel. The wheel whined like a shamed puppy. The heroine pulled out a stage axe and began hacking at the mast holding the Faceless's crow's nest. One by one, the Night Masks began to attack her, but, one by one, she knocked them out with a quick bonk on their heads with the side of her axe.

"Now," Dragonbait said excitedly, tugging on her sleeve.

Rising out of the water beside the ship came the halfling, pulled by someone in a costume that looked as if it had been put together from the parts of two other costumes, one the body of a crocodile, the other the head of a horse (now painted green). Alias laughed out loud. It was nothing like Dragonbait, but it could be no one else. She shot a look at her companion, who looked as proud as a new father.

The halfling was really damp, and he carried a bucket that appeared full. The stage Alias finally got the crow's nest chopped through, but the Faceless leaped down beside her at the last moment. Jamal landed a little awkwardly, though, and fell on her rear end. When the heroine had to help the villain to "his" feet, the audience applauded and roared with laughter. The halfling strode purposefully toward the Faceless, with his bucket poised for attack. The actor playing Dragonbait grabbed the Faceless's cloak. The Faceless tried to run, but succeeded only in limping quickly in circles around the stage Dragonbait as the halfling chased after him.

The girl playing Alias led the crowd in jeers as the Faceless tried to avoid being soaked. Finally, she and the halfling cornered the Faceless at the very front of the stage. The halfling swung the bucket forward just as the Faceless ducked. As one, the audience near the stage held up their hands to hold back the expected splash of water.

A cymbal crashed, and the bucket rained a spray of shiny blue confetti over the crowd.

The audience cheered and applauded, and those who'd just avoided a drenching cheered the loudest. The stage Alias and Dragonbait each set a foot on the Faceless's prone form and took their bows. Then they dragged the Faceless off the stage by her arms, leaving the halfling to lead the crowd in one of those interminably long halfling songs. Alias recognized the chorus, but the lyrics of the verses had been twisted into a commentary on House Thalavar's supposed cheapness:

> *"Some say the Thalavars are fools,*
> *But I think they're pretty bright.*
> *They hire halflings by their weight,*
> *But pay them by their height!"*

"You look insufferably pleased with yourself," Alias noted to her companion as the crowd bellowed the song's chorus.

"A small part, but vital to the plot," Dragonbait replied. "Given time and good reviews, I could see that character carrying the entire show. On the whole, I think its a valuable artistic inclusion."

"Well, patron of the arts, I suppose your fifty gold was well spent. I wonder where Jamal gets all her information."

"I was wondering that myself," Victor Dhostar said behind them.

Alias spun about in surprise. "However did you find us in this crowd?"

"I saw you leaving your inn and followed you here. I've just come from the Tower, where Durgar was reluctantly reviewing your victories to Father. He sounded rather put out, claiming that you'll clog all his jail cells before the magistrate can deal with the cases. Father suggested he should just have a watch patrol and a magistrate follow you around, and we could dispense with the jail and send the Night Masks right to the dungeons."

Alias shook her head. "I'm afraid they'd make too much noise and warn off our prey."

"Hadn't thought of that," Victor replied. "I guess that's why you're the pro. At any rate, the performers seem to be right. You are giving the Faceless a drenching."

"We've made a start," Alias replied, trying not to overemphasize their progress. "So what brings you here?" she asked.

"Well, Family Dhostar is commissioning a new trading

ship tomorrow evening and capping the event with a party on board. I'd like to extend an invitation for you to be my guest at the party."

Alias shifted uncertainly, remembering how Luer Dhostar had reprimanded his son yesterday for planning to have dinner with her. "Does this invitation come from your father as well?" she asked.

"Father? Why do you—" Victor paused as insight dawned on him. "Just because my father hired you for your sword, I don't see why I shouldn't have the chance to practice my courtly graces on you. Unless, that is, you'd object to that?" Although Victor's voice sounded light, there was the trace of nervousness in his question.

Alias flushed, but she recovered her composure quickly. "I can't think of any objections. I would be delighted to accept your invitation."

Victor broke into a smile. "Good. Um. Will Dragonbait be chaperoning you?"

Alias gave the paladin a questioning glance.

"Trapped on a ship filled with partying merchants and traders?" the saurial harrumphed. "I'm sure I can find a less tedious way to spend my evening. But you go without me if you think it might amuse you."

"Dragonbait says, 'No, thank you,' Alias replied.

"Well, then, that's settled. I'll send my carriage tomorrow around sunset. Dress is semiformal. No need for armor. Weapons must be peace-bonded. I'm afraid I won't see you again before the party. I have several pressing duties."

"I understand. I'll look forward to tomorrow night," Alias replied, offering him her hand.

Victor took up her hand and bowed low over it. Alias could feel his breath on her wrist. He stood again, but seemed reluctant to release her hand.

"Until tomorrow evening," the swordswoman replied, drawing her hand away ever so gently.

"Until tomorrow evening," the noble replied. He spun about and waded away through the crowd.

Dragonbait studied the swordswoman. For the first time since he'd known her, Alias seemed oblivious to her surroundings. He might have taken the opportunity to remind her they were in the heart of Westgate, a town whose hobby was crime, home of the deadly Night Masks, but he didn't have the heart to spoil her moment of bliss.

On stage, the halfling song was winding down with one final verse:

> *"The Thalavars are nettled*
> *By nasty Night Mask boasters*
> *They need to get an Alias*
> *Just like the lucky Dhostars!"*

Alias went red, hearing the lyrics, while the crowd applauded and stomped feet.

"Let's get nearer the stage," the swordswoman said. "I want to make sure Jamal got Mintassan's message that we wanted to talk to her. We need to find out how she knows so much about the city and the Night Masks. And watch your purse in this crowd. Night Masks work the day shift, too."

Dragonbait chuckled and nodded.

# Nine
# Parries and Ripostes

"So you want to know how I know so much about the Night Masks," Jamal said as she turned over the cool, wet cloth covering her swollen ankle. "It's not that complicated, really." The thespian paused, assuring herself that she held her audience's complete attention. Dragonbait leaned forward on his stool. Alias fidgeted impatiently, hating Jamal's theatrics. Although the actress had refused to let Dragonbait heal her injury, she had accepted the adventurers' help back to Mintassan's. Now they were seated once again in the mismatched chairs around the heavy table in the sage's cluttered workroom.

"*I* have the sense the gods gave geese," Jamal said.

Mintassan, who hovered in the doorway of the side alcove waiting for the tea water to boil, called out, "Are those the geese that walk barefoot in burning buildings and then jump out of crow's nests for the amusement of the rabble?"

Jamal shot an annoyed glance at the sage. She turned back to the swordswoman and the paladin. She motioned them to lean closer, and when they had, she whispered, "I listen carefully, and I know how to put two and two together."

Alias leaned back and sighed. "Could you maybe give us an example of putting two and two together?" she requested.

"First I consider my source of information. Take the halflings. They have it in for the Night Masks, and not just because the Masks exclude them from their guild. It goes back to a blood feud started when the Masks first sprang up in this town. Now while halflings aren't always reliable reporters, they aren't going to lie on behalf of the Masks. So if a halfling who works for Lady Nettel Thalavar tells me Her Ladyship won't pay protection to the Night Masks, I'm inclined to believe him. If all the halflings working for Lady Nettel confirm his story, I'm going to accept it as fact.

"Then when a halfling tells me a certain type of misfortune strikes the Thalavar trading house, I consider who would benefit from such misfortune. If a Thalavar ship laden with goods sinks in the harbor, I suspect the Faceless's wrathful hand. If the ship sinks but it was emptied out first, I suspect that another merchant family hired the Night Masks to pick up the goods for them. The merchants hate waste, even if it benefits them, with the exception, in my opinion, of Family Urdo. The year of the summer brushfires there was never quite enough corn to meet demand, but enough for House Urdo to make a killing."

"So how do you know who to talk to?" Alias asked.

"Oh, I don't seek out my sources," Jamal replied. "They come to me. You see, I have many loyal fans, and, of course, some people just can't resist the temptation to see their story played out."

"And others can't resist the five copper she pays per story," Mintassan added as he joined them with the tea tray.

"So you're an information broker," Alias stated.

"More of a collector," Jamal corrected. "I don't sell what I get, but I do put it on display—in my performances. Like a sage, I specialize. All things Westgate: local lore, noble gossip, Night Masks, the city's new cheap hero, Alias the Sell-Sword. Congratulations, by the way, on taking down Littleboy, and nabbing Timmy the Ghast and Bandilegs's bunch."

"Who told you about all that?" Alias asked.

"Oh, I never reveal my sources. They trust me because of that," Jamal explained as she accepted the teacup Mintassan handed her.

Alias thought of all the people who knew about her activities last night. The thieves themselves, the scullery maids, the Turmishmen, Big Edna and her customers, the watch, and no doubt lots of people looking down from windows, too afraid to go out at night, but curious enough to watch the street.

Jamal sipped her tea, then said, "Littleboy's fall and Timmy's bath are part of our afternoon performance, if my stand-in thinks he's ready for the job."

Alias sighed with exasperation. "Why can't you tell stories about other heroes. The Knights of Myth Drannor, the Harpers, the Swanmays?"

"Those are *old* legends," Jamal argued. "They're fine for summer stock theater. But a fresh, young, cheap hero, walking the street where people can point her out to their children, that's going to inspire people. They've lived in silent fear of the Night Masks, certain the guild could never be defeated. You prove otherwise, and now they can't help but talk about you. Soon talk becomes action. I've already heard that last night, over on Thunn-side, a crowd pummeled three Night Mask bully boys who beat up a barmaid. They'll be part of the performance, too. Eventually there'll be cheap heroes popping up all over the city. Courage is contagious."

"Courage can also be dangerous," Alias pointed out, "as you may have noted when they burned your house down."

"True," Jamal agreed, "but the Faceless won't focus on the anonymous cheap heroes. He'll focus on you."

"Perhaps I shouldn't be staying at Blais House," Alias commented.

Mintassan handed Alias a mug of tea. "Blais House is exactly where you should be," he insisted. "It has . . . protections of its own. Consider it a safe haven. It's on the street that you'll have to watch your back."

"Durgar thinks the Faceless and the Night Masters are myths," Alias said.

"Durgar hasn't got my sources," Jamal countered.

"What sources?" Alias demanded.

"The Night Masks themselves, for one. They aren't about to go to the city's judge and tell him about the

Faceless. They talk business, though, in taverns where a certain disguised actress can get work as a barkeep any time. And then sometimes the branded ones are angry enough to come to me."

"The branded ones?" Alias asked.

"The Faceless has a magical item with the power to burn a domino mask brand into the face of someone who's earned his displeasure. Sometimes the brand is too deep to be healed without leaving a scar. Then the branded one has no choice but to flee the city. About seven years ago a man claiming to be a Night Master came to me with such a brand. In exchange for safe passage from the city he told me a lot about the Night Masks organization. He said that the original Faceless, the founder of the Night Masks guild, had been assassinated by some new person who'd just taken up the old Faceless's magical regalia, and hence the office of the lord of the Night Masters. The new Faceless branded this Night Master when he'd challenged him over the right to hold the office.

"Later that year, another Night Mask, some second-story man, came to me. There had been a steep increase in the Night Master tax—the cut every thief pays to the guild. The tax was doubled for guild members and tripled for free-lance thieves working in the city. When this second-story man and some others refused to pay, they were brought before the Faceless and branded. The second-story man confirmed a lot of what the branded Night Master had told me."

"So why is he called the Faceless?" Alias asked.

"According to the branded Night Master, the first Faceless had a face like a lump of clay. The Night Master thought the first Faceless might have been a doppelganger. The new Faceless's face is a blur of colors. The Temple to Leira, goddess of illusion, once possessed a magical helmet that caused exactly such an effect. The helmet was of mesh chain covered in platinum coins struck with the goddess's glyph. Shortly after the Time of Troubles Leira's temple was looted and burned and the magic helmet went missing."

Dragonbait asked, "Will it really hurt the Night Masks if Alias captures the Faceless, or will it only make room for some Night Master to take the place of their lord?"

Alias translated the paladin's question for Jamal.

Jamal was silent for several moments as if considering her answer very carefully. Mintassan drummed his fingers on the tabletop in the silent pause. Finally the actress replied, "I think if you can seize the Faceless's treasury, you'll have dealt them a mortal blow. According to the branded Night Master, the treasury contains an artifact discovered by the first Faceless. It protects his identity and that of all the Night Masters. With it, Durgar could detect them or any who tried to take their place. My sources estimate there are at least two thousand Night Masks, but without the Faceless and the Night Masters they won't be anywhere near as organized. Also in the treasury are magical items the Night Masks have used to rescue *or kill* members who know too much and who've been caught by Durgar's watch."

Alias sipped her tea thoughtfully.

"If I might make a suggestion," Jamal said.

"Murf?" Dragonbait prompted the actress.

"House Thalavar brought in a wine shipment yesterday," Jamal explained. "One hundred twenty barrels of fire wine from the Old Empires—dark, strong, spicy, and worth more with every mile it moves west. If the wine makes it to the tables of Waterdeep, it means a major profit for the Thalavars. If not, they stand to lose a great deal. It's sitting in the Thalavar warehouse until it can be loaded on caravan wagons tomorrow morning. Odds are good that the Night Masks will try to steal it or destroy it. Instead of roaming the streets looking for trouble tonight, why not see if you can get trouble to come to you. Stand guard in the warehouse. My guess is you'll round up at least a dozen Night Masks, and if it rains, you'll stay nice and dry."

Alias tilted her head suspiciously. "You know, I smell a halfling behind this plan. Probably the same one who took your copper pieces for her story about yesterday's incident on the docks. I don't suppose it came from an annoying redhead named Olive Ruskettle."

"Oooh, I can feel my ears burning all the way out in the street," a new voice declared from the doorway. Alias didn't need to turn around to know that Olive Ruskettle had entered Mintassan's shop. The halfling joined them at the table, climbed into a chair, snitched a sugar cube from the tea tray, and popped it in her mouth.

"Olive tells me you're well acquainted," Jamal said.

"Oh, yes," Alias replied. "I hadn't realized until now that you knew her, too."

"We're both in the entertainment business," Olive explained.

"So, you're expecting me to do your guard duty for you?" Alias asked the halfling.

"No. Thalavar halflings can do their own guard duty," Olive retorted sharply. "As a matter of fact, Lady Nettel is secretly going to put all her available guards on this consignment at the risk of leaving her other properties undefended. We're not worried about defending the wine, but capturing Night Masks is a little harder work. Since you're so keen on sending them in to Durgar, I thought I'd offer you this opportunity. You won't find more Night Masks roaming the streets tonight. It's already started to drizzle. They'll all be tucked in front of warm fires sipping ale—except for the ones assigned to plunder House Thalavar."

"She may have a point, Alias," Dragonbait said.

The swordswoman succumbed to Olive's logic. Privately, however, she suspected she might actually find a fruitless evening of hunting in the rain more enjoyable than hiding out in a warehouse with a gang of halflings.

* * * * *

Alias and Dragonbait met Olive shortly after sunset at the gates to Lady Nettel's castle. The family sheds were located in a shallow vale between castles Thalavar and Ssemm. Olive, however, led Alias and Dragonbait outside the city walls to the Thalavar stockyards. There, in a horse pen beside the city wall, sheltered from view by a copse of trees, was a secret tunnel leading beneath the city wall. The halfling guided them through the tunnel to a ladder that climbed up into the warehouse inside the city walls, where the wine was being stored.

The building was a windowless fortress of solid stone walls and a clay tile roof. There was one door large enough for a wagon and a smaller one for people, both bolted shut. The only other way in, aside from the trapdoor in the floor that led to the secret tunnel, was through one of the five skylights used for ventilation. These were covered with hinged doors, also bolted shut.

The Thalavar halflings were all hidden behind crates stacked in the loft overhead. Olive and Alias took up a position beside the cribs holding the wine barrels, while Dragonbait paced the perimeter of the shed, both upstairs and down, checking on the halflings stationed about and using his *shen* sight on the walls around them. Then they waited.

Alias wrapped her cloak around her. For a summer evening the air was cool, and cooler still inside the warehouse, like an outpost on the edge of the Negative Material Plane. By the light of the hooded lantern beside her, the swordswoman could see her own breath. She was beginning to think it might have been warmer out in the rain; it certainly would be less boring. She lost track of time in the dark, but it seemed as if she'd been here for hours.

"Apricot?" Olive offered. The sweet, pungent aroma of the dried fruit rose from the sticky paper bag she held out. Alias waved her hand to refuse the fruit. Already tonight Olive had consumed numerous bags of various comestibles, including hazelnuts, Moonshae chestnuts in syrup, candied cherries, pears, carrots, mushrooms of Brost, golden raisins from Berdusk, and a bag of what looked like chocolate-covered spiders.

Alias steamed. "This could be a colossal waste of time. We don't even know they're coming."

"Day're cummin'," Olive mumbled through a mouthful of apricot. When she had swallowed, she reiterated, "They're coming. This shipment's worth a small fortune.

The Night Masks won't be able to resist. They're compulsive about their vengeance—"

Something thumped somewhere overhead.

"Alias!" Dragonbait called out in Saurial. "They're climbing to the roof."

Alias translated for Olive, who pocketed her apricots and whispered a warning to the other halflings to put out their lights and take their places. Hooded lanterns all about the warehouse went dark.

Alias slipped behind a stack of crates by the wagon door. Olive had disappeared into the darkness. The warehouse felt colder in the dark and, oddly enough, closer, as if ghosts were pressing in around them.

In a minute Alias could hear feet scraping across the tiles above. She couldn't estimate from the sound how many thieves there were, but one of them was heavy-footed and not very agile, stomping up the roof, sliding down, then stomping back up again. Alias wondered if they'd brought an ogre for a backup.

Next came the sounds of nails popping and wood cracking as thieves armed with crow bars made short work prying the skylight doors from their hinges. A more artful crew, Alias thought, might have found a way to slide back the bolts using a drill and a wire, but the Night Masks seem to prefer brute strength and destruction.

Rain began to drizzle into the warehouse as the skylight shutters were thrust aside. Someone above lowered a lantern down to the warehouse floor, and a moment later whispered, "All clear." Five rope ladders rolled down into the warehouse, and five figures began climbing down each ladder. They all wore dark clothes and caps and domino masks—the costume of the Night Masks.

All but one of the Night Masks were armed with daggers and heavy dwarven hammers. The one exception was a tall, heavy man with long, puffed-out black hair, which he had not bothered to tuck into a cap. Inexplicably, he wore a scabbard and sword. The scabbard caught in a ladder-rung, and its wearer, while extricating it, lost his footing and fell the last three feet to the warehouse floor. He landed with a thump and a curse.

Alias had to cover her mouth to keep her laughter in. Several other Night Masks laughed, but one, apparently their leader, hissed, "Silence," and they all shut up instantly.

"We're in," the leader called up to the roof. Someone above cut loose the rope ladders and slid the hatch doors back over the skylight. He'll keep lookout from up there, Alias realized. She made a mental note to collect him from the roof when they'd taken the others.

The leader pointed to three men, saying, "You open the wagon door and take care of the watchman out there. The rest of you start shifting the wine."

Alias put two fingers to her tongue and whistled.

At that signal, twenty halflings pulled back the shutters on their lanterns, bathing the Night Masks in a bright yellow glow. The Night Masks all jumped in surprise, but lost no time drawing their weapons and turning outward in a defensive circle.

Alias stepped out from behind the crates and into the light. She held her sword at the ready. "If you put down your weapons and surrender, you won't be harmed," she said.

"It's that common she-dog the Dhostars hired," the Night Mask with the sword shouted, advancing on Alias with his blade. "Kill her now and our names are made!"

All around the warehouse, the restraining locks on the halflings' crossbows clicked off. The swordsman halted in his tracks.

The Night Mask leader, a tall, well-muscled, fair-skinned woman, pulled the man back by his shirt. "Let's be reasonable," she said, addressing the halflings in the loft rather than Alias. Her accent screamed Zhentil Keep, and Alias instantly detested her. "There is more than enough here for all. What say you arrived late, chased us off, and managed to save only, mmm, a third of the shipment? Yes, a third would be reasonable. Or we can arrange to move that amount for you, privately, if you wish to tell Lady Nettel you lost everything."

"You seem to forget," Alias said, stepping forward until she was directly in front of the tall woman, "that *we* have *you* surrounded."

The Zhentish woman grinned wolfishly at Alias. "*You*
forget, *we* have your precious wine hostage." She
motioned swiftly with her hand, and, before any of the
halflings could react, one of her men slammed his heavy
dwarven hammer into the base of the nearest wine barrel, smashing the wood to splinters.

Instead of wine gushing to the floor, only dry bits of
wood clattered about the hammerer's feet. In a fury, he
smashed at a second barrel. Without warning, the lid of a
third barrel popped open, and a slightly rattled Olive
Ruskettle rolled out, shouting, "Surrender or die!"

The hammerer aimed a blow at the halfling, who
yelped and dived for cover as half a dozen crossbow bolts
pierced her would-be attacker. The hammerer fell to the
floor and remained still.

About half the Night Masks threw down their weapons,
but the rest dived for the cover of the crates. Six were hit
by more crossbow bolts and joined their comrade on the
floor. Three of those remaining began making for the
halflings in the loft. The first one up the ladder to the loft
caught a crossbow bolt and a halfling foot in his face. He
fell back, landing with muffled thump.

Alias chased the Zhentish Night Mask leader and the
clownish sword-wielder down an aisle of crates. She cornered the pair against the warehouse wall. The Night
Mask leader gave the sword-wielder a slap on the shoulder,
and he stepped forward to challenge Alias with his blade.
He adopted a first-year swordsman's training position.

Alias snarled with annoyance that she would have to
deal with this fool while the Night Mask leader was
climbing a wall of crates to the loft.

"Now you will die for challenging the true rulers of
Westgate," the swordsman announced dramatically.

Alias snorted derisively, but resisted the temptation to
run him through. She feinted high with her sword, and
when the Night Mask caught her blade on his own she
closed in on him and delivered a punch to his belly.
Assured that the man wore no armor, she slugged him
twice more before he collapsed in a groaning heap at her

feet.

Free from distractions, the swordswoman began climbing the crates, following the Night Mask leader.

The Zhentish woman had leaped from the top of the pile of crates into the loft. She was bending over a lantern when Alias came up on her. Alias poked her sword in the woman's back. The Night Mask whirled around, holding a tube of metal with a burning candlewick hanging from one end.

Alias froze. She'd never seen the device the woman held, but she'd heard about it. It was some magical explosive made with smoke powder, so simple that even a thief could use one. It could be deadlier than a wizard's fireball. The Night Mask leader backed away until she stood in the section of the loft above the cribs of wine barrels.

"Kiss your wine good-bye, Dhostar lackey," the Night Mask said with a laugh.

"The wine's not in those barrels," Alias replied with a smirk. "It's hidden behind the crates on the other end of the warehouse."

The Zhentish woman glared at her opponent. She glanced back down at the warehouse floor, where two halflings stood guard over the Night Masks who had surrendered. They'd made the Night Masks lie with their faces to the floor. The Night Mask leader scowled down at her former troops who had surrendered so easily.

She dropped the explosive tube down on their backs.

"No!" Alias screamed. "Get behind the crates!" she shouted at the people below. One of the halflings looked up at her with a confused look on his face.

The tube exploded with a flash and a great boom, which rocked the empty wine barrels and the crates in the loft overhead. Smoke poured up from the floor of the warehouse.

As Alias turned around to confront the Night Mask leader, the Zhentish woman smacked her on the side of the head with her hammer. The swordswoman reeled backward and lost her grip on her weapon. Her attacker lunged toward her, dagger drawn. Alias lashed out with a kick, catching the Night Mask squarely in the chest. The

Zhentish woman toppled over the low loft railing, landing
with a sickening, deadly thud on the stone floor below.

Through the clearing smoke Alias could see Dragonbait examining the bloody carnage of bodies below.
Intent on a prayer to heal a bleeding halfling, the paladin
was oblivious to the recovered Night Mask swordsman,
who was now sneaking up behind the saurial. Just as
Alias cried out in Saurial, Olive Ruskettle dashed out
from behind a pile of crates and smashed the Night Mask
on the knee with a hammer pillaged from one of his com-
patriots. He crashed to the ground, swearing profusely.
Dragonbait continued praying over the halfling.

With their leader dead, and most of their party killed—
eight of those torn apart by the explosive device wielded
by their own leader—the remaining Night Masks were
easily rounded up and convinced to surrender.

The second halfling caught in the explosion was
beyond help from even Dragonbait's prayers. The other
halflings glared at their remaining eight prisoners, muttering angrily. Olive had the sense to send the two
halflings who muttered the loudest out for the watch,
and two more to fetch down the Night Mask on the roof.

Despite the hostility of his captors, the Night Mask
swordsman could not resist taunting Alias. "You'll only
live long enough to regret your interference in this matter," he declared.

Alias tried to ignore him as she watched the halflings
cover the face of their fallen companion.

"You don't know who or what you're dealing with." The
swordsman sneered.

Alias whirled around and closed on the arrogant captive. The halflings standing guard over him with loaded
crossbows all held their breath, half anxious, half eager
for her to hit him.

Alias snatched off the swordsman's domino mask. "I
don't care *who* you are, because I know *what* you are. An
ugly brute who'll stand accused as the accomplice of a
dead murderess. Fortunately, I don't have to deal with
you. That's Durgar's job."

The Night Mask snorted. "Durgar. That old relic can't

touch me."

Fearing she would lose out to her anger and hit the arrogant thief, Alias left the prisoners to Olive and the halflings. Just outside the warehouse door, six halflings swarmed over an empty wagon meant to carry away the Thalavar wine. The halflings held the driver and his companion at crossbow-point.

Alias raised her head to the sky, letting the raindrops cool her face and wipe away the tears she couldn't stop. Dragonbait came up beside her and stroked the tattoo on her arm.

"If I hadn't taunted that Zhentish witch about the wine being hidden, she would have just blown up the empty barrels," the swordswoman accused herself.

"There were other halflings around the barrels, Alias," the paladin reminded her. "Someone would have gotten hurt anyway. More halflings might have died if you hadn't been here."

"Fifteen Night Masks dead, thirteen captured, and all it cost was one halfling's life. Was it worth it? If Jamal is right and there are nearly two thousand Night Masks, are we getting anywhere? I'm beginning to know how Durgar must feel," the swordswoman whispered.

"Their leader, the Zhentish woman, was very evil, as bad as Kimbel. It's good that she can't hurt anyone else," the paladin replied. "I'm sure by stopping her you've dealt the Night Masters or the Faceless a direct blow. You've hacked off a bough of this evil tree."

"But the Faceless is the root. I have to find some way to get him," Alias insisted.

\* \* \* \* \*

Somewhat later, in the subterranean meeting hall of the Night Masters, the mood was angry and close to mutinous as each district reported on the detrimental effect the Dhostars' sell-sword was having on their trade. Usually intimidated victims were showing more spine, and there were more than a few reports of agents being set upon by mobs of townsmen. The report given by the head of Enforcement did nothing to quell the passions of those present.

"Although my spies cannot determine exactly what happened," Enforcement explained to his fellows, "the retaliation mission on House Thalavar seems to have ended in disaster. Our operatives were to acquire or destroy a wine shipment from the Thalavar warehouse. The entire team has been killed or captured. The team leader, one of my best operatives, is reportedly dead. My spies heard a great explosion, but they cannot tell if the wine was destroyed. Alias the Sell-Sword was seen at the warehouse."

The Night Master in charge of Noble Relations piped up, "On the plus side, one of the operatives who was arrested is Lord Ssentar's youngest son. I've sent someone to stir His Lordship up, get him good and riled so he'll make trouble for this sell-sword."

Finance Management reported on the bottom line. "With the exception of tonight's loss of a team leader, the swordswoman, and those inspired by her, have targeted only low-level agents. Still, bringing in new recruits and training them takes time. And recruitment, though not ordinarily a problem, is more difficult in light of the perceived risk. Some agents have decided to lie low, while a few others have chosen to retire or take their business elsewhere."

"Rats leaving a sinking ship," Gateside muttered, just loud enough to be heard.

"Consequently," Finance Management continued, "income for the past two days is down ten percent in Gateside and four percent elsewhere. If this trend continues, we foresee stagnation within the next tenday. Beyond that, there is a possibility that by summer's end we will show a loss owing to our overhead costs. This will severely set back our long-range goals for next year."

A panicked grumbling spread among the Night Masters.

Throughout the reports the Faceless had remained silent. He interrupted the grumbling now, commanding, "Order." The tone of his metallic voice was cool. "Thank you for your reports," he said. "Is there any other business?"

Gateside rose to his feet, rather quickly for a man of his portly size. "Any other business!" he cried out in a strangled voice. "In two days, this common little sellsword has laid waste to years of profitable operations. Everyone here, even Enforcement, is taking this on the chin. Take is down, and we're being hissed in the streets by rabble. And you ask if there's any other business?"

A hush fell over the room as the other Night Masters waited for the Faceless's reaction. The Night Mask lord allowed the silence to grow longer, increasing not only Gateside's, but all the Night Masters' uneasiness. "You needn't be so perturbed, Gateside. Within a few days, the matter will be under control."

"The only way you're going to get the matter under control is to whack this Alias. I say we hire an outside professional."

"Really?" the Faceless replied with a bone-chilling tone. "If we attempt to 'whack' the swordswoman and we fail, we will have enhanced her legend, making our agents fear her more. If we succeed, Jamal will make a martyr of her, and the rabble will turn on our agents more ferociously than ever. It may take us years to return to our current strength. Only a fool would implement such a heavy-handed, unoriginal scheme."

The blood drained from Gateside's face so that his exposed chin was as white as his mask. He mustered all the courage he possessed and asked, "But you do have a plan, don't you?"

"I do," the Faceless replied, drumming his fingers on the arm of his chair in irritation.

"I ask that you share this plan with us," Gateside retorted, then softened his demand by adding, "respectfully."

"Request denied," the Faceless responded, then added in a tone dripping with sarcasm, "respectfully."

Gateside raised his voice so that it echoed off the stone walls surrounding the Night Masters. "And what am *I* supposed to do while I wait for this mystery plan of yours to take effect? She's biting into *my* profits." The normally emotionless professional manager of the Gateside district had become an angry, bellowing merchant.

The other Night Masks shifted uneasily. No one shouted at the Faceless with impunity.

"I suggest," the Faceless replied coolly, "that you suspend all activities in your region for a few days. You will lose fewer resources that way."

Gateside's pale skin turned an apoplectic scarlet. His eyes widened with astonishment, and his mouth moved for several moments before his words could come out. "If I call off my boys, I won't have *any* resources in a few days. This little witch is not going get tired and move on. She's dangerous!" Gateside was screeching now. His voice had climbed several octaves.

"I'm growing tired of your hysterical impatience," the Faceless snapped, and the other Night Masters drew their chairs back from the table as if their lord had just drawn a weapon.

"And I'm tired of your arrogant inertia. I'm not going to sit around on my nether cheeks while Dhostars' little dollymop rips my operation to shreds!"

"Enough!" the Faceless growled. He rose to his feet, pointed at Gateside with a ringed finger, and uttered one word, *"Kreggarish!"*

A field of energy rippled across the room, and Gateside's mask began to glow; the white porcelain shined golden from something beneath the mask.

Gateside fell forward across the table, screaming in agony. Enforcement and Thunnside, who flanked him at the table, rose from their chairs quickly and backed away. None of the others came to the portly thief's aid. A few touched their own masks nervously, though they knew perfectly well it was the Faceless's power that attacked their fellow.

Instinctively, Gateside clawed at the mask covering his burning skin; still the glow persisted around his face. The Night Master continued screaming, and his frame writhed in agony. Enforcement and Thunnside could detect the scent of charred flesh.

*"Jokash,"* the Faceless intoned, and the glow faded.

The Faceless's spell had burned the flesh around Gateside's eyes, leaving the image of a domino mask in bright scarlet.

"Consider that a warning," the Faceless said coldly. "I might have let the fire burn long enough to sear your skull, but, in deference to your usefulness, I've left you with only a temporary scar.

Gateside slumped back into his chair. His eyes were tearing profusely, and his sobs were broken only by his gasps for breath.

"Your hysteria endangers us all. Now that I've marked you, you have no choice but to remain hidden for the next few days. Night Masks are not very popular at the moment. If you do not reveal yourself, you will not be in danger, and neither will we. Once the scars have begun to scab, a priest will be able to heal the damage. Consider it a test."

Gateside summoned enough energy to nod weakly.

The Faceless turned to the others and asked, "Is there any other business? Does anyone else have doubts about my ability to deal with this sell-sword? No? Good. Enforcement, help Gateside out. This meeting is adjourned."

The Night Masters shuffled silently from the meeting hall. Gateside leaned heavily on Enforcement, but he found the strength to turn for one last look at Westgate's hidden master.

The magical blur about the Faceless's head continued to mask his features, but Gateside was sure the fiend was smiling.

# Ten
# Power Plays

If Alias had been more attuned to city politics, the puppet show might have served her as a warning. Unfortunately, she hadn't understood the show completely, so she headed unwittingly into the storm.

As usual she'd risen late in the morning, but this morning she did not feel rested. She'd slept badly, due, she knew, to the halfling's death. Upon waking she remembered Jamal's comment that the Night Masters had magic to kill or free any of their people imprisoned by the watch. Alias thought about the arrogant but ineffectual Night Mask swordsman. While she couldn't believe he would be worth the Night Masters bothering over, she became too uneasy and restless to return to sleep. She decided to visit the Tower and assure herself that Durgar was dealing adequately with the thief.

Dragonbait had left her a note that he'd be with Mintassan, so she snatched up some breakfast rolls and set out for the Tower, where the watch and Durgar were headquartered.

At the edge of the market, a Turmishwoman was hawking short wooden skewers laden with roasted, spiced meat. The smell was not only enticing, but brought back memories of her old friend Akabar, who had once prepared her meat the same way. The Turmishwoman caught her eye and thrust out a stick laden with meat, saying, "Lady, you look hungry."

Alias laughed. "I am," she admitted. She bought two sticks of meat, and while she was wolfing down the drip-

ping lamb, she noticed Jamal's troupe. They were set up
in the corner of an open-air cafe, apparently with the
owner's blessings, for he was doing a booming business
selling chowder in bread bowls to the audience.

There was no sign of the Faceless. Evidently Jamal
was still in no condition to perform and her understudy
did not feel up to the role. The actress who usually
played Alias was present, as were the halfling juggler
and the actor wearing the Dragonbait costume.

On the stage were six small kegs stacked in a pyramid,
representing, Alias realized, the barrels of wine in the
Thalavar warehouse. One of the three stage Night Masks
carried on her shoulders a cyclops head puppet—the
symbol of House Urdo.

Alias tried to figure out the appearance of the Urdo
puppet. Was House Urdo behind the raid? To get the
wine?

There was the usual slapstick swordplay until the
Night Mask carrying Urdo blew up a paper bag and
popped it in the halfling's face. Black powder billowed
from the bag, and the halfling and the other two Night
Masks dropped to the stage and lay still.

Alias swallowed back a return of last night's grief. The
audience reacted with an angry mutter, but their anger
was not with the serious turn the troupe had suddenly
taken; it was aimed at the Night Masks. Although
human-halfling relationships were sometimes strained
in Westgate, the general consensus was that only a cow-
ard would kill a halfling.

In the play, Alias's reaction was swift and sure. She
yanked the Urdo puppet away from the remaining Night
Mask and kicked the thief off the stage. The Night Mask
lay still at the audience's feet. Dragonbait pulled out a
miniature prison stocks, and Alias locked the Urdo puppet in it. The audience participated immediately, throwing scraps of food and rocks at the puppet and booing
loudly.

The halfling rose from the stage and called out, "This
collection's for the family of Maxwell Berrybuck. He's left
behind a wife, a stout son, and two fine little girls." As

the musicians played a dirge, the Night Mask actors yanked off their masks. All the actors took up the small kegs and plowed their way through the audience, collecting far more coin than Alias had ever seen any of Jamal's shows earn.

There was the trill of a watch whistle in the distance, and the entire acting troupe looked up. While Jamal might go toe-to-toe with the local authorities, her people obviously recognized the better part of valor. Wrapping themselves and their kegs of coin in their cloaks, they disappeared down one alley, the musicians down another. Although the actors had plenty of time, they made no effort to retrieve the food-spattered Urdo puppet, but left it sitting in the stocks.

Discretely, Alias stepped into the shadow of a building and looked down the street in the direction of the whistle. A phalanx of guards, headed not by Sergeant Rodney, but by the humorless, freckle-faced officer, bore down on the cafe. Of course, by the time they arrived, there was no one but innocent cafe customers picking at their chowder-soaked bread bowls and a puppet. The freckle-faced officer's reaction to the puppet locked in the stocks surprised the swordswoman. He pulled the puppet out and ordered one of his men to hide it beneath his cloak. The patrol then turned and marched back toward the Tower.

Alias gave them a friendly nod as they went marching past her, but they all kept their eyes locked forward and did not acknowledge her presence. She shook her head with disdain at their rigid attitude. Not wanting to arrive at the Tower on the heels of the patrol, Alias strolled more casually through the market.

The market was a rainbow of tents and stalls erected each dawn and removed, by order of the watch, before sunset. Here all the merchants of Westgate were out in full force, extolling the virtues of their wares and pressing them into view of all potential customers. Even merchants who had a shop in town kept a stall in the market to hawk their best items.

A bolt of shining yellow fabric caught Alias's eye, and she paused for a moment to finger the shimmering cloth.

A moment was all the stall's salesman needed to notice her interest and descend on her. He was a short young man in saffron robes and a long, long plait of hennaed hair. He had the most ridiculous patter about how silk from Kara-Tur was harvested from great purple worms herded by giants and spun into cloth with the aid of magic.

Alias had fought purple worms before and knew that the beast's tail was armed with a scorpionlike stinger, not spinnerets, but she knew better than to reply. She'd learned from Akabar that such fanciful tales were a common merchant's trick along the southern coast. If the potential buyer believed the tale, the product was enhanced. If not, any time spent arguing about the tale kept the buyer looking at the product, and, hopefully, increasing her desire to own it. Alias smiled wordlessly at the merchant and passed on. She could hear him tell another passerby how Mulhorand silk was made from moonspiders who tried to snare Selune each night from her orbit.

The swordswoman paused by a jewelry stall. As she lingered over a large display of silver and gold earrings, she began wondering what she would wear for the Dhostar boat party. She traveled light, and she suspected that nothing in her backpack would be suitable. She'd brought plenty of money to buy something, but there wasn't time to have anything sewn.

Lost in her own thoughts, it was a few moments before Alias noticed the stall's saleswoman, a southerner who, being quite tall and dressed in a gown splatter-dyed with every imaginable color, was hard to miss. Yet while the woman watched Alias curiously, she kept a respectful distance, allowing the swordswoman to browse without pestering her.

Alias examined three sets of earrings. The first was a pair of tiny daggers with blue stones in the pommels. The daggers were beautifully crafted, but Alias decided they were too fierce. The second set of earrings was a moon engraved with Selune's face, matched with a dangling set of tears—the shards that followed the moon across the

sky. The moon and tears, while clever, reminded her
uneasily of the arguments she'd had with Finder Wyvernspur over his song *The Tears of Selune*. The third pair, a
set of interlocking stars, reminded her of the stars in the
Dhostar trading badge. Victor, she thought, would appreciate the connection. She held out the earrings to the
saleswoman asking, "How much?"

"No charge," the large woman said, shaking her head,
"I recognize you. You're Alias."

"I couldn't do that," Alias replied with a smile as she
reached for her purse.

The saleswoman's face clouded for a moment with hurt,
"Please, take them," she insisted. "You have done so much
good. Consider them a gift on behalf of all of Westgate."

Alias chuckled, "The last time I received a gift on
behalf of a whole town, I'd just killed a kalmari. I haven't
done that much yet here."

"Hmmph," the woman said dismissively. "Kalmaris are
nothing. Night Masks, they're trouble. You take those.
Don't feel bad. Once I tell people Alias-Who-Unmasks-
the-Night wears my jewelry, I'll sell it all." She smiled
broadly, revealing two rows of perfect white teeth.

Alias grinned at the woman's sales acumen and nodded in agreement. As the merchant held up a mirror of
polished steel, Alias pulled out and pocketed the emerald
studs she normally wore and slid in the silver wires
attached to the stars. She shook her head and smiled
with satisfaction. She could hear the small, interlocked
stars jingling softly, and they twinkled in the light. Now
all I need is an outfit to go with my jewelry, she thought.
Bidding the merchant farewell, she strolled deeper into
the heart of the market, toward the Tower.

The Tower was a circular stone keep five stories high
situated on a low hillock in the center of the market. The
hillock, Alias suspected, was artificial, built up to cover
not only the tower's foundation wall but the first level of
dungeons beneath. Two later additions abutted the east
side, made of similar though not perfectly matched stone.
The larger addition held rooms for public business: the
registry offices for imports, exports, and other licenses

and the courtroom. The smaller addition was a guarded
entrance into the tower itself. Within the Tower the city
kept its counting house and treasury, the nobles kept
offices and meeting rooms, and the watch kept its armory
and some barracks. Beneath the tower, an unspecified
number of subterranean levels served as jails and
dungeons.

Outside the entrance hall flew the banners of those in
residence at the moment: the watch, Durgar, several
other noble lords, and the croamarkh. The doorway of the
entrance was a stone oval, which could be barred by an
iron portcullis, which hung overhead, a security design
repeated at the other end of the hall—at the entrance to
the tower itself. There wasn't a speck of rust on the
heavy gates, and the chains that operated them were
dust free and gleamed with oil. Durgar, Alias realized,
must run a tight ship to keep in perfect working order
gates that hadn't been necessary for decades.

The entrance hall was abuzz with people coming and
going—the watch, messengers, servants dressed in the
livery of their respective noble houses, local petitioners
and foreign merchants waiting to speak with the nobles,
and, on occasion, an individual whose wealthy garb and
wake of bodyguards, supporters, and supplicants indicated a member of a noble family. Only nobles and their
parties were allowed to pass through the second
portcullis unchallenged. All others seemed to be required
to register their name and business at a desk stationed
with three watch officers before being told to wait or go
ahead. There was a long line before the desk.

Alias took her place in line behind a woman dressed in
the full crimson regalia of a Red Wizard of Thay, who was
speaking in hushed tones with a dwarven mercenary
dressed in black. Two Turmish merchants, complaining
in their native tongue about some tariff, took their place
behind her.

The swordswoman wondered uncertainly if she might
not be wasting her time. While she really wanted to be
sure the Night Mask swordsman was sentenced severely,
Durgar might get officious on her and refuse to discuss

his prisoner. He might even be too busy to see her. Just as she considered stepping out of the line, a member of the watch came up to her—the first female member she'd seen.

"Alias the Sell-Sword?" the guard asked.

"Yes," Alias said with a nod.

"I'm Rizzi, Ma'am. I'm to fetch you up to the croamarkh."

"Actually," Alias explained, "I've come to see Durgar."

"He's with the croamarkh, Ma'am. Please, follow me."

Alias did as requested, glad at least to be free of waiting in line.

As she stepped through the entrance into the main section of the keep, someone going the other way slammed into her, hard, jamming his elbow into her side. More surprised than harmed, Alias retreated back two steps and instinctively checked for her money pouch.

A short but powerfully built, scar-faced man with annoyingly familiar, but unplaceable features stood before her. He was dressed all in gold and black, with a huge black opal set in a medallion around his neck.

"Terribly sorry," the man snarled, his eyes glittering with undisguised hatred. "You had better be more careful," he added. It was the most threatening apology Alias had ever heard.

With a sense of confusion, the swordswoman watched the man and his entourage stream out of the tower until Rizzi touched her shoulder and whispered, "Ma'am?"

Alias turned and followed the guard across the vast, open hall on the first floor of the tower and up one of the two staircases that climbed along the outer wall. What, she wondered, did the croamarkh want? Merely a congratulatory meeting? Considering the croamarkh's emphasis on performance, that was unlikely. Perhaps some command for special protection of some place or thing. The swordswoman studied her escort for a moment before asking, "What's going on?"

Rizzi shook her head. "Better you should speak with the croamarkh, Ma'am." At the top of the first flight of stairs there was a curved hallway with a doorway at each

end and a third along the inner curve. Two of the doors
were solid oak, but the one at the far end of the corridor
was oak carved with dragons and stiff-limbed elves. Rizzi
led her to the more ornate door and knocked softly. Durgar opened the door, and, upon seeing Alias, motioned
the swordswoman through the door. The priest dismissed
Rizzi with a quick nod and closed the door.

The room was a meeting suite decorated in neutral colors. Consequently, while everything was impeccably
matched and well built, the room hadn't the least hint of
creativity. The rugs on the oaken floor were a mottled
black, gray, and white. The pattern woven into the tapestries covering the walls was a repeating abstract in
cream, tan, and brown. No one's mind was likely to wan-
der staring at the floors or walls. The round oaken table
was covered with a white cloth and surrounded by twelve
oaken chairs padded with white cushions. The chairs
were of the heavy, thronelike variety favored by merchants in cities where they had no need to worry about a
king who might take offense that they sat in cushier
chairs than royalty.

Croamarkh Luer Dhostar sat at the far end of the
table, dominating the room with ill humor. He glared like
a basilisk as the swordswoman entered, and drummed
his fingers impatiently on the arm of his chair as he
waited for her to approach. Victor, seated on his father's
right, looked nervous and worried, but smiled weakly.
Kimbel, who stood behind the croamarkh, to his left,
blinked like a lizard. Alias strode over to the table and
stood behind one of the large chairs.

"Last evening you attacked a group of individuals
breaking into the Thalavar warehouse," the croamarkh
announced.

Alias wondered if she should nod in confirmation, but
the elder Dhostar stormed on, "One of these individuals
was Haztor Urdo, the youngest son of Lord Ssentar Urdo.
Lord Ssentar has just been in here to demand an apology
for your mistake."

With a flash of insight, Alias realized that Lord Ssentar must be the rude merchant noble who'd slammed into

her as she entered the tower. And Haztor . . . "Haztor Urdo?" she asked. "He wouldn't be an arrogant young man with mediocre skill with a blade and black hair that pigeons could nest in, would he?"

"That's him," Victor agreed in a whisper.

"I made no mistake," Alias said coolly. "Haztor Urdo may be a pitiful excuse—"

"You made a mistake!" the croamarkh interrupted with a bellow. "I know you made a mistake, because Lord Ssentar informed me that his son is innocent. And because I need the support of the Urdo family in council, I had to a-pol-o-gize." Lord Luer spat out each syllable of the last word as if it were poison. "Apologize for someone in my employ, even if her position is on a trial basis."

Angrily Alias replied, "*As* I was saying, Haztor Urdo may be a pitiful excuse for a thief, but he is a Night Mask, albeit a petty one."

"He is not a Night Mask!" exploded the croamarkh.

"Because Lord Ssentar said so?" Alias asked in disbelief.

"Lord Ssentar is a long-time ally from a noble merchant house. His word holds more weight than that of a common little sell-sword who blew in on the wind," the croamarkh snapped.

Alias smiled the tight smile that came to her lips whenever she was about to lose her temper. She pulled out the chair before her and sat down in it. This not only established her attitude that she was on equal footing with the merchant lord, but kept her from lunging across the table and wringing his arrogant neck. The seat cushion was warm, which probably meant the chair had just been vacated by Lord Ssentar or a member of his retinue. Alias laid her hands on the table, one over the other, looked Luer Dhostar in the eye, and spoke. "A sell-sword I am, and common those may be, but *I*, Lord Luer, am not common, a fact you no doubt recognized when you offered me a thousand gold retainer for ten days of work. Should you wish to *break* our contract, I will accept two hundred as a penalty fee and two hundred for the two days of service I have rendered to date."

Luer Dhostar looked astonished by the swordswoman's

nerve, but there was also a hint of dismay in his expression. He quickly returned to the offense, though, insisting loudly, "I have no intention of canceling our contract. I want you to fulfill the terms without harassing any of the merchant houses."

"So you're going to let Haztor Urdo go free?" Alias asked.

"He's already been released," Durgar said from the doorway.

"Well, then, Lord Luer, I don't see the problem," Alias replied with her tight smile. She kept her voice at a low rumble as she explained, "I will continue hunting Night Masks. Should any of them turn out to be Haztor Urdo or some other thieving noble merchant scion, you may feel free to apologize all you want to their parents and grant them freedom. That's your business. I will not, however, agree that I have made any mistakes just to soothe your misplaced anger. I've fought assassins, a sorceress, a lich, an ancient dragon, a mad god, and a fiend from Tarterus, and all in my first year as an adventurer. If you think you can subdue me simply by shouting, you are most amusingly mistaken."

The croamarkh heaved himself to his feet and glowered down at the swordswoman as he growled, "In all my life, I've never had so disrespectful a hireling."

"Or, I'll wager, one with an eye for detail equal to your own," Alias answered.

"Detail? What detail?" Luer demanded, leaning over the table toward the swordswoman.

"The Night Masks used a smoke powder explosive last night. Recently you caught House Urdo attempting to smuggle smoke powder."

"We confiscated that shipment. The Night Masks did not get it," Lord Luer snapped.

"Not *that* shipment, but no doubt there have been others you've missed. That's why you've finally decided to hire a mercenary, someone for whom you did not have to be fully accountable. Fourteen years ago, the Night Masks were just an annoying thieves guild, so you ignored them. In the past few years, however, smoke

powder has become less rare, like Amnite sugar cubes.
Ordinary thieves can do more damage with it than powerful wizards can with fireballs. You realize that more
and more smoke powder is being smuggled in. Whether
it's brought in by House Urdo or House Anybody, you
can't afford for the Night Masks to build a reserve,
because if they do, it's just a matter of time before they
start deciding who the next croamarkh will be. With the
right threats, they might convince some of the houses to
vote for a compromise candidate—Haztor Urdo, now
wouldn't *he* be perfect. His father certainly stands behind
him."

Luer Dhostar waved his finger in Alias's face. "You
take care of the Night Masks. I'll take care of the merchant houses," he said. "Victor will see that you receive
your full retainer today so that there will be no more discussion of broken contracts." The croamarkh motioned
with his finger from his son to the door. "That will be all,"
he finished and sat back down in his chair.

Alias rose and followed Victor to the door.

"Durgar," the croamarkh said, "please assign some
members of the watch to escort this not-so-common sell-
sword back to her hotel with her retainer. We wouldn't
want her robbed."

"Yes, Your Lordship," Durgar replied. He opened the
door and followed Victor and Alias from the room. Once
he closed the door, Victor clapped Alias on the shoulders.
"You were wonderful," he said. "Wasn't she wonderful,
Durgar?"

Durgar raised an eyebrow, but did not reply.

"I've never seen anyone square off against Father as
well as you. Fifteen minutes ago, he was threatening to
fire you, now he demands you remain. You should be a
merchant. Shouldn't she, Durgar?"

"Considering that House Dhostar is paying her a hundred times the salary of a guard of the watch, she certainly has the financial outlook," the priest replied dryly.

"House Dhostar isn't paying me to be a watch guard,
Your Reverence," Alias retorted. "They're paying me to
bring down Night Masks. As to your father's firing me,

Victor, it wasn't likely. He knows that if he did, and I continued to catch Night Masks, he couldn't take the credit
for it."

"That may be so, but he was sorely tempted," Durgar
said as he motioned for Alias to climb the staircase to the
next level. "The noble merchant houses are sacrosanct as
far as Lord Luer is concerned, as well he should be."

Alias turned and climbed the stairs backward as she
looked back down on the priest and Victor behind him.
"Are you saying you approve of freeing Haztor Urdo, Your
Reverence?" she asked with some surprise. "I would have
thought you of all people would expect the law to apply to
all."

"I am a pragmatist, young woman. I understand the
importance of bending some laws so that society remains
orderly. The croamarkh is elected the first among his
equals, his equals being the other noble merchant lords.
Some nations obey their monarch because they believe he
has a divine right to rule. Tyrants hold sway with armies
or fell magic. Here in Westgate, the croamarkh rules by
the consent of the noble merchant houses. He needs their
support to rule, and without him to rule, there would be
anarchy in this city."

"You mean the common people might be free to block
traffic if they want to watch a puppet show?" Alias
teased.

"And powerful merchant families with money to hire
mercenaries would be free to run those common people
down with impunity," Durgar retorted. "The croamarkh's
laws protect the weak as well as the strong. Now you
must excuse me, I have other duties. I will arrange for
two guards to meet you at this door with a porter. Good
day." The priest continued down a corridor, leaving Victor
and Alias standing at a guarded doorway.

Victor pulled out a key hanging around his neck and
unbolted one lock of the doorway. The guard, with his
own key, unbolted a second lock and pushed the door
open. The room within held two accountants, four more
guards, and enough coin to satisfy a young dragon. Victor
wrote out an order for Alias's payment, and the guards

gathered up twenty small sacks filled with fifty gold each
and piled them into a box.

Alias signed a receipt and hefted the box under her
arm. As she and Victor left the room, Alias could hear the
guards on the other side relocking the bolts. She and Victor sat on a bench beneath a window beside the counting
room door.

"So what do you think of all this?" the swordswoman
asked the young merchant.

"Well, no one loathes Haztor Urdo more than I," Victor
said with a laugh, "but my father and Durgar have a
point. The croamarkh must stand united with those
who've elected him. We've had a croamarkh ever since
Verovan's death. For a hundred and twenty years, that's
protected us from another tyrant. Any of the merchants
would be better than someone like that, and Father is the
best of all of them."

"How about a croamarkh who isn't a merchant, elected
and supported by all the people?"

Victor looked at Alias with astonishment. "You can't be
serious. Where did you get such an idea?"

"It's the way Dragonbait's people elect their leaders,"
Alias said.

"Alias, I don't know much about the saurials, but they
must be different from humans. Not all humans are able
to make important decisions like voting."

"Human adventuring groups elect their leaders that
way, too," Alias argued.

Victor shook his head. "It could never work, not for a
city like Westgate," he said. "I'm glad you're with us,
though. The other merchants will look after themselves,
but with you we can look after the weak, like Durgar
said."

"How do we do that?" Alias asked.

"By fighting the Night Masks. It's true, they prey on
the merchants, but it's the common people they hurt the
most." Victor's voice grew more impassioned, though
unlike his father he did not need to raise his voice to
reveal the intensity of his feelings. "When the Night
Masks rob or burn the warehouse of a bigger merchant,

the merchant loses some goods, perhaps some guards, a little business. It's a nuisance. But when the Night Masks go after the common folk, it devastates their lives. To the common people, a bolt of fabric or a crate of wine could be their whole inventory, a wounded guard is a breadwinner without work, a little business is the whole profit margin. If we can take care of the Night Masks, the people will be better off."

The young merchant spoke with the same earnest and hopeful tone he had when he'd revealed his dreams to find Verovan's treasure and use it to improve Westgate. Alias put her hand on his. "We will take care of the Night Masks," she assured him.

"I know. Do you think, as a favor to me, you might try at least to keep from offending the merchant houses while you're doing it. I'm not saying letting scum like Haztor Urdo go, but, um, maybe you could let me in on your plans, then if there's anything politically treacherous involved, I could at least warn you."

Alias withdrew her hand from Victor's. Although she truly wanted to please the young lord, she was unable to resist the sarcastic comment that came to her lips. "Maybe I should just work the Shore," she suggested, referring to the slums just outside the city's western wall, "since there's nothing there any merchant could want."

"Yes. That would be good," Victor agreed, oblivious to her sarcasm. "The Shore is full of transients who don't like to get involved with the watch. The watch doesn't even patrol there regularly, so the Night Masks strike at the inhabitants with the most impunity."

Alias smiled at the innocent way Victor had taken her suggestion.

"That's settled then," the merchant lord said. "Now, about the party on the ship tonight. You will still come, won't you?"

Alias grimaced. "Perhaps I'd better not. The other merchant houses might object to the presence of a common little sell-sword who's arrested one of their own."

"You know I don't feel that way. You've performed your

duties with honor, and I think you deserve respect. I want to set an example by hosting the hero of Westgate on our cruise."

"Thank you, Lord Victor. I'd be honored to accept."

"It will be my honor to show off the most intriguing, lovely woman in all of Westgate."

Alias laughed at the flattery. "I've been looking forward to showing off my new earrings, so I may as well come."

Victor leaned closer, examining the earrings. "Three stars. They're very becoming on you," he whispered with his mouth so near her ear that she could feel his breath move the tiny stars. "Might I hope you choose them in honor of the Dhostar trading badge?"

"I choose them in honor of you," Alias whispered.

Someone nearby coughed politely.

Alias and Victor moved away from one another and looked up. Sergeant Rodney and the watch guard Rizzi stood at the top of the stairs; the porter stood behind them.

"His Reverence sent us to serve as escorts, Your Lordship," Sergeant Rodney said to Victor.

"Just a moment, please," Victor told the guards. Turning back to Alias, he said, "I must be on the pier to greet all our guests, but I'll send my carriage to your hotel a little before sunset."

"I'll meet you at the pier," Alias agreed. The porter came up and hefted her box of gold on his shoulder. Alias gave Victor's hand one last squeeze before she followed her gold and her escorts down the stairs.

# Eleven
# Stalking From the Outside In

Back in her room at Blais House, with the money she'd just been paid, Alias planned what to do next. She wanted to work in the afternoon to make up for the time she'd lose tonight at the party. In the daylight she'd have to rely on a disguise, which would be easier if she went without Dragonbait. She returned to the market, where, once she'd purchased a new tunic to wear to the party, she started picking through second- and thirdhand rags. She found a stained, long-sleeved tunic to cover her tattoo, a pair of badly patched, baggy trousers to hide her scabbard, and a scarf to cover her red hair. With the addition of some mud and a layer of dust, she would pass for a drover. Back at Blais House, she lay the outfit for the party—a blue silk tunic trimmed with silver embroidery—on the bed with her new earrings and changed into her newly purchased rags. Then she headed for the Shore via the Water Gate.

The city wall made more or less a half-circle around Westgate, but owing to a steep cliff in the northwest, it turned inward sharply, running along the top of the cliff until the cliff reached the shoreline. The Water Gate opened over this cliff onto a steep staircase and a path leading down to the Shore. While the Outside, the district of Westgate surrounding the city wall, was predominantly open grassland for grazing herd animals, with the stockyards of the leading merchants pressed against the city wall, the neighborhood of the Shore, wedged between the cliff wall and the sea, was a slum.

It was, as Victor had said, populated mostly by transients,

unable to afford the silver for board and lodging within the city walls: drovers, day workers, and down-on-their-luck adventurers. The Shore offered flophouses for a few coppers a night, and food stalls in the neighborhood sold stale bread and bruised fruits and vegetables for less. Many of the inhabitants relied on the sea for added nourishment. As Alias made her way down the steep cliff staircase, she could see hundreds of them on the beach, digging for clams and crabs.

The buildings were cobbled together from lumber scavenged from broken-down carts and driftwood from shipwrecks. None of them looked as if they could withstand a serious storm. Lean-tos, tents, and tarps filled in the spaces between the buildings. Sewage meandered through fly-lined trenches to a creek, which spilled into the sea.

What with the steep staircase and the stench, Alias could understand why the watch did not make a regular patrol of the area. Although Finder had given her detailed memories of Westgate, she had no recollection of the Shore, beyond the fact of its existence. Not even the curious, adventurous Harper bard had come down here.

Despite her costume, Alias couldn't have felt more out of place if she'd come down in a white coach pulled by six horses. People scurried ahead of her in fear, and she could feel jealous eyes following her down the street. It couldn't be her hidden weapon people feared or her rags they envied, but something she couldn't pinpoint.

From a low pen beside a ramshackle hovel came a vicious-sounding *skronk*. Alias peered into the pen. Inside was a mother pig and six piglets. Two of the piglets were fighting over a moldy cabbage stem. None of the piglets was plump (apparently there wasn't even enough garbage to feed them), but the two piglets fighting were just a touch less scrawny than the other four who lay, like their mother, in an exhausted slumber brought on by too little to eat and no hope of more.

I don't fit in because I look well fed, Alias realized, and willing to fight for my food if I get hungry again. The swordswoman slouched, shuffled her feet, and kept her eyes down in an effort to dispel her warriorlike appearance. She joined some people at a well and waited her turn for a scoop of water. After she drank, she sat down near a lean-to where three drovers were playing dice, with penny stakes.

As she stared up the cliff at the city wall, Alias could pick out the newer stone in the section that had been rebuilt after the corpse of the dragon Mist had collapsed on top of it eleven years ago. The wyrm had been enlarged by a magical spell at the time, and Alias shuddered, imagining how much damage the dragon must have caused when it toppled over the cliff and landed on the slum below.

She was wondering who had scavenged the ancient dragon's skull when she noticed a lean but aggressive-looking young man approaching her. He wore a new tunic of brilliant green, and Alias thought he was handsome enough to serve one of the merchant houses, until he smiled and spoke. Only half of his teeth were still in residence, and his manner and his speech were too uncouth to recommend him to such a post.

"Ya jus' get ta the city?" he asked her.

Alias nodded, keeping her eyes down.

"Gotta pay the visit tax," he said.

"Not staying in the city," she answered. "Sleeping under the stars."

"Don't matter. Gotta pay the visit tax. It's a copper a night."

"Suppose I don't have a copper?" she asked.

"Then ya gotta stay out past the 'ill of Fangs, wit' the beasts and goblins. Wanna be safe near the city, gotta pay the visit tax."

Alias made an elaborate display of pulling the copper coin from her boots, secretly pleased that she'd managed to convince him she was just another victim. The man dropped her coin in a sack he wore about his neck. "Anyone else bother ya, tell' em ya paid Twig," he said, then moved off.

It wouldn't be worth it, Alias thought, to bring him in for extorting a copper. She watched Twig "tax" the camping

drovers, then move toward the hovels around the well. At
each hovel he demanded coin for every inhabitant he saw.
The tax was two coppers for those in a "real" house. Even
the day workers who weren't new to the region paid Twig,
though their money was probably labeled a "residence tax"
or "insurance."

Rather than stop Twig, Alias wanted to get a feel for
how far his dealings reached. The Night Masks, she realized as she followed Twig from a discreet distance, had
found a way to draw blood from stone. Even if Twig collected for a tenth of the district and paid as much as a
fifty percent cut to the Night Masters, he'd earn at least
two gold a day, twice the salary Dhostar paid a watch
guard, all that for no more labor than the asking, collecting, and, no doubt, the occasional act of violence.

Alias had no trouble keeping Twig's bright green tunic
in sight. He did not seem concerned that he might be followed. The watch didn't come down here, and the inhabitants weren't about to challenge the Night Masks. Alias
kept waiting for some show of resistance, but no one
made any trouble for Twig. After half an hour, the collector turned and made a beeline due west. Alias paused at
the outskirts of the neighborhood and watched Twig
cross an empty field. Across the field, in front of a thick
woods, was Lilda's, a large festhall with a reputation for
tolerating rowdy customers.

Alias moved toward the woods and crept up on the
building from the rear. One wing had suffered a recent
fire. Scorch marks ran from windows up the plaster walls
of the building, and charred bits of wood, the remains of
the shutters, hung beside the windows. The smell of
smoke was still strong. Piled in the rear were remnants
of Lilda's business, which someone had managed to rescue from the fire: scorched feather-filled ticks, bedsteads
covered with soot, tapestries stained with smoke, a painting of a female sphinx reclining like an odalisque.

Recalling the arson of Jamal's home, Alias wondered if
the Night Masks had been involved in this fire, too. The
damage here wasn't extensive, but perhaps the thieves
guild had meant only to frighten Lilda into making

"insurance payments" more promptly, without actually destroying her lucrative business.

The sounds of hammering and sawing echoed inside the building. Lilda apparently had enough stashed away to cover emergency rebuilding.

Alias slid along the end of the burned-out wing and peeked around the corner. Twig stood on the front porch, shifting his weight impatiently from foot to foot as another man, seated at a table, counted it out. The counter was a tall, skinny man with a long braid of gold hair hanging down his back. Twig's boss, Alias guessed. He shoved some coin back at Twig and poured the rest into his swelling belt pouch. Twig's cut was smaller than Alias had supposed; he received only a quarter of the take, one gold worth of copper coin, but that was still a lot for a few hours of unskilled "labor."

After Twig left, his boss yanked a knife out of the porch floor boards and proceeded to whittle a small stick into a smaller stick. A few minutes later, a pair of children showed up with their collection. The pair were maybe twelve to fourteen years old, a brother and sister by the looks of them. They brought in somewhat more than Twig, but received the same quarter share. The boss whispered something to the girl, which Alias did not hear, but from the girl's weak smile and uncomfortable squirm and the boss's lewd wink, the swordswoman could guess the content. She fought off the temptation to blacken the boss's winking eye, deciding it could wait until sometime later, but not too long from now. The girl noticed Alias watching from around the corner, and for a moment Alias worried that the child might point her out to the boss. The girl remained silent, though. She pocketed her and her brother's cut, then the pair ran back to the Shore. The man resumed his whittling.

The next collector came three whittled sticks later. He was a powerful-looking man, made mean and miserable by personal neglect and overconsumption of ale. The whittler growled at him for being the last one to arrive, as usual, and the collector snarled something back to the effect that the boss had nothing to do but sit on his rear end and wait. He turned his collection over, sullenly pocketed his take, and stomped into the undamaged section of Lilda's festhall.

The boss rose, threw away his stick, sheathed his knife, and strode west, toward the road. Alias wondered if it would be possible to follow the money all the way up to a Night Master.

Guessing that Twig's boss would take the road back into the city, the swordswoman dashed southward, climbed a fence, and cut through the Dhostar stockyards. Two yard hands approached her as she reached the southern stables, obviously intent on bringing her in for trespassing, but after identifying herself, they let her pass without further challenge.

Spotting her quarry heading farther south, the swordswoman cut through the Thorsar stockyards as well. She reached the city wall in time to see Twig's boss heading toward her. She passed through Mulsantir's gate just ahead of the man. As she strolled idly down the main street, the Night Mask passed her, and she followed him through the city. There was just enough foot traffic for her to blend in with the crowd, but not so much that she couldn't keep her eye on her quarry's blond braid. Twig's boss entered a tavern within spitting distance of the Ssemm sheds. The tavern's sign read "The Rotten Root," and pictured a particularly malevolent-looking treant.

Alias adjusted her scabbard so that it could be seen, took a deep breath, and plunged into the tavern's smoky darkness. Her eyes adjusted to the dimly lit common room just in time to see Twig's boss being escorted into a private room in the back by a large man with gnoll-sized biceps.

Alias slid into a booth with a view of the back room door. The muscular man returned to his post a moment later. He wore an apron over his leather armor, leading Alias to believe he served not only as a guard for the Night Masks, but a bouncer for the bar as well.

None of the regulars seemed to give her a second glance, but Alias was quick to establish a reason for her presence. When the barmaid came by to take her order,

Alias help up two fingers, telling the woman she was expecting a friend. Two ales looking suspiciously like harbor water arrived. As the swordswoman sipped at the beverage, she thought harbor water might have been tastier. The barmaid stood waiting for payment, and Alias handed her some copper from a pocket of her boot.

Alias nursed first one drink, then the other, with the diligence of a condemned man lingering over his last meal. Twig's boss spent about five minutes in the back room, then returned to the common room. He ordered an ale and downed it without paying. He was either well-known enough to run up a tab, or the Night Masks had an arrangement with the tavern to serve free refreshments to their collectors. More importantly, Alias noticed that the collector's belt pouch slapped nearly empty against his thigh.

So the watering hole was the next drop-off point for scam and protection operators. Alias remained while Twig's boss disappeared out the tavern door.

Every few minutes, someone would arrive and approach the door to the private room and the guard would escort the person in or, with a jerk of his thumb, make him or her wait in the bar until the previous arrival left. Occasionally someone would leave the room looking chagrined, but most left smiling.

The visitors to the back room were mostly rough-looking men, a scattering of women, and a few children too young to be collectors themselves, no doubt working as runners for the collectors. Save for one dwarf, who muttered a string of curses as he entered and another as he exited, the visitors were all human.

After about a half hour, midway through her second, carefully nursed ale, Alias noticed that the guard let a visitor in before the last had left. Then it happened a second time. Either the master of the back room was keeping them for a reason, Alias realized, or, more likely, there was a back exit.

Alias gladly abandoned the last of her ale and left the tavern just as the guard was escorting a new arrival through the door. She headed right, down the street, counting the buildings until she hit a cross street, then made another right. She slipped down the alley and counted buildings until she'd reached the rear of the Rotten Root. She slowed as she approached.

Ahead of her she spied someone already watching the doorway from behind a stack of crates. Although the watcher had her back turned to the swordswoman, she seemed familiar. Alias slowed and increased her stealth.

"Hello, Alias," Olive whispered, without even turning around. "Duck behind these crates before someone spots you."

Alias stepped into the shadows behind the crates. "How did you know it was me?" she demanded.

"I saw you in the tavern common room, when I peeked in the front door. Since you were watching the front of the counting room, I thought I'd keep watch over the back. I saw you slip into the alley. Even at that distance I recognized your amusing drover's costume. You're not as noisy as your average human being, but you're still not stealthy enough to sneak up behind me. How's the house brew?"

"Miserable," Alias reported. "They'll have to improve it once we break up this operation, or lose their clientele."

"I think we should hold off on breaking it up," Olive said. "I followed my money from a young shake-down artist to a local tough to here. I'm very curious to see if I can follow this loot to its final resting place."

"I had the same thing in mind," the swordswoman admitted. "How about if I keep watch back here and you sit it out in the common room? Your cast-iron stomach could probably handle their ale better than mine."

"I'll give it a go, but they may not welcome halflings," Olive remarked. "If the climate seems too frigid, I'll be back in a few—"

Olive halted in midsentence and stepped deeper into the shadow, pulling Alias with her. The iron-clad back room door banged open, and someone within tossed out a teenaged boy.

The boy slid along the damp alley until he hit the wall of the building behind the bar with a thud. Two large

men followed him out the door. They were dressed in
leather armor like that worn by the muscle-man guarding the room's front door.

One man closed the door firmly while the other grabbed
the boy by his arms and pulled him up from the ground.
The boy struggled, but the man gripped him more firmly
and slammed him hard into the wall.

The boy let out a whimper, which made his attacker
laugh. He slammed the boy twice more before presenting
him to his companion. The second thug had just finished
wrapping his knuckles with a leather band.

"Following the money's just lost priority," Alias said as
she slid her sword from her scabbard.

"I can't disagree," Olive replied.

The second thug backhanded the boy once across the
face before Alias managed to cross the alley. He would
have noticed the swordswoman, but he was too engrossed
in his mayhem against the boy to warn his companion of
her presence. Alias brought the hilt of her weapon down
on the back of the first Night Mask's skull. He slid to the
ground with his prisoner. Meanwhile Olive had run up to
the boy's other attacker and smacked him in the knees
with a war hammer. The attacker crashed to the ground,
and, with a blow from Alias's sword hilt, joined his companion in unconsciousness.

Alias knelt beside the boy and helped him sit up. It
looked as if the thugs had worked him over before they
had brought him out to the alley. One of his eyes was
nearly swollen shut, blood trickled in a thin stream from
his mouth, and his uninjured eye appeared unfocused.
"Are you all right?" the swordswoman asked. The boy
waved his hand in his face as if to ward off a blow.

"He's not going anywhere," the halfling said. "Let's get
Brothers Bane and Bhaal here trussed and hidden just in
case someone else comes out," she suggested as she
pulled out a ball of thick twine and began hog-tying one
of the Night Masks.

Alias sheathed her sword and dragged the thugs down
the alley, stashing them in the well of a basement door.
When she returned, Olive was helping the boy rise to his

feet. From the way he hopped and leaned, it was obvious he'd injured a leg, too.

"Easy, child," Alias said, holding the boy's upper arm to steady him. "You're safe now."

"Na' a chil'," the boy retorted and shook off Alias's grip, but he was so disoriented that he began to fall backward. As Alias steadied him, he insisted, "I jus' nee' a minute. I'll be fine."

Alias guided the boy back to their hiding place behind the stack of crates. After a minute of steady breathing, he seemed to regain his balance and his senses. He touched his sore jaw and let out a string of curses—an imaginative array of gods' names coupled with parts of the human anatomy that might have been amusing were he not so young.

"So what's this all about?" Olive prompted the boy, all the while keeping her eyes fixed on the back door.

The boy shrugged. "Nothin'. My fault. There was some foolsilver in my payments, some bogus coins. They said I had to be made a 'zample for th'others."

"Made an example? Who said that?" Alias demanded. "Who ordered those men to hurt you?"

The boy looked at Alias with suspicion. He withdrew into himself and would not reply.

Alias shook her head as she studied the boy. While nothing about his appearance attracted attention, making him the ideal delivery boy, he was obviously neglected and abused. His dark brown hair had been trimmed crookedly, probably with a knife, and certainly hadn't seen a comb within the last month. He was rail thin and smelled heavily of unwashed flesh. His clothes, ragged gray trousers, a dingy white shirt, and a moth-eaten vest, were probably washed only when their wearer was caught in a rainstorm. Only his good eye, shining with savvy and cunning, set him apart from a zombie.

"Who was it?" Alias asked again.

"Leave me go," the boy muttered. "I'm fine." He turned and spat out some blood.

"You're the picture of health," Olive retorted. "Don't let him bolt," she warned Alias. "He'll be right off to the head man to warn him about us."

Knowing Olive was right, Alias positioned herself so that the boy could not slip past her. She couldn't bring herself to play the bully, though. She pulled out a gold coin from the money belt beneath her tunic and held it out, twisting it so that it glittered in the late afternoon sun. "Tell me who gave those men orders to hurt you, and this is yours," she offered.

The boy eyed the coin longingly but remained firm. "You think I'm stupid?" he asked. "One-Eye'd kill me if I told you anything. There's nothing she don't find out."

"One-Eye?" Alias repeated.

"She?" Olive added.

Realizing he'd let slip this information, the boy muttered another string of curses. Then, apparently deciding he would be safer betraying his rescuers to One-Eye, he suddenly began shouting, "Help! Help!"

Alias shoved her hand over the boy's mouth and pressed him against the wall. The boy struggled, trying to push her arm away, and when that failed, nipped at the swordswoman's hand. "Be still and stop shouting," she hissed. With her free hand she yanked her scarf off her head and shoved it in the boy's mouth.

"Hold him tight," Olive warned in a whisper. "Someone's coming out."

The back door swung open, and a short, dark-haired woman stepped out. She was dressed all in black leather, and her severe haircut and sharp facial features gave her a hawklike appearance. When she turned to look down the alley, Alias and Olive could see a black patch over her right eye. She held the straps of a heavily laden backpack, which clinked like chain mail when it bounced against her black-clad legs. She looked very annoyed.

"Knost!" she called out, then more uncertainly, "Marcus?" She looked up and down the alley, tapping her black-booted foot impatiently.

Alias noticed the boy had ceased struggling and had begun shaking with fear.

"Damned fools," the black-clad woman muttered. She went back inside the tavern.

"One-Eye, I presume?" Alias asked.

"Undoubtedly," Olive replied.

One-Eye reappeared in the alley, this time with the muscle-man, who doubled as a bouncer.

"—damn fools probably went too far again," One-Eye was saying. "They'd better pick a better spot to dump the body this time. Come on," she said, handing the muscle-man the backpack. He shouldered the pack and followed on One-Eye's heels.

"You'll have to hold onto the kid," Olive said, "so I can follow the money."

Alias nodded. "Be careful," she whispered.

"You never let me have any fun," the halfling sniffed. Then she sneaked off after the pair of Night Masks.

After a few minutes, Alias released the boy, prepared to grab him again at the first sign of trouble.

The boy pulled the gag out of his mouth, but he made no trouble; he was too intent at staring, his eyes wide as saucers, at Alias's sword arm.

Alias followed his gaze. In his struggles the boy had pushed up her tunic sleeve, revealing the azure tattoo, which seemed to swirl of its own volition.

"You're her—that Alias witch," the boy gasped finally. "Oh, Cyric-on-a-stick, I'm really dead."

Alias shook her head, insisting, "You're *not* dead."

"You kill Night Masks," the boy said in a trembling voice. "Knost said you sliced up fifteen men last night." Behind his fear there was a hint of curiosity in his voice, as if he hoped she would confirm her bloody spree to him.

"Knost is a liar or a fool, probably both," Alias retorted.

"You're not going to kill me?" the boy asked in a small voice.

"I just saved your life," Alias pointed out.

The boy shrugged as if that didn't mean much in his line of work.

"What's your name, child?" the swordswoman asked.

"I'm not a child," the boy insisted. When Alias did not respond, but waited patiently, he answered her question, full of bravado, "My name's Kel, like in Kelemvor the death god."

"As in Kelemvor the judge of the dead," Alias corrected. "He was a hero before he was a god. Anyway, you look like you were born before the Time of Troubles. You're too old to have been named for him. Where are your folks? Do they know you work for the Night Masks?"

"Mom took off when I was little. Don't remember her. Dad was a collector for the Masks 'til he got stuck with a dagger in the back by a poacher after his take. Knost gave me a job carrying, but said I was too small to collect—yet. You gonna let me go?" Kel asked.

Alias considered his request. She didn't think she could trust him to keep his mouth shut. He might start bragging that he'd escaped as soon as her back was turned. One-Eye might have Kel brought in and beaten into confessing he'd identified her. One-Eye would then know she'd been followed by the halfling and would warn whoever she was taking the extortion money to.

Then there was the question of the boy's condition. His left eye was swollen shut, and he was still spitting blood. No one was looking after him, and he needed looking after more than ever. When One-Eye found and released Knost and Marcus, they'd go looking for the boy.

"No, I'm not going to let you go," the swordswoman replied. "I'm going to have to take you into custody."

"Nay, ya can't. Ya got no proof I did nothin'. Not even old Durgoat'd hold me just for bein' beat up."

The boy's arrogant grasp of Westgate's justice system made Alias's hackles rise. "I didn't say I was turning you in to the watch," she retorted. "I said *I* was taking you into custody."

\* \* \* \* \*

When Alias arrived at Mintassan's, Jamal and Dragonbait were in the midst of a lively discussion. Jamal did most of the speaking, but the heavy table was littered with paper covered with Dragonbait's tiny script, indicating that he was keeping up his end of the conversation. Mintassan was sitting at the desk, counting and measuring the feathers of living pigeons he pulled from a cage.

When the sage finished with a bird, he recorded the numbers in a log, then let the bird loose. Freed birds fluttered around the back and front room of the shop until they found the open half of the front door and made their escape.

Kel, who'd boasted all the way to the sage's home that Alias would never be able to hold on to him, looked around dumbfounded at all the dead things cluttering Mintassan's workroom; the boy even looked a little nervous.

"What have we here?" Jamal asked.

"I brought Mintassan a specimen," the swordswoman explained. "Westgate human juvenile—descendant of the Night Masks." She smiled at the sage and asked him, "Think you could have him mounted for me, so he doesn't run off?"

Mintassan grinned fiendishly. "Hanging or freestanding?" he asked.

"Freestanding, I think," Alias said. "It's creepier."

Dragonbait, who eyed the boy with disapproval, asked, "If he's one of them, why did you bring him here?"

"He's given Olive and me a little information. I thought I might return the favor."

"She's lyin'," Kel snarled. "I didn't peach on no one. She tricked me into it. Hey! You never did give up that gold piece," he complained to Alias.

"Two Night Mask leg-breakers worked him over. He could be hurt even worse than he looks," she said to the paladin. "Would you help him, please?"

The saurial rose and approached the boy, but Kel, terrified of the saurial, backed into Alias.

"He won't hurt you," Alias said, holding him still.

"Murf," Dragonbait commanded, holding a clawed finger up to the boy's face. He placed his hands on the boy's shoulders and began reciting his healing prayer.

Kel relaxed as he felt his battered flesh mending. His eyes widened in surprise. "He a priest?" the boy asked.

"Sort of," Alias replied.

"Alias," the paladin said, "I know he is only a child, but the Night Mask's have twisted his soul. In time you might fix what is wrong, but for now you cannot trust him."

"I know, but I need to keep him off the street so he doesn't talk to his boss. A few days should do it, I think," Alias said in Saurial. She turned to Mintassan and asked, "You wouldn't happen to have a dungeon, would you?"

"Not exactly, but I'm sure I could arrange something," Mintassan said. "I suppose you'll want him fed, too?"

"Gruel and water at the very least," Alias replied.

"I hate gruel," the boy muttered.

"Well, I was just thinking I could use a hand tidying up around here. If you're willing to work for your supper, I could arrange some roast pigeon," the sage said to the boy, holding up the bird in his hand.

"Pigeon's good," the boy agreed.

Mintassan, not expecting his joke to be taken seriously, paled. "There, there, girl," he said, stroking the bird in his hands. "He didn't mean it." He let the pigeon go free.

"You can't be serious, Mint," Jamal argued. "Letting a child loose in a sage's home is like giving a necromancer the keys to the crypt. It's a recipe for disaster."

"As long as he doesn't touch any boxes labeled 'Danger' or 'Keep out' or 'Hope,' he'll be fine."

"Can't read," Kel said.

"What do you mean, you can't read?" Mintassan asked.

Kel shrugged. "Never learned. No need."

"How can you grow up in Westgate and not learn to read?" the sage demanded.

"How can you grow up in Westgate and not realize it's full of people who can't read?" Jamal snapped at Mintassan.

"Yeah!" Kel seconded.

Mintassan looked taken aback. "Well, I guess *I've* been told." He looked Kel over. "I suppose we ought to get you cleaned up before we let you sit on the furniture. Come on, boy. Follow me."

Kel looked uncertain, but Alias gave him a shove toward the sage, and the boy followed Mintassan up the stairs.

"I'd better get back to Blais House and get cleaned up myself," the swordswoman said. "It's not too long till sunset."

"What happens at sunset?" Jamal asked.

"Victor Dhostar's sending his carriage for me. He's invited me to a party on his family's new ship."

"Ah, mixing with the Westgate snobs. How—" Jamal stifled a mock yawn "—exciting."

"Victor is very nice," Alias said. "He stood up for your theater the other day."

"He was just trying to impress you with his power. He's a merchant, my dear, to the core. Granted, he's a very good-looking merchant, and possibly a good-humored one, but he's still a merchant."

"What do you have against merchants?" Alias demanded.

"Ah, well, that's a long story. It boils down to the fact that merchants know the price of everything and the value of nothing. Rather like this ship you'll be on—*The Gleason*, named for the family of Luer Dhostar's late wife. The Dhostars spent a fortune on a ship to protect their goods from pirates, but they can't protect the people of Westgate from the Night Masks."

"They've paid me a good deal to try," Alias pointed out.

"The price of a set of *The Gleason*'s oars would cover your retainer," Jamal retorted. "Not that I want to encourage you in this ill-fated fraternization, but what are you wearing?"

"Victor said it was semiformal, so I bought a full-length silk tunic. It's blue with silver embroidery. I thought I'd wear it over my leather britches."

"Ah," Jamal sighed blissfully, "they are so egalitarian about dress up north, aren't they? Let me give you some motherly advice. You can't do that. First of all, the slightest whiff of leather will get you shown to the back door with the bodyguards. Secondly, the ladies of Westgate wear inconvenient, uncomfortable clothing to semiformal affairs to remind them how perilous social arrangements are in this city. You'll want to wear an undergown. I have a white bliaut that should fit you and goes with blue. You'll want to double gird the tunic with two silver belts. I've got a set I've just polished. One can hold your scabbard, peace-bonded of course."

"I don't want to impose," Alias insisted.

"You don't want to embarrass Lord Victor either. Trust me on this. A tunic over a gown will look a little old-fashioned, but anyone who's really worth impressing will find that charming. The rest you shouldn't care about. Come with me. We'll get you fitted," the actress ordered, rising to her feet. Alias followed Jamal up the staircase, noticing that the older woman was no longer limping.

Jamal pulled Alias into a back room lined with boxes of costumes. Alias stripped off the clothing she'd worn as a disguise while Jamal rummaged through the boxes and pulled out a plain, short-sleeved gown of white silk.

"What were you and Dragonbait discussing?" the swordswoman asked as she slipped the gown over her head.

"Oh, old times. Cassana, Zrie, you."

"Me?" Alias asked, suspicious.

"You look too much like Cassana to be a *distant* relative, as you said," Jamal replied as she fastened the clasps at the gown's side. "I thought you must be a daughter or a niece. Dragonbait explained how he stole you from Cassana when you were young—that you felt no loyalty to her."

Alias nodded slowly. Dragonbait had stolen her the day she'd been created. "I hated Cassana," she assured the actress.

"That's what your friend said."

"What else did you talk about?"

Jamal shrugged. "Nothing much."

"The Dragonbait effect," Alias noted. "Everyone talks to the silent saurial. Tells him things they won't tell other people."

"Just boring stories of an old woman's life. Nothing that could interest you." Jamal pulled two glittering silver belts off a hook on the wall and handed them to the swordswoman.

"But they do," Alias insisted. She struggled for some way to explain why Jamal interested her, without giving away the feelings she had for the woman, feelings that Finder had implanted in her for some reason. "My father," she said, "was in Westgate in the Year of the

Prince. He died two years later. He told me about a woman he'd met here—an actress named Jamal with red hair." Finder had never actually told her any such thing, but he had to have known Jamal. "I thought you might have known him."

"Who was your father?" the actress asked.

"Finder Wyvernspur. He wouldn't have used that name, though. At the time, he called himself the Nameless Bard."

Jamal sat lightly on a trunk, looking a little stunned. "The Nameless Bard was your father?"

"You did know him?" Alias asked.

Jamal nodded. "It was the Year of the Prince, like you said, in the spring. I was running from a squad of Night Mask muggers, and he stepped out of an alley with his sword and saved my neck. Then he saved my spirit."

"Your spirit?" Alias asked. "How?"

Jamal took a deep breath and sighed. Then she explained, "I'd lost my daughter the year before. I nearly grieved myself into the grave beside her. Nameless . . . he convinced me I still had things to live for."

Alias felt her throat drying. "You had a daughter?"

Jamal nodded. "She died in Deepwinter, in the Year of the Worm."

The year before I was created, Alias thought.

"She was murdered by a vampire when she was twelve."

"I'm so sorry," Alias said.

"The vampire was a merchant noble's daughter, and they shielded her whereabouts from Durgar and the watch."

"Which merchant noble?" Alias asked.

"It doesn't matter which one. All the merchants knew about it."

"So the vampire escaped?" Alias felt sick with horror.

Jamal shook her head. "I hired an adventuring group to do what the watch couldn't. They tracked the vampire down to its lair and killed it, then brought the body back to Durgar. When Durgar realized that the nobles had kept him from investigating the area of the lair, he was ready to quit. Luer Dhostar had an awful time convincing him to stay."

"So you and Nameless spent some time together?"

Jamal grinned. "Only two weeks, but they were a good two weeks. Then he disappeared without a word."

"Cassana had him locked in her dungeon," Alias explained. "Then the Harpers ordered him to Shadowdale."

"He'd told me he was a Harper," Jamal said. "Later I'd heard he had some falling out with them, but after he died, they cleared it up."

Alias nodded. "So how close were you and Nameless?" she asked.

"Well, actually, that's none of your business," Jamal said with a sly smile. "But he was a fine figure of a man, no doubt about it." She handed Alias a pair of white silk slippers embroidered with silver thread. "Try these on."

Alias pulled the slippers on. They fit snugly, but well enough for a few hours leisure. "My tunic is sleeveless. Do you think I need to cover my tattoo?"

"Not unless you're attending incognito. They all know you have one. There's no point in hiding it. They've seen plenty of foreign merchants with markings. What jewelry are you wearing to this party?" the actress asked.

"A pair of silver earrings—three interlocking stars."

"Over a wagon wheel?" Jamal teased. "A gift?"

"Just stars, no wheel, and I bought them myself."

"At least you don't have to wear Dhostar livery. That tawny color looks awful on us redheads."

"Very sweet," a high-pitched voice said from the doorway. "I'm out tracking down evildoers, and you decide to play dress up."

Alias and Jamal turned to Olive Ruskettle. The halfling looked as if she had run halfway across Westgate and still had a full head of steam up.

"Our warrior is mixing with high society tonight," Jamal explained.

"From the back alleys to the castles in a matter of hours, eh?" Olive said. "What a whirlwind life you lead."

"What did you find out?" Alias demanded.

"Well," the halfling began, "I followed One-Eye and her

bodyguard south to a big manor house right on the edge
of the city. She went in, spent about ten minutes, just
enough to count that sack of money. Then she and her
friend left and parted company." Olive paused for dramatic effect.

Alias glared. She hated these pauses. "And?" she
prompted.

"I didn't see the occupant," Olive replied, "but I asked
around. "The house belongs to a wealthy vintner named
Melman. Melman bought the place ten years ago, after
the former occupant died. Guess how."

"Night Masks?"

"Nope. Guess again."

Alias let out a sigh of exasperation. "Olive! Spit it out!
How did the former occupant die?"

"She took a blast from a staff of power. Her name was
Cassana."

"Melman's living in Cassana's house?" Alias asked, a
smile of glee creeping across her face.

"Yep. The same place we all knew and loathed."

"The one with the secret tunnel into the secret basement," Alias said with a twinkle in her eye.

"The very same," Olive said, rubbing her hands
together.

# Twelve
## Maiden Voyage

Olive accompanied Alias and Dragonbait back to their inn, making plans for a little breaking and entering. Although the halfling agreed it would be safer to wait until long after dark, she was disappointed that they could not leave immediately. Alias suspected that were she and Dragonbait not on the scene, the normally cautious halfling might have plunged recklessly ahead even before sunset. There was an eagerness in Olive that went beyond a desire to check out the Night Mask Melman's hoard of ill-gotten gain. Olive really wanted to bring the Night Masks down. It was a side of the halfling that Alias would never have expected to see when the two first met, eleven years ago.

Inside Blais House, Alias hurried to wash up as Dragonbait escorted Olive to their room. When Alias joined them, fresh from her bath, she noticed Olive eyeing the sacks of gold containing her retainer from the Dhostars. "You should have gotten more," the halfling said.

"Olive, you know I don't need the money," the swordswoman argued as she pulled her new silk tunic over Jamal's white undergown. "Neither do you, for that matter. I might have ended up fighting the Night Masks even if the Dhostars hadn't offered to pay me."

"It's the principle of the thing," Olive insisted. "Never sell yourself cheap, and always charge rich humans through the nose. The Dhostars are richer than old Misty was. It's up to people like you to see to it that their floor doesn't give under the weight of all that coin."

"Is that what you're doing for Lady Thalavar?" Alias

asked as she slipped her new earrings back in her ears. "Seeing to it that her floorboards don't give?"

"House Thalavar is nothing like House Dhostar," Olive insisted. "Lady Nettel has more noblesse oblige in her pinkie than all of the remaining merchants in this city combined. She makes a profit, yes, but she doesn't invest in things just to see an obscene return. She invests in little businesses so the owners can make a living and patronizes musicians and artists and donates wells and fountains and park land to the people of Westgate."

There was a knock on the door, and Olive opened it. Mercy stood on the threshold, eyeing the halfling with the same wide-eyed look she'd given Dragonbait and Alias on their first day as guests. The girl, Alias thought, must have too few opportunities to meet other people. The swordswoman introduced Olive as a long-standing friend. Mercy curtsied politely, then informed Alias that there was a carriage waiting downstairs.

"Please tell him I'll be down in a few minutes, Mercy. Then you can come back and take Olive and Dragonbait's orders for dinner."

The half-elf hurried off to do as she was bid.

Alias slid her scabbard onto the lower of the two belts Jamal had loaned her and secured her sword to the scabbard with a piece of silk ribbon tied in an elaborate knot that she could release instantly by pulling it in just the right place. She tugged on the white silk slippers and ran a comb quickly through her hair. Turning about, she asked the others. "How do I look?"

"Very nice," Dragonbait replied.

"Better than Lord Victor probably deserves," Olive answered.

Alias hurried downstairs and out to the street. The reins of Victor's carriage were in the hands of the same old man who'd held them at the Harbor Tower that first day she'd met Victor. The bent, gray-haired servant bowed with earnest deference, and Alias could see he looked at her with a certain approval as he handed her up into the carriage seat. Jamal's advice on dress pleased at least one elderly member of House Dhostar's staff. The servant climbed into the seat beside Alias and urged the horses forward.

The carriage pulled up to a pavilion at the western end of the docks, where a footman in Dhostar livery handed Alias down to the ground. The swordswoman stared uncomfortably at the crowd of strangers all about. Most of them appeared to be errand boys, bodyguards, and ladies-in-waiting, left beneath the pavilion to await the returns of their masters and mistresses. Alias smiled politely at a bodyguard dressed in Malavhan livery, but was met with a grim stone face. Too late, she realized he took her for one of the nobles, and in Westgate the servants did not fraternize with the nobles.

Alias turned to thank Victor's driver, but he had already evaporated, coach and all, to whatever demi-plane hid such utilities until they were called for again. Another, larger carriage was pulling up to debark its passengers. The footman asked Alias politely to please move down the pier to join the other guests.

Down the pier there were small mobs of nobles, from dandies to grand dames, in tight little constellations. Wandering planets of individuals only casually acquainted with the brightest stars would graze the edges of the constellations, but finding insufficient gravity to hold them, they would soon look for new orbits. Eventually, in twos and threes, guests drifted up the gangplank of *The Gleason*. Since she had no acquaintances among any of those on the pier, Alias made straight for the gangplank, but she paused halfway down the pier to stare in awe at the Dhostars' new ship.

*The Gleason*, Alias realized, was a galleass. She had heard that Sembia was building such ships, but the Dhostars' was the first she had seen. It was basically a larger and more heavily armed version of the great galley, one hundred sixty feet long and forty feet across the beam. The sails were lateen-rigged from three huge masts, though at the moment they were tightly furled, tied with cords of black and gold. Tonight the ship would be powered by oar. Alias counted fifty oars, painted bone white and so large that each could be manned by several rowers. A twenty-foot iron-clad battering ram jutted out from the bow. Tarpaulins covered what Alias guessed was a pair of ballistae mounted on a massive turret on the top of the foc's'le. Both the foc's'le and the sterncastle, which towered two stories over the deck, featured narrow archers' slits.

While the fighting capabilities of the ship were not hidden, tonight the vessel was obviously decorated for festivities. The rowers' benches were curtained off, screening them from view of the guests, and vice versa. A giant banner emblazoned with the wagon wheel and three stars of House Dhostar draped down from the top story of the sterncastle, reaching nearly to the waterline, while a smaller House Dhostar banner and the banners of the croamarkh and the city of Westgate fluttered from poles fore and aft. The stern lantern, fitted with magical light stone, was covered with a square of fine red silk, bathing the ship's deck and the dockside with a rosy glow.

The pier rattled, and Alias turned to see a chair on wheels, with an awning, like a miniature carriage, rolling toward her. The wheeled chair was white, with a green feather painted on the side panel, and pushed by six halflings. The passenger was an ancient human woman attended by a pale, blonde girl in her teens. The girl's main duty seemed to be to keep the halflings from pushing the chair into other guests in their zeal to move the device toward the gangplank. Several guests broke away from their constellations to chase after the chair, with as much dignity as they could muster, until the vehicle came to rest at the end of the pier. Then the followers paid their respects to the elderly passenger.

Someone brushed up against Alias, and the swordswoman turned quickly, expecting a pickpocket despite the standing of the crowd all about her. She faced the back of a woman in an elegant gown of yellow satin hemmed and edged with fox fur, with a tiny golden dagger dangling from her gold-link belt. Her dark hair, which hung down her back, was swept back from her face with a barrette fashioned like a basilisk. The woman turned and murmured an apology, which Alias accepted with a nod and a weak smile.

The woman smiled broadly. "You're new," she noted with a tone of delight and surprise.

"Yes," Alias admitted. "I feel like a fish out of water. I'm afraid I don't know anyone here."

As Alias spoke, the other woman took full stock of her, her gaze fixing at last on her right arm. The stranger's eyes became glassy, and her face seemed to petrify. "No," she replied frostily. "You wouldn't." She turned on her heel and made for the next little group over, leaving Alias staring at her retreating form and the eyes of her basilisk barrette.

Alias frowned. Obviously the woman had recognized her from her tattoo. She couldn't believe she'd been snubbed just for being a swordswoman. Surely Westgate merchants socialized with adventurers on other occasions. She continued moving toward the gangplank, scanning the crowd for a friendly face. As she passed the woman with the basilisk barrette, the group the woman now stood with broke into gales of laughter. At least two other women turned to look at the swordswoman, then hurriedly looked away.

Alias spotted a flash of blue and purple, and thinking it might be Durgar, moved in that direction. At this point, even the opinionated priest would be welcome company.

Fortunately, her rescue was much more pleasing. She spied Victor bolting down the gangplank in long, swift strides. His eyes were fixed on the pavilion at the end of the pier, where the carriages were still unloading guests. He could be looking for someone else, but Alias was determined not to let him hurtle past her without speaking to him. She stepped into his path with her hands folded in front of her as he approached.

Victor checked his stride so suddenly that he almost tripped himself. The anxious look he'd worn was fading into one of delight. "I'm sorry I wasn't at the pavilion to welcome you. There were so many last-minute—" The young noble interrupted himself. "You look radiant. I'm so glad you came."

Alias smiled. "So am I," she said. "Now. You look nice, too," she complimented him. He wore a three-quarter length tunic of cream-colored silk, trimmed in brown satin, and his hair glistened in the lamplight. Tonight he looked every bit the nobleman.

As Victor took her arm and ushered her up the gangplank onto the ship, a herald began announcing the ship's imminent departure. All guests, the herald insisted, should board the ship now.

There was a flurry of activity as the guests tried to move toward the gangplank quickly, yet without looking hurried or rudely jostling one another. Still, many people on the pier remained where they were, without moving.

"They don't all seem to believe your herald," Alias commented.

"They haven't *all* been invited," Victor explained. "They're petty nobles, lesser merchants and their hangers-on, come to see the boat off, hoping for some last-minute invitation."

Alias looked down and saw the woman who'd snubbed her among those not chosen for the voyage. The woman shot Alias a glare as killing as that of the basilisk that adorned her hair.

The last to board the ship was the ancient woman from the personal carriage. She hove herself out of her chair and ambled up the gangplank, leaning on a large, ornately carved staff on one side and the pale, blonde girl on the other. Despite the supports, there was nothing feeble about the woman's appearance. Her back was as straight as an elm tree, and she carried her head high.

"That's Lady Nettel Thalavar," Victor whispered in Alias's ear. "She's the only one of the merchant nobles who has even a dram of old Verovan's blood in her. She's a third cousin, two generations removed. She's outlived three husbands and rebuilt her clan's fortunes to nearly what they were in Verovan's day. The girl on her left is her granddaughter, Thistle."

"She's quite pretty," Alias said. "The granddaughter, I mean."

"Hmmm?" said Victor. "I can't look at her without

remembering how she used to tear through the streets as a child with her halfling nannies chasing after her. She was almost as troublesome as the halflings themselves. Her nickname back then was Dervish."

On the turret where the ballistae were mounted, a small group of musicians had set up two rebecs, a larger viol, and a dulcimer, led by a bard with a songhorn. The players launched into a soft, somber number that drifted along the length of the ship. The ship's first officer bellowed an order to cast off. As crew members unfastened the lines to the pier, the oarsmen on the near side began pushing off with poles. A moment later, Alias could feel a slow, steady beat on the floor, and all the oars moved, as one, in rhythm with the beat. The musicians picked up their tempo to match the beat, and the Dhostar's new galleass pulled out into Westgate's harbor.

Most of the guests stood at the buffet tables lined up down the center of the ship. The tables were laden to the groaning point with expensive delicacies and elaborately prepared dishes. Servants dressed in crisp white sailors' shirts replenished empty trays and answered questions about the food.

"Care for something to eat?" Victor asked.

"In a bit," Alias declined. "I'd like to see the ship first."

From Victor's smile, Alias could see he was inordinately pleased with the chance to show off the new ship. Taking her arm, he steered her toward the bow as he began a lecture that sounded spontaneous, but must have been partially rehearsed.

"Most of the ships in our family's fleet are carracks, multisailed roundships," the young noble explained. "Useful for hauling large shipments of cargo, but not very fast, with maneuverability still dependent on the wind." Victor pointed to a Dhostar carrack in dock. It was, Alias realized, the same one that had been cut off at the harbor entrance by the Thalavar ship two days ago.

"For the past ten years," Victor continued, "while merchants along the Sword Coast have been adding even larger carracks, the so-called galleons, to their fleets, merchants of the Inner Sea, including House Dhostar, have invested instead in great galleys. Such ships are large enough to carry perishable and luxury cargoes: silks, spices, perfumes, wines, fruits, messengers, and passengers. They are also maneuverable enough to guarantee safe entry into any harbor.

"Most importantly, they are quick enough to outrun the swarms of pirates haunting the Inner Sea: those making their homes in the Pirate Isles, as well as those along the coastline of Thay and Mulhorand, nations that are not exactly quick to rout out such predators. Should a great galley, despite its speed, be boarded by enemies, the rowers can abandon their oars for swords in the ship's defense." Victor led her up a staircase to the top of the foc's'le. Standing behind the musicians, they were able to look out over the bow.

*"The Gleason* is classed as a galleass," Victor said. "It's basically a refitted great galley. It's much wider and somewhat longer, for more cargo space. It has fewer but larger oars, giving the captain more flexibility in assigning duties. Finally, of course, the galleass is fitted with more armament." Victor gave a nod toward the battering ram mounted in the fore and then removed a tarp from one of the ballistae to show it off. Alias peered at its well-oiled parts as Victor said, "We choose to have the ballistae manufactured in Neverwinter—their mechanisms are superior to any others. The local Gondsmen suggested we use bombards of smoke powder, but we consider that far too dangerous to transport. For projectiles we've settled on iron shot, and oil and flaming arrows." Victor flipped the tarp back over the ballista and led Alias back down the foc's'le stair.

"This is our first ship of this sort. We plan to use it as an escort for our carracks traveling to the Easting Reach."

"Have the other merchant houses in Westgate been building galleasses?" Alias asked.

"House Guldar built two, but they were lost at sea, no doubt due to the treachery of Thay's Red Wizards. House Vhammos has had one even larger than this half-finished in dry dock for a year, as they muster the resources to finish it. House Athagdal had one nearly finished two years ago, but their dockyard was prey to a mysterious fire, and they lost it as well as three other ships."

"Night Masks?" Alias asked.

"They may have started the fire," Victor answered, "but it's very likely they were paid to do so by House Thorsar. Thorsar and Athagdal have a long-standing feud, fueled by petty jealousy."

At the bottom of the foc's'le stair stood a tall, heavy man with long, puffed-out black hair—Haztor Urdo. Alias remained on the stair, glaring down at the Night Mask merchant, her hand resting on her sword.

With a venomous look at Alias, the young merchant greeted Victor with a simple, "Dhostar."

"Urdo," Victor responded in kind, his tone chill.

"Hiring swordswomen for your company now?" Urdo taunted Victor with a sly grin.

With an expertly executed shove, Victor pressed Haztor against the wall of the foc's'le and held him there with a finger pressed against the younger man's windpipe. With his face close to Haztor's, Victor replied, "Considering the company you are known to keep, you would do well to keep your mouth shut."

Victor turned to Alias, and in a mild and pleasant tone asked, "Would you excuse me for a few minutes? I have some business with this scion of the Urdo clan. Please, help yourself at the banquet table. I'll join you there."

Alias considered asking Victor to ignore the insult. Urdo wasn't the first to snub her this evening, and he probably wouldn't be the last. She recognized, though, that there was more to the conflict between the two men than an insult to herself. The young Urdo had challenged Victor's power on his own turf. "I *am* hungry," the swordswoman replied, and, slipping past Haztor, drifted over to the buffet tables.

A number of portly merchants were parked in front of the tables where beef, pork, and mutton were being served. At a table laden with seafood, several young men were challenging each other to down unhealthy portions of some of the more exotic offerings—fish eggs, pickled cuttlefish, and raw squid. Alias slid up to a table featuring a huge, edible centerpiece of fruits surrounded by slices of wine cheeses fanned out like playing cards. Accepting a plate from a servant, she filled it with pieces of Vilhon Blanc and Turmish brick, and some grapes plucked from the centerpiece. Another servant provided her with a slipper of mead. With her hands full, Alias backed away from the table.

The swordswoman took a sip of the wine. She started with surprise as the taste blossomed in her mouth. She took another sip to confirm her suspicion. Evermead! A wine made in only one place—the elven island of Evermeet, twenty-nine hundred miles away. The Dhostars had imported it all the way to Westgate. Alias was more impressed by this feat of transportation than the building of all the galleasses on the Inner Sea. She sipped blissfully at the sweet wine with her eyes closed, remembering, as if in a dream, simpler days and friends long gone.

When she'd finished the wine, the spell was broken. She looked toward the bow, where Victor was speaking with Haztor Urdo. Victor seemed relaxed and friendly, while Haztor looked tense and nervous.

"Your glass is empty," someone at Alias's side noted.

Alias turned to find herself face-to-face with Lady Nettel Thalavar. It was like turning the corner in a cavern and running into a dragon, a smiling dragon. The old woman was far more imposing than any Westgate noble Alias had met yet. She stood as tall as Alias and held her ground. There was none of Luer Dhostar's bullying or Ssentar Urdo's viciousness about her. She was simply a strong woman, unafraid of strangers.

Compared to the other guests, the noblewoman was dressed quite plainly, in a conservative black-velvet gown. Her white hair was twisted into a bun at the top of her head. Her only jewelry consisted of a gold wedding band, a strand of pearls, and a brooch of a stylized feather fashioned of copper aged to a green patina. The elderly woman motioned toward Alias's glass, and a servant appeared immediately to fill it from a wineskin.

"I am Lady Nettel," she introduced herself. "And you are Alias of the Magic Arm," the noblewoman stated as she regarded Alias through a set of lenses mounted on an ebony rod.

Alias, unused to the description, did not reply immediately.

"Alias the Sell-Sword. Ruskettle's friend. Jamal's cheap hero. Dhostar's young champion. Stop me if I mention one you prefer," Lady Nettel requested with a grin.

"Just Alias," the swordswoman replied and bowed formally at the waist. "I'm pleased to meet you, Lady Nettel. Olive speaks very highly of you."

"As she does of you," Lady Nettel answered. "I am very grateful for the assistance you rendered to her protecting my wine. Thank you."

"You are most welcome," Alias replied. "I only wish it had ended better than it did."

"Yes," Lady Nettel agreed. "Please, allow me to present my granddaughter and heir, Thistle."

Thistle Thalavar, who had been staring wide-eyed at Alias, lowered her eyes and curtsied. She was dressed rather more elaborately than her grandmother, in a white gown trimmed with miles of pink ribbon. Her yellow hair was elaborately plaited all about her head and decorated with tiny flowers. She wore a diamond necklace that must have been an heirloom, since it was far too expensive for so young a woman.

"You are the talk of my household," Lady Nettel announced, "with the halflings hailing you as Ruskettle's warrior companion, the servants raving about your street theater antics, and the youngsters speculating about you and Victor."

Alias smiled politely, hoping she would not blush, but Thistle looked horrified. "Grandmama!" she said after a gasp.

Grandmama held up a hand, and Thistle hushed. "Young people are always gossiping, trying to figure out where everyone around them fits into society. Such a waste of time."

"Because the people themselves don't even know where

they fit in?" Alias asked.

Lady Nettel smiled and shook her head. "Because we weren't meant to *fit* into society. We must be what we are, and let society fit around us. That is how I have always lived my life. And you?"

"That's always been my choice," Alias agreed.

"Like your tattoo?" Thistle asked, her words starting to spill over each other. "You chose that. Did it hurt? Do you regret it?"

"Thistle," Lady Nettel spoke in a warning tone.

"How else will I know?" Thistle insisted.

Lady Nettel sighed. "Please excuse her. We had an argument that had nothing to do with you."

"That's all right," Alias said. She turned to Thistle. "My tattoo was not really my choice. Someone branded me when I was a captive. It didn't hurt, because I was unconscious at the time. It's not a regular tattoo, though, but magical. I cannot regret it, since I had no choice in its existence, but it can be very tiresome. It is not something one can remove like a dress or jewelry. It is always there, the same design, the same color. Once I hated it, but no longer. It reminds me of a special time in my life and of the bonds I share with my brother and my sisters and with my father."

"I see," Thistle said, more thoughtful. "Thank you for telling me."

Lady Nettel raised her glass to someone behind Alias. A moment later, Alias felt a hand on her shoulder as Victor Dhostar took a position beside her.

"Lady Nettel," Victor greeted the elderly noblewoman, adding a deep bow. He winked at Thistle and asked, "How are you, Dervish?"

Thistle colored deeply at the nickname and tried unsuccessfully to appear too haughty to notice the young Dhostar.

Lady Nettel chuckled. "Congratulations on your new vessel, Lord Victor," she said. "It hasn't sunk yet under the weight of Westgate's pride. It must be well-constructed."

"I'll pass your compliments on to father," Victor

answered.

"Hah!" Lady Nettel replied. "If those compliments belong to anyone, they're yours. For all his meddling, Luer hasn't peeked in a shipyard for six years. Can't take the dust. This is your victory, young man, and everyone knows it."

Victor bowed his head wordlessly.

"Well, I'll let you steal away with your guest," Lady Nettel said. "I'm sure she's not here to entertain me." With that, she moved off with Thistle, followed by a wake of other guests all vying for the Thalavar matriarch's attention.

Alias offered Victor some cheese from her plate. The ship was rounding the harbor entrance now, and everything on the ship cast two shadows, one from the stern light, the other from the lighthouse. Looking across to the Westlight plaza, Alias saw a group of people scurrying around in the twilight, setting up some sort of display on the northern shore of the peninsula.

"What's going on out there?" she asked Victor.

"Ah, well, that's a surprise. You'll just have to wait and see," the nobleman said.

Alias nodded. "I shouldn't ask, but how did your business go with young Urdo?" the swordswoman queried.

Victor grinned conspiratorially. "We discussed how easy it was to make an apology. Taking my cue from my father, who apologized for his arrest, I thought I might just apologize in advance in case Haztor happens to fall overboard and no one notices. Should he falter in his attempt to swim ashore or, gods forbid, should the quelzarn happen to devour him, I assured him that my apologies to his family would be profuse if not sincere."

"There isn't really a quelzarn, is there?" Alias asked, knowing that such giant sea serpents were reputed to be very rare.

"Of course there is," Victor insisted. "What do you think eats all the garbage tossed into the bay?"

Alias gave the nobleman a suspicious look. "Have you ever seen this quelzarn?" she demanded.

"Many times," he replied, then added, "though only on

foggy nights, when I'm alone, without, alas, any witnesses to back up my story."

Alias laughed. "So where is Haztor now?" she asked.

Victor looked around the deck, then shrugged. "I've no idea," he answered, raising his eyebrows theatrically.

"Victor, you wouldn't—" Alias looked around the deck uncertainly.

The young nobleman chuckled. "He's over there, hugging the mainmast. I don't imagine he'll go anywhere near the rails this evening. He's not a strong swimmer."

Alias looked in the direction Victor had nodded. Haztor Urdo was surrounded by several young men and women who chatted with him amicably, but he was indeed keeping the mainmast at his back.

"I haven't seen Ssentar Urdo," Alias noted. "Wasn't he invited?"

"Each noble house is invited, and each sends at least one representative so the rest of the houses cannot gossip freely about it. Ssentar Urdo, however, is prey to seasickness. Ordinarily Ssentar would send his oldest son, Mardon, and Mardon's wife. By sending Haztor in his stead, his father is showing Haztor his support. Haztor, despite the scandal of being arrested as a Night Mask, will remain a power. Consequently, sycophants will flock about him, seizing this opportunity to offer their support. Such people are liable to snub you, given a chance. They aren't worth worrying about."

"Considering the company I'm in, I doubt I should notice them," Alias replied. She set aside her empty plate and glass. "Shall we continue our tour?"

Victor smiled, took her arm, and steered her aft. "The masts and keel," he explained, "were fashioned from redwood logged in the far north, around Hartsvale, land of giants and giant trees."

"And where do you get the oarsmen?" Alias asked, "Sentenced criminals?"

"Sometimes," responded Victor. "This particular crew, however, is made up of shareholders."

"Shareholders?"

Victor nodded, "Of course. You didn't think we'd risk

all the heads of Westgate in a boat with a crew of criminals, did you? People work better when they have a stake
in the outcome. In this case, fight better and row better.
They get a small portion of the profits this ship will make
for House Dhostar. Any who agreed to serve for this frivo-
lous maiden voyage gets a double share of the first venture. We have no trouble finding rowers."

At the deck level, the stern castle was open to the fore.
In the rear, two sailors manned the tiller, but the rest of
the area was taken up by tables for the guests. Luer
Dhostar and most of the noble clan elders sat at a table
in the front of the sterncastle, drinking, playing dice, and
telling sea stories from their past. The croamarkh nodded briefly at his son. He gave no indication of noticing
Alias. Durgar, who sat on the croamarkh's right, smiled
ever so slightly at the swordswoman, but then turned his
attention back to some elderly noble describing a run-in
he'd had with pirates back when the world was young.

Victor led Alias past the tables to the stairs in the
back.

"Up or down?" Alias asked.

"Up," said the young noble. "Down is storage and
berths for the crew."

Alias climbed the steep stairs and paused at the first
level. Victor gave her a peek into the officers' and guests'
quarters. All but the captain's cabin looked cramped, but
all were snug and smelled pleasantly of fresh pine.

They climbed another set of steep stairs and stood
alone on the roof of the sterncastle. There was no one else
up there. They could look down on the party below, but
when they turned their backs, it seemed to disappear.
Alias looked up into the darkness overhead, but due to
the glare of the stern light, the lighthouse, and the waxing moon, she could pick out only the brightest stars. Victor strolled to the stern railing, and Alias drifted behind
him.

For the first time Alias felt as if they were truly at sea,
and not just because they'd left the bay. A stiff breeze
shot across the port side. Alias shivered in the wind.

"I forgot I might need a cloak out here," she said.

"In the interest of chivalry, I feel obliged to offer you an arm around your shoulder," Victor said.

"In the interest of encouraging chivalry wherever I find it, I feel obliged to accept," Alias replied.

Victor slid his arm around her back, and Alias leaned against his side. The wide sleeve of his tunic served well as a shawl, and the warmth of his hand on her shoulder was wonderfully pleasant.

Westgate was ablaze with lights that rivaled the stars above: the lighthouse, the streetlights, the campfires on the shore.

"It's beautiful, isn't it?" Victor said, regarding the city. "Lit up on a clear night like this, it looks every bit as magical as Evermeet, as exotic as Kara-Tur, as wealthy as Zakhara. Like a place of make-believe, a place where legends can be born."

Alias made an agreeable and noncommittal, "Mmmm," unable to put out of her mind the Night Mask rot at the city's heart.

As if he could read her thoughts, Victor added, "If only we could excise the Night Masks without damaging the city."

"Well, we may be another step closer," Alias said. "I've traced a protection racket from the Shore back to a wealthy vintner in the city. His name's Melman. I wanted to be sure he wasn't some noble's cousin or brother-in-law."

Victor furrowed his brow in thought. "Melman. My father and I have exported some of his wine. No, he's not related to any of the noble houses."

"Good. I'm hoping he's a high-ranking Night Mask or will lead us to one."

"I've heard some stories. His house has an evil reputation," Victor said. "Promise me you won't go there alone."

Alias nodded. She didn't mention she knew the house well, or that she planned to visit it later this very night. There was no sense worrying the young nobleman.

"Better still, why not just have Durgar arrest the man?" Victor asked.

Alias shook her head. "Jamal," she said, "has suggested

that if we can just find the Faceless's treasury, we should be able to capture the artifact that keeps him and the Night Masters magically sheltered from scrying and divinations. I'm hoping Melman might lead me to the Night Masters' lair. He's not going to cooperate, locked in a cell in the Tower."

"How does Jamal know all this?" Victor asked.

"She has a network of her own informants," Alias answered.

"I realize she must be a friend, but, well, she seems to know so much. Are you certain—do you think it's possible that all this theater against the Night Masks is maybe a smoke screen? She could be one herself. She could be the Faceless, for all we know."

Alias shook her head with a scowl. "That's no more likely than your father being the Faceless."

"Father! That's ridiculous."

"Is it? You said he refuses to pay the Night Masks protection, yet the Night Masks haven't wreaked their revenge on your operations as they have on House Thalavar."

"That's because they're afraid that Father would make good on his threat to start a war in the streets."

"Or they have orders not to harm your oper—" Alias halted, struck by a sudden idea.

"What is it?" Victor asked.

"Or they've been geased not to harm your family. Kimbel would certainly make an excellent candidate."

Victor shook his head. "I keep an eye on Kimbel. If he were running a thieves guild on the side, I would know. But I'm also sure the Faceless is not Father."

"So am I," Alias agreed.

"But you just said—"

"I was just pointing out that there are some inconsistencies. I suspect your father pays the Night Masks, but is too proud to admit it. He's simply not a logical candidate. He has more money than an ancient dragon and the most powerful position in the whole city. He has no reason to belong to the Night Masks."

Victor remained silent for too long.

"What's wrong?" Alias asked.

"Nothing," Victor assured her, shaking himself. "I was just thinking about how much my father wants to be croamarkh. You might almost say he covets the post. After his first two terms, I was sure he'd recommend me, but then he insisted the time was wrong for a new man and he offered himself for the third term. Then, after Lansdal Ssemm made such a mess of his four years, father told me he had to take up the next term, so I wasn't blamed for any problems Ssemm left behind. I know I'd make a good croamarkh, but I need father's support to be elected."

"I know you'd make a good one, too," Alias said.

"I have such plans."

"I know. You told me about them the day we met."

"Those are just the plans if I find Verovan's treasure. I have others I'd start without it. Build a navy to protect our trading ships from pirates, for one, and train an army of Westgate citizens, not mercenaries, to protect our caravans from brigands, for another. I've even begun to toy with your idea of offering more people a vote in the council. Not everyone, like you said. That would be chaos. But smaller merchants and important artisans and craftsman. Bring in some new blood, like my father said about you."

"You should be croamarkh," Alias said. "Don't wait for your father anymore. When his term is up, tell him you're running with or without his support."

"I don't think I'd have enough support to defy him."

"You might be surprised," Alias said. "Lady Thalavar thinks highly of you. She said everyone knows *The Gleason* was your victory. If I've managed to bring in the Faceless by then, everyone who stands against the Night Masks will support you, too."

Victor turned toward her, his face only inches from her own. "And you? Would I have the support of one clever, beautiful warrior?"

"Of course," Alias replied, "though I don't think my support means much in this city."

"With you by my side I feel like I could conquer the

world. What—why are you laughing?"

Alias worked hard at stifling a giggle. "I'm sorry. You just sounded for a moment like the hero in an opera."

"Opera's drawn from real life, after all," Victor replied. "Maybe if you close your eyes and listen hard you'll hear music, too."

Alias closed her eyes. She felt Victor's lips brush against hers.

"I do hear that music," the swordswoman whispered as she slid her arms around the nobleman's waist. "It sounds very far off, though. We need to bring it closer." She pulled Victor toward her and pressed her lips against his.

At the base of the Westlight, Kimbel checked his hourglass, then nodded to the waiting servants. With smoldering sticks the servants began lighting the fuses of the smoke powder novelties imported from Kara-Tur. They spiraled up into the darkness on columns of sparks, finally exploding in flowerlike bursts of light. The sky above flashed with color, reflected in the bay below. A few citizens of the city, those who'd actually witnessed magical fireball attacks, were bemused by this new toy of the wealthy. The less experienced, especially the children, were delighted with a spectacle they could share for free. Aboard *The Gleason*, although they were careful not to indicate how impressed they were by the display, the nobles all agreed it was a fitting signal for the end of the ship's maiden voyage.

# Thirteen
## Conversations Ashore

"Ooh, that's a pretty one," Jamal exclaimed as a golden marigold blossomed on the horizon. Mintassan harrumphed politely.

When the first explosions sounded Jamal had insisted they run up to Mintassan's aerie—a balcony reached from a window of his attic. The sage's home was far enough up the hill for them to have a clear view of the fireworks blossoming over the bay.

The sage and the actress reclined in heavy iron garden chairs which, after years of exposure to the elements, looked as if they'd been gnawed upon by rust monsters. Kel, newly scrubbed and dressed in some old clothes of the sage's, leaned out over the balcony railing with all the disdain for personal safety a teenaged boy could muster. Fireworks were still so rare an occurrence that the young thief was unable to hide his pleasure beneath his usual veneer of apathy. From his shouts and applause it was obvious he preferred the noisier explosions to the more visually elaborate ones.

Jamal rearranged the faded, mildew-ridden cushion at her back and took another sip of her wine. "Ever think of getting some new furniture out here?" she asked the sage.

"Not much reason to sit out here anymore," Mintassan grumbled. "Since they added that blasted magical light to the harbor tower, the sky's too bright. Can't see the stars I chose to observe for my treatise on astronomy."

Jamal looked up at the sky. "The ones you can still see are lovely enough."

"I suppose," the sage said with a shrug. He was eyeing Kel nervously, certain that the boy would flip over the railing any minute, requiring a magical flying spell for his rescue.

The sage leaned nearer the actress and murmured softly, "He—" Mintassan indicated Kel with a jerk of his head "—was looking over the silver tea set, estimating its resale value. He could calculate a twenty-seven percent cut in his head, but he can't read. He said he doesn't need to learn to read. How can he say that? How can he think that?"

"No one's given him reason enough," Jamal replied. "Although I'm sure a clever man like yourself can find some motivation for him."

"Me? Why me?"

"Well, it's not likely he'd want to imitate an old lady with modest thespian skills. Boys need to look up to men."

"Because I'm a man my home has become a shelter for homeless actresses and underage rogues?"

"More likely because you're a powerful mage, remember?" Jamal retorted.

Mintassan shrugged off the comment. "I'm beginning to dread it when Alias goes out after Night Masks. Who knows what she'll bring back next?"

"Maybe she'll bring back young Victor Dhostar," Jamal suggested.

Mintassan scowled. "I'm not taking him in. I don't even know why I agreed to take Kel," he complained.

"Because Alias asked you, and she's a clever, pretty woman," Jamal stated.

Mintassan flushed ever so slightly. "I'm simply extending her a courtesy because she's a friend of Grypht's," he argued.

"Is that what Victor Dhostar is doing by inviting her to his posh party—simply extending a courtesy?" Jamal asked, peering with concern at a firework that exploded a little too low on the horizon. "I don't imagine he's failed to notice how attractive she is."

"I noticed she was pretty. Said so the first night she

came in here. I can't understand why she would have anything to do with Victor Dhostar, though. She's a bright, experienced adventurer. He's a puffed-up greengrocer," Mintassan declared, using the adventurers' term for a merchant.

"Well, when he's not standing in his father's shadow, people seem to think he's pretty capable," Jamal remarked. "If Luer were to die this millennium, Victor might take his place as croamarkh."

"Croamarkh. Oh, that's different," Mintassan said contemptuously, his face illuminated by the light from a distant skyrocket. "King of the greengrocers."

"And he and Alias do have something in common."

"What? What do they have in common?" Mintassan demanded.

"A desire to rid the city of the Night Masks."

"I don't especially like them either," the sage pointed out.

"But you don't care much about Westgate."

"That's not true. I grew up in this city, the same as you."

"And you left it just as soon as you could to go gadding about the planes and other bizarre places. You only think of this city as a convenient place to store all the junk you bring back from adventuring."

Mintassan paused thoughtfully, then shrugged. "All right, I admit it. I find cities boring, full of boring people, present company excepted, of course. Alias wasn't interested in Westgate either when she first came. Dragonbait and you talked her into this job."

"I think Victor Dhostar had more to do with it than we did," Jamal replied.

"Sure. Rub it in," Mintassan grumbled into his wine.

"Still, as you pointed out, Victor Dhostar's just a greengrocer. He really can't do too much to protect her. It wouldn't hurt to have a wizard watching her back."

"She can't be scried, remember?"

"You don't get close to a person by watching her through a crystal ball. I was thinking you might involve yourself in a more active role. Offer to go with her the next time you have a chance," Jamal suggested.

"I think behind this request to look out for your cheap hero is an ulterior motive—playing matchmaker," the sage noted.

"I'm too busy to worry about nonsense like that. My ulterior motive is to unnerve the Faceless," Jamal replied. "He relies on the neutrality of people like you, Mintassan. I'm hoping he'll grow anxious and careless if he perceives the balance shifting against him."

"You're bringing out all your reserves for this battle, Jamal. So certain you can end the war this season?" Mintassan asked.

The actress sighed. "Not really, but the fight is beginning to wear me down. I'm giving it all I've got before I get another year older."

The horizon lit up with the firework's finale, a shower of multiple bursts that raced along the length of the peninsula. Scattered applause broke out from watchers in the street.

Kel climbed down from the balcony railing, his eyes wide and alert.

"Did you enjoy the fireworks?" Jamal prodded him.

The youth's eyes took on a wariness common to all young people when called upon to pass judgment on adult endeavors. "It was all right," he allowed with a shrug. He was too excited to remain indifferent for long. "I want to be able to do that some day," he admitted.

"You want to work with fireworks?" Mintassan queried, bemused.

"No," the boy corrected, shooting Mintassan a look suggesting the sage was as dumb as a rock. "I want to be a great thief, like the Faceless, or an important merchant, like one of the Dhostars, so I can afford to have fireworks every night. Then I'd get some serious respect."

Mintassan looked down at the youth with astonishment. It took him more than a moment to recover and ask, "You think their wealth is something to respect?"

"Sure," Kel answered. "What could be better?"

The sage harrumphed and rose to his feet. "How 'bout this?" he responded. Pointing to the iron chair he'd just vacated, he intoned, *"Quesarius Amano Illusar Jho!"*

A miniature sphere of orange-and-white flame formed at his fingertip, then streaked toward chair, emitting an ear-splitting shriek. A second and a third sphere formed and sped after the first. As the flaming orbs hurtled passed, Kel could see on their surfaces tiny faces with howling mouths.

The fiery spheres orbited around the iron chair, faster and faster, spinning a cocoon of white light. The cocoon began to stretch and deform as something within grew and pushed outward. An iron claw slashed through the cocoon, and an iron muzzle poked out. With the sound of shattering glass, the cocoon dissipated into myriad light motes, which sparkled and vanished to reveal a miniature iron dragon. The wyrm flapped its wings, arched its neck, and gave a low roar. Smoke, smelling like burning mildewy cushions, streamed from the creatures' nostrils. Then the beast settled back on its rear haunches, folded its wings, and became still.

Kel, his eyes as wide as saucers, reached out gingerly and touched the transmutated iron chair, now an immobile sculpture of ornate detail and great beauty.

Holding Kel in place with a hand on his shoulder, Mintassan lifted the boy's chin so that their eyes met. *"Knowledge* is better than wealth," the sage said. "It cannot be stolen. It cannot be bought. Once you possess it, it is yours for life. You can accumulate knowledge by observing, listening, and questioning. The truly wise can do so by reading and writing as well."

Kel squinted with a doubtful look, trying to analyze the truth of Mintassan's arguments. "If I learn to read, can I do that?" he asked, pointing at the iron dragon.

Mintassan snorted derisively. "Reading isn't a skill you acquire to learn parlor tricks. Reading lights the pathways to all knowledge. The ability to travel each pathway varies with the individual, but reading makes the journey easier."

The expression on Kel's face indicated he was struggling to understand the sage's metaphor. He glanced back at the iron dragon as if it could offer him illumination. Then he looked back at the sage. "So, how do I learn this stuff?" he asked.

"First, you get a good night's sleep," Mintassan said. "Lessons are learned better in the morning."

The boy clambered back into the attic and bolted for the stairs, as if speed would bring the next day closer.

"You really know how to motivate a child," Jamal said with a grin.

"Great thieves and rich merchants. What sort of heroes are those for young boys to have?" Mintassan asked with a shake of his head.

"The sort that fade into obscurity when better men make an effort to impress them," Jamal replied, giving the sage's shoulder a grateful squeeze. "Good night," she murmured as she slipped through the attic window.

Mintassan remained on the balcony for a while longer, alone with his thoughts.

\* \* \* \* \*

"The fireworks have been over for half an hour now," Olive said. "She should be back soon." The halfling stood at the open window. Although the second story of Blais House did not offer a clear view of the harbor, she had been able to catch sight of the higher skyrockets and, of course, hear the entire display.

Dragonbait, his attention focused on the chessboard, made a noncommittal noise. He'd beaten Olive at two games already, and he had been winning a third when the halfling had abandoned the game to watch the fireworks. Not surprisingly, when the fireworks ended, the saurial had been unable to coax Olive back to the board, so now he was continuing the game solitaire—playing both sides.

The chess pieces gilded in white gold represented the Cormyrian forces, those in yellow gold, the Tuigan Horde. Dragonbait made a clicking noise with his tongue and dragged Vangerdahast diagonally across the length of the board to capture a Hordelands horseman. Then the saurial switched positions at the table and considered the halfling's crumbling defenses.

Olive peered out into the darkness, where she could just make out the Westlight. "I wonder what's going on out there," she said, not for the first time that evening. "On the boat, I mean. This Lord Victor seems genial enough, for a human, but he is still one of the merchant nobles. The most poisonous snakes are the most brightly colored, my mother used to say."

Dragonbait made the same disinterested huffing noise he'd made the last three times Olive had tried to draw him into a discussion of the party on *The Gleason* or Victor's character. He maneuvered the remaining Horde-lands horseman to threaten the Cormyrian sage Dimswart, but the move only delayed the inevitable. Olive had left her Tuigan forces in complete disarray.

This time Olive would not be deterred from her speculations. "Jamal says Lady Gleason, his mother—Victor's, that is—died young. Considering Lord Luer's reputation for arrogance, one has to wonder how Lord Victor turned out to be so pleasant. Maybe he had a halfling nanny or something. She's out there alone. Alias, I mean. Not even a chaperon."

Dragonbait changed sides and stared at the situation from the Cormyrian side. From behind the King Azoun figure it looked like mate in three moves. He couldn't imagine what Olive was worrying about. Alias had once taken on a dragon single-handedly. How the swordswoman could have trouble on a two-hour cruise eluded him. More likely, the saurial reasoned, Olive was trying to cover her nervousness about their planned excursion to Cassana's old house.

A long pause ensued as Dragonbait changed sides again and tried to discover a way out of his self-inflicted attack, but an escape was denied the Tuigans. Mate in two now. At least the Tuigans should have something more to show for it. He took the Dimswart piece with the horseman.

"At least she has her sword with her," Olive said.

Dragonbait toppled the Tuigan khan and growled.

Olive turned at the saurial's guttural roar. In the

thieves' hand cant the paladin signed, *She'll be all right. Don't worry.*

"Don't worry?" Olive retorted. "Alias is out there alone with that greengrocer. Give me one good reason why I shouldn't worry."

*Alias is in good hands*, the paladin signed. *Lord Victor is an honest, valiant, and worthy young human.*

"She's spent most of her life in the Lost Vale with your people."

*And now she should spend time with her own people.*

"You can't just throw her into this society alone."

*You didn't have any of these objections when Giogi Wyvernspur married her sister Cat.*

"That's because I knew Giogi well enough to trust him. He was a really nice boy."

*I've looked into Lord Victor*, the paladin signed, the closest the hand cant could come to expressing his *shen* sight. *His intentions are good.*

"Well, we all know what road good intentions pave."

*Alias can take care of herself*, the paladin signed hard and fast, and the halfling could detect the chickenlike scent of his impatience.

"Physically, yes," Olive agreed, "but emotionally? She's still just a child."

*Her feelings have grown more quickly the last few years.*

"Even worse," Olive retorted. "That would make her a teenager, impulsive and reckless."

*Why does this worry you so?*

"I do think of her as my friend, you know. I don't want to see her get hurt making the same mistakes I did when I was young."

*Lord Victor could be as nice as Giogi Wyvernspur.*

Olive looked doubtful. "Even so, that leaves us with another problem. I don't know how it works among your people, but among the fur-bearing races of halflings and humans, love wreaks havoc on us. It's like pouring sand into the fine gearwork of the mind. When you should be thinking about your enemies' position and your defenses and where to strike, your mind is wandering off and you're thinking about his eyes, or his smile, or what he said last."

The paladin thought of Alias's own comments about the lovers by the fountain on the day they arrived in Westgate. With eyes only for each other, they were sitting ducks, she'd said. *Alias knows enough to guard against that*, he signed.

"Hah," Olive declared. "Shows what you know. 'I'll never be that stupid' is what every woman thinks until it happens to her. Then, too, something could happen to Lord Victor. He could be hurt or kidnapped. Alias wasn't all that rational when she thought Finder was threatened. What would she be like if something happened to someone else she'd grown attached to?"

The halfling's warnings were cut short by the sound of horses' hooves on the cobblestones outside.

The halfling and saurial exchanged glances, then Olive padded over to the window. Standing in the shadow of the curtain, she looked down onto the street. After a moment, she waved Dragonbait to approach.

The saurial sighed and ambled forward, but the halfling grabbed his tunic and jerked him to the side. "Stand in the shadows," she hissed. Feeling a little foolish, and a little guilty, but also a little anxious, the paladin did as instructed before looking down on the street. He shifted nervously, made uncomfortable by the sight below.

Victor's carriage stood outside the hotel door. As Lord Victor helped Alias down, she slid into his arms, threw her own around his neck, and pressed her lips against his. The pair remained embracing, lips locked against each other for an embarrassingly long period to witness.

Dragonbait pulled Olive away from the window, back to the chessboard and made her sit down opposite him. They both stared at the chessboard without seeing the pieces, waiting for Alias's return.

\* \* \* \* \*

When Victor finally released her, Alias drew in a deep breath and giggled.

"You make me feel so good," Victor whispered.

"Good as in virtuous?" Alias teased, gently nibbling at his ear.

"Lucky, happy, fortunate, fated, delighted," the young noble burbled. "I've never had anyone I could really talk to. Knowing you understand, that you're with me—" He faltered for words. "Are you sure you have to go?"

The swordswoman nodded. "It's late. We both have a lot to do tomorrow."

"It's already tomorrow," Victor murmured, sliding his hand up and down her back.

"Exactly," Alias retorted, and she slipped gracefully from his grasp and began climbing the steps to the hotel door.

Lord Victor reached out and grasped her wrist. "Alias?" he entreated her.

"Yeeessss?" the swordswoman answered, making no attempt to pull her captured arm away.

Lord Victor moved closer, standing on the step just beneath hers. He looked up into her eyes. "Give me a token," he demanded with a grin, "or I shall never let you go."

"A token?" Alias replied with a little laugh, not certain she'd heard him correctly.

"A token to show your regard for me, at least, that is, I hope you have some regard for me, for my feelings, for what you mean to me. Please. Some trinket to remind me of you when we're apart."

Alias thought of her new earrings, but somehow they didn't seem enough a part of her. "I don't think I have . . . " she started to say, then she thought of something appropriate. "Wait. You have to let go of my hand first, though."

Victor released her and held out both his hands cupped together, waiting for his boon.

With a deft motion Alias released the peace-bond knot tying her sword to her scabbard. She drew out her sword and raised it to her head. She held out the strand of hair she wore in an ornamental braid and sliced the braid off with the blade of her weapon.

She slid her sword back into its scabbard. After curling

the braid into a tiny loop, she laid it in the young noble's palms. "Your token, milord," she whispered.

"Accepted gratefully, milady," Victor replied, bending briefly to one knee. He tucked the red ringlet into his shirt, then his arms snaked out again and grasped the swordswoman about her waist. He pulled her toward him until they stood lips to lips.

They kissed again.

Finally the young noble released the swordswoman. Alias ran up the steps and into the hotel. Lord Victor climbed back into his carriage and urged his horses forward.

* * * * *

As the carriage rolled away, the halfling and the saurial could hear Alias moving toward them in the hallway, singing a love song.

"Oh, yeah. She seems really guarded to me," Olive mocked the paladin. She sat back down beside the chessboard and righted her overturned king. "Your move, Dragonbait," she said.

The paladin sat across from the halfling, his brow furrowed as the hamlike scent of his anxiety wafted out the open window.

# Fourteen
# Melman's Place

It took the swordswoman only a few minutes to change from her finery back into her armor, but in that time the weather had turned. Clouds rolled in from the east, veiling the moon, and mist rolled up from the bay and the river, shrouding the streets. Despite the cover this provided the three adventurers, Olive insisted they take one extra precaution to elude any possible Night Masks who might be spying on them—leave the city via the Thalavars' secret underground tunnel.

Once outside the city, Olive crept southward, keeping in the shadow of the city wall, with Alias and Dragonbait following behind. Since only the halfling had been both conscious and free of the sorceress Cassana's magical controls when they'd last used the tunnel that led to Cassana's former home, they had to rely on Olive to lead them to the outside entrance. They sneaked over the fence into the Ssemm family stockyards and made their way to the eastern end of the yards.

As the halfling rustled through an overgrown dry wash searching for the entrance, Alias and Dragonbait kept watch at the wash's rim. The moon broke through the clouds for a few moments, and then Alias could make out seven mounds to the southeast.

There was a good deal of activity in the stockyards to the west of the dry wash. Caravans were being readied for departure in the morning. Alias shifted nervously, worried that she would be discovered trespassing, and Orgule Ssemm would add his complaints to those of

Ssentar Urdo, further annoying the croamarkh.

"Olive," she whispered. "What's taking you so long?"

"I'll bet the passage hasn't been used since Finder and I came through it. The gully is really overgrown," the halfling whispered back.

An eternity of heartbeats seemed to pass before Olive called out to report her success. Dragonbait, able to detect the heat of the halfling's body in the dark, took Alias's arm and led her to Olive's location. The halfling crawled out from beneath a thicket of wild raspberry. "I don't think either of you could get through like I could," Olive reported. "You'll have to hack at the brush some."

The two warriors drew their swords and cut into the briars until they'd cleared a path into a tributary of the gully.

"There!" Olive whispered excitedly, pointing into the hillside.

The doorway was partially blocked by mud and rock carried by heavy rains, but the door was still visible. Fortunately it opened inward, so they weren't required to do any digging. Alias pushed up the latch with the tip of her weapon and nudged the door open with her foot. The door's hinges made an alarming squeal, and a decade's worth of dust assailed the swordswoman's nostrils.

Dragonbait whispered "Toast," in Saurial, causing his enchanted blade to blaze. Igniting a straw from the paladin's sword, Alias used it to light a conventional lantern. Dragonbait took the point; Alias followed behind him. Olive, after one last look down the dry wash to be sure no one had observed them, slipped through the door behind the warriors.

The passageway beneath the city wall was so narrow that the adventurers had to go single file. Olive's nose twitched in the dusty, sepulchral air. "Smells like Zrie Prakis," the halfling complained.

Remembering the lich's smell, Alias shuddered in spite of herself. Prakis had been among the alliance of evil beings who'd created her. Each being had had some evil purpose for the swordswoman, but it was Prakis's purpose that had unnerved Alias the most. Prakis had had a

long-abiding love-hate relationship with Cassana, even
after he'd become undead. He wanted an enslaved Alias
to replace Cassana.

"That's good, though," Alias said, "if it means that no
one has been using the passage since then. Look, ours
are the first footprints in the dust in years."

"Maybe because it's haunted," the halfling suggested
unhappily.

Spiderwebs across the passage crackled and fizzled
away, ignited by Dragonbait's fiery blade as they moved
forward, but there was nothing they could do to keep the
dust from swirling up into their faces. Olive, who was
closer to the floor, had to put up with more, and she muttered nonstop complaints all the way down the passage.
Alias began to sense that the shorter woman was fighting a growing sense of panic. The halfling had also been a
prisoner in this house, in all but name.

"They're all dead, Olive," Alias said, trying to reassure
the woman. "Nothing but dust is left of them," she added,
then realized as Olive puffed at the dust in the air that
that probably wasn't the most reassuring thing she could
have said.

Olive laughed, a little nervously.

They reached a dead end in the passage—a wall of
solid rock. Dragonbait sniffed at the blockage, trying to
discern any breeze or whiff of fresh air that would reveal
a hidden mechanism.

"Allow me," the halfling said, stepping forward. "Coming out of Cassana's, the catch to move this wall was on
the right. We can probably reach it from the left going in
this direction."

Olive ran her hand along the wall until it disappeared
into a hole in the rock. There was a click, which echoed
down the secret passage behind them. Olive stepped
back. "I've done my bit. Now it's your turn. Push here on
the right side. The wall pivots. You'll have to put some
muscle into it to get it started, but then its weight swings
it around."

Alias set down the lantern and began shoving at the wall.
After a moment, she felt it begin to move, but something

seemed to be jamming it on the other side. Dragonbait held his sword out for Olive to hold. The halfling took the heavy weapon with some trepidation. The paladin put his back into the labor along with Alias. The door moved another inch, then another.

"Just like old times," Olive said in an excited whisper. "My brains, your brawn. A dusty dungeon, the hint of danger. Now all we need is—"

The door rotated a full ninety degrees, and something clattered to the ground behind it. Gold coins glinted in the lantern light as they rolled across the floor.

"—treasure," Olive concluded, handing Dragonbait back his weapon. With a squeal of delight, she pressed her way past the two warriors.

The cellar floor was carpeted with a layer of shifting gold coins and a smattering of silver utensils, bowls and tea services. It appeared that a mound of treasure had been piled up against the secret door. Olive went scuffling through the coins like a child kicking up fallen leaves in the autumn, humming happily. Her practiced eye made a quick survey for gems, jewels, or particular stunning pieces of silver, but there were none of those. She contented herself by rolling about atop the coins and washing her hands in them with a laugh.

"Not bad at all," the halfling said with a sigh. "It doesn't appear that the current owners know anything about the secret passage, or this treasure wouldn't have been left so conveniently in our path."

Alias frowned as she peered at the glistening walls around the dungeon. "Olive," she whispered, "do you remember the walls down here being damp?"

"Bound to be some seepage in a basement this deep," the halfling replied, scooping handfuls of coins into her pockets. The halfling giggled as she moved down the corridor. "I can just picture whoever settled Cassana's estate trying to sell the old place. Yes, Madam, the walls of the basement *do* leak, but that's a minor inconvenience when you consider the value. Four bedrooms, single bath, prison cells in the basement. The previous owner was a notorious sorceress. She lived here quietly with her undead lover. Did I mention the secret passageway—"

Olive froze in her tracks, literally, one foot poised over the ground in a step that never came down. She remained motionless and, even stranger for Olive, speechless.

Dragonbait took a step toward the curiously immobile, suspended halfling, but Alias caught him by the arm. She bent down, grabbed a handful of coins, and flung them down the corridor. The air about them seemed to ripple and surge for a moment, then the coins hung in the air, just as did the halfling's foot.

Realizing now what caused the walls to glisten, Alias raised her sword and sprang forward. "It's a gelatinous cube!" she shouted. "It's swallowed Olive. We've got to cut her out before she suffocates!"

The scavenging monster had been practically invisible in the lantern light, but the adventurers could now see it rippling as the creature, alerted to their movements, slithered toward the secret door in an effort to engulf them. It had no intelligence, so its attack was purely instinctual, and it towered over them and blocked the passage completely.

Alias struck first with a sweeping semicircular cut along one side of the cube, wide enough to miss the imprisoned halfling but close enough to loosen the monster's grip. Dragonbait began slicing at the jellylike creature with his flaming sword, creating great scorching gashes in its side. The smell of burning flesh permeated the air. With her free hand Alias grabbed Olive's shirt collar and pulled hard. There was a soft sucking sound as the cube attempted to draw the halfling deeper into its digestive interior.

Knowing that the gelatinous cube exuded a slime capable of paralyzing even the largest of prey, Alias shifted backward to avoid contact with the creature and nearly lost her grip on the halfling.

The warrior woman stabbed the creature and released the hilt of her sword. With both hands clenched on the halfling's shirt, she yanked with all her might.

There was a squishing noise, and the slime-encrusted halfling erupted from the side of the cube. Alias slipped

on the carpet of coins and fell over backward, Olive landing on top of her. A layer of clear ooze still covered the
halfling, but separated from the host body the goo could
not survive and began to evaporate in a thin mist.

The creature sent out a protrusion that crested over
the heads of the two woman like a wave. Before the wave
could overwhelm them, the saurial slashed it from the
body of the gelatinous cube.

The wave, cut off from its parent, began to steam
into nothingness before it hit the ground. Alias's sword
clattered into the coins as the creature, damaged
beyond its ability to hold its shape, slumped to the
ground in a puddle of steaming goo.

Alias rolled Olive on her back and pushed on her stomach. The halfling gagged and coughed up a slimy bubble,
then took a gasp of air. Alias breathed a sigh of relief.

"Is she all right?" the paladin asked as the halfling
stirred feebly while ooze steamed off her body.

Alias nodded. "She walked into it with her mouth
open," she explained. "Probably paralyzed her vocal
chords. Maybe we'll get some quiet for a while," she said
with a grin.

"That's not funny," Olive retorted in a hoarse whisper.

They took the time to investigate the rest of the cellar.
Dragonbait stood staring thoughtfully into the prison cell
where he'd once been chained awaiting death, the cell
where he'd sworn to the Nameless Bard that he would protect Alias. Except for the glistening slime left by the gelatinous cube, everything was just as he remembered it.

Alias, who had no clear memory of the place, was busy
investigating bits of litter on the floor mixed in with the
gold coins and the remains of the jelly creature. Several old
rat skeletons, the skull of a very large cat, fruit peelings,
moldy cheese, some bloody bandages. The swordswoman
studied the ceiling. There was a hole overhead.

"Melman must be using the cellar as a midden," Alias
guessed. "If it weren't for the gelatinous cube cleaning up
down here, we might have had to wade through garbage.
Melman probably threw the poor creature down here
when it was just a bud."

"The door between the house upstairs and the cellar is secret, too," Olive explained. "Melman may not even realize that there's anything down here. He may think there's just an old well or sewer. I'll bet this treasure is all Cassana's original horde. Prakis said she stored it down here. Probably in there." The halfling pointed to a side room with a missing door. The hinges remained suspended from the door frame. "The door must have been wood. After several years the gelatinous cube dissolves it, slips into the treasury, drags the coins around beneath it, leaving them piled in front of the secret passageway."

Dragonbait extinguished the flame of his sword, and Alias covered the lantern so that only the faintest light showed. Then the trio climbed the spiral staircase leading to the first floor of the house. At the top, they halted and listened for any sounds that might indicate they'd been heard. The house seemed preternaturally still. Alias wondered if perhaps Olive had been spotted tailing One-Eye to the house, causing Melman to bolt. Olive, her ear to the secret panel, looked suspicious, but she finally pushed on the section of wall that released the secret panel. The curved section of wall slid easily enough until it caught on something in the alcove on the other side.

Olive was just able to slip through the crack in the secret entrance. There she discovered the obstruction immediately. In Cassana's time there had been on display in the alcove a stone statue of a particularly voluptuous succubus. The new owner had replaced it with a brass sculpture of a masked warrior driving a spear through the heart of a maggot-ridden mastiff. The end of the spear was blocking the secret panel from sliding all the way open.

Grunting and shoving with all her might, Olive found she could not shift the sculpture. She solved the problem by hanging on the end of the spear until it bent downward, out of the door's path. On the halfling's signal Alias shifted the panel open all the way and she and Dragonbait stepped into the hallway beside Olive.

The three adventurers moved down the hallway until they stood at the base of the staircase to the second floor.

There was a light on in a room upstairs, and voices drifted down the stairs. It sounded like a man and a woman arguing, but Alias could not make out any distinct words. She frowned anxiously. If the shouts came from the master of the house and some female friend, it was likely there were also servants awake and about.

As the shouting grew closer, Alias motioned Dragonbait into the hallway behind the stairs. Olive had already faded into some other shadowy recess of the house.

"And you call yourself a healer!" the man above bellowed.

"There are limitations to every craft," the woman snarled back. "You are lucky I could ease your pain. Perhaps after it scars I can help further, but not now. The wound's magic is still too strong!"

"So you say," the man shot back. "What good is a healer who will not heal? I think you're in league with him!"

Someone now stood on the first landing, casting a shadow down the stairs and into the hallway. "If I were," the woman argued, "why would I come here in the middle of the night? Let it scar, then I'll call again. Until that time, I recommend you keep a *very* low profile. Good night."

Someone stomped very deliberately down the stairs and paused at the bottom. Alias peeked around the railing. It was a woman dressed in a tunic and leggings made from satin fabric printed with a harlequin diamond pattern. She wore a mask of black fabric that covered her face from her forehead to her nose. Around her neck was an iron necklace of a stylized mask—the unholy symbol of Mask, the god of thieves. The woman wrapped herself in a voluminous cape of wolf fur, nodded, and waved to someone down the hall, then let herself out the front door.

Alias waited anxiously for several moments, expecting a servant to come down the hall, but only Olive appeared.

"Did you see who she waved to?" the swordswoman asked the halfling.

"The sculpture we were pushing around. Its supposed to be of the god Mask stabbing Kezef, the Chaos Hound,"

Olive explained. Her voice was still a hoarse whisper. "Wishful thinking on the part of Mask worshipers. She's a priestess of Mask. She was just making an obeisance to the image of her master."

Alias nodded as she wondered what was wrong with Melman that he required a healer in the middle of the night, and why couldn't the priestess heal him?

Alias checked the door to what had once been Cassana's laboratory. The door was securely locked. Olive pulled out a tiny wire and began working at the lock as Alias and Dragonbait proceeded to investigate all the other first floor rooms.

It didn't take them long to ascertain that there was no one else in the other rooms. If there were servants in the house, Alias suspected they were quartered upstairs. Throughout their search she could hear pacing upstairs, punctuated by a man cursing occasionally.

Alias took the precaution of securing and locking the front door against any other evening visitors. Then she and Dragonbait returned to the entrance of the previously locked laboratory. The halfling stood within, her lantern propped up on an accounting table. A huge smile graced her face. With its window bricked up, the room had been converted to a treasure vault. All about the halfling were sacks, crates, and chests, each labeled with a tag. Alias read the nearest one. In a crabbed, tight handwriting was the notation, "500 gold, 100 platinum, Duck Statue stolen from Family Urdo for later ransom."

Quite a hoard for a simple vintner," Alias noted. "Grapes must have been exceedingly good these last few years."

Olive pointed to the last pages of a thin red leather-bound ledger lying on the accounting table. "According to these figures, Melman's profits are minimal. Not even enough to require payment of business taxes.

"So all this is just spare change he's found lying in the street," Alias commented.

Olive held up a finger for Alias to wait, then thumped deftly on the side of the accounting table and a small, secret drawer sprang out. From it the halfling pulled out a second ledger.

"This," Olive said, cracking open the ledger and taking several moments to peer down the page, "shows that our man Melman is a major player in Westgate. He's got his thumb in extortion, fencing, smuggling. It's all written down here."

"So we've caught ourselves a big Night Mask," Alias whispered with glee.

"Actually," Olive said, lifting a false bottom out of the secret drawer and pulling out yet a third ledger, "we've caught ourselves a big Night Mask who cheats. First ledger for the law, second ledger for his criminal cohorts and bosses, third ledger—well, that will have the numbers closest to reality. Melman was not only skimming off the top, but he was collecting outside his own territory. Here's today's entry from One-Eye in the second ledger. Two hundred gold, Gateside Protection, it says. In the third ledger it's entered as three hundred gold, Gateside and the Shore."

"Let's see if Melman is interested in talking about his books," Alias suggested.

Just as the adventurers began climbing the stairs, they encountered their man turning on the landing, coming down toward them. He was dressed in a long nightshirt and slippers, and oddly enough, a full cloak with a very deep hood, which concealed his features.

For such a heavy man Melman moved very quickly. The moment he spotted them, he grabbed from the landing a halfling-sized urn filled with dried flowers, tossed it down the stairs, and bolted back up to the second story.

Dragonbait dodged aside, but longer-legged Alias leaped over the obstacle and charged after her prey. Olive caught the urn and fell back down the stairs with a curse and a crash.

In the upstairs hallway, Alias caught sight of Melman disappearing into the only lit room in the house. He tried to slam the bedroom door closed, but he caught his cloak in the door frame and was forced to reopen it to pull the robe free. Alias threw herself against the door before the Night Mask could manage to lock it.

The force of the swordswoman's entry flung the vintner into the center of the room. His hood fell back, revealing his face, and Alias felt her throat constrict in horror.

This must be what Jamal had meant when she spoke of the branded ones, Alias realized. Melman's face was hideously burned all about his eyes, in the shape of a domino mask. The damaged flesh was covered with great white blisters and bright red all about the edges. Blisters even covered his eyelids, and in the brightly candle-lit bedroom his eyes squinted as if the light pained them.

Alias recovered quickly from her shock and leveled her sword at the man's chest.

"It's you! Alias the Sell-Sword!" Melman gasped. "When I saw you on the stairs I thought you were a burglar," he explained. Meekly, he raised both hands, shaking back his sleeves to reveal there were no weapons concealed there.

"I'm glad to see you recognize me, Master Melman," the swordswoman said. "We have a lot to talk about."

"I haven't got anything to say to you," the vintner insisted.

Dragonbait and Olive entered the room.

Olive whistled at the sight of Melman's brand. "I can see why he needed a priestess," the halfling muttered.

"The rest of the house is empty," the paladin reported in Saurial.

"I can summon the watch, you know. You're all trespassing!" Melman declared, his voice rising in pitch.

"It appears you've let all the servants have the night off," Alias noted. "Didn't want them to catch sight of your face? No matter. I'm sure Olive will be glad to fetch the watch for you . . . if you're serious. The watch will probably be fascinated with the trove of treasure you've got downstairs. Especially those pieces that are undeniably stolen property. Then, too, there are the ledgers. So many different accounting books."

Olive made for the door, suppressing a grin, but she halted when Melman called out, "No need for that. What do you want? As you already saw, I can offer you a great deal."

Alias motioned for Melman to have a seat. "What I want from you, Master Melman, is information. Let's start with the Faceless."

Melman sat down on the bed. "Who?" the vintner asked, but there was a quiver in his voice that belied his ignorance.

Alias leaned forward. "The Faceless, Master Melman. You remember him. He's the man who burned your face."

"This," Melman said, pointing to his face. "An accident. Walked into a torch."

"Very funny," Alias said. "We'll see if the watch finds you so amusing. You should get along with His Reverence Durgar. He doesn't know anything about the Faceless either. The Faceless, however, knows something about you. He probably knows you'd be dangerous in Durgar's custody. I understand Night Masks do not always survive once they are taken by the authorities."

Melman flinched, and he licked his lips nervously. "Try to understand," the man pleaded. "If this is my punishment for arguing," the vintner pointed to his face again, "imagine what will happen if I betray them."

At a nod from Alias, Dragonbait stepped forward. He spread his clawed fingers to touch the perimeters of Melman's shocking wound. At first the vintner shrunk back, but when it became clear that the saurial was not attacking him, he relaxed considerably. The paladin's whispered prayer invoked the same healing blue aura over his hands as ever, but the blue light seemed to spark and dissolve as it formed. Melman's face remained as damaged as before.

The saurial looked at Alias and growled and clicked, "There is some evil force preventing the healing. I've never encountered anything like it."

"Is that what happened when the priestess of Mask tried to heal you?" Alias asked Melman.

The man nodded. "He said it wouldn't heal until it scabbed over."

"He who? The Faceless?"

Melman nodded.

Alias felt her stomach twist with excitement. An admission of the Faceless's existence was a major concession from the man. Now if she could just press her advantage.

"So basically the Faceless has made it impossible for you to leave your home for the next several days," Alias pointed out. "In the meantime, you're a sitting duck."

Melman did not reply.

"You didn't think we were burglars when you spotted us, did you? You thought we might be Night Masks assassins," the swordswoman guessed.

"That's ridiculous," Melman retorted, but without much conviction.

"Is it? I don't think so. This is the deal, Master Melman. You tell us all you know about the Faceless and the Night Masters, and if you're telling the truth, I'll help you escape from Westgate."

Dragonbait radiated the scent of his displeasure with this idea, but he said nothing, instead shifting toward the window.

"You hold out on us, though, Melman, and I'm going to have to leave your fate to Durgar's discretion."

Melman shuddered. "I'll—I'll tell you what I can," he said.

"Good. Let's start with you. Are you one of the Night Masters?" the swordswoman asked.

Melman nodded wordlessly.

"Why did the Faceless brand you?"

"I argued with him in council. I wanted you killed, but he insists he has some other plan to take care of you. He's playing some bizarre power game that's liable to ruin business for good. None of us have any idea who or what he might be."

At Alias's prodding, Melman described the last several meetings of the Night Masters, highlighting the parts of the discussion that dwelt on her and Jamal. As he began covering the details, Melman began to relax, until finally it was as if he were sitting with other merchants in the bar, chatting about business.

"The Night Masters report to the Faceless every other evening," Melman explained, "always at low tide. The entrance to the hideout is on the western bank of the

Thunn, beneath the River Bridge. It's covered at high tide. It's hidden by magic, but if you have the key, you can see through the illusion."

Melman reached into his shirt. Alias raised her sword just an inch. The Night Master gave her an uneasy smile and pulled out a chain around his neck. Hanging from the chain was an iron key with a circular grip. He held out the key, and Olive took it from him.

"You look through the grip," the Night Mask explained, "and you can see the door. The tide is just turning now. You won't be able to see the door until tomorrow afternoon. The next meeting of the Night Masters won't be until tomorrow night—"

"Alias," Dragonbait interrupted in Saurial. "There's trouble coming this way. Night Masks. Assassins."

"Olive, check outside," the swordswoman ordered.

The halfling moved toward the window and peered out from the side. "I don't see—wait. Hmmm. Night Masks, nine that I can count. Probably more around the other side of the house. Hanging in the shadows across the street. Surrounding us."

Melman's face went white from shock, making the red markings of his burned mask stand out all the more. "He's found me out already! Those are assassins! I shouldn't have talked to you!" The vintner stood up, looking as if he might try to run past Alias, but Dragonbait pushed him back onto the bed.

"Don't be foolish," Alias snapped, keeping her voice calm and even. "No one knows we're here, and we can't be detected magically. More likely the Faceless had already decided to bring your career to an end. You're lucky we're here to get you out of this."

"Looks like they've gathered a quorum," Olive quipped. They're starting to cross the street."

"They'll soon regret gathering here," Dragonbait said, drawing out his sword.

Alias put a hand on the paladin's arm. "It's better they don't discover we've been here. Faceless won't suspect we've learned anything from Melman. We'll sneak out through the basement. Let's go," she said. Picking up the lantern, she headed for the staircase.

Dragonbait prodded Melman to his feet and out of the bedroom.

"He knows everything," the vintner insisted, his voice climbing an hysterical octave.

"Look, you've been cheating with your phony ledgers for over a year," Olive pointed out, following from behind. "If he knew everything, he'd have killed you sooner. If you just keep your mouth shut and keep moving, we'll get you out of this. No sweat."

They were just coming down the lower flight of stairs when someone began pounding on the front door with a mailed fist and shouting Melman's name.

Dragonbait halted in the front hall and hissed at the door.

Alias pushed Melman toward the secret passage and pulled on the saurial's tunic. "Remember how they burned Jamal's home?" she whispered. "We've got to keep moving."

The paladin growled with displeasure, but he followed Melman down the hall and guided him to the passage behind the statue. As Alias followed behind them, the pounding on the door stopped, replaced by the sound of someone or several someones throwing their shoulders against it. Alias set down the lantern and turned about to usher Olive down the stairs, but the halfling was nowhere in sight.

"Olive!" the swordswoman shouted.

Outside, the Night Masks began smashing windows all around the house, including the transom window over the front door. Something thumped in the dark hall, and Alias could see a tiny flame glowing on the floor. It was the same explosive device the Night Masks had used in the Thalavar warehouse.

The halfling appeared in the doorway of Melman's treasure room, loaded down with two sacks.

"Olive, get down!" Alias screamed, throwing herself at the halfling, knocking her halfway into the treasure room.

The explosion rocked the house, and the noise was

deafening. The swordswoman was just rising unsteadily
to her knees when a second, third, and fourth bomb went
off.

"We've got to get out of here, Olive," Alias shouted, but
the halfling did not reply. She was still breathing, but her
leg was oozing blood where a piece of twisted metal had
cut a gash through the flesh to the bone. There was no
time to bind the wound. Alias slung the woman over her
shoulder and stumbled to her feet. She cursed under the
weight, realizing a good deal of it was gold coin.

Out in the main hall, the wall hangings were ablaze
and the house was filling with smoke. Alias took a breath
of the still-untainted air of the treasure room and dashed
down the hall to the secret panel.

Dragonbait stood at the top of the stairs, anxiously
looking for the swordswoman.

"Pull the panel closed behind us," Alias ordered as she
half ran, half tumbled down the secret stair with her
halfling load.

Dragonbait tugged on the panel, but the statue of
Mask had toppled into it, wedging it into place. Sheathing his sword, the saurial moved out into the corridor to
shove the statue over.

The front door burst open, and a large wooden keg
rolled into the front hall. The paladin wasted no more
time on the secret panel. He slipped into the stairwell
and flew down the steps.

Overhead, an even bigger explosion rocked not only the
house but its foundation as well. Brick, mortar, and wood
began pouring down on the paladin's head, and the spiral
staircase, which Dragonbait had just stepped off of, fell
over into the basement. No one was going to notice that
the secret panel was out of place, the paladin realized. In
the dark he could sense the heat coming off Alias, Olive,
and Melman, and he hurried down the passage to where
they waited in the dark.

He pulled his sword and whispered the command for it
to ignite. By the light of the flame he could see Alias
holding her hands over Olive's leg, trying to stanch the
blood that oozed from a great wound. Melman stood

pressed against a wall, breathing heavily, his eyes wide with terror.

Thinking they would be safe enough in the basement for at least a few minutes, Dragonbait handed the flaming sword to Alias and bent over the halfling to heal her wound.

Alias stood up and was instantly aware of how much warmer the air near the ceiling was than the air at the floor. The flames from Dragonbait's sword flickered toward the ruined secret staircase. Air coming in from the secret passage to the outside was feeding the fire above.

Something overhead spattered to the floor and spread out with a gleam. Alias looked up in astonishment. One of the heavy floorboards beneath Melman's treasure room had cracked in the last explosion and molten gold was now dripping into the basement.

"I've stopped the bleeding, but she's still unconscious," the paladin said. His mouth dropped when he caught sight of the shower of gold. "Pity she'll miss this," he added.

Alias thrust the flaming sword back in the paladin's hand. "Get Melman out," she ordered. She scooped the halfling over her shoulders again and ran after the paladin and the Night Master. At the secret door, she hesitated. She could leave it open, feeding the fire so that there would be nothing but ash left—making it certain the Night Masks wouldn't expect to find Melman's bones. Concerned that smoke might drift out and reveal the passage's existence, though, she decided against it. With a quick tug, she pulled the door closed and hurried down the passage.

It was quiet in the passage, but Alias hustled them through it, fearful that it might collapse. When they finally reached the dry wash, she set down the halfling and took a rest. Melman collapsed on the ground.

Dragonbait stood over the Night Master, assuring himself that Melman didn't try to escape before Alias was through with him. "What are we going to do with this one?" he asked the swordswoman.

"Well, I had thought we might lock him up in one of the cells below his own house," Alias said. She peered over the edge of the dry wash and watched the flames dancing along the roof of Melman's former abode. "I don't think we should bring Lord Victor into this, considering the deal we've made with Melman."

"You're going to have to impose on Mintassan again," the paladin noted.

"I know," Alias sighed. In the south of Westgate, a false dawn blossomed as the roof of Melman's house collapsed and the flames shot higher into the air. "He's not going to be happy about my turning his house into a home for retired Night Masks."

"But he will oblige you, I think."

Alias nodded, realizing uncomfortably that, while House Dhostar was paying her to take out the Night Masks, other people were shouldering even greater shares of the burden to get the job done.

# Fifteen
# The Lair of the Faceless

The fog that had drifted through Westgate's streets the night before now climbed as high as the city's wall and poured into the outlying countryside. The midday sun, covered with layer after layer of clouds, was powerless to burn off the mists. From the top floor of the Tower Alias surveyed the few islands of solid matter high enough to poke above the gray shroud: the towers of the merchant nobles' castles, the heaven-aimed spire of the Temple to Ilmater, the Westlight, and the Tower, where she stood.

She'd come to the Tower to see Durgar, but he'd gone out to investigate the remains of last night's mysterious fire. Taking one last look at the covered city, Alias hurried back downstairs to meet Dragonbait and Olive, who had waited for her in the reception hall below.

The halfling, who had regained consciousness soon after they'd left the secret tunnel, now paced up and down the hall, unable to hide her eagerness to hunt for the Faceless's lair. She bore a long, jagged scar on her leg, but Dragonbait had healed her wound sufficiently so that it gave her no pain. Dragonbait stood very still beside the gate, but from the twitch in his tail Alias could see that he, too, was anxious to be going. He had even grown less annoyed by Alias's promise to Melman that she would free him later; an attitude that would hold only as long as it appeared Melman had been truthful with them.

"Looks like we go alone," Alias said after explaining Durgar's absence. "The watch captain on duty says he doesn't have the authority to send a patrol out to investigate unless the peace is being disturbed."

The three adventurers donned their heavy cloaks, and Olive lit the lantern she carried before they went outside. Westgate was like a ghost city, for the fog shrouded commerce as well. There were no booths or carts set up in the market; very few shops appeared open, and those that were had no customers. Even those people hardy enough to venture the streets at night remained indoors in the fog. Alias wondered if even the Night Masks avoided working in the fog.

The sound of their footsteps was muffled by the water in the air so that the adventurers appeared to be three wraiths gliding along the streets. Dragonbait squinted, concentrating on using his *shen* sight so that they wouldn't be surprised by anything coming out of the fog. They strode due east on Silverpiece Way to the bridge that crossed the River Thunn.

Five stone arches supported the River Bridge, and the road across it was wide enough for two large wagons and several extra pedestrians to use at once. The bridge was not only a masterful feat of engineering but a dumping ground for stone carvings looted from King Verovan's castle when he had died. Brooding gargoyles held out stone braziers flickering with oil flames, which pushed ineffectually at the foggy darkness. Curling sea serpents made up the bridge's railings. The statues of ancient historical figures lined the center, dividing it into two distinct lanes.

At high tide, the river below would slam into the rising waters of the sea, creating a surging wave that ran the width of the river just downstream from the bridge. Now, at low tide, the two bodies of water collided near the mouth of the bay, no more than a mere rill on the water's surface. The river level also dropped down a few feet, uncovering a wide expanse of muddy sandbank beneath the bridge. The adventurers veered from the bridge and made their way down to the sandbank.

"This must be a good place to dig for clams," Alias noted.

Olive shook her head. "According to the halflings in the

Thalavar household, there's some sea serpent called the quelzarn that lurks in these waters. People who come down here tend to disappear.

"Disappearances no doubt arranged by the Faceless to conceal his lair," Alias guessed. She pulled Melman's key from her pocket, and, holding the key loop up to her eye, scanned the stone embankment. She pointed to a featureless spot a little ways downstream at the foot of the embankment. "There," she said, handing the key to the halfling.

Olive peered through the key loop. It was like looking through a soap bubble. Rainbows of color swirled before her eye, but when she looked toward the spot where Alias pointed, a hot white light shone before her eye. She offered the key to Dragonbait, but the saurial declined to use the magic item, disdainful of handling any Night Mask magic unless absolutely necessary. Out of habit, Olive ran her finger down the teeth of the key, registering its shape, before returning it to the swordswoman.

Once more Alias held the key up to her eye. She strode purposefully toward the stone embankment. Olive could detect only slight, irregular frost cracks in the rock. Alias reached out with her hand and touched a spot on the rock. "There's some sort of keyhole here," she said. Then she guided the key to the hand she held on the wall like a woman trying to unlock a door in the dark.

The key slid smoothly into the rock; Alias twisted it, and from beneath the ground came the sound of a huge bolt being thrown.

The erratic pattern of cracks joined in the shape of a rough-hewn door some three feet across by five feet high. The door popped a few inches out of the wall. Dragonbait grasped its edge and muscled it open.

Behind the entrance lay a tunnel several feet wider and higher than the door. Alias looked around. An outcropping of rock in the muddy bank blocked any view from the bridge. The riverbed widened considerably just below the bridge, so no one standing on the opposite shore at night would be able to see more than the light of their lantern. It was a location well hidden in plain sight.

Olive thrust her lantern into the inky black tunnel. Brickwork lined the walls, floors, and arched ceiling as far back as they could see. All three adventurers drew their blades and slipped through the door. Dragonbait growled the command for his blade to ignite.

There was a ring attached to the back of the door. Alias gave it a tug, pulling the door nearly closed so that it did not attract visitors behind them, but leaving enough of a gap that they could flee the tunnels easily should the need arise. Then the trio plunged into the darkness.

Thirty feet down, the passage emptied into a larger tunnel with an uneven floor and a canted ceiling cut directly into bedrock. This tunnel appeared to be far older. Along its length were several side passages, all of which were bricked up. The older tunnel went on for some distance straight ahead.

Finally the passage widened slightly. On one side were ten empty sconces, and on the other, ten empty pegs.

"At *last* we've found the cloak room of the Faceless," Olive joked.

Another ten feet ahead, the passage spilled out into a large vault cut out of the solid stone. The walls were bare, and the furnishing was sparse but impressive: a massive obsidian table streaked with veins of gold, polished to a liquidlike luster. Ten large wooden chairs, five to a side, stood about the table, and at the head, on a raised dais, stood a throne of the same black-and-gold material as the table. On the table sat a brass brazier, unlit but stoked with fresh charcoal. Beside the brazier lay a black cloth covering a small object.

Alias lifted the black cloth. Beneath it was a white porcelain mask, a domino mask painted about the eyes and a glyph on the forehead.

"The mark for Gateside," Alias noted. "Melman's district."

Olive proceeded around the room, tapping the walls and looking for secret access ways.

"Is the Faceless simply letting the others know of Melman's death or informing them that he himself was responsible?" the paladin mused.

Alias shrugged and laid the black cloth back over the

mask.

"Yes!" Olive whispered from the wall behind the obsidian throne. She knocked again, and they all heard the distinct hollow sound. Olive could just make out with her fingertips the hair-thin crack that betrayed the edges of a secret passageway. After several minutes searching, though, she was still at a loss for a handhold, button, or switch to open it. Alias pushed on the edges of the door in case it pivoted, but without result.

"Try Melman's key," the halfling suggested.

Alias peered at the closed passage through the handle of the iron key. "Nothing," she reported.

"Guess it was too much to hope that Melman would have access to the Faceless's inner sanctum," the halfling muttered.

"We may need a mage for this," Alias said with a sigh, wondering just how many times she was going to have to go to Mintassan for help.

"Boogers," Olive cursed.

There was a sharp crack, and the entire wall panel swung slightly outward and upward, revealing another stone passage.

Alias looked at the halfling, stunned.

"I guessed the secret word!" Olive cried out excitedly.

From behind them came the clicking sound of the saurial's laughter. Dragonbait was standing behind the obsidian throne with a clawed finger resting on a panel in the back of the throne. As they watched, the saurial pushed the panel and the door swung closed.

"I would have thought of that next," Olive said with a sniff.

Dragonbait reopened the door. Just inside was another empty sconce. Most notable about this passage, though, was the damp, pungent smell, not of the sea, but of sewage. Wrinkling their noses, the adventurers proceeded through this new tunnel, Olive in the lead, with Alias and Dragonbait just behind her.

Despite the lantern she carried, Olive did not see the chasm that abruptly crossed the passage until she was right on top of it. Fortunately, the stench and the sound

of running water had warned her to slow down and she
was able to back away from the edge before she stepped
into the yawning void. Alias and Dragonbait halted
beside her, and they all peered downward. Across their
path lay a circular sewage tunnel lined with brick. They
stood near the top of the tunnel. On the other side, nearly
twenty feet away, the passageway to the Faceless's lair
continued on. Ten feet below them the sewage of Westgate churned and surged past.

"You'd think the Faceless would be concerned that a
sewer inspector might stumble on this place," Olive
quipped.

"Cities the size of Westgate have enough underground
sewers, pipes, and cisterns to confuse a dwarf. They probably built this tunnel before King Verovan's time and
promptly forgot it," Alias retorted.

"How're we going to cross it?" the halfling asked.

Alias shrugged. "The Faceless must have some way
across," she said.

Dragonbait picked up a handful of pebbles from the
floor and tossed them into the chasm. They skittered horizontally in midair, some finally tumbling into the dark
water below, but others remained suspended, resting on
an invisible surface.

"Aren't you clever," Alias said, smiling at the saurial.

The paladin shrugged. He could detect the bridge from
the way it masked the heat flowing up from the sewage
below.

Alias stepped out into the void. Assured that the
bridge was sturdy beneath her feet, she continued across,
using her sword as a cane to tap out the edges of the
bridge. It was only two feet wide, but flat and smooth.
Nonetheless, when she reached the opening in the sewer
wall at the opposite end and stepped off the bridge, she
breathed a sigh of relief. She turned and waved for the
others to follow.

Olive began crossing next, using her own sword as a
guide. The halfling moved more quickly than the
swordswoman had, but when she was halfway across the
bridge, she froze.

Alias furrowed her brow in puzzlement. Olive had never been afraid of heights, yet now she stood motionless, looking down into the water. "Come on, Olive!" the swordsman whispered urgently.

"I can't," Olive retorted through clenched teeth. "I want to move, but I can't! Feels like magic, maybe some kind of trap."

Alias had just set one foot back on the bridge when something erupted from the water below. By the light of Olive's lantern the swordswoman could make out a great serpentine beast—its body stretching out far longer than the lantern light could make out. Its back was covered in a diamond pattern of green and brown scales, and a green fin ran the full length of its eel-like body. It reared its head, revealing a yellow belly, and filthy water dripped from the slimy moss coating its scales. Thrusting upward toward Olive, it roared with a mouth large enough to swallow the halfling in a single gulp. Needle teeth glistened by the light of the halfling's lantern. In the beast's eyes Alias imagined she could detect intelligence and cunning. "It's the quelzarn!" Alias shouted. "Olive, you have to move!"

Olive, unable to comply, looked into the maw, wondering if she could cut her way out from the inside. She realized with a sickening dread that her chances of doing so were not good even if the magic that now held her disappeared once she was swallowed.

Just as the sea serpent's head arched over Olive, the saurial scooped the halfling up in his arms and dashed across the bridge to the other side. The quelzarn snapped its jaws on empty air, squealed with annoyance, and slid back into the water.

Dragonbait set Olive down gently. The halfling was breathing so heavily that Alias was afraid she might pass out before she regained control.

"Why do these things always happen to me?" the halfling moaned. "Why didn't it use magic to hold you in place?"

"Maybe it just wanted a light snack," Alias teased. "It probably noticed your lantern. I went across without one."

"Or you're more resistant to its magic." The enchantment holding Olive dissolved suddenly, and she started like a sleeper in a dream. "Boy, I really hate magic, sometimes. Now I'm all pins and needles," she complained, rubbing her limbs.

They finally got Olive back on her feet again and continued onward. The passageway on this side of the sewer sloped upward, ending in a short staircase. Alias wondered if they might be climbing into the basement of a building by the river, but she realized they must be somewhere beneath a hill when they reached the top of the stair and they stood in one more underground cavern carved out of solid bedrock. Magical lanterns bathed the cavern in a bright yellow glow, leaving them no doubt that they had discovered what they'd been seeking.

"Jackpot!" Olive whispered in awe.

Alias nodded in agreement.

The Faceless's treasury made Melman's hoard look like the collection plate at a dead god's church. Great sea chests, closed and locked, were stacked against one wall. A multitude of weapons, from swords and polearms to wands and staves, hung from another. Dozens of open amphoras stood in an alcove, stuffed to overflowing in the southern fashion with jewelry and gems.

On a workbench in the center of the room stood a rack like a tree—with twelve long pegs branching out from its central pole. Hanging from the peg branches were eleven white porcelain masks, each with a different glyph painted over the domino mask markings about the eye slits. A twelfth branch was empty—no doubt the one that had once held Melman's mask. A large mirror was mounted on the wall to the right of the workbench. To the other side stood two rows of statues. Behind the workbench a fountain pool gushed water in a burbling rhythm.

"I always say there's nothing like the sound of a fountain for relaxing at the end of a hard day's extortion and murder," the halfling joked.

Alias held up a hand to silence the halfling. She thought she saw movement near the statues. She

motioned for Dragonbait and Olive to take up positions
on either side of the workbench as she moved around it.

The statues were iron, covered with a thin film of oil to
ward off rust. They were about twice Alias's height,
molded in a humanoid form but with dragon heads. Alias
was sure they were some sort of golem—automatons
capable of serving as deadly guards. Those constructed of
iron often breathed poisonous gas, and Alias found herself holding her breath as she approached them.

She reached out and touched the nearest statue. It was
cool and remained immobile. If the statues were iron
golems, they did not appear to be activated. They were
set in a military formation, two rows deep. It was in the
back line where she thought she saw movement.

The warrior woman slid between the two ranks, moving as silently as a cat. She saw a flash of light on metal
behind the second rank. Swinging around the line, Alias
raised her sword, prepared to skewer whatever skulked
back there.

Fortunately, her mind analyzed what she saw before her
instincts took over. She recognized the man in fine silk
vestments who stood before her gripping with white knuckles a sword held out in an awkward defensive position.

"Victor!" Alias gasped.

Victor Dhostar lowered his sword and held his other
hand over his heart as if to keep it from leaping out of his
chest. His eyes were wide with both fear and astonishment. "Alias!" he exclaimed, breathing a sigh of relief.
"Am I glad to see you!"

"Come on out," Alias ordered, holding her sword level,
still ready to strike. Magical creatures sometimes used
the face of a friend as a ploy to get adventurers to lower
their guard.

Victor stumbled forward sheepishly, nodding at the
saurial and the halfling as they approached him warily.
"Dragonbait. Mistress Ruskettle. How do you do? I was
afraid you were the Faceless."

Alias looked at the paladin for some confirmation of
Victor's identity.

Dragonbait concentrated his *shen* sight on the man

before him. There was nothing but the sky-blue of grace
in his soul. If he was not Victor Dhostar, he was his twin
in all respects. The saurial nodded.

Alias exhaled and sheathed her sword. Then she
leaned in toward Victor and snapped angrily, "What are
you doing down here?" Her voice rang through the chamber like a bell clapper.

Victor sighed. "Being a damned fool," he answered. "I
thought I could help you find the Faceless's lair. I followed up a few clues and found this place. I was investigating it when I heard a voice down the hall. I hid
because I thought it might be the Faceless."

"How did you get past the quelzarn?" Olive asked suspiciously.

Victor blinked twice. "There was a quelzarn? I mean,
there really is one?" he asked.

"Perhaps it didn't attack because it failed to hold him
magically, just as it let me across," Alias suggested.

Olive was not mollified. "So how did you get in?" she
demanded of the merchant noble.

"This," Victor said, pulling out from his vest pocket a
key on a pink ribbon. He handed the key to Olive. It
appeared identical to the one Alias had from Melman.
"There's a secret door on the banks of the Thunn. You
look through that hole in the grip to see it, then the key
opens the door."

"How did you find the secret passage beyond the meeting room?" Olive demanded, running her fingers along
the teeth of the key before handing it back.

"The latch behind the throne. King Verovan had something like that over a hundred years ago. Now it's a fairly
standard release for the merchant houses to use in their
treasuries."

"Where did you get the key?" Olive demanded.

Victor looked down at his hands as if examining them
for dirt. "I'm afraid I can't tell you that," he said coolly.

"Can't or won't?" Olive pressed.

"Olive," Alias said in a cautioning tone.

Victor met Olive's intense gaze. "Won't," he retorted.
"Certainly not to an employee of a rival house." He looked

at Alias. "I will explain all to you later," he said, "when we are alone."

Alias accepted the noble's terms with a nod, but she had to ask, "Lord Victor, if you had some clues, why didn't you contact me?

Victor sheathed his sword. "There was some indication that another noble house was involved, so I thought I had better check it out first, to spare you another incident like yesterday's with the Urdos," the young man explained.

"You shouldn't have come down here alone. You could have been killed!" the swordswoman exclaimed.

"I realize you think of me only as a merchant, but I am capable with a sword and I can take care of myself," Victor replied.

There was a chill in the nobleman's tone that stung Alias like an icy rain. I've offended his pride, she realized, and although she couldn't help think of the awkward way he'd held his sword up only a moment ago, she knew she couldn't bring herself to challenge him. "Victor, this isn't about your being able to take care of yourself," she began carefully. "This is about your life being too important to risk on such a reckless excursion. Your father, the croamarkh, needs you. Westgate needs you." The swordswoman held his eyes with her own and, in a whisper, added, "*I* need you."

"How absolutely precious," a harsh whisper echoed through the cavern. "I'd nearly forgotten how amusing mammal love is."

Alias and Dragonbait held their swords up at the alert and wheeled back to back in a long-practiced maneuver. Without discussion they kept Lord Victor between them. Olive ducked quickly into the shadow of the iron statues.

The pool at the far end of the room began to bubble and hiss, and from it rose a great dragon's skull. "Hello, children." The words seemed to come from the dragon's skull. Its tone was mock cheerfulness. "It's good to see you again, even in my reduced circumstances."

It took only moments for all three adventurers to place the voice, but it was Olive who replied first.

"Misty!" the halfling chirped, sheathing her sword and stepping out from the shadows. "Long time!"

"So nice to be remembered," the dragon skull said as the water finished dripping from its sides. "I have not forgotten you either, Mistress Ruskettle. Or you, Champion. Or you, Alias, you red-headed witch."

Alias moved cautiously toward the skull. "Mistinarperadnacles. You're an ally of the Faceless, aren't you?"

"No, witch. I'm merely a pawn," the dragon skull answered. "Just as is everyone in this city, yourselves included."

Victor stepped forward. "I am no man's pawn, dead thing," the young lord declared.

Mist's laughter rang all about them. "You are one of the biggest pawns of all, Dhostar pup. Pawn to your father, pawn to your ambitions, pawn to your . . . desires.

"As for you, Alias of the Inner Sea, you are a pawn of the Faceless's. He has plans for you. He will make himself your master."

"An evil sorceress, a lich, a fiend from Tarterus, a mad god, and an assassins' guild all tried to master me. All are now dead," Alias retorted.

"True," Mist replied. "If your luck is still as it was, you may defeat the Faceless. I will aid you in exchange for a boon."

"What boon, wyrm?" the swordswoman demanded.

"Swear that you will free me from this bondage of my spirit so that I may rest in peace, and I will tell you three of the Faceless's secrets."

"I so swear," Alias agreed. "First. The device that shields the Faceless and the Night Masters from detection. Tell me all you know of it."

"It sits there on that table," Mist answered, turning so that one eye socket seemed to look at the tree rack hung with the white porcelain masks. "It was crafted by the priests of the temple of Leira, the deceased goddess of illusions, and stolen by the priests of Mask, god of thieves. A doppelganger imitating the Shadowlord of Mask's temple stole it and used it to build the Night Mask guild. The masks must hang there on that rack for a day to recharge their magical powers. Anyone wearing one of the masks for one hour is protected from all magical detection and divination for four days. The Faceless sets them out for the Night Masters to wear just before the meeting they attend every other night so there is no chance of their being discovered. Even the Faceless dons one beneath the coin mask he wears to conceal his features from his own servants, including myself."

"So you don't know who old Faceless is. Too bad," Olive sighed.

"She didn't say that, Olive," Alias replied. "She said the Faceless concealed his features from her. But an old wyrm like you can see with more than her eyes, can't you, Mistinarperadnacles?"

"So true," the dragon said. "Is that the second secret you wish me to reveal?"

Alias hesitated, sensing a trick on the dragon's part. Mist had no love for her. Vengeance might still override her desire for a peaceful death.

"We don't need her to answer that," Victor declared. "All we need to do is destroy these masks—" The young lord yanked a mask from the tree rack.

"Victor, no!" Alias shouted. "It could be a trap!"

"Oh, yes," Mist said. "Did I fail to mention the masks must be removed from the rack in a particular order?"

With a shocked look, Victor set the mask back on the tree rack, but it was too late. The floor began to shake as all around the cavern hidden gears and levers of massive proportions began to turn and move. A panel in the workbench slid open and the tree rack containing the masks dropped down into it. An iron gate dropped down over the alcove where the gem-laden amphoras were kept. Larger grates dropped over the walls with the sea chests and weaponry.

Mist laughed. "Oh, dear. It does not look like we shall be able to complete our little transaction after all. Ah, well. I have no regrets, knowing this will be your end. Die well, Alias of the Inner Sea. And fond good-byes to you, Mistress Ruskettle, Champion. Lord Victor, it was a pleasure dealing with you." The dragon skull sank back into the pool.

The level of water in the pool began to rise until it poured over the edge, splashing to the floor.

"This doesn't sound good," Olive whispered.

The sound of the gears grinding stopped and there was a moment of relative silence. Then they all heard it: the sound of rushing water, as loud as the ocean itself.

Vast amounts of water began pouring down on the adventurers from the ceiling, extinguishing Olive's lantern. The force of the flow was enough to knock Olive off her feet. Dragonbait grabbed the halfling by her cloak and helped her stand upright.

"We've got to get across the bridge!" Alias shouted. She sheathed her sword and snagged Victor's arm, pulling him toward the stairs to the bridge. Dragonbait splashed behind her with the halfling in tow.

The stairs had become a rushing cascade of water, and Dragonbait's flaming sword was their only light now. The swordswoman was forced to press her hands against both sides of the narrow corridor in order to keep herself upright. She could feel Victor, Dragonbait, and Olive bumping into her from behind. As Alias touched down on the last step, she felt it shift beneath her feet. With a sickening dread, the swordswoman tried planting her feet more firmly on the slick stone, but to no avail.

A wave of water crashed down from the ceiling above the stair, knocking all the adventures off their feet and carrying them at a breakneck speed down the corridor toward the bridge and the sewer.

First Alias could hear the water plunging down into the sewer. Then there was a sense of weightlessness as the current shot her out across the chasm of the sewer. Just as she took a great gulp of air, she had a glimpse of light—Dragonbait's flaming sword. Finally, there came the flesh-bruising impact of her body against the fetid sewer water below.

Alias's lungs were screaming for air before she managed to break the surface and take a gulp of the foul air. The water was flowing faster, fed by the stream from the Faceless's water trap, carrying her with it.

"Dragonbait!" Alias screamed. "Victor! Olive!"

She spotted the paladin first, still clutching his flaming sword. Olive bobbed alongside him.

"Where's Victor?" she shouted.

"Here," the nobleman called from just behind her.

Alias strained to face the young lord's direction, relieved to see that he seemed to know how to stay afloat. Her chain mail shirt made treading water tiring enough. She didn't think she could manage helping a fully grown man as well.

"Try to stay close to the near wall," the swordswoman shouted to the others. "There have to be some side passages we can—"

Alias gasped. Something large had pushed against her, and she knew what it had to be.

The quelzarn's head broke the water just beside Dragonbait, attracted perhaps by the light from the paladin's sword. The sea serpent's teeth gleamed in the flaming light.

Alias screamed the paladin's name in his own tongue. The quelzarn dived down, taking the saurial with it. The sewer darkened, but a dim light shone beneath the water's surface.

The female warrior took a deep breath and plunged beneath the surface, heading for the light. As long as it shone she knew Dragonbait had not yet been swallowed.

The foul water stung her eyes, and visibility below the surface wasn't more than a few feet, but that was enough to detect a great shadow looming before her. Alias grabbed the monster's fin and hung on with all her might as it wriggled and writhed beneath her. With her arms aching from the strain, the swordswoman pulled herself along the length of the fin, making for the quelzarn's head. Just when the fire in her lungs grew too intense to bear, the creature broke the surface of the water again, and Alias was able to gasp for air. A dark stain seemed to be flowing from the light beneath the surface. Alias was sure it was blood, but whether the saurial's or the sea serpent's she could not tell.

The creature looped backward on itself, and Alias had

a clear glimpse of Dragonbait. The saurial had one
clawed foot jammed against the beast's lower gum and
one hand thrust between two needlelike teeth of the
upper jaw so that the monster could not snap its jaw shut
and swallow its prey. Blood poured from the paladin's
foot and hand as well as from a gash in his thigh. With
his flaming sword the paladin was lacerating the monster's upper palate.

Alias pulled her dagger from her boot and launched
herself at the quelzarn's head. She managed to catch the
fin beside its gill. She could still not reach the beast's
eyes, so she tore a V-shaped gash into the flesh behind
the gill. Then she began pulling back on the flesh, stripping it away like whale blubber.

The beast breached from the water with a shriek and
slammed itself and the swordswoman against the sewer
wall, dislodging the saurial in its mouth and the human
woman at its gill.

Alias wasn't sure what happened in the moments she
was stunned, but when she next opened her eyes, Dragonbait, his hands clenched in her hair, was holding her
head out of the water. The saurial was a powerful swimmer, and he was towing the swordswoman toward a side
sewer where Olive and Victor stood shouting.

The side sewer was eight feet in diameter; the water
level in it was only two feet high, so the adventurers'
could work their way against the current. The halfling
and the nobleman helped pull the warriors inside. They
moved down the tunnel about ten feet, but had to stop to
catch their breath and tend to their wounds.

Dragonbait, after first assuring himself that Alias had
suffered no life-threatening injury, handed his weapon to
the swordswoman and turned his attention to the wounds
the quelzarn had given him.

As the scent of the paladin's prayer filled the air, a
great roar blasted down the tunnel. The quelzarn thrust
its head a few feet into the side passage. Victor, who
stood directly in its path, fumbled in the tangles of his
cloak, trying, Olive thought, to reach his sword in its
scabbard.

The halfling was sure the young lord was about to become the last of the Dhostar line when the quelzarn slid back out of the tunnel and disappeared.

Victor gulped and backed farther from the tunnel exit. "That was too close for comfort," the nobleman said. "If the tide were in and the water higher, it would have come in after us for sure," he said.

Olive nodded, her eyes wide with amazement at the young man's close call. She followed him down the corridor, wondering with suspicion what he seemed to be holding with his hand, which remained buried in his cloak pocket.

"I believe we should be able to follow this sewer to an opening near a street," the nobleman said.

"Yes," Alias added. "And if we're lucky, the fog will still be thick, and no one will notice us."

"They'll smell us before they see us," Olive predicted.

# Sixteen

# Suspicions

The sewer passage surfaced in a storm drain. After taking a moment to get his bearings, Victor pointed them in the direction of an outdoor ale garden called the Rosebud. There the merchant noble sent a runner for his carriage, and tipped the proprietor generously for the use of his well in the back. Pouring buckets of fresh water over each other, the four managed to scrape all of the sewer muck and most of the smell off their skin and clothes. Olive, gathering up her sopping cloak, excused herself, declaring she had a previous engagement. Alias didn't argue. She was anxious to grill Victor about the source of his key, and she knew the merchant lord would say nothing in Olive's presence.

Shortly after the halfling had gone, a young serving boy brought them three mugs of mulled wine. Alias allowed herself a few minutes to enjoy the sensation of warmth creeping back into her bones, then she forced herself to return to the business at hand.

"Victor, you have to tell me where you found the key," Alias insisted.

Victor stared hard into his mulled wine as if an answer might appear in the mug. "I began thinking about what you said last night, that maybe Father was paying the Night Masks on the side but was too proud to admit it. I started searching through his desk in secret. I couldn't find anything about payoffs, but I found this key. It was in an envelope with instructions on how to use it."

"And the instructions?" Alias asked. "Were they written in your father's hand?"

"Yes," Victor admitted. "I thought I should check it out by myself, in case it wasn't anything important."

"Or in case it was," Alias commented.

"It doesn't prove anything," Victor insisted. "There could be a perfectly good reason why he had the key. You have a key, too?"

Alias nodded.

"How did you get it?" the noble asked.

"I took it from Melman shortly before the Night Masks blew up his home with him in it," the swordswoman explained.

Dragonbait looked at Alias with surprise. She was deliberately misleading the noble to believe that Melman was dead.

"Victor, did you tell your father I was checking up on Melman?"

"When I got home last night. We had this stupid argument. He said I was distracting you from your duties. I told him what you told me at the party about Melman." The young man's eyes widened in surprise. "You don't think—he couldn't. It's just a coincidence. My father is *not* involved with the Night Masters!"

Now it was Alias's turn to look down into her mulled wine for a reply.

"You said yourself, last night, that you didn't think Father was the Faceless, that he had no reason to be involved with them. He hired you to get rid of them," Victor argued. "Wait! He could have gotten the key from Kimbel after Kimbel tried to assassinate him."

"Then why didn't he turn the key over to Durgar?" Alias asked.

Unable to come up with a ready excuse, Victor shifted tactics. "What would you do if you found the key in the possession of someone you loved? If it were, say, in Dragonbait's purse?"

Alias exchanged a look with the paladin. "I would ask him about it," the swordswoman replied.

"You wouldn't just take it to Durgar first, would you?" Victor retorted.

Alias sighed. "Victor, Dragonbait is like a brother to me. I've known him all my life."

"I've known my father all my life, too," the merchant noble countered.

"Very well," Alias said. "I'll ask your father about the key before I mention it to Durgar. I will give him a chance to explain."

"No!" Victor exclaimed. "That is, I'm asking you to give me a chance to ask him. He's my father, and, well, I think I should be the one to ask."

Alias couldn't imagine Victor getting a straight answer from his verbally abusive father, and, if Luer Dhostar should actually be involved with the Night Masks, there was a chance Victor would be in danger.

"I know what you're thinking," Victor said, "but you're wrong. My father would never hurt me. He has a good reason for having this key. You'll see. Let me handle this."

Alias nodded reluctantly. "All right," she said. "I have to report to Durgar about the lair today, so he can send the watch in at the next low tide. I will tell him you accompanied us there. I will not mention you had a key just yet. But, Victor, I can't keep that from him for long. I must have some explanation from your father by tomorrow."

"Tomorrow, then," the young merchant agreed. "I have all sorts of tasks to finish for the ball. We can discuss it then."

"Ball?" Alias asked.

"Yes. Oh, I almost forgot." Victor replied with a sheepish grin. "I'm afraid your invitation is just a little damp." He reached into his cloak pocket and drew out a soggy sheet of parchment folded in thirds. The sealing wax was marked with the croamarkh's insignia. Victor held it out to her.

Alias held up a hand as if to ward the invitation away like an evil spirit. "Victor, I'm supposed to be uncovering the identity of the Night Masters and the Faceless. I can't be rushing off to every party in Westgate."

"This isn't just a party. This is the Regatta Masquerade Ball," Victor argued. "It's the major social event of the season. In King Verovan's day it was called the Naval

Ball, but since the king's demise, we celebrate it as a commemoration of his folly. Everyone will be there."

With a sigh, the swordswoman took the folded document from the merchant and turned it over. It was addressed to her and Dragonbait.

"Besides, we have a reason to celebrate. You've found the Faceless's lair. I know I ruined our chances trying to capture him by setting off that water trap, but once you get Durgar's men down there at the next low tide to clear out his treasury and that mask thing that protects him and his lieutenants—well, it will really only be a matter of sweeping up, won't it? Please, say you'll come." Victor reached out and took her hand. "You'll need to come anyway to hear what my father has to say—about the key. Besides, I've really been looking forward to dancing with you."

"I'll come, to hear your father explain the key to me and Durgar," Alias said. She tucked the invitation into the vest beneath her chain mail. "*Maybe* I'll dance," she added, "if I think then that I have something to celebrate."

The young serving boy came out to announce that Lord Victor's carriage was waiting at the front gate. Alias declined the merchant noble's offer of a lift back to Blais House.

Between feeling shy in front of both the carriage driver and Dragonbait and feeling less than attractive with her hair plastered against her head and the scent of sewage lingering about her, Alias was prepared to see Victor off with no more than a friendly squeeze of his hand. The young merchant apparently did not feel similarly inhibited. He pulled the swordswoman close and stole a quick kiss from her before he climbed up beside his carriage driver. "Until tomorrow," he said.

Alias nodded.

As the nobleman's carriage pulled away, Alias turned and looked toward the River Thunn. "I wonder how quickly the tide comes in."

Dragonbait did not reply. He was staring at the back of Victor's carriage, which seemed to have picked up a small, wet, halfling-sized bundle on the rear boot.

"Maybe," Alias said, "if we can get Durgar to hurry, we'll be able to clean out this lair before nightfall."

\* \* \* \* \*

One of the few joys of being half the size of the dominant race of Faerûn, Olive reflected as she hung on to the low-slung storage area at the rear of Victor's carriage, is that unless someone is on the lookout for you, it's easy to hide just beside them. Even if the day were not ridden with fog, it was unlikely that she would be detected. She looked just like an old horse blanket someone had thrown in the back, and she was too light a stowaway for the horses to seem burdened. She kept her ears pricked during the ride through the city, out the West Gate, and through the countryside to Castle Dhostar, but Victor and his driver did not even attempt a conversation with one another. The halfling was not surprised. According to her mates at the Thalavar household, the Dhostars were very strong believers in the separation of stations.

Things might have been dicier for the halfling had their destination been a real castle with a curtain wall and guards at the portcullis, but Castle Dhostar was really just a very large manor house. Victor hopped down from the carriage, and, as the driver pulled away, Olive rolled out of the boot and slipped into the shadow of a yew tree by the drive. There were no guards at the front door, but, as Victor let himself in, he called for someone named Kane, and a butler appeared to take the merchant lord's sewer-drenched cloak.

Olive sneaked into the front hall as the butler was pulling off Victor's muck-encrusted boots. She slipped into the shadow beneath a table against the wall. As the servant handed the nobleman a pair of comfortable house slippers, Olive caught the words, "Your father . . . the library . . . soon as you arrive."

The halfling listened for the sound of Victor's retreating steps, and, as soon as the butler disappeared with Victor's wet things, she slipped down the hallway after the merchant lord.

Fortunately, Castle Dhostar was an easy place to sneak around in. Apparently Luer Dhostar did not believe in wasting money on candles to light the halls. The servants all carried their own lights, so Olive could see as well as hear them coming and take cover in a shadow as they passed. There were plenty of shadows cast by the usual bric-a-brac of the wealthy: out-dated armor, stuffed animal trophies, stone statuary, ancient urns on pedestals.

Olive pressed her ear against several doors without hearing Victor's or Luer's voice. Then, from a room just ahead, she heard the croamarkh shouting. Victor had left the door open, so Olive peered inside. Luer Dhostar sat at a desk; his son stood before him, receiving a paternal dressing down.

"In the sewers! Gond's gears! What were you thinking? You could have been killed! "You are a Dhostar, not some cheap hero from the street plays. You hire people to take risks for you, then you stay away from those people. That way, when they make mistakes, you don't suffer directly."

When *they* make mistakes? Olive wondered. What mistakes?

"Anyone could have set off that trap," Victor replied. "You can't blame Alias because a halfling couldn't resist handling things."

He's blamed me for picking up that mask! Olive thought with a huff. What a little rat.

Just inside the open door was a large stuffed displacer beast mounted rampant, its forepaws and tentacles batting the air. Lord Luer or one of his ancestors was quite the accomplished hunter. Olive slipped into the library, positioning herself behind the trophy beast.

"I hired this woman to take care of the Night Masks, not drag you on dangerous jaunts into the underworld. It's bad enough you've been neglecting your duties—"

"I have not been neglecting my duties," Victor snapped in a low growl. "There isn't a single obligation to you, the family business, or Westgate that I have not fulfilled."

Luer Dhostar drummed his fingers on his desktop. "First you champion her acting friends in front of the rabble," he accused his son. "Then you spend last night's cruise almost exclusively in her company, time you might have spent with your peers, men and women of your own rank. Now I find you've been diving into sewers with her. That is not the life of a Dhostar."

"No, the life of a Dhostar is all cold figures and hard cash. There's no room in it for honor or courage," Victor taunted, stepping forward and wringing his shirt sleeve out on the accounting books spread out before his father, leaving puddles in the blue ink.

Lord Luer turned several shades of red, though Olive couldn't be sure whether he was more angered by his son's words or his reckless disregard for bookkeeping. For a moment it seemed as if Victor, faced with his father's apoplectic wrath, showed a moment of fear, a recognition that he had gone too far, for he backed away suddenly from his father. In the next moment, however, the young man's back stiffened, and he stood his ground.

Several moments of icy silenced followed, then Victor said, "I've issued Alias and her companion an invitation to the masquerade ball."

"And you expect the other noble families to accept her because you keep dragging her into their presence?" Luer said with a laugh.

"I don't care about the other families. I expect you to honor her for the service she's done us. She's discovered the Faceless's lair for you. Within a few days she may have his identity."

"That's what I've *paid* her for. I am not required to reward her success with invitations to socialize with her betters," Luer growled. "Since you have so injudiciously invited her, I suppose there is nothing I can do. Welcome her to the ball, introduce her as your guest, dance with her. I will not be there. I will not watch my son cavorting with a common adventuress or seem to give my approval with my presence."

"Father, you cannot mean that. You are blowing this all out of proportion. I haven't forgotten my rank or hers. I am simply extending a courtesy to a very useful employee. I assure you I have no intentions of forming an alliance beneath my station."

*Funny you forgot to mention that to Alias,* Olive thought.

"Your lack of propriety is not my concern," Luer replied to his son. "It is the appearance of impropriety I cannot tolerate. If that girl is there, I will not attend the ball."

Someone rapped at the door frame, and Luer barked, "Enter."

Kimbel stepped into the room. "Excuse me, Lord Luer," the assassin-turned-servant begged. "Lord Orgule has sent his son with a message. He awaits your reply in the hall." Kimbel proffered a scrap of parchment.

Luer read the message and cursed softly. "Orgule could foul up a one-horse parade," he muttered, pushing himself out of his chair. "I'll speak with the boy myself," he said as he stalked over to the door. Just before he stepped out of the room, he whirled about to address Victor once more. "Get into some dry things," he ordered, "before you ruin the carpets."

When the croamarkh had gone, Kimbel closed the door softly behind him. Victor flopped into his father's chair and propped his feet up on the desk.

"He is a fool, you know," the young lord said.

"So you have informed me," Kimbel replied without a trace of irony or humor.

"He refuses to see how useful Alias is," Victor steamed.

*Useful!* Olive thought angrily. *Is that all you have to say about a girl who's welcomed you with her arms and lips and given you a token of her regard? You Westgate nobles are so romantic.*

"The rabble is rather taken with her, thanks to Jamal," Kimbel noted, "but, aside from House Thalavar, the noble families are cool."

"Short-sighted fools," Victor muttered. Olive could see his jaw clenched in irritation.

"It's hardly surprising," Kimbel pointed out. "Every one of them has some involvement with the Night Masks, which they wish to remain hidden. They do not perceive this Alias as an ally. You do not want to offend them. After all, it is still the noble families who choose the croamarkh."

"Hah!" Victor laughed, and there was a bully-like tone to his amusement. "Imagine how they'll all look when they discover that their very own croamarkh is the leader of the Night Masks."

Olive almost gasped with surprise.

"It should leave them in a decided quandary, sir," Kimbel replied as calmly as if he and the merchant lord were discussing the price increase of Selgaunt marble.

Victor laughed the same unpleasant laugh again. "They'll be no better off than the rabble they consider their inferiors. The only way they'll manage to hold on to their power is by choosing a popular candidate—the one wearing the token of Alias of the Inner Sea—the woman who freed them from the yoke of the Night Masks." Victor took a small case from his tunic, opened it, and displayed the braid of hair that Alias had cut off and given him. It was now fastened to a pin. "If the nobles are frightened enough by the Faceless's plot to destroy them all, they may even be convinced that it is time to restore a monarchy, return Westgate to the status of a kingdom."

"Is it certain then that the croamarkh will be revealed as the Faceless?" Kimbel asked.

"Alias and her companions stumbled upon me investigating the Faceless's lair. I got in with this key," Victor said, holding up the key he'd shown Olive earlier. "Unfortunately, like a fool, I touched off a water trap and we were all washed out to the sewer, where we barely escaped the quelzarn. I had to admit to Alias that I found the key in my father's desk. She has given me time to ask him to explain the key. I do not think he will do so."

"No," Kimbel agreed.

"Alias should be with Durgar now, planning to check out this lair at the next low tide. In the meantime, you and I both have lots to do," the noble said, rising to his feet. "Come along."

Victor strode to the door. He passed so close to the mounted displacer beast Olive hid behind that the halfling could feel the breeze of his passing. Olive held her breath as the nobleman exited the room.

Kimbel paused for a moment by the doorway, and the

former assassin's eyes narrowed, much the same way, Olive thought, as Dragonbait's did when the paladin was using his *shen* sight. Kimbel stared directly at the displacer beast. Olive knew he could not possibly see into the dark shadows of the ill-lit room, but she grew acutely aware of the sound of her heart pounding in her chest, and if she could have stopped it from beating at that moment, she would have. Her fingers tightened about the hilt of her sword, prepared to draw it in a hurry.

"Kimbel!" Victor called from down the hall. "We haven't got time to waste!"

The geased servant's head snapped back at an unnatural angle as if against his will. He turned to the door and exited the room without looking back.

Olive breathed as silently as she could. She did not move from her hiding place until the sound of Kimbel's footsteps had faded into nothingness.

\* \* \* \* \*

When Alias and Dragonbait returned to the Tower, Durgar was still out sifting through the ashes of Melman's home, no doubt making sure the treasure found in the basement was thoroughly catalogued before it could be looted. The two adventurers left a message for the priest and hurried to Mintassan's.

There they found Jamal in the middle of a lesson with Kel. The boy seemed much more subdued. Apparently the young Night Mask had gotten a look at Melman's branded face when he had brought the former Night Master his lunch, and now he was seriously rethinking his original career choice.

Mintassan sent Kel off to study on his own. Once the boy was gone, Alias told the actress and the sage of the afternoon's adventure just as she intended to relate it to Durgar—not mentioning Victor's second key. She felt just a hint of guilt deceiving Jamal, but the alternative, she knew, was to have the key and the croamarkh's reputation called into question in Jamal's very next street performance.

Mintassan, eager to get a glimpse of the quelzarn, asked if he could join the next party down to the lair.

"You're on," Alias agreed. She'd been secretly hoping the sage might be enticed into lending his expertise to the expedition. "I was hoping we might make it down there again before high tide."

"Then we'd better not waste any time," the sage replied. "Jamal, you game? We'll take a shortcut." He took up Jamal's hand in his right hand and Alias's in his left hand. Jamal snagged Dragonbait's arm. "Silver path, Thunn Bridge," the sage intoned.

Alias felt a buzz in her ears, and a moment later she, Jamal, Dragonbait, and Mintassan all stood in the center of the bridge over the River Thunn. Although she realized Mintassan must possess far more powerful spells than teleportation, the swordswoman was a little taken aback by how casually he used it. "A little showy, aren't you?" she teased the sage.

"Just lazy," Mintassan retorted with a grin. He moved over to the edge of the bridge and peered at the riverbank through the fog. "Where's this door?" the sage asked.

"It's hidden from the view of the bridge by some rocks," Alias explained. The fog was no thicker than it had been this morning, but Alias was unsuccessful in locating the rocks. The rocks, along with the sandbank, were already under water. "It could be tricky getting back in. We'll have to do some wading."

"In the Thunn's current, with a sea serpent in the water!" Jamal exclaimed. "Better count me out."

"Which way does the door open?" Mintassan asked.

"Out," Alias explained, realizing with disappointment that the water would make the door very difficult if not impossible to budge.

"I could pass us though the door with a dimensional portal," the sage suggested.

"Most unwise," a voice said from behind them, and out from the mists stepped Durgar, flanked by a large contingent of the watch. "But then you were always a bit reckless, weren't you, Mintassan?"

"Not everyone wants to live to be as old as you, Durgar,"

Mintassan taunted.

Durgar smiled coolly at the sage. He held up the note Alias had left for him at the tower. "This door is the entrance to the alleged Faceless's lair?" he asked Alias.

The swordswoman nodded. "I obtained this key from a Night Mask," she explained, handing over the magical key that Melman had given her. Briefly she described how she, Dragonbait, Olive, and Victor had explored and then been expelled from the Faceless's lair. Just as she had before, she omitted any mention that Victor had also had a key and had been in the Faceless's lair before she'd arrived.

"This site is now under the jurisdiction of the watch," the priest declared. "As such, you may not explore it without an official escort. And since I neither expect nor will allow any of my own people to attempt any magical entry that might endanger their health, we will wait until low tide, when the door can again be opened."

"That won't be until hours after midnight," Mintassan growled.

"We can't get in, they can't get in," Durgar pointed out. "I plan to station men in hiding about the bridge and the shore. Perhaps we will catch some Night Masks attempting to enter."

"I don't think that's likely," Alias argued. "As elaborate as the water trap was, I can't imagine that it didn't also include an alarm to warn the Faceless, wherever he might have been at the time."

"Well, we shall see," Durgar said. "If, a half hour after low ebb, no one has appeared, then I shall go in with my men. I'd appreciate your presence at that time as guides," he said, addressing both Alias and Dragonbait.

"And can I come, too?" Mintassan asked, imitating a schoolboy begging a favor of an adult.

"If you choose to bring another advisor," the priest said to Alias, eyeing Mintassan somewhat disapprovingly, "that's your business. You, though, woman," he addressed Jamal, "have no business here."

"Jamal's advice, Your Reverence, has been crucial in helping me locate this lair," Alias argued.

"That may be," Durgar replied, "but, as she is not known for her discretion, she is not welcome. As you will recall from your discussion yesterday with the croamarkh, your employer, there are more serious aspects to these investigations than feeding the curiosity of theatrical vagrants."

"Theatrical vagrant. I like the sound of that," Jamal said with mock indignation. "Certainly a step up from being a lackey to the likes of Haztor Urdo." She sneered.

Durgar's eyes narrowed, but he did not reply to the actress's implied insult.

"We'll be back at low tide," Alias said. Mintassan reached for her hand, no doubt prepared to whisk the two women and the saurial away with magic, but Alias said, "I'd like to walk." She proceeded down the bridge with Jamal at her side.

"Very well," the sage sighed, and took a position alongside Dragonbait, following the two women.

As they strode through the streets, Mintassan began expounding on the varying legends about quelzarns. Dragonbait listened intently, eager to learn all he could about a creature he might battle again, but Alias drifted back a few paces to apologize to Jamal for Durgar's insistence that she be left out.

"Don't give it a second thought. I certainly haven't," the actress reassured her. "Besides, I'll squeeze the story of your expedition out of you later."

Alias felt another twinge of guilt, reminded of how she'd kept secret the croamarkh's key. The loyalty she felt she owed Luer Dhostar as an employer remained intact only because she hoped, for Victor's sake, that the croamarkh had a good reason for possessing the key to the Night Masters' lair. She felt a stronger loyalty, though, to Jamal, and not just for all the advice the woman had given her. She was still haunted by the phantom memories of a mother who looked just like the actress. In addition, the connection Jamal had to Finder Wyvernspur made Alias feel a certain warmth for her. She wanted something to make up for the key that stood between them.

"Lord Victor's invited me to a masquerade ball tomorrow night," she confided. "Dragonbait and I."

"My goodness, how egalitarian," Jamal said with a grin. "I wonder what he's playing at?"

Alias shook her head. "He's not playing at anything. He just likes my company."

"A likely story," Jamal retorted, her tone laced with dramatic suspicion.

"I suspect I'll need a fancier gown from all Victor said about this event."

"Definitely," Jamal agreed. "Fortunately, I know a dressmaker who owes me several favors. Why don't we just pop into her shop now?"

The two women excused themselves from the company of the sage and the saurial and made their way down a side street.

Jamal's dressmaker was an elven woman called Dawn, who greeted Jamal with a suspicious look. She broke into a string of expletives when the actress explained Alias's needs and time constraints. Jamal insisted that a designer of her talents was surely up to the challenge.

The elf eyed Alias critically for several moments. Finally she said, "The shoulders. None of these Westgate witches can compete there. Lady Nettel forty years ago, but none of the wilting lilies of this generation. We'll leave the shoulders bare."

"How will the dress stay up?" Alias asked.

"Elven magic," Jamal chuckled.

For the next half hour the swordswoman fidgeted through measurements, pinnings, and some rather rude appraisals of her features. At last Dawn announced that Alias was free to go. Providing the swordswoman came by tomorrow for a final fitting before noon, the gown would be ready an hour before the ball.

"Her scabbard belt will spoil the gown's lines. She'll need a baldric for her sword," Jamal informed the elf. "You were planning to wear your sword, weren't you?"

"In this city, I wear it everywhere," Alias confirmed as she studied the dozens of masks that lined the walls of the shop. For Dragonbait she picked out a half-mask covered in feathers and for herself a simple full face done in glazed porcelain. The mask's arched eyebrows seemed to express exactly how she was beginning to feel about all the twists and turns her visit to this city had taken.

"This is actually getting exciting," Jamal laughed as she and Alias left the shop and made their way through Westgate's fog-bound streets. "It reminds me of a song Nameless sang about the Westgate nobs—something about battles at the balls."

"Their battles are fought at the ball," Alias corrected, in measured rhythm. She knew the song perfectly well, though she had never known before that Finder had sung it about Westgate. She turned to Jamal and spoke as openly as she dared. "I'm so glad we've met. I'm glad Finder knew you, glad that I got to know you, too. I'm going to bring down the Faceless for you, Jamal. I promise."

The actress looked taken aback for a moment, but then she smiled and draped her arm around the swordswoman's shoulders. "I appreciate that," she said, giving Alias's shoulders a friendly squeeze. "I think, though, that you look exhausted. You should get some rest before you throw yourself back into the fray."

Back at Blais House, Alias found she could hardly keep her eyes open as she took her leave of the actress. Leaving Mercy with instructions to wake her at midnight, the swordswoman retired to her room to nap. Dragonbait was already there sleeping.

*　*　*　*　*

By the time the sandbar was uncovered again, the fog had cleared. The crescent moon shone brightly on the untrampled approach to the Night Masters' lair. It was the perfect secret entrance, Alias thought. The tide washed away all signs of the Night Masters passing after every meeting.

There had been no sign of any Night Masters approaching the site, despite the fact that, according to Melman, this would be the night of their regular meeting. The

Faceless had learned of their trespass, Alias realized, and had warned his followers. The Night Masters and their lord would elude Durgar this night, but soon much of their wealth and the magical source of their obscurement would be in the hands of the watch.

With a keen sense of satisfaction, Alias showed Durgar how to use the key to the lair, and she, Dragonbait, Mintassan, and twelve armed members of the watch followed the priest into the dark tunnel by the River Thunn.

Half the watch carried hooded lanterns, and Mintassan produced a small silver wand, which glowed with a magical light.

As the party moved into the conference room, Dragonbait tapped on the table. "Melman's mask is missing," he said in Saurial.

"Damn," Alias whispered. A leaden feeling of failure settled over her. "The Faceless must have some other way in," she said to Durgar, and she explained about the missing mask. "He might have come in the way we left, through the sewer," Alias suggested.

"Or used magic," Mintassan pointed out.

Dragonbait pressed the panel that operated the secret door. Alias nearly ran through the secret passage. She hesitated only a moment at the chasm over the sewer to check with her sword that the bridge was still intact and crossed over the sluggish water below.

Dragonbait clucked with annoyance at her impatience. He remained behind to present the invisible bridge to Durgar, Mintassan, and the watch. Dragonbait and the sage stood guard as the watch crossed, but the quelzarn did not appear. As the others trooped up the next passage, the sage stood looking over the chasm's edge with disappointment. Dragonbait had to tug on his sleeve to get him to follow the others.

"I guess a watched quelzarn never surfaces," the sage said as he continued on.

They found Alias in the empty treasure room, leaning dejectedly against one wall, staring at the shards of the mirror that had been mounted on the wall. Save for the broken mirror, the room was stripped of all trace of the

Night Masks' treasure. The chests, the weaponry, the wands and staves, the iron golems, the table holding the tree of masks—all were gone.

"The mirror," Alias muttered. "I never thought about the mirror. As if the Faceless would need a mirror to check how his hair looked before his meetings. I'm such an idiot."

Mintassan bent over and picked up a larger sliver of the broken, silver-backed glass. "Nice workmanship," the sage commented. He held it out to Durgar. "Late monarchical period. Legend has it that there were several of these magical portal mirrors in Verovan's castle. They disappeared in the looting that followed his death."

"So all the Faceless had to do was pop through the mirror and carry the stuff back to wherever he has another mirror," Alias noted.

"No," Mintassan corrected, "all he had to do is order the iron golems to carry the stuff through. Much easier."

Alias glared for a moment at the sage.

"Then, unable to carry the mirror through itself," the sage continued, "the Faceless had to smash it so no one could walk through it and discover where he'd gone."

"Well," Durgar said, "while I'm willing to concede this might have been a meeting place of Night Masks and even a hoarding place for their ill-gotten goods, I can see no evidence before me of any creature known as the Faceless."

"There is a Faceless," Alias snapped. "Mist confirmed it when we spoke with her."

"Mist? Ah, yes. The dead dragon. She might have been lying to you. Dragons will do that, you know," Durgar pointed out.

"Mist's skull is gone," Dragonbait noted, peering into the pool, which had lately held the earthly remains of their former foe.

"I think, to be on the safe side," the priest murmured, "we should leave before the tide turns and traps us down here."

Durgar ushered the watch back down the stairs toward the sewer, but Alias remained behind, pacing the cavern floor with a barely concealed fury. There would be no end to the evil the Night Masks brought to Westgate unless she captured the Faceless. She thought of the rag man who had died when the Night Masks burned Jamal's home, and the halfling who'd been killed in the explosion in the warehouse, and all the other people who were dead because of the thieves guild. With his minions and his smoke powder, the Faceless would continue to terrorize the whole city—no doubt he considered himself master of Westgate. Now he was somewhere safe, with all his power still intact, laughing at her failure. Alias let loose with a tremendous shout, a battle-cry from the north, a call for vengeance.

Durgar, who'd just looked back to ask the adventuress if she were leaving with them, took a step back in surprise, nearly tripping down the stairs. Mintassan felt his blood run cold from the emotion he sensed emanating from the swordswoman.

The saurial touched Alias's tattoo, kindling the link they shared, trying to infuse some of his inner calm into her wild spirit.

The warrior woman shook herself out of her rage. "I will find him again!" she declared. "He cannot hide from me much longer."

# Seventeen
# Accusations

The Faceless looked over his nine surviving minions, and from behind his two masks, one of porcelain, the other of coins, he smiled. They had responded well, and promptly, to his summons. Each had received, from a messenger they'd never seen (nor would ever see again), a single scrap of paper with the code word "kudzu." They all knew what this meant. It had happened on rare occasions before, when some local activity near the bridge prevented them from using the entrance to their lair in secret. They were to meet at a different site, but at the same time as usual. So the Night Masters' business continued uninterrupted while Durgar and his watch were occupied examining a lair that had since been pillaged and abandoned.

Two Night Masters who lived near the bridge had apparently detected the watch's interest in the sandbank and were now informing the others in hushed whispers. They were like nervous cattle milling in the path of an approaching storm, the Faceless reflected. They needed only that sharp crack of lightning to turn them into a stampede. The Faceless was prepared to be that lightning.

The Night Masters' lord sat at the head of a wooden table, in a tavern that had closed for business two hours earlier. Behind him stood two rows of dragon-headed iron golems, arranged like obedient troops, to remind the others of the power he commanded. He drummed his fingers impatiently on the tabletop.

First the stick, the Night Masters' lord thought. He began the meeting by tossing Melman's mask on the table.

The glyph that labeled it as Gateside's had been scratched off the porcelain. "Gateside is dead," he announced. The effect on the assemblage was immediate. To the Faceless, their fear and uneasiness was palpable . . . and exquisite.

Now the carrot, the Faceless prompted himself. "I have at this time no plans to turn the management of his district over to anyone else. It might be better, I think, to divide his duties and his income among those of you who remain." A tingle of excitement passed though the Night Masters. It was a great risk, being a Night Master, but the rewards were what made the risk worthwhile.

And finally the challenge: "Before Gateside died," the Faceless declared, "he betrayed us to Alias the Sell-Sword. Before his betrayal, this Alias was nothing more than a mercenary, a trumped-up member of the watch. In betraying us, though, Gateside made her into exactly what he feared her to be—an enemy capable of destroying our organization."

The Faceless paused, letting his words sink in. It took his minions a few moments to shift their thoughts from their own greed to their own self-preservation. He ignored their impassive masks, but studied instead the pursed lips, the clenched jaws, the trickle of sweat along the cheek of Finance Management. Aside from fearing the loss of their wealth and freedom, some of them, he knew, had a childlike terror of being killed by this red-headed witch.

After a few moments, the Faceless continued. "I had not expected Gateside to betray us." It was an admission that he was, after all, only human, but one that also laid the blame squarely on the deceased. "Once I was made aware of his betrayal, I did everything in my power to keep the damage to a minimum. Our secret identities remain unthreatened." It was important to make them aware that he alone had preserved them from their enemies.

"The loss of a secure meeting place is a minor loss. Our treasury and our armory remain in our possession." Now to give them blood, the Night Masters' lord thought. "This swordswoman has lunged at us with all she had," the Faceless growled, "but we have parried her attack. Now it is time for our riposte."

Around the table, heads bobbed up and down in agreement.

"It is time to show this mercenary witch and all the people of Westgate that we are the true commanders of this city. It is time to let the merchant nobles know they cannot simply hire someone to free them from our rule."

Smiles of satisfaction beamed from the Night Masters.

Finally, the Faceless thought, it's time to reveal my plan. "I propose," he declared, "that we use our long-hoarded troop of magical warriors in a single strike that will end the career of Alias the Sell-Sword and at the same time break the power of the merchant nobles once and for all. In light of Melman's betrayal, I will not go into the details of my plan, for security reasons. Are there any questions at this point?"

There should have been questions. Seven years ago, when the current Faceless had managed to wrest the title and power from the doppelganger who'd created this guild, there would have been questions. There had been at least three Night Masters then whose ability to reason, and consequently their power, had been strong enough to argue with him. Over the years, though, the current Faceless had skillfully eliminated these challengers. Melman had been the last. With his demise, there was no one left who would voice what the others hardly dared think, no piece of grit around which a pearl of wisdom might form.

Last of all, the Faceless thought with a cynical grin, display for them an illusion of their power and choice. "I call then for a vote, allowing me the use of these resources"—he motioned to the golems—"to use at my discretion." He pulled a short dagger from his belt and held it out. The blade glistened with a drop of greenish ichor. There was a sharp collective intake of breath from the Night Masters. All wondered if another compatriot would perish at this meeting.

"How say ye to my proposal?" the Faceless asked. "Yea or nay?"

Nine resounding yeas echoed around the table, each Night Master eager to prove his or her loyalty by the zeal with which he or she replied.

Visual aids, the Faceless reflected, never failed to
smooth the course of democracy. He smiled with pleasure
at the wisdom of his minions.

\* \* \* \* \*

Dragonbait awakened instantly at the knocking on the
door. Alias was gone already. He vaguely recalled her prodding him earlier to tell him she was going with Jamal back
to the dressmaker's. He considered rolling over and ignoring the knock. After the late hour he had finally retired, he
felt he was owed more sleep, even if it was nearly noon. If it
was Mercy at the door with a breakfast tray, the half-elf
girl would let herself in and leave it on the table.

There was the sound of a key rattling in the lock, then
the sound of another key, then another. Then a wire slid
through the keyhole.

Dragonbait swung out of bed warily and grabbed his
sword.

The door swung open, and Olive Ruskettle slipped into
the room and shut the door behind her. "It's such a pleasure to find a challenging lock for a change," the halfling
said in place of a greeting. She pushed her lock-picking
wire into her hair.

The saurial lowered his sword and set it back against
the wall. *Good morning to you, too*, he signed, sitting
down on the edge of the bed. *Alias has gone out with
Jamal*, he explained.

Olive hopped up into a chair by the table. "I know. I
waited until I saw her leave. I wanted to talk with you in
private.

The saurial yawned toothily. Impatiently he signed,
*What is it now, Olive?*

"It's about Victor Dhostar."

*What about him?*

"He can't be trusted. You've got to convince Alias somehow to drop him like the slimy toad he is, and fast."

The paladin glared at the halfling for her effrontery. *I
told you I've already studied him with my* shen *sight*.

*There is nothing evil in him. I trust him completely.*

"Well, I think the old *shen* sight's going, pal," the halfling retorted.

The paladin bristled. To say his *shen* sight was wrong was the equivalent of suggesting he had slipped from the grace of his god.

Smelling the fresh-baked bread scent of the saurial's fury, the halfling hurried to put a different tone to her words. "It's like Elminster always says—good and evil aren't always. You've been tricked somehow. Instead of relying on this paladin magic all the time, you should use the evidence of your other senses. Like my mom used to say, 'Handsome is as handsome does.' And Lord Victor doesn't at all, at least not handsomely."

*What evidence?* the paladin signed, barely in control of his temper.

"Well, the key he had, for starters," Olive said.

*He explained the key to Alias and me.*

"Yeah, I know. He told you he got it from his father. I heard him admit it when I followed him home."

*Yes. I saw you stow away on his carriage. He is only trying to protect his father the way you used to cover for Finder Wyvernspur's crimes. It proves only that his judgment is poor, not that he cannot be trusted.*

"The key he had wasn't the same as the one Alias had."

The saurial cocked his head in confusion. *What do you mean?*

"It wasn't the same cut. It was nothing like it."

The paladin shrugged. *Different kinds of keys can open the same door*, he signed and pointed to the door to the room, *as you so aptly demonstrated.*

"Yes, if they have certain similarities. Melman's key and the key Victor said he got from his father, they're as different as night and day. And I know my keys, as I so aptly demonstrated."

*There might be magic on the key that opened the door*, Dragonbait argued. *And magic is not your forte.*

"Then there's the question of footprints," Olive continued, undaunted. "There weren't any on the sandbar as we approached the door. If Victor had entered by the same door, we would have seen his footprints."

Dragonbait struggled to remember the sandbar the afternoon before, anxious to dispute the halfling, but, truth to tell, he had not noted the condition of the sandbar one way or the other. *He could have waded in earlier before the tide was at complete ebb, and the water carried away his prints*, he signed.

"His boots weren't wet, and there were no wet footprints in the sand on the other side of the door," Olive argued. "He not only failed to mention there was another way in, which he must have used, but he also lied to us to cover that fact."

Dragonbait thought of the smashed magical portal mirror they'd found in the lair last night. He scratched his head, trying to think of some excuse for the young noble. Covering for his father was one thing, but neglecting to mention a second entrance indicated something far more serious.

"Then there's the quelzarn," the halfling continued. "Those things aren't dumb animals. They cast magic. There were four tasty morsels in the water. One with a sword and scales—you—one with chain mail—Alias—one in leather—me—and one with no shell on him at all—Lord Victor."

*It was attracted to the light of my sword*, Dragonbait argued.

"A quelzarn hunts by scent first. They say one can smell blood in the water a mile away," Olive commented. "If you hadn't smelled juicier, it would have taken me. More importantly, it was upstream from all of us. It had to pass Lord Victor before it surfaced beside you and me. Then there's the moment in the side tunnel when it lunged at Lord Victor. He had his hand in his pocket, fingering something. I'm willing to bet he has some charm against the creature."

*They sell such charms on the docks*, Dragonbait pointed out, *to anyone willing to pay two silvers.*

"But I'll bet his works better than those," Olive replied.

*It does not prove your point*, the paladin insisted.

"Not alone. You have to study the whole body of evidence," the halfling retorted. "Allow me to continue."

The paladin remained silent.

"There's the question of Victor's only known confidant—the person with whom he discusses his day-to-day problems."

*His father?* Dragonbait queried by hand.

"Hardly," Olive replied. "Oh, to be sure, he kept the croamarkh informed of Alias's discovery and our expedition into the sewers. He also reassured the old man that, where Alias is concerned, he has no intention, and I quote, 'of forming an alliance beneath his station.' But the most sinister point of all—guess who it is that Victor Dhostar has chosen as a confidant, who he trusts with all his schemes. Go on, guess."

The saurial shrugged.

"Kimbel."

Dragonbait shook his head in disbelief.

"Yes!" Olive insisted. "Kimbel, the geased assassin. The man whose idea of an amusing afternoon is torturing halflings. He and Victor both know that the croamarkh is the Faceless. They were talking about it."

*If Victor knew for sure, he would have told Alias*, the paladin insisted.

"Oh, he'll tell her," Olive said. "But not until the time is right."

*What time is that?*

"When he's certain he's properly positioned to be installed as croamarkh. The halflings at House Thalavar think he's had his eye on the position for eight years, ever since his father cheated him out of it by running for his third term. Lord Victor's an ambitious little viper, but he can't just squeal on his father. He has an image to uphold as the dutiful, loyal son. If Alias accuses Luer, she'll be the one to take the brunt of the nobles' anger for insulting one of their own. Victor will get the credit for helping her fight the Night Masks, but won't be blamed for turning on his father. He's using her, using the way everyone feels about her."

*You are speculating*, the paladin signed.

Olive hopped down from the chair and strode up to the paladin with her hands on her hips. "I am not speculating," she growled, stomping her foot soundlessly in the plush carpeting. "I heard him plotting to overthrow his father, plotting to take over as croamarkh, plotting to use Alias. Now, you have to decide who you're going to believe. There's me, who you've known for eleven years, who helped free you and Alias and Finder from the clutches of Cassana and Zrie and Phalse and who helped you free your people from Moander's slavery. Then there's this silver-tongued green-grocer who you don't know a thing about except that he looks good to your *shen* sight."

Dragonbait folded his hands together. He did not reply immediately, but Olive could tell from the hamlike scent of worry wafting from his neck glands that she'd gotten through to him. Finally he signed, *I must think more about this.*

"You do that," the halfling answered. "And while you're at it, think about how you're going to break it to Alias. She's likely to be upset, but she can't be kept in the dark. She's up to her neck in all this, and Westgate politics are even deadlier than the Westgate sewers. I'm going back to House Thalavar. I've managed to wrangle myself into duty as one of Lady Nettel's personal attendants for the ball, so I'll see you both there."

The halfling let herself out, leaving the paladin to brood over her words. It wasn't until Mercy came in with a tray of fruit and bread an hour later that the paladin even moved. He returned the girl's smile and curtsey with a brusque nod, then returned to his thoughts. The young half-elf shook her head at the stuffy smell in the room and opened a window before taking her leave. She couldn't think why the room smelled so of smoke, but then she was unaware that that was the scent of the saurial's fervent prayers.

\* \* \* \* \*

Lord Victor surveyed the robe and sash he'd had made especially to match Alias's gown. The swordswoman's elven dressmaker had been obnoxiously discreet about what the swordswoman was wearing. Victor had had to visit her personally to talk her out of the information. It was worth his trouble, though, since it was important that people associate him with Alias tonight. Costuming was only one of several subtle but effective methods to achieve that end.

Almost everything was in place for tonight. Before he dressed for the ball, though, he had one last piece of business with his father.

The croamarkh was where he'd been yesterday afternoon at the same time, indeed, where he could be found every afternoon, in his library, balancing the business accounts personally, double-checking the figures of his accountants, ship captains, customs agents, and warehouse guards. Any discrepancy resulted in angry bellowing to send for the person responsible for the error, even if the error was in the Dhostar clan's favor.

Victor entered the library and stood before his father's desk. "Father?" he said.

"Victor," Luer Dhostar replied curtly, looking up with irritation at the disturbance, his pen paused in midstroke. There was a trace of concern in his eyes. He never knew these days what his son might tell him next.

Victor remained standing silently in just the right spot to cast a shadow over the account book.

Finally the elder Dhostar asked, "Is there something you need?"

"Many things," Victor replied smoothly, inwardly pleased that he had managed to make his father ask him. "But first and foremost," he said, "I need to know if you have changed your mind about attending the masked ball this evening."

"You know I have *not*," Luer retorted, snapping off the last word like a dry twig. "You are consorting with the help. It's no different than being caught in a compromising position with a chambermaid. I will not be seen appearing to endorse such a relationship."

"I think you should reconsider," Victor stated. "This evening Alias is going to unmask the Faceless."

The croamarkh's forehead creased deeply with concern. He set down his quill pen and closed his account book. "She knows who the Faceless is?"

"She is very close," said Victor, "and she'll have the proof she needs by tonight."

"Why hasn't she come to me with this information?" Luer demanded. "That's what I hired her for."

"Why hasn't she?" Victor parroted. He shrugged. "Perhaps consorting with Jamal and her little troupe has given her a flair for street theater dramatics. Will you reconsider coming tonight?"

Luer shifted uncomfortably in his seat, remaining silent as he considered his options. After a few moments, he shook his head. "Send for her. She must tell me first. I can't have half the nobles up in arms if she is wrong."

Victor frowned down at his father. "She can tell you in private at the ball," he argued.

Luer's face clouded with anger. He rose to his feet and shouted, "I will not attend this cursed ball! Send for Alias now!"

A look of rage spasmed across Victor's face, but the croamarkh was not unaccustomed to his son's temper. Luer held his ground. In a moment, the younger Dhostar mastered his emotions, and his face transformed back to a mask of civility.

Victor lowered his eyes to the table and whispered, "I'm sorry, Father. It's over now."

"I should think so," Luer snapped. "These tantrums are beneath you. Now do as I ask, please."

Victor shook his head sadly. "I mean it's over for you. We know that you're the Faceless."

Luer's face turned scarlet, and for several moments, though his mouth moved, he seemed unable to reply. Finally, the words exploded from him, "That's preposterous! If that's what this cheap sell-sword thinks, I want her here now, before she does any more damage!"

"That's what she will think, and she has proof." Victor produced the key he'd shown to Alias and explained, "I found this among your possessions. It's the key to the former lair of the Night Masters and the Faceless."

"I never saw that key before," Luer declared.

"So you say, but I do not think that Alias will believe

you."

"We'll see about that," Luer growled. He reached out and yanked on the bellpull. Almost immediately Kimbel appeared in the doorway.

"I want you personally to fetch Alias and bring her here immediately," the croamarkh commanded the servant.

Kimbel looked at Victor. The younger Dhostar shook his head. Kimbel entered the room, closed the door behind him, and stood before it, silent and still.

The veins in Luer's face throbbed visibly. "What is the meaning of this?" he demanded.

"Tonight," Victor explained, "Alias, under my direction, will identify you as the Faceless, leader of the Night Masks. Enough evidence will be found among your possessions to offer proof of this accusation." The young noble slid around the desk and put a hand on his father's shoulder. "There is still a way out for you. A ship to Mulhorand is putting out to sea tonight just before the ball. You can take passage on that ship, leaving a document behind that will abdicate leadership of House Dhostar to me and recommend me for the post of croamarkh. I, in turn, will ensure that these awful revelations are never made public."

"If you believe me guilty, why would you do that?" Luer Dhostar asked with a laugh.

"To preserve the power of the nobles and the power of this family," Victor retorted. "There will be talk, naturally, but nothing will come of it. Then, in a few years, when the Night Masks are under control and all of the rumors have died, I will send for you. You can return as an elder statesmen." He gave his father's shoulder a reassuring squeeze.

"You think I will leave this house, this city, in your hands, knowing you have allied yourself with these criminals?"

Victor's brow knit in confusion. While he hadn't expected his father to accede readily to his demands, he was not prepared to meet with a counteraccusation. "It is not I who've aligned myself with the Night Masks, but you," he insisted, throwing his hands up in the air.

"I know about the smoke powder," Luer said.

"Smoke powder? What about it?"

"It occurred to me when Alias noted how much more common smoke powder is. She thought perhaps we weren't able to stop it from being smuggled in. She didn't know how efficient the sniffer dogs at the customs check are or just how much we've confiscated. It's all been recorded in the customs records. There should be quite a stockpile." The croamarkh poked a hard finger in his son's chest. "A stockpile I entrusted to you," he growled. "A stockpile I have since discovered has been seriously depleted. You've been selling it to them, haven't you? You've been supplying the Faceless with the smoke powder he uses in his evil schemes. You've made yourself his pawn."

Victor snorted derisively. "I am no one's pawn, old man. I control this game, and when it is through, Westgate will no longer be a squabbling collection of petty nobles, but a powerful kingdom—something I might have already accomplished if you had supported me as croamarkh. We might have avoided this whole ugly mess if only you had given me a chance to prove myself."

Luer's features softened for a moment, and he put his hands on his son's shoulders. "Whatever you've done," he said, "whatever hooks the Faceless has in you, I can put things right again. Escape yourself on that ship to Mulhorand, and I'll sort matters out on this end. Gods know, you're not the first noble scion I've had to pull from the mu—"

Luer's voice faltered, and he gasped and looked down at his chest. A dagger jutted from between his ribs, and Victor, who held the blade's handle, thrust it in deeper.

The green ichor in the blade's groove sizzled as it came into contact with the croamarkh's blood, and a black stain spread across the croamarkh's tunic.

Father looked at son with an unbelieving stare. His lips tried to issue the word "Why?" but the sound was blocked by a bloody foam pouring from his mouth.

A moment later, Lord Luer Dhostar, Patriarch of Clan Dhostar and Croamarkh of Westgate, crumpled to the floor in a heap.

"I'll pull *myself* out of the mud, Father," Victor replied coldly. "It is too bad you wouldn't do as I asked. It would have been so much more convenient for both of us." He looked up at Kimbel. The servant was grinning.

"I fail to see any humor in the situation," Victor snapped.

"It's the irony," Kimbel retorted. "Where the warrioress has been led astray, an accountant comes to the truth."

Victor sniffed in recognition of Kimbel's point, then ordered, "Get the body to the new hideout. When you finish that, begin to search and mark all the books with references to smoke powder so I have evidence of the former croamarkh's pilfering."

"And may I inquire as to your plans, Your Lordship?" the former assassin queried as he opened the library door.

"I have to get ready for the masquerade ball," Victor said with a laugh as he strolled from the room. "You know us merchants. Banes of the dance floor and dessert tables."

# Eighteen
# The Masquerade

Alias returned to Blais House in the late afternoon, lugging a red velvet gown made from so much fabric it weighed nearly as much as the adventurer's sword. Jamal accompanied her, carrying the baldric and the masks Alias had chosen for herself and Dragonbait. The saurial had gone out, but he returned just as Jamal was buttoning up the side of Alias's gown.

To Alias's questioning look the paladin explained in Saurial, "I've been to see Mintassan about a few matters."

"Anything in particular?" Alias asked as she slipped the diamond-patterned baldric over her head.

Dragonbait shot a glance at Jamal. The actress was beginning to fuss with Alias's hair. "It would be better in private," he answered.

On the pretext that Dragonbait was too modest to change with the actress about, Alias asked Jamal to excuse herself. The actress agreed, promising Alias she'd be waiting in the hotel lobby to see them off.

"Well?" Alias prompted once she'd closed the door behind Jamal.

"Olive was here earlier," the paladin explained.

"And?"

Dragonbait shifted uncomfortably. He didn't really know that he credited Olive's story, which made it very difficult for him to present it at all. Of course, if he actually believed the halfling, the truth would be even harder for him to reveal.

"She doesn't trust Victor Dhostar," the saurial said.

Alias chuckled as she worked her way into the white slippers Jamal had loaned her. "Neither does Jamal. It seems to be a way of life in Westgate—mistrusting all the noble merchants. According to Jamal, it should be a crime for people to make that much money for so little labor or talent."

"What do you think?" Dragonbait asked.

Alias tied her scabbard to the baldric she wore. "Well, I'm sure there's more than a few Haztor Urdos among them."

"I meant about Victor," the paladin explained.

Alias smiled. "Victor's different," she said. Dragonbait said nothing, but continued to stare at Alias until she felt obliged to elaborate. "He's wonderful, charming, clever, thoughtful, and, to use a phrase Jamal's fond of, he's a fine figure of a man."

"Olive thinks he lied to us about the key, that he did not enter the Faceless's lair the way he claimed, that he knows his father is the Faceless, that he is using you to depose him."

Alias glared at her companion. "That's ridiculous," she snapped.

"You do not think he suspects his father?"

"Of course he suspects his father. He's just loyal to him, the way I was to Finder, like you said. Remember? The day you told me how sky-blue virtuous he appeared?"

Dragonbait nodded. "Suppose I hadn't told you that. Would you think the same of him?"

"Of course I would," Alias said in an exasperated tone. "Because he is. It's not his fault his father might be a criminal."

"Olive thinks Victor must have used a different entrance to the lair and lied to us about using the key."

"Oh, and Olive has never been one to jump to conclusions," Alias said with sarcasm. "I'll find out about the key from Victor tonight. We'll get this settled then. You should be getting dressed. Victor will be here soon." She turned to the window and began vigorously yanking a brush through her hair.

Dragonbait changed into his best tunic and strapped on his sword. As he peace-bonded his weapon with a cord of silk, he said, "I spoke with Mintassan about the magic that makes the Faceless and the Night Masters undetectable."

Alias turned about. "Probably something like what makes me undetectable. Cassana could have bought or stole the skill from the priests of Leira. Durgar won't believe in the Faceless because he can't be detected by magic. I wonder, if he tried to detect me, would he conclude I don't exist, do you think?"

"No," the paladin replied. "Not if it contradicted the evidence of his eyes. Mintassan suspects that the Faceless's helmet of disguise was not the only piece of magic looted from the Temple of Leira before it was burned. There might have been objects that could misdirect other sorts of magical detection. Perhaps even something that could blind my *shen* sight."

From the street outside came the sound of carriage wheels rumbling on the cobblestones.

"That could explain why you read the croamarkh as completely neutral, if he is the Faceless, " Alias noted as she turned to look out the window.

Dragonbait nodded, but did not add his worse suspicion. He was unwilling to admit there was any magic that could thwart his *shen* sight, which was, to his mind, a gift from his god. Without proof, he could not bring himself to slander Lord Victor.

"That's Lord Victor's carriage," Alias announced, snatching up her porcelain mask. Her gown rustled as she swept toward the door in a most unladylike dash.

It was too late to say anything more, the paladin realized, picking up his own feathery mask. The timing was all wrong. She would not hear it anyway. Although she had made no admission, it was clear to him that she loved Victor Dhostar.

"Come on," Alias chided from the hallway. "I don't want to keep him waiting."

Dragonbait followed his companion from the room.

Victor stood at the bottom of the stairs, looking up at Alias with delight written all over his face. Was it possible, the saurial wondered, that the merchant's pleasure could be a ruse? With his *shen* sight, the paladin studied the man as he bowed low before Alias. Once more he saw nothing but the cool blue flame that symbolized virtue. Dragonbait shook himself. It was entirely possible that Olive was wrong and that Victor was everything he appeared. The paladin descended the stairs, determined to make no more judgments until he'd heard what the merchant noble had to say about the key and his father.

Victor made a polite, although less dramatic, bow to greet Dragonbait. From the corner of his eye the paladin caught sight of Jamal in the shadow of a pillar. She winked conspiratorially at the paladin as Victor ushered his guests out of the hotel.

From the anteroom behind the actress, a small voice noted, "They've dressed alike."

Jamal turned to face the little half-elven servant girl, Mercy. "Pardon?" the woman asked.

"Lord Victor and Mistress Alias," the girl explained. "The fabric of the sash about her waist is the same as her baldric—the same diamond design. And his tunic is dark red velvet, too. A darker shade than Mistress Alias's gown, but close. He has her favor on his tunic, too."

"Her favor?"

"She gave him a lock of her hair the other night. I saw her cut it off. I was watching from my window," Mercy admitted. "It was so romantic."

Jamal frowned. "It looked romantic. That's not always the same as being romantic," she muttered.

"No, Ma'am," the girl replied, too well trained to argue. She scurried off to avoid any further disagreeable comments. The aging actress leaned back against the pillar, realizing she must sound like an ill-tempered old maid. It was a curse, knowing so much. It made it impossible for her to suspend her disbelief and accept a fairy-tale romance as fact. Westgate nobles did not court for love, and they certainly did not court commoners. What was Victor Dhostar up to? she wondered.

\* \* \* \* \*

The ride to the Tower, where the ball was to be held, was brief but lively. Victor steered the carriage skillfully through streets full of people apparently gathered to watch the pageantry of the nobles in their splendor. The crowds recognized not only Lord Victor but Alias as well, and cheers and shouts greeted them all the way to the market. Still, Alias felt compelled by Dragonbait's dour look to lean over and ask the merchant noble, "Have you spoken with your father?"

Victor nodded and returned a wave to a gathering in an outdoor cafe. "I'll tell you about it later, in private."

The watch was posted around the perimeter of the market, allowing only those who had an invitation to the ball to approach. Victor pulled his carriage up to the edge of the green. A member of the watch in buffed leather armor and a white capelet with a white plume jutting from his helmet helped Alias down from the carriage. Victor's elderly driver stepped up from the green to take the horses' reins from his master and move the carriage out of the way of newer arrivals.

Lord Victor donned his mask, a mere strip of red velvet with eyeholes bordered with gold stitching. Alias and Dragonbait did likewise, then their host led them up a path covered with ornate carpets. The market had been cleared of its mercantile trappings, leaving the crowds about the green a clear view of the nobles as they climbed the path to the Tower.

The Tower was alight with magical faerie fire, which formed the symbols of all the noble houses of Westgate, from Athagdal to Vhammos. Alias shuddered to think about all the nobles' homes guarded only by sleepy servants. The Night Masks must make quite a haul on nights like these, she realized.

There was a small queue of glittering nobles inside the Tower's entrance.

"What are we waiting for?" Alias whispered.

"This is a formal ball," he explained. "We must be announced, so the others present know we are here."

"And can give us the once-over," Alias mused.

"Don't worry," Victor said. "You look radiant."

When they reached the front of the queue, Victor leaned over to give their names to the acting seneschal, another member of the watch with a white capelet and white plume.

"Lord Victor of House Dhostar," the seneschal announced. "Alias, Foe of the Faceless, and Dragonbait, Companion of Alias."

"Foe of the Faceless?" Alias repeated with disbelief, her laughter muffled behind her mask.

"It's the thought on everyone's mind, here," said Victor. "You might as well admit it."

Dragonbait pushed on his mask, which kept slipping up on his reptilian muzzle. He wished irritably that the Foe of the Faceless had not chosen him a mask with feathers. They kept tickling his eyes.

The interior of the Tower was awash with light. Hundreds of candles burned from a large central chandelier of cast iron, and all about the perimeter hung magical globes of light enchanted to appear as if salamanders and efreeti were dancing inside the orbs. Two great mirrors hung opposite one another, reflecting back into the room all the light they caught and creating the illusion of two infinite corridors filled with revelers.

The watch officers' desks had become buffet tables, and a ten-piece orchestra was playing a rondo. A dozen couples occupied the center of the floor, spinning in their own little orbits around an imaginary central point. The stairs to the upper levels were blocked by more of the watch, decked in white plumage.

The guests' clothing was rich and varied, but it was the masks that impressed Alias the most. They ranged from simple domino masks and silk veils to full face sculptures of papier maché and enamel. There were silvered globes of the sort worn by priests of Leira, the goddess of illusion, and more than a few veils of strung coins or beads. Most amusing were the masks that were common to street theaters everywhere: the Merchant, the Gossip, the Red Wizard, the Cat Burglar, the Twins.

Alias spotted Durgar dressed in his silvered armor but wearing the mask of the Doctor, a pompous character in street plays who always offered bad advice. With its high forehead, bulbous nose, and thick handlebar mustache, the mask looked like a parody of Durgar's own face. The swordswoman would never have credited the priest with such a sense of humor.

Catching sight of Haztor Urdo's black, puffed out hair, Alias paused to watch him. The Night Mask noble was wearing the mask of another theater staple—Captain Crocodile, the foolish, brash young warrior who blusters, but at heart seeks only love. Haztor was flirting with a woman dressed in an extremely low-cut gown made of fabric covered in mirrored facets and a silvered globe mask. Alias watched them just long enough to see the woman slap the young man and stalk off.

Alias chuckled. "Their battles are fought at the ball," she quoted.

"Pardon?" Victor asked.

"A song that my—" She hesitated a moment. "That Finder Wyvernspur wrote about nobility in general," she explained. In a low voice audible only to Victor and Dragonbait, adjusting to the rhythm of the orchestra, Alias sang softly:

> "For all of their dancing,
> Posturing, prancing,
> They'll fight with their backs to the wall.
> Till then they are eating
> And drinking and meeting;
> Their battles are fought at the ball."

Victor smiled. "That sounds like Westgate," he agreed. "Good evening, Lady Nettel," he said.

Alias turned to greet the elderly Thalavar matriarch. The noblewoman was dressed as before, in a black velvet gown and her verdigris feather brooch, her only concession to the masquerade a bit of white silk tied about her eyes, with eyeholes cut into it. In her wake she pulled her niece, Thistle, and Olive Ruskettle.

Olive cut a dashing figure in the green-and-white Thalavar livery, which included a huge, floppy hat bedecked with a great green plume. She wore a mask of silver glittering with fake emeralds. Alias could see other halflings in the crowd similarly costumed.

Thistle wore a veil of fine white lace over her face and was bedecked in a pink gown with a very high collar and short, ballooning sleeves. Long pink gloves covered her lower arms. As she approached Alias, her eyes were glittering with excitement.

"See what I have?" the young woman exclaimed, holding out her right arm for Alias to see.

Thistle's right glove was embroidered with a blue stitchwork very similar to Alias's own tattoo. Waves and thorns crested from wrist to elbow, but where Alias's pattern displayed a rose, the young noblewoman's featured a thistle.

Alias nodded politely, grateful that her face was masked and her amusement hidden.

"It is a compromise," Lady Nettel explained with a smile, "one that might keep her from attempting any major transformations in her appearance for a few months. Victor, I do not see your father here."

"My father was . . . detained," Victor replied, avoiding Alias's look. "He's asked me to stand in his stead until his arrival."

Alias was about to pull Victor aside and demand that he elaborate on his last statement, but Olive was tugging on the swordswoman's bodice to get her attention. "Did you and Dragonbait talk?" she whispered anxiously.

Alias frowned down at the halfling, wishing now that the mask she wore did not hide her displeasure. "This is not a good time, Olive," she growled.

Olive lowered her eyelids suspiciously, but with Lord Victor so near she did not dare elaborate. "Fine. I guess I'll go check out the buffet table."

Alias turned back to Victor, who was making excuses to Lady Nettel that he needed to circulate. Thistle asked Dragonbait to escort her and her grandmother about the room. The paladin nodded his assent. As he let each Thalavar woman take an arm and draw him off, he tilted his head in Victor's direction. His meaning was perfectly clear to the swordswoman.

"You said your father was going to be here," Alias

declared heatedly.

"He is," Victor replied, nodding at a passing Thorsar dignitary. "We . . . talked this afternoon. When I showed him the key, he looked surprised, but he wouldn't speak about it. He promised that he would come later to talk to you and Durgar before the end of the ball."

"Victor," Alias stressed, "you have to go to Durgar with this right now. Your father could be using this time to flee the city."

Victor shook his head. "My father isn't going to flee. This is his city. I think maybe the key belonged to another noble, and Father is covering for him. He just needs time to decide how to handle this gracefully."

Alias shook her head at Victor's stubborn loyalty to the croamarkh. Part of her wanted to bolt the party immediately and track down Luer Dhostar, while the other part was willing to wait for Victor's sake, even though it probably meant losing the Faceless. She sighed and nodded. "I'll wait," she said.

"Good. Then, since you're waiting, we may as well dance. Would you do me the honor?" Victor asked, extending his arm. He froze for a moment as an uncomfortable thought occurred to him. "You can dance, can't you?" he asked.

"I can manage," Alias replied with a laugh.

Victor called the dance a Westgate procession, but Alias knew it as a Shadowdale reel. It was simple and repetitive, but Alias found herself enjoying it nonetheless. The orchestra was skilled and lively, and the nobles on the dance floor at least showed her no animosity. She looked into Victor's blue eyes, and her heart soared.

Along the sidelines, Dragonbait stood listening politely to Thistle as the young woman explained the origins of all the different food on the buffet table. All the while, he stared at Victor Dhostar, wondering whether Olive could be right.

The halfling popped up beside him, munching on a sticky roll. "*Shen* sight still out of focus, eh?" she taunted, noting the look with which he fixed the croamarkh's son. "You could stand on your head. Maybe that would turn everything right side up." She wandered off to another table for some liquid refreshment.

The saurial glared after her for a moment, then smiled. Only Olive could suggest something so ridiculous that might actually have merit. Not upside down, but backward, the paladin thought. He turned about to face the buffet. As Thistle chattered on about the longer growing season required for melons, the paladin closed his eyes and reached out with his *shen* sight.

He let the myriad colors slide along his consciousness. He stopped, focusing on a very dark purple to his right. He peeked out one eye. Kimbel, the former assassin, stood on a staircase, watching the guests from behind the guards.

Dragonbait closed his eye again. In a moment, he could sense a deep red hatred speckled with green jealousy. The paladin confirmed his guess. Haztor Urdo, hating Alias, jealous of Victor's pleasure in her company.

With his eyes squeezed tightly shut, the paladin let the colors wash over him longer, until he could sense their pattern as they moved about the blue that he knew must be Alias, as they stepped back from her, circled around her, pulled her close.

Blackness like a shroud covered the blue flame of Alias's spirit, blackness so dark, it devoured the light from her, giving up none of it. Blackness was the lust for power, the voracious appetite for control over all others, the desire that swallowed its tail and devoured the being's own universe.

Dragonbait whirled and glared at the man holding Alias in his arms. Once again, where Victor stood, the paladin saw the blue flame so like Alias's. Now he concentrated on what lay beneath the blue. As if Victor's soul were a canvas, he stared at it for the pentimento that lay beneath the illusion of virtue painted on the surface.

Then he could see it—the image that lay beneath what Victor had seemed. There were pits of blackness filled with black serpents, all poised to devour whatever came their way. As Victor reached a hand out to the swordswoman, Dragonbait saw a serpent wind about the flame of Alias's spirit, prepared to crush the life from it before making it a meal. Despite himself, Dragonbait let out a mewling cry and nearly toppled forward.

It was a moment before he could gather his *shen* sight back into whatever spot it rested when not in use. He saw a flame of blue, tinged with a little green jealousy just before his vision cleared. Thistle stood before him, her hands resting gently on his shoulders. "Are you all right?" she asked slowly, in a manner that presumed that because he did not speak her tongue, he could not hear or easily understand it.

The paladin nodded, tapping his chest to indicate he'd only swallowed something the wrong way.

As Thistle turned to get a glass of water for the saurial, Dragonbait watched Victor with new insight. He remembered how Mist had claimed the noble was a pawn to his ambition and desires. The wyrm always did have a talent for understatement, the paladin thought with a wry sense of amusement.

The dance ended, and Alias strode from the dance floor, hand in hand with Victor. Dragonbait excused himself from Thistle and moved toward the couple.

"I must speak with you," the paladin said to Alias in saurial, "alone."

"Can't it wait?" Alias asked, eager to reach the refreshment table and ease her parched throat.

The paladin shook his head to indicate it could not. With a sigh, the swordswoman excused herself from Lord Victor's company. She followed the saurial to a less-crowded section of the room.

"What is it?" Alias asked. She removed her mask and spoke in Saurial so that she would not be overheard. "Night Masks?"

"No, it is Victor," Dragonbait replied. "Olive is right. We cannot trust him."

"Would you forget about Olive? She doesn't know what she's talking about."

"It is not just Olive. I have seen it with my *shen* sight. He is corrupted. He is an evil man."

"Four days ago your *shen* sight saw he was virtuous,"

Alias argued heatedly.

"I was deceived somehow. Some illusion covered the truth."

"How do you know you aren't being deceived now?" Alias demanded.

"Olive convinced me that I was wrong."

"I think Olive talked you into seeing something that isn't there," Alias snapped. She burst into a tirade, which consisted of several growls and clicks audible to the other party goers around them, and a few of them glanced nervously in her direction. "I'm tired of hearing about your *shen* sight, of the way you judge everyone with it. There's more to people than your paladin visions. What they say and what they do is what really matters. That's how I *know* Victor is good," she declared. She spun around and bolted off.

\* \* \* \* \*

While the swordswoman and the paladin argued, Kimbel slipped up behind Lord Victor.

"Is everything in place?" the merchant asked.

"Yes, but there may be a problem," the servant whispered. "The lizard was studying you and seemed to have an attack of some kind. I suspect he has seen past the illusion projected by your amulet of misdirection."

"Bloody hell," Victor muttered. "He's talking with Alias now."

"I suggest you continue with the plan," Kimbel said. "If there is a problem, you can deal with her once you are alone. I can deal with the lizard."

"Remove him, but do not kill him yet," Victor ordered. "She might be able to sense that somehow. Make it appear innocent."

"As if he left town in a fit of paladin snobbery," Kimbel suggested.

"Yes. Nice touch," Victor agreed. "Go."

The former assassin slipped away. Victor looked in Alias and Dragonbait's direction. Alias appeared to be arguing with the paladin, which was certainly a good sign. The merchant lord spotted Thistle Thalavar standing beside her imposing grandmother. The girl was as good a pawn as any, Lord Victor thought. He hurried over to ask her to dance.

Alias returned to the spot where she'd left Victor, only to discover he'd escorted Thistle Thalavar out to the dance floor. She slipped her mask back on, grateful for the way it hid her fury. She watched as Thistle seemed to hang on Victor's every word. The merchant lord may think of her as a child, but it was obvious the young girl thought of him as a hero. Alias felt miserable standing alone in the room full of people, but she could hardly blame Victor for abandoning her. After all, he was supposed to mix with the guests. The swordswoman was just toying with the idea of finding herself another dance partner when Victor and Thistle parted company. Thistle moved in Dragonbait's direction and Victor came toward Alias.

The young noblewoman soon cornered her quarry and dragged the saurial onto the dance floor for a quadrille.

"I thought your friend could use a little coaxing onto the dance floor," the nobleman explained as he rejoined the swordswoman. "He looks far too dour for a celebration. Thistle said she'd see what she could— Alias, what's wrong?"

"Nothing," Alias retorted hurriedly. "What makes you think something's wrong?"

"Well, you're shaking, for one thing," Victor replied as he placed his warm hands on her shoulders. "And, well, with your complexion, you do tend to color when you're angry. Even your shoulders are red. Perhaps we should talk in private. Come upstairs with me."

The white-caped guards on the stairs parted for the son of Luer Dhostar and his guest. Halfway up the stairs, Alias shot a glance down at the dance floor. Dragonbait was acquitting himself admirably, keeping up with Thistle's steps, but the swordswoman could tell his heart was not in the motions.

Victor hesitated before opening the door to the conference suite. "I need to explain something. I was planning on asking you up here to—to talk. I realize maybe this is a bad time for it, so please don't misunderstand."

He swung open the door, and Alias felt her heart melting despite her anger. The drab conference room had been transformed into a romantic faerie realm. The large table was glittering from lit tapers of perfumed wax. Bolts of silk fabric and oversized pillows covered the floor between the table and the hearth, where a fire blazed and crackled. A bottle of Evermead, two glasses, and a platter of fruits and cheeses sat on a tray beside the hearth.

"We can just sit at the table, if it will make you more comfortable," Victor said.

Alias stepped into the room, and Victor followed, pushing the door closed behind them. Feeling a little foolish, she walked past the table and sat down on one of the pillows. She inspected the bottle of Evermead. It was more than a hundred years old.

"Now, tell me what's wrong," Victor insisted, sinking onto a cushion beside her.

Alias shook her head. "It's nothing, Victor . . . really. Dragonbait and I just had an argument. He can be so—so—Oh! It just doesn't make any sense! Victor, have you been telling me the truth about your father?" she demanded.

Victor looked into the flames of the fire. "No," he admitted softly.

Alias removed her mask, then reached up and untied the strings of the fabric covering Victor's eyes and pulled it away. She laid both masks down on the pillow beside her. Then she said, "Victor, you have to tell me everything you know."

"You have to understand," Victor said, looking her in the eye. "I love my father. I'm sure he thinks somehow what he's doing is right. He's not an evil man, Alias. He's just—well, he's just so certain that he's always right."

"You know he's involved with the Night Masks?"

"I've suspected it for some time. There hasn't been any money missing, but I guess he's been making some other kind of payments. He's in charge of all the smoke powder the city confiscates. There's a lot of it. It isn't all in the warehouse where the books say it should be. When I told him I'd found the key, I also told him I'd discovered about the smoke powder. He seemed pretty shaken. He asked me to cover for him, to give him time to take care of some personal matters. He promised me, though, that he would come here tonight and explain things to you and Durgar."

The young man looked away, and Alias could see there were tears in his eyes. "It doesn't look good, does it?" he asked.

"No. It doesn't," Alias agreed.

"You'd better go back downstairs," Victor said. "It would be better for you if you weren't seen with me, I think."

"Why not?" Alias demanded.

"My father is going to be the center of a scandal, Alias. He could be involved with the Night Masks. Gods! He might even be the Faceless. I have to stand beside him, but there's no reason for you to be involved."

"Victor, no," Alias said, feeling her heart breaking for the young man's pain. "Look. I can't approve of your father, but I love you. I'm not going to abandon you because of something your father did."

"I love *you*," Victor replied, "which is why I can't allow you to stay. I don't want your name dragged down with ours."

"If you love me," Alias whispered vehemently, "you'll let me stay."

Victor smiled sadly. He ran his finger across her cheek, then down her neck and along her shoulder. "You are so very beautiful," he whispered. "You made me feel so lucky."

Alias put her hand behind the nobleman's neck and pulled his face close to her own. "I am not leaving you. You say you love me. Prove it," she demanded, and she threw her arms about his neck and pressed her lips against his own.

Lord Victor slid one hand about the swordswoman's waist to pull her closer as his other hand rested over Alias's porcelain mask, covering its eyes completely.

\* \* \* \* \*

Below, in the main room of the Tower, the interminably long quadrille had ended and Dragonbait excused himself from Thistle Thalavar's company as quickly as good manners allowed. Now he scanned the crowded room for either Alias or Victor. In the end, it was Olive who found him. She tugged anxiously on the hem of his tunic.

*Where is she?* he signed surreptitiously.

The halfling jerked her finger in the direction of the stairway. "With Lord Victor," she growled. "Didn't you talk to her?"

Dragonbait cursed in Saurial and began pushing his way through the crowd, toward the stairs. He managed to climb four steps before his way was blocked by a wall of leather armor and white plumes.

Dragonbait hesitated, considering whether he should fetch Olive to translate his need to the guard or whether he should just shove his way past them. He had just decided on the more forceful option when the screaming began.

The paladin wheeled just in time to see a huge figure leap down from one of the mirrors mounted on the wall and land with a great *thoom* on the stone floor. The creature was twice the size of a human, kettle black, with a head shaped like a dragon's. An identical creature had already landed on a young noble, who screamed as his legs were crushed beneath the monster's weight. The saurial recognized the figures as iron golems from the lair of the Faceless. A third appeared in the mirror, pausing only for the first two to move out of the way before it, too, leaped down onto the floor.

The crowd was already panicking, driving like a herd of cattle for the entrance, only to find that the portcullis to the entrance had been lowered. Those in the rear were being decapitated by blows from the iron golems' fists, while those in the front were being crushed by their fellow guests.

A fourth and a fifth golem emerged from the mirror before the guardsmen poured off the stairs to meet the assault.

Dragonbait hovered uncertainly. He could search upstairs for Alias or battle the creatures. As a sixth golem appeared in the mirror, he knew he must act. With a sharpened claw, he cut the peace-bonded cord from his weapon and drew his blade. Then he launched himself at the magical mirror, swinging his sword.

The mirror shattered in a burst of light. Glass rained on the guests, but if there were any other golems, they would not be entering the Tower as easily as the first six had.

The paladin crunched broken glass beneath his feet as he landed. He turned in time to witness Haztor Urdo, with his sword drawn, run toward the sixth golem. The nobleman feinted to the right, then struck the creature on the opposite leg, but his blade broke on the monster's iron surface. The golem grabbed the youth by the arm, slammed him hard against the wall, then released him. Haztor's body slid down the wall, leaving a long, bloody smear, his Captain Crocodile mask still smiling.

With a snarl, the paladin leaped onto the shoulder of one of the creatures. He knew heat helped such creatures repair themselves, so he did not ignite his sword. Fortunately, the weapon carried other powerful enchantments, so the blade bit deep into the side of the creature's face, parting it like butter.

The golem reached up to grab the saurial, but the ornate dragon head prevented it from reaching its assailant. Dragonbait struck again and again with his sword, reducing the golem to spinning around in place while swatting ineffectually at the saurial.

The other five golems were not so distracted. The swords of the watch did not carry the necessary enchantments to slice through magically enlivened iron, and the monsters carved a wide swath through watchmen and party-goers alike. The frightened nobles' only hope was to dodge between the beasts.

Durgar's voice rose above the din, and Dragonbait caught a glimpse of the old priest, his mace glowing with its own eldritch power, smashing huge dents into one of the iron creatures. The golem was swift enough to grab Durgar by the arm, however, and it tossed the old man aside easily and moved back into the crowd, punching and crushing anyone in its path. The priest of Tyr landed heavily, but he rose, albeit unsteadily, and returned to the fray.

A smattering of magic missiles *plinked* without effect on a golem's surface, indicating a few nobles were not above learning the Art. At least one mage must have had some advanced training, for he sent a lightning bolt arcing across the room. The bolt struck two golems and a handful of nobles. The humans collapsed to the ground, but the golems were slowed.

The situation was deteriorating quickly. With the golem beneath him cracking along its entire length and breadth, Dragonbait leaped clear and vaulted up the stairs, three at a time. Alias could help turn the tide of the battle, if he could only find her.

Kimbel stood waiting at the first landing, with a double-loaded drow crossbow aimed at the paladin. Dragonbait could smell as well as see the resinous putty smeared on the bolts' tips, but he wasn't quick enough to dodge the missiles. The first caught the saurial in the shoulder, the second in the chest. Dragonbait hissed and lunged in an attempt to skewer the assassin, but he fell short and crumpled into a heap on the stairs.

"Looking for your mistress?" Kimbel taunted, lowering the crossbow. "I'm sorry, but she's occupied right now." He motioned for two men in guardsmen uniforms to collect the saurial's body.

On the main floor, a tight knot of halflings surrounded Lady Nettel as Olive Ruskettle tried with limited success to keep any approaching golems from turning their attention on the matriarch. Lady Nettel was leaning heavily on a spear, which she had plucked from a fallen guardsmen. Just when it seemed as if Olive had managed to send one golem off to seek easier prey, Lady Nettel shrieked, "Thistle!"

Olive spotted the young noblewoman collapsed on the floor with a golem hovering uncertainly over her.

Olive dashed forward, but Lady Nettel was faster. The head of House Thalavar barged through her ring of bodyguards and stepped right between the iron colossus and her granddaughter. The old lady swung her spear to ward off the monster, but the shaft snapped like a twig against the creature's iron arms. As Olive dragged Thistle back to the uncertain safety of the ring of halfling bodyguards, the golem lifted Lady Nettel in both arms and squeezed. Even above the din, Olive swore she could hear the sound of the old woman's back breaking. Then the monster, disinterested in the dead, dropped Nettel Thalavar's crushed, mangled body and wandered off.

Olive dashed over to Lady Nettel's broken form; Thistle followed directly behind her, ignoring the bodyguards who tried to hold her back by tugging on the skirt of her gown. Astonishingly, the old woman still breathed, but she was twisted in an odd, inhuman fashion, and Olive could tell she was fading before their eyes. The dying woman called for Thistle.

Thistle bent close to her grandmother's face. "You are . . . my heir," Nettel Thalavar wheezed. "Take . . . the feather pin."

Thistle began to cry, but Lady Nettel pushed her aside and grabbed Olive by the tabard. She gasped once, then whispered vehemently, "Protect . . . my . . . granddaughter!" The noblewoman never drew another breath. Her face spasmed into a contortion that looked anything but peaceful and froze.

Thistle Thalavar, new leader of House Thalavar, gently unpinned her grandmother's copper brooch. As her tears splashed on her grandmother's corpse, she fastened the brooch to her own gown. Then she and Olive fled to the halflings' last defensive position, under a buffet table.

# Nineteen
# The Unmasking

Ultimately it was a mild-mannered gate crasher who managed to turn the tide. Yielding to Dragonbait's request, Mintassan had been keeping an eye on the proceedings at the ball. Cloaked in an invisibility spell, he had slipped past the seneschal and stood quietly in the corner, wearing the mask of a bearded, graying wizard with pipe clenched between his teeth. The paladin had not been able to even guess what might go wrong at the ball, but once the golems had arrived, the sage knew exactly how to bring the situation under control.

Magic being nearly useless against such monsters, Mintassan teleported back to his home. There, on his desk, tucked in box full of straw, was the remedy for iron golems. He had prepared it this morning after realizing the Faceless still controlled a troop of the creatures. Arriving in the back of his workroom, the sage dashed to his desk, prepared to scoop up his secret weapons and teleport back immediately. He halted before the desk and nearly froze in panic. The objects he sought were missing.

Fortunately, Mintassan was far more levelheaded than his reputation credited him. He also was not so old that he could not remember being a boy and the sorts of things boys enjoyed doing.

"Kel!" he hollered, dashing up the stairs two at a time. He threw open the door to the boy's room and gave a great sigh of relief. The box lay on the bed, three glass globes packed within. Kel sat on the floor, waving a nail in front of a fourth glass globe. Within the globe a tiny insectlike creature pawed frantically at the glass ball, causing it to roll after the nail almost as if the ball were magnetically attracted to the iron.

"I was just playing," the boy insisted.

Mintassan snatched up the box and the fourth globe and hissed, "Silver path, tower stair."

Before Kel's astonished eyes, the sage vanished.

Mintassan reappeared in the Tower on one of the staircases. Grimly he assessed the battlefield. Only one golem had actually been felled, lying in two twitching halves on the floor. Durgar was hammering on a second golem's legs with such determination that the creature was limping noticeably, but then so was the old priest.

With an uncanny aim, Mintassan threw one ball each at the remaining four unscathed golems. The glass smashed against the iron monsters, releasing the tiny creatures within. They grew as they fell, so that by the time they hit the floor they were five feet in length, each sporting four insectlike legs, an armor-plated back, a long, bony tail with a paddle-shaped tip, and, most importantly, long mobile antennae. They were easily recognizable by the few experienced adventurers present as rust monsters—normally docile animals with a voracious appetite for all things iron.

The first freed rust monster struck its antennae against the legs of the iron golem looming over it. The golem's legs turned brown and crumbled beneath it, so that it toppled to the floor, crippled.

The second rust monster took a moment longer to get its bearings, giving the golem beside it time to reach down and grab it—a serious error on the golem's part. The rust monster's antennae wrapped around both arms like whips. The golem's arms crumbled to rust, freeing the rust monster it had just grasped. The golem stumbled off as the rust monster chomped on the rusted remains of its arms. Though able to move, the golem was now unable to continue grappling or punching at the guests, though it continued to chase them.

One rust monster was slain by a powerful strike of a golem's fist, but as the iron behemoth pulled away, it lost its hand at the wrist, struck by one of the dying animal's antennae. The fourth and final rust monster scrambled on top of its golem, rusting it from the head down to the shoulders and arms, through the torso, and down to the knees. The ferrous-loving animal rolled about in the huge pile of rust as it chomped on it like a cat in a field of catnip.

Having thrown all his weapons, Mintassan looked about for Dragonbait. Just before he'd teleported to his workshop to fetch the rust monsters, the sage had seen the paladin slashing at one of the golems. Now, however, the saurial was nowhere to be seen. There had to be nearly fifty people dead and dying on the Tower floor, but the saurial was not among them.

As the watch, under Durgar's direction, dragged a rust monster in the direction of one of the remaining mobile golems, some other members of Durgar's forces had managed to raise the portcullis to the outside. Nobles streamed out of the Tower like ants from a flooded nest. The sage was just about to teleport to the temple of Ilmater to fetch some priests to heal the wounded, when he spied Kimbel exiting through the portcullis.

The Dhostar manservant looked not only uninjured, but completely unruffled, as did the two guards in Dhostar livery who followed him carrying a lumpy, rolled up tapestry. With a suspicious frown, the sage reached in his pocket for a spell component and whispered, "Lightpass." His large form went translucent, then transparent, then invisible. Once transformed, the mage hurried after the former assassin, his minions, and whatever it was they found necessary to cart off.

\* \* \* \* \*

Upstairs, isolated from the noise of the attack by the massiveness of the Tower's construction, Alias lay with Victor Dhostar before the fireplace of the conference room. Shaking off the elegant torpor that enthralled her, she raised her head from Victor's chest and looked up at him. "I love you," she whispered.

"I love you, too," the nobleman replied, "but now that

you have your proof of that, we really should be getting
back to the ball."

Alias nodded. She rose to her feet and shook out the
wrinkles in the skirt of her gown. Victor handed her her
baldric and sword. She slipped the decorative belt over
her head.

As soon as Victor opened the heavy oaken door, Alias
heard disturbing sounds coming from the hall below. The
thunderous crash of something heavy falling to the floor
echoed up the Tower. When she reached the stairs, Alias
could hear people screaming and moaning. She raced
down the stairs. Halfway down, she spied Mintassan in
front of her, but he vanished before her eyes. When she
reached the spot where the sage had stood, she was
aghast at the destruction she witnessed.

Members of the watch were pulling on a rope wrapped
about the legs of an armless iron golem in an effort to topple
the monster. Several other bits of iron golem lay strewn
about the floor, surrounded by dead and wounded nobles.
One last golem, missing only a hand, was hovering over a
desk that was serving as a buffet. The monster looked as if
it were trying to decide what to eat, but Alias spied something rustling beneath the tablecloth and realized the golem
was deciding how to get at whomever hid below.

Just before the golem struck the desk with his remaining hand, crushing it to splinters, Olive Ruskettle and
Thistle Thalavar dashed out from beneath the tenuous
cover. They ran toward another desk, with the creature
plodding after them. When it had them against the wall,
Olive Ruskettle whirled about, her sword raised, in a
hopeless effort to ward off the creature's blow.

Alias released the peace knot tying her sword to her
scabbard and drew her weapon. The swordswoman
leaped from the stairs onto the golem just as it raised its
remaining fist. Her sword connected with the golem's
dragon-shaped head, sending sparks flying as the steel of
her magical blade cleaved through the iron skull.

The beast spun about and seemed to examine Alias for a
moment. Then it turned again, pivoting slowly, stopping
when it finally faced Olive and Thistle. Alias realized she

was being ignored for a target of higher priority—either
Olive or Thistle. Yanking free the tablecloth from the
smashed desk, Alias whirled it like a net over the golem's
head.

"Olive, Thistle, quick! Hide," the swordswoman shouted
as she slashed at the creature's leg with her sword.
"Then stay very still."

Olive dragged Thistle down behind the remains of a
deceased noble, pulling the dead man's cloak over their
bodies. Thistle started to argue, but the halfling stifled
her protest with a quick elbow in the ribs.

Alias slashed into the golem's leg, and the monster
turned toward her as it tugged the tablecloth off its head.
Upon spying the swordswoman, however, the golem once
again ignored her in favor of scanning the room for its
previous prey.

From the staircase, Victor looked on the carnage in
shock and muttered, "Sweet Mystra," an oath to the goddess of magic. Hearing the nobleman, the golem turned
toward the stair.

"Victor, get back up the stairs and stay there!" Alias
ordered, shifting so that she stood between the monster
and the staircase. "It seems to be interested only in the
nobles."

Alias couldn't tell if the nobleman obeyed her, but the
golem spun about, once more checking for targets. Then
it turned again. Finding no more nobility to smite, it
made its way for the exit.

A rust monster, bloated from gorging on more iron
than it usually ate in a year, made a halfhearted wave at
the retreating golem with an antenna, but did not bother
to pursue the iron creature. The golem passed beneath
the portcullis and trundled from the Tower.

Durgar, who knelt beside a bloodied but still breathing
member of House Athagdal, looked up at Alias. "Follow
the golem," he ordered her. "I will follow when I can. Go
with Alias," he instructed three of his watchmen, who
stood by uncertainly.

Alias dashed from the Tower with the watch behind
her.

The injured golem was halfway down the Tower hill, moving northwest. Alias had no trouble keeping up with the monster, which even at top speed was ponderously slow. The swordswoman remained behind it and instructed the watch to do likewise. With mounting excitement, she realized the golem may actually lead her back to its point of origin—the Faceless's new lair.

Alias was just wondering what had happened to Dragonbait when Victor ran up beside her, sword in hand.

"You shouldn't be here," she said vehemently.

"I have to see where the golem goes. As long as I don't let myself get cornered, I can always outrun it," the nobleman argued.

Alias nodded, unable to counter Victor's logic or his desire to see this through to the end.

The golem moved through the streets without incident. Any nobles that were left in the city were no doubt at home piling furniture in front of the doors, and no one else in the streets was so foolish as to challenge the monster.

Finally the golem halted before a ramshackle warehouse near the House Urdo docks. It banged once on the door, which swung open, bathing the golem in a yellow glow. The monster disappeared inside.

Alias ordered Victor and the watchmen to remain at the warehouse gate as she crept up to the door. The golem stood just inside, unmoving, as if awaiting instructions. Alias slipped past the creature, turned about, and tapped on its chest with the tip of her sword. The creature loomed over her, but remained perfectly still.

The swordswoman waved for the others to join her. Alias kept an eye on the golem as Victor entered the room, but the noble's appearance did not reactivate the monster. Its killing spree was over for the time being.

The room was a cavernous vault. In the center stood a great table of ebony stone glittering with veins of gold, a twin to the one in the Night Masters' last conference room. Most of the ten chairs surrounding it were pushed out, a few overturned, but the tenth chair remained against the table. What appeared to be a man was slumped in the chair. The man's face was obscured by

some strange magic, which blurred its features like rain
damages a chalk portrait. A bloodstain clotted his robes.
He was as immobile as the golem.

On the table before the figure lay a sheet of paper.
Scrawled in blood was the message, "Death to all who
betray and defy our will, noble or common, Night Mask
or outsider. So say the Night Masters."

As Alias was examining the sheet of paper, Durgar
entered. He had battled the golems until they were no
longer a threat, then spent his last remaining energies
casting magical curative spells on the wounded. The old
priest looked drained, but he would not, Alias realized,
forsake what he perceived to be his duty.

Durgar stepped forward and took the paper from
Alias's hand. He scowled angrily at the words. Without
ceremony, his face as emotionless as the golems', the
priest ran his hand down the dead figure's face. A jingling mask of threaded coins came away in his hand.

The illusory blur of the Faceless became the features of
Croamarkh Luer Dhostar.

Alias reached out to steady Victor, who swayed in
shock and gasped, "Sweet Mystra! It can't really be true."

Durgar collapsed into the nearest empty chair, drop-
ping the mask onto the table and cradling his head in his
hands. "The croamarkh in league with the Night Masks.
I can't believe it," the old priest whispered.

"It's true, Your Reverence," Alias said. "We have other
evidence linking him to them. No doubt they turned on
him for some perceived betrayal. Perhaps they decided to
turn their golems loose against the nobles, but Lord Luer
fought against them. Perhaps the golems perceived he
was a noble and turned on him first. Perhaps—"

"Perhaps once I have recovered my powers I should
cast a spell to speak with Luer's dead spirit," the priest
said gravely. "Then we will get to the heart of the matter.
There will be no— Look out!" Durgar shouted suddenly.

Alias spun about, her sword at the ready, just in time
to see the golem bat away the watchmen who stood guard
over its form. The swordswoman threw herself in front of
Victor before the monster could harm the nobleman, but

instead the creature strode toward the dead body of the croamarkh.

Durgar rose, drawing his mace, but, with its remaining hand, the golem flipped the table onto the priest. Then the creature hefted Luer Dhostar's body over its shoulder like a sack of potatoes and began plodding toward the door. Alias was prepared to follow, to battle the golem for the croamarkh's corpse, but Victor held her back.

"Durgar will be crushed!" he exclaimed. "We have to get this table off him."

Alias nodded. Victor was right. The priest's life had to take priority. She laid down her weapon and helped Victor heft the table from Durgar's pale form. Durgar groaned, but he still breathed.

The golem had left the warehouse. Alias could hear members of the watch shouting and banging on the monster with their useless weapons. She retrieved her sword and rose to leave, but Victor grabbed her gown. "Where's Dragonbait?" he asked. "We need him to heal Durgar."

"I don't know," Alias said. "Victor, I have to go after the golem."

"Why?" he demanded. "Why risk your life for my father's body?"

"Without it, Durgar can't speak with his dead spirit. We might never learn the truth," she replied.

"I've seen enough. I don't think I want to learn any more," the merchant lord declared. "There's no guarantee my father will answer in death any questions he would not answer in life."

Gently Alias took Victor's hand from her gown and gave it a sympathetic squeeze. "We still have to try," she said. Then she raced off after the iron monster.

By the time Alias caught up with the fleeing golem, it stood at the edge of the harbor, teetering on the thick wooden pylons that protected the shore. The watch soldiers had the monster cornered. Alias shouted for them to get a rope on it, but she was too late. Ponderously the creature rocked back, then forward, pitching headlong into the water with a tremendous splash.

The ripples spread outward until they hit the pier and

bounced back. The moon was nearly full, but Alias could detect no bubbles or turbulence in the dark water below. She returned to the ramshackle warehouse. Victor was ordering one of the watchmen to fetch a priest for Durgar. The old man lay on the floor of the warehouse, his breathing strained and shallow, his complexion turning gray.

"It's just cracked ribs," Durgar assured Alias. "After years of combat wounds, I can tell," he added with a grim smile.

Alias reported on the fate of the iron golem and Luer Dhostar's body.

"Damnation," Durgar growled with annoyance. "It could walk across the bottom of the bay and be halfway to the Pirate Isles before it corrodes. We'll never get Luer's body back now."

The watchman Victor had sent out returned with a stern-faced young man in white robes, a follower of Ilmater, god of suffering. The others maintained a respectful silence as he knelt beside the elderly priest and began intoning a curative chant, his hands hovering over Durgar's chest. When the young man had finished, Durgar took a deep breath, then another, and his complexion began to grow rosier.

"I just can't believe it," Durgar said as Victor helped him to sit up. "I've known Luer for years. I can't believe he was—he was . . . Victor, I'm so sorry," he concluded, patting the merchant lord's hand.

"It's all right," Victor said softly. "He hid it well. I couldn't believe it either, at first."

"But your father lived for this city and for his business!" the old priest insisted. He picked up the Faceless's coin mask and sighed. "Luer's greatest pleasure was going over his books," he said, still unable to grasp his friend's treachery. "We used to work together in the Tower for company's sake, me with my arrest records, he with his account books. Not two nights ago—no, three— he spent the whole evening tracking down an error in bookkeeping that proved one of his ship captains was skimming off his shipments. He used to say it was easier to catch a thief with an accounting ledger and an abacus than it was with a sword. It was nearly dawn before he found what he was looking for, but when he did, he was elated. Of course, it didn't last. Ssentar Urdo came in to holler about Haztor's arrest. Still, for those few moments, he was so happy. You can't imagine a man's a scheming criminal when he's that happy doing his work."

Durgar got wearily to his feet. "I'd best be getting back to the Tower to see what assistance I can give the survivors." His shoulders were bowed—the weight not of his responsibilities, Alias knew, but of his grief. Magical spells could cure broken ribs, but not spirits. Victor walked the priest to the door, speaking to him in a hushed whisper. The noble returned to the swordswoman's side as all the watchmen followed behind their leader.

"I should return to the Tower, too," Alias said to Victor. "I have to find Dragonbait. I haven't seen him since we left the ball."

"I did, just after you left to chase the golem. He was behind the stair, healing an injured member of the watch."

"Then he was all right?"

"Looked all right to me, though I'm no expert on how saurials are supposed to look," Victor said. "I guess there's really nothing more I can do until morning. All the nobles who were still able ran off to bolt their castle doors. Durgar's seeing to the injured."

The young man looked back down at the chair where his father's corpse had been. "I don't know if I want to be alone right now. Would you come back to Castle Dhostar with me?"

Alias hesitated. It was hardly an invitation Victor could have made were his father still alive, she knew. It was bound to cause talk. Victor could use her support, though, especially after all he'd been through. There was really nothing else she could do tonight, either, and she was beginning to feel weary. She nodded her consent.

They walked back to the market green, where Victor found his carriage, attended by his driver. He dismissed the driver and took up the reins himself.

The drive from the city was quiet and uneventful. They leaned on each other, but neither spoke much. No one greeted them at the door, and Victor explained that, save for Kimbel and his carriage driver, the servants had all been given the evening off in honor of the ball.

Victor ushered Alias down the hallways and into the library, where Kimbel was tending a blazing fire in the hearth. After all the violence and the chill of the night air, the room seemed blissfully warm and peaceful, in spite of the malignant servant. Kimbel bowed and left the room without a word. Alias noticed that there was another bottle of Evermead on the table, with two glasses.

"Were you expecting me to return with you?" Alias asked.

Victor shook his head. "The other glass would be for my father. I just realized, Kimbel probably doesn't know yet that Father is—is dead." He sighed. "I suppose I can wait until morning to tell him, if he hasn't picked it up in the servant hall by then."

The nobleman poured them each a glass of Evermead as Alias wondered if the Dhostars ever drank less expensive wines. "You look lovely," he said as he handed her a glass.

Alias laughed. "My hair's a rat's nest, I've torn my gown, and I'm covered with iron golem rust."

"You look lovely to me. He sat down at the desk, but Alias stood warming herself before the fire.

"I spoke with Durgar before he left us," Victor said. "He agreed to call a meeting for tomorrow morning of all the surviving heads of the noble merchant families. It doesn't look good, I'm afraid. From what I could see of the casualties, most of the noble merchant houses are going to end up in the hands of third children or second cousins. Do you think it's possible what you said, that the Night Masters killed my father for opposing the use of the golems on the nobles?"

"It makes a certain amount of sense. But then, so do a lot of other scenarios," Alias said as she laid another log

on the fire. "Your father might have wanted to use the
golems on the nobles to consolidate his grip as croamarkh. The Night Masters might have realized he was
using them, and fearing he would betray them, destroyed
him. What I can't figure out is why the Night Masters
went to so much trouble to be sure we found your father's
body but then made sure the golem took it away from us.
I'm surprised they left his coin mask, too. A piece of
magic that powerful—why didn't they take it from him
after they killed him?"

Victor reached calmly into one of the desk drawers and
pulled out an ornate ring, set with a huge black opal.
Pushing a tiny nub forced the opal to slide aside, revealing a needle tipped with poison. Alias, staring thoughtfully into the fire, did not notice the merchant lord's
actions.

"It was as if they wanted us to discover that your
father was the Faceless. Did they think I would stop
hunting for them if they slew their leader? Unless—"

"Unless what?" Victor prompted as he leaned back in
his chair.

"Unless he really wasn't the Faceless, and the real
Faceless wanted to pin it on him," Alias said excitedly.
"Surely the real Faceless couldn't have been killed so easily. He could have them all on the floor in agony with just
a spell word. It was one of the Faceless's powers. He used
it just two, no, three nights ago . . . but— Victor, that's it!
You're father is innocent! They did set him up! They
probably planted the key as well!"

Alias turned suddenly from the fire and looked down
at the young nobleman. Victor stood suddenly. "You can't
be serious," he said.

Alias paced before the fire. "Durgar said three nights
ago he and your father sat up all night balancing their
accounts and going over records, right?"

Victor nodded.

"Until dawn, when Ssentar Urdo came by," Alias continued as she swung about. "But, according to Melman,
the Faceless was attending a meeting that night with all
the Night Masters."

Victor seemed to be scowling, unable to understand what she was saying.

"Don't you see? Your father could not be the Faceless or even a Night Master," Alias explained, "because he was not at that meeting. He was with Durgar."

"Are you sure of the night of the meeting?" Victor said with an anxious tone. "Melman could have lied about the night, or you might have misheard him."

"No problem," Alias said. "We'll get Durgar to do a *detect lie* spell and ask him again."

"Ask—" Victor gasped. "Ask him? He's alive? You've captured one of the Night Masters alive?"

"Yes," Alias said. "I told you I got the key to the Faceless's last lair from him."

Victor looked aghast. "I thought you'd stolen it— I mean that that halfling Ruskettle acquired it for you. Why didn't you tell me?" he demanded.

Alias sighed. "When we talked about it before," she explained, "I was afraid your father was a Night Master, maybe even the Faceless, and I thought you might be passing information on to him—innocently of course. Then, too, I knew you might not approve of the arrangement I'd made with Melman. I agreed to let him go, providing he told me everything he could, and providing he wasn't lying."

Victor looked stricken. "So where is Melman now?"

Alias looked slightly guilty. "He told me all he knew, and it checked out. By now he's on a boat bound for Cormyr. But we could have Mintassan meet him in Cormyr and bring him back for something as important as clearing your father's name."

Victor nodded thoughtfully. "It shouldn't be too hard to find a branded Night Master," he mused aloud.

Alias nodded in agreement, then paused. "How did you know Melman was branded?"

Victor opened his mouth and closed it. "Didn't you mention it?" he asked, perplexed.

Alias frowned, reviewing in her perfect memory every conversation she'd had with Victor concerning Melman. She'd said the Faceless had branded someone, but not who. "No, I'm certain I didn't," she said.

Victor crossed to where Alias stood and laid a warm hand on her shoulder. "My love, I have my own sources."

"What sources?" Alias demanded. "Victor, I have to know. You can't keep hiding things from me."

"Alias, I have other friends besides you who have been investigating the Night Masters for me, but I can't reveal their names. You have to trust me. You do trust me, don't you?"

Alias was about to assure him that she did when she looked up into his eyes. There was something calculating there, and the words died in her throat. Dragonbait's warnings came back to her immediately. She thought, too, of Kimbel. The former assassin had been at the ball, but had avoided the golem rampages, then returned to the castle and sat quietly at the fireside, prepared for Victor's return, unruffled by the affairs of the evening.

She was suddenly overly conscious of Westgate's reputation for intrigue and betrayal. "Of course I trust you," she managed to say, but she knew her voice sounded hollow.

Victor took her glass of Evermead from her hands and sipped at it. "We need to be careful in the next few days," the noble said, his eyes pinning her in place. "After all that has happened, the city is going to be full of rumors and unrest. I think we should tell the people that we've found the Faceless, that he's dead. It will help settle things down more quickly."

There was something hypnotic about Victor's voice, and Alias had to shake herself to throw off its influence. She raised a hand to touch Victor's cheek, trying to reassure him of her loyalty even as she argued with herself. "Victor, a *lie* like that is a two-edged sword. It can help you at first, but in the end it can cut you in half. We have to tell the truth, that we found your father murdered wearing the Faceless's regalia, but that the Faceless may still be at large."

"As you wish," Victor purred. He bent his face down and pressed his lips against her own, but there was nothing gentle or warm in his kiss. It was indifferent and brief—a farewell kiss to a dismissed lover.

Alias grabbed at the nobleman's sleeve. "Now is the time to pursue the Faceless even harder," she said, still anxiously trying to convince him she was right. "He must think he's safe, having framed someone else. He's likely to get careless—"

Victor slashed the back of his hand across her face, tearing at her flesh with a spiked ring much like the one sported by the extortionist Littleboy. Alias gasped as a searing pain streaked down her left cheek.

The adventuress jerked away from the nobleman and tried to draw her sword from its scabbard, but her muscles failed her. The sword felt as heavy as lead, and her hand spasmed uncontrollably, so she could not grip the hilt. The poison on the ring was quick-acting. Her face, her throat, and her arm burned with an inner fire.

The room seemed to sway like the deck of a tempest-tossed ship. Alias tried to focus on Victor, who stood there sipping the Evermead from her glass. Despite her swollen tongue, she managed to slur out the words, "Victor, why?"

Victor laughed harshly as he set down her emptied glass. "I gave you the chance to lie for me, but you could not do so, could you, my darling? It's just as well. You make a better legend than a lover. Besides, I really don't feel like sharing my city with anyone."

Victor chuckled some more, amused by her feeble, jerking steps in his direction. When her knees gave out beneath her, the nobleman stepped forward to catch her, his eyes sparkling with a sick delight. "You poor dear," he said, looking into her wildly dilated eyes. "You served me so well, but I'm going to have to let you go. Still, I ought to thank you properly for all your help."

He kissed her with a cruel passion, ignoring the way her body twitched and spasmed from the poison running through her veins. He was possessed with a feeling of absolute power. Like a vampire in a bloodlust, he didn't pull away from her until he felt sated—sated on the control he'd taken of her emotions, of her actions, of her very life. By then, although the swordswoman was still twitching slightly, her breathing was shallow and irregular. It was only a matter of time before the poison reached her heart and stilled it in an icy grip.

Victor lifted the swordswoman, a little surprised at how heavy her dead weight was. He carried her from the library, through the main hall, then down a narrow spiral stairs to the wine cellar. He pushed on a bottle of wine, and a section of wall slid away, revealing a hidden passage. At the other end of the passage was a secret room.

Kimbel was waiting there, in the company of two prisoners shackled at the neck, wrists, and ankles to a thick iron post in the center of the room—Dragonbait and Mintassan. The saurial had been muzzled. The sage wore a disjointed, idiot's expression on his face, and his tongue lolled out of the side of his mouth.

The lizard paladin lunged toward Victor, hissing through his iron muzzle, but he was halted by the iron collar around his throat. The sage fixed Victor with a desperate look and gibbered in a high voice.

Kimbel lifted an eyebrow at the appearance of the noble's burden. "Is she dead?" he asked, curious.

"Not yet," Victor replied as he laid the swordswoman down on a worktable. He smiled gleefully as Alias shuddered. "To what do we owe the honor of Mintassan's company?" he asked.

"He spotted me carrying off the saurial," the assassin explained, "but he fumbled his ambush attempt. I had someone from the Temple of Mask place him under a feeblemind spell until you decide what to do with him."

The sage gibbered hysterically, beseeching the nobleman with his clouded eyes. Victor turned from the figure in cold disgust. "You'll have to kill him. You can destroy the lizard, too, now that we are finished using his mistress. Make sure none of the bodies are found."

"No one is going to believe all three just left town," Kimbel pointed out.

Victor peered down at Alias. He stroked the tattoo on her sword arm. "Have her lovely arm wash ashore at low tide, clutching a domino mask. Nice and ambiguous. The Faceless can reassure the Night Masters that he was responsible for the death of their foe, and Lord Victor can tell his people that a victory has been struck against the Night Masks, albeit at a great cost—the death of his love, the hero Alias. I won't need to keep up the worried lover act. I can go straight to being the mourning lover—so much more sympathetic. See to the details."

"Yes, milord," Kimbel replied. "This one may last a while yet," he noted, staring down at Alias, who still drew gasping breaths.

"Well, I've dismissed her. She's no longer in House Dhostar's employ, so she's yours to play with," Victor said. "Just not here. Be a good flunky and make sure she expires someplace where her vengeful spirit can't haunt me. When you're finished taking care of the bodies, loot the sage's workshop. Do it 'legally.' Kick Jamal out on the street. With Mintassan gone, we can take care of her at our leisure."

"And what will you be doing, milord?"

"I'll be sleeping. I'm worn out from my battles at the ball," Victor said with an evil chuckle. He left Kimbel alone in the workshop with the prisoners.

The assassin could hear his master's voice drift down the spiral staircase. The merchant lord was singing the jaunty tune he'd learned from Alias:

> *"For all of their dancing,*
> *Posturing, prancing,*
> *They'll fight with their backs to the wall.*
> *Till then they are eating*
> *And drinking and meeting;*
> *Their battles are fought at the ball."*

# Twenty
# Stirring the Ashes

The next afternoon found Olive Ruskettle slipping through the alleys of
Westgate, her spirit deeply troubled.
The light of day and the official procla-
mations from the Tower had done little
to clear her confusion. She needed to
speak with Jamal; the actress often
helped her get her thoughts straight even
as she was plying the halfling for information.

Olive was about to step out on the main road and cross
the street to Mintassan's house when she spotted the
symbols on the cobblestone. There were two of them,
scrawled in charcoal, in a most inexpert manner, but
there was no doubt about their meaning. The first symbol
was used by Harpers to mean danger. The second symbol
was used by thieves to mean danger. Both were aligned
to indicate Mintassan's.

Olive stood in the shadow of the alley, studying all the
approaches to the sage's house. In a few moments, she
spotted Kel, lurking in a doorway down the street. The
halfling moved out into the main street, striding in the
boy's direction, without looking at him. She stopped by
the door, pretending to study a slip of paper for an
address.

"You put out those symbols, Kel?" she asked, without
looking at the boy.

"Yeah. Jamal taught me to write 'em. Did it right,
didn't I?"

"Did it fine," the halfling assured him. "What's up?"

"Supposed to warn Jamal's friends not to come by.
Dhostar's spider Kimbel's taken over the house, tossed

Jamal and me out. Jamal's up at Blais House."

"Thanks. Keep up the good work," the halfling said. She kept going, then slipped down the next alley to make her way to Blais House.

At the hostel, Mercy escorted her two flights up to a guest room far smaller than Alias's and Dragonbait's suite. The room was cluttered with Jamal's costume wardrobe, puppets, and theater props. Jamal was seated at a table, scribbling furiously in a small black book. "I was hoping you'd come by," the actress said.

"What is going on?" Olive demanded.

"I thought you could tell me," the actress said in exasperation. She blotted the ink in her book and slipped it back into the bottom of her jewelry box. "That worm Kimbel came by Mintassan's this morning with an officious-looking scroll claiming House Dhostar is supposed to oversee Mintassan's estate in the sage's absence. It had Mintassan's seal on it, and Kimbel had seven large Dhostar guards with him, so I wasn't in a position to keep myself from being thrown out on the street. I left Kel to warn off my friends. I don't want all my contacts running into Kimbel or vice versa. The manager of Blais House is willing to let me stay here for a while."

"Where are Alias and Dragonbait?" Olive asked.

Jamal shrugged. "No one saw Alias and Dragonbait return last night, but Mercy says Alias's armor is missing. I guess Alias came back for it before going back out to hunt more Night Masks. I'm used to Mintassan disappearing into the night for weeks on end, but I'll confess I'm getting a little nervous that Alias and Dragonbait haven't returned. What happened at the meeting of the merchant nobles this morning?"

"Durgar recapped the events of last evening, giving us the final tally of the dead," Olive reported. "The heads of Houses Guldar, Ssemm, Thalavar, Urdo, and Vhammos were killed by the Night Masks' iron golems. Houses Ssemm, Urdo, and Vhammos also lost their recognized heirs. The croamarkh wasn't at the ball, but Durgar claims that a golem got him anyway and carried his body into the sea. Then Lord Victor says that his hireling Alias, with her companions Dragonbait and Mintassan, found a clue last night that led them into the sewers to search for the Faceless. Finally, at Durgar's suggestion, the heads of the merchant houses—mostly inexperienced cousins and youths—unanimously voted Victor Dhostar in as interim croamarkh. They're supposed to make an official proclamation tomorrow, after the funerals."

"Durgar said a golem killed Luer Dhostar?" Jamal asked.

Olive nodded. "Yes. Why?"

"I think it's time we throw all our cards on the table and see if we come up with a full deck," Jamal suggested. "I've got a source in the watch who says they found the Faceless dead, stabbed in the ribs. Durgar unmasked him, and it was Luer Dhostar, but Durgar has ordered the watch to keep mum about it."

Olive laughed. "Making all Lord Victor's hard work in vain. Victor Dhostar knew his father was the Faceless. He's been feeding Alias clues, hoping she'd unmask Luer for him. Then the nobles would be disgraced by the knowledge that the Faceless turned out to be their own elected croamarkh, and they'd have to pick a candidate popular with the people."

"Alias?" Jamal asked in astonishment.

"No," Olive corrected, "the noble responsible for hiring her—the noble who's wearing her token—Victor Dhostar."

"Well, that's how it ended up, anyway," the actress said.

"Not exactly," the halfling replied. "The nobles haven't been disgraced, and they've only made Lord Victor interim croamarkh. If anything, the Night Masks' attack last night has made people feel more sympathy for the nobles."

"No kidding," Jamal said. "I tried a puppet show this morning portraying the nobles as sheep running from the wolf. It was not well received."

"You should have known better than to kick a dog when it's down," Olive retorted.

"Even I make mistakes," the actress replied with a

shrug. "So, Lord Victor was planning to turn on his own kind and reveal all, but Durgar stopped him. If we could get him out from under Durgar's influence, he might prove useful—a noble who cares what the people think."

"The only one Victor Dhostar cares about is Victor Dhostar," Olive snapped. "He was manipulating Alias into uncovering the Faceless, he manipulated Durgar into proposing him as the new croamarkh, and, given half a chance, he'll manipulate you and anyone else in Westgate fool enough to support him. He doesn't just want to be croamarkh. He wants to be *king*."

Jamal raised an eyebrow in surprise. "Never happen," she replied. "Not in Westgate. Not after Verovan. No one will ever go for it. Not the merchant lords, and certainly not the people."

"Wrong," Olive retorted. "If the people start clamoring for it and the merchant lords are weakened, they might have no choice."

"The people don't want a king. They want to rule themselves," Jamal argued.

"Jamal, I've studied you humans for years. Humans don't want to rule themselves. Only a few humans want to bother with the mess it takes to rule themselves. The rest want to be left alone. Your average Westgate citizen wants the Night Masks taken care of, but for over fifteen years they've been waiting for the merchant nobles to handle it. Some of them look at a nation like Cormyr, with a king who's managed to purge the land of assassins and who exiles convicted thieves, and they think maybe the gods favor monarchies. Should a popular candidate come along, some of them might start dusting off Verovan's regalia," the halfling concluded.

Jamal looked for a moment as if she might explode. Olive knew she'd just called into question a basic tenet of the actress's beliefs. A moment later, though, Jamal sighed. "Just because people won't take charge of their own lives doesn't mean they can't," she argued.

"I'm not saying that," Olive replied.

"Well, you may be right about the king thing," the actress conceded. "I have heard people talking about

Azoun of Cormyr as if he were the gods' gift to the people. Are you sure about Victor Dhostar, though? Alias seemed to think he was all right."

"Even Alias makes mistakes, something I intend to correct just as soon as she and Dragonbait get back from the sewers," Olive said. "In the meantime, Lady Nettel's dying request was that I protect her granddaughter. House Thalavar lost three halfling bodyguards to the golems last night, so I've spent the last twelve hours not letting Thistle Thalavar out of my sight. I think the girl was getting tired of me. After making all the arrangements for her grandmother's funeral, she locked herself in the study to go over House Thalavar's account books and Lady Nettel's personal journal. I should be getting back to Castle Thalavar to keep an eye on visitors offering their condolences. When Alias gets back—"

"You'll hear from me," Jamal promised.

\* \* \* \* \*

It was nightfall before the actress sent Kel around with a message for the halfling, but all the note said was that Alias had not returned, and neither had Dragonbait nor Mintassan. Olive penned a reply that Jamal should sit tight. The sewers were vast. It might take a little more time to explore them. The halfling did her best to keep from sounding worried when she handed the message to Kel.

Thistle finally came out of her grandmother's study for supper. Olive pressed her for permission to hire more bodyguards. The young girl fingered her grandmother's brooch like an amulet, then nodded her agreement.

The next morning brought a similar note from Jamal. Alias had not returned, but a fisherman had relayed a rumor that Alias was seen battling a fire elemental in the plaza around the Westlight. Jamal had checked with the watch stationed around the lighthouse, only to learn that some itinerant wanderer had started a trash fire by the water to keep herself company.

That afternoon, after Lady Nettel's funeral, one of the

Thalavar halflings returned to the castle with the rumor
that the Faceless was holding court in a tavern in Gateside. With Thistle again locked in the study with her
account books, Olive hurried down to the tavern in question, but discovered only an outlander in a heavy cloak.
He was not holding court, only recruiting bodyguards for
a caravan going south, and he kept his face covered with
the hood of his cloak to hide a particularly ugly scar
received from brigands.

Olive spent the afternoon interviewing halflings to
serve as guards for the castle, for the warehouses, and,
most especially, for Thistle. While she found several
sturdy, sensible recruits worth training, no one with any
real combat experience came forward.

By evening, Jamal sent another negative note. The
adventurers had not returned. A beachcomber down by
the river claimed to have seen Dragonbait battling the
quelzarn in the water below the bridge. After interviewing the witness, Jamal had concluded he was into his
third tankard of ale and was seeing anything the actress
could suggest to his vivid imagination and besotted
brain.

The third morning after the ball brought a new rumor
to the servants' quarters of Castle Thalavar: the Faceless
was dead. Night Mask activity was so low for the past
two days, people had begun to believe that perhaps the
Night Masks were in mourning for their leader. Speculation was rife that perhaps one of the deceased nobles had
been the lord of the Night Masters. Olive wondered if
Victor had had a hand in spreading the rumor.

Kel appeared at the Thalavar castle gate right after
breakfast. Olive realized he brought something more
than rumor. The boy had been crying. This time he
hadn't brought a note. "Jamal's at the Old Beard," he
reported. "She says come now." Still crying, Kel ran off.

Olive arrived at the tavern near the river just as House
Dhostar's massive carriage was pulling away. People were
pouring out of the tavern. Olive hurried inside. Jamal was
sitting at a table, looking pale and shaken.

"What is it?" the halfling asked.

"A fisherman found it near the Athagdal docks," Jamal explained, "where the Thunn runs into the harbor."

"Found what?" Olive demanded.

"Alias—Alias—her—oh, gods!" The actress broke into sobs.

Olive looked up at the tavern's host. "It was an arm," the man explained, "covered with a tattoo of thorns and waves, with a rose at the wrist."

"I found it floating in the water," a young fisherman said. " 'Tweren't chewed up or anything. Someone had hacked it off at the shoulder. It had a domino mask clutched in its hand—in a death grip."

"Where is it?" Olive demanded through clenched teeth.

"Croamarkh Victor took it," the tavern owner said. "Wept over it like it were the lady 'erself. Wrapped it up in a piece o' velvet and said it would be laid to rest in the Dhostar family crypt in honor o' 'er service to the croamarkh."

Olive nudged Jamal to her feet, anxious to get her away from the somewhat crowded tavern.

As they walked down the street, Jamal explained. "I sent Kel as soon as I heard. I thought you might be able to tell for sure—tell if it were hers. You said it was a magic arm. You could tell if it were a fake, couldn't you?"

"Maybe," Olive said. "Why'd you let Dhostar take it?"

"He was weeping. He asked the fisherman and the people in the tavern if they would let him take it. No one could turn him down. If he's really as bad as you say, he's the best actor in Westgate," the actress said. "I don't think I could show more grief than he did."

"If you're not careful, he'll make your troupe obsolete," the halfling snarled.

If rumors flew before, now they teleported from place to place. Some said that the severed arm meant that Alias had battled the Night Masks and lost. Others insisted that the fact that the arm's fist clutched a domino mask meant she had won, even though it had cost her her life. A third faction held that she, her companions, and all the Night Masters, including the Faceless, had never fought at all, but just been eaten by the quelzarn.

Olive told herself Alias could have survived losing her arm. Dragonbait and Mintassan might be with her even now. It was impossible, though, to come up with a reason why they didn't return, why Mintassan didn't just teleport them back to his home to reassure their friends that they were safe. Olive's hope began slipping away.

Five days after the ball, Olive Ruskettle, captain of the House Thalavar guard, self-declared bard, and self-declared Harper, was making a halfhearted attempt to drink herself to death. She sat on the open patio of the Black Eye tavern, with its excellent view of the market and the Tower. Three days had passed since the funerals of the croamarkh and the other felled merchant lords. The official period of mourning completed, the market was once again blanketed by a tapestry of motley—the wares of both minor and noble merchants being offered for sale.

That, if no other reason, was enough to keep Olive ordering round after round of a highly potent southern drink known as Dragon's Bite. She was disgusted by the way this city shrugged off its losses and returned diligently to the task of making money. There had been no funeral for Alias, Dragonbait, or Mintassan, no official period of mourning for the heroes who had so selflessly risked their lives for this town of money-grubbing greengrocers. Not that three days of mourning could be enough to honor adventurers of their caliber—adventurers who'd been her friends.

She wanted to blow this festhall of a city, to leave it to fester in its own greed, to head north where adventurers weren't treated like carpets for merchants to wipe their feet on. Still, Westgate held her in its thrall. She had business here still.

First, of course, she felt obligated to honor Lady Nettel's dying request to protect Thistle. Lady Nettel had been really decent. She would have made a good halfling. As for Thistle, Olive had actually grown to like the human child. She was a serious, hardworking girl, something Olive admired without actually emulating, of course. Three days of interviewing the halfling popula-

tion of Westgate, and even some of the humans, had left
Olive with the certainty that there was really no one else
as qualified as she was to be the girl's bodyguard.

Yet Thistle had walled herself up with her books, and
there wasn't much challenge in guarding a hermit. Olive
had wiled away hours outside the door of Thistle's study
reorganizing every aspect of security for House Thalavar,
its castle, its warehouses, its stockyards and its docks.
The halfling was distracted to the point of madness waiting for the Night Masks to renew their vengeful attacks,
but the thieves guild really did seem to be on hiatus.
Thistle Thalavar, her castle, and all her property
remained undisturbed.

The tension was enough to drive a halfling to drink.
Olive drained her glass and thumped it on the tabletop,
demanding a refill. House Thalavar would pick up the
tab, making it possible to order drink after drink without
actually plunking any money down or keeping track of
how much one spent on liquor. Olive wasn't sure that was
a good thing, but it was certainly a comforting one.

Her second order of business in Westgate was what to
do about the new croamarkh, Victor Dhostar.

When the evil mage Flattery had disintegrated her
friend Jade, Olive had wasted no time avenging Jade's
death. Of course, then she'd had some formidable allies:
Giogi Wyvernspur, who could shapechange into a wyvern;
the mage, Cat; and the wizard, Drone. Here her only
allies were an aging actress, a boy who had only just
retired from his career as a Night Mask, and a castle full
of pampered halflings. Then there was the question of
popularity. No one had liked Flattery—all agreed he was
a sick menace to society. Victor Dhostar, though, was a
slick piece of work, friendly, smiling, concerned. Whatever emotion or reaction was appropriate to the situation, he could summon it to the surface. Even Alias had
been fooled. Milil's Mouth, he even had me charmed that
first day, Olive recalled. On top of all that charm, he was
croamarkh. While he was not quite a king, plotting his
destruction certainly smacked of regicide, a serious crime
even in a place like Westgate.

More importantly, without more information, she couldn't really assess the extent of Victor's guilt. He might not have anything to do with Alias's death. The swordswoman was, after all, always taking risks. The Night Masters might have destroyed her whether or not Victor Dhostar was a nice guy. Victor could just be a selfish, power-hungry jerk who'd used Alias. The world was full of them. Olive fumed whenever she thought of the way he'd carried off the swordswoman's arm, as if he owned it. Victor Dhostar was definitely one more reason to drink.

A pottery mug of Dragon's Bite hovered at eye level, carried by a slim female halfling about half Olive's age. The younger woman was dressed like a Luiren schoolteacher, in a long, black divided skirt and a starched white blouse buttoned tight at the wrists and to the top of its high collar. Her reddish blonde hair was twisted into a severe bun at the back of her head. She wore a bitter, no-nonsense expression on her severely angular face, which Olive thought might actually stop a beholder in its tracks, if beholders could leave tracks.

"You're drinking too much," the younger halfling said, setting the mug down none too gently. She sat down at the table across from Olive.

"Never would have guessed," Olive snarled, taking a long pull on the fresh mug. She glared across the table at the new arrival until it became clear that her guest was not going to politely evaporate. "Was there a shift change? Are you my new waitress?" she asked.

"I'm not a waitress," the newcomer informed her. "You're Olive Ruskettle," she said, not really questioning, but not quite certain either.

"Maybe," Olive muttered.

"And you're employed by House Thalavar."

"Maybe," Olive said with a sigh. She took another gulp of her drink.

"And you were a friend of Alias of the Inner Sea," said the other halfling.

Olive slammed her mug down hard. "What in the Abyss do you want, child?"

The other halfling blinked for a moment, as if shocked by Olive's outburst. Finally, she replied, "My name is Winterhart. I met Alias last summer in the Dalelands. I understand she is dead, and you were her friend. Please accept my condolences. I am also seeking employment. I've spent most of my days as an adventuress, so I have little experience as a servant, but Alias said I could use her as a reference. Does House Thalavar have use for a capable halfling?"

Olive seethed silently. The friend-of-the-dead trick was an old halfling con. She was insulted that someone thought she was good enough to play it using Alias's name, and insulted that anyone thought her fool enough to fall for it. "You were a friend of Alias, too, hmm?"

"We met and talked," Winterhart responded calmly. "I was impressed by her. I am truly sorry she is dead."

Well, Olive thought, at least she's smart enough not to claim that Alias was an old friend from way back. Aloud she asked, "And you knew her from the Dalelands?"

"Yes." Winterhart's head bobbed just a tad.

"Then you know what song she first sang in the taproom of the Old Skull Inn," Olive said offhandedly.

"It was *The Standing Stone*," Winterhart said, displaying the first trace of a smile, "an old elven tune with words by Finder Wyvernspur, the Nameless Bard. That was an easy one. Want to ask what her favorite color was?"

"Her favorite color was blue," Olive lied, waiting for Winterhart to take the bait.

"Red," Winterhart corrected. "Blue reminded her of her tattoo, which she thought of as a symbol of her previous enslavement. Shall I tell you how she first met Elminster, or how she nearly skewered Giogi Wyvernspur, or in which boot she kept her throwing dagger?"

Olive smiled, delighted to be convinced of something for a change. "What is it you can do, Winnie?" she asked.

"The name is Winterhart, and I prefer *Miss* Winterhart," the younger halfling corrected. "I would make a suitable lady's companion. I am trained in human customs and dress. I am also skilled with the sword, dagger, and bow, and can provide protection for the young mistress."

Olive looked with some surprise at Winterhart. "Think fast!" she snapped and threw her half-full mug at the younger halfling.

Miss Winterhart dodged slightly to her right, her left hand snaking up and snaring the mug by its handle. She set it down smoothly without spilling a drop and slid it back in Olive's direction.

Olive's reflexes were too deadened by drink to stop the mug in time. It slid into her lap, drenching her with its contents of liquor-laced ale. Olive stood up and cursed.

"Drinking is a filthy habit," Winterhart declared. "I have no truck with it."

Olive cursed some more as she tried unsuccessfully to brush the liquid from her leggings.

"And bad language is another thing," Winterhart added primly. "Foul words lead to foul deeds."

Olive did not reply. She studied Winterhart as carefully as she was capable of in her inebriated condition. The girl had fast reflexes and a strong will. If she was telling the truth about being skilled with weaponry and proved to have a modicum of halfling sense, she might be just the sort of woman suitable to take over as Thistle's bodyguard.

There was something else about Winterhart that impressed Olive. It was not the woman's sobriety and primness, but what Olive sensed, or imagined she sensed, lay behind those traits. Winterhart had been hurt somehow, in the past, and she held herself tightly in check so that she didn't fall apart. It didn't make her a powerful ally, but it meant she had just the sort of strength Olive lacked. Nothing, Olive realized, could take away the pain of Alias's death. With Winterhart behind her, however, Olive knew she would find the courage to avenge the swordswoman's death. She would make the Night Masks pay for Alias's murder, and if she found out Victor Dhostar was involved, she would make him pay, too.

Had Olive been sober, such an unrealistic goal might never have occurred to her—she was far too cautious. She was not sober, though, and she saw in Winterhart not just a halfling seeking employment, but a sign from the gods.

"Mistress Ruskettle, do you have an answer for me?" Winterhart demanded.

Olive smiled grimly at the other halfling. "All right," she agreed. "I'll give you a trial period. But I'll be watching you like a hawk!"

Miss Winterhart nodded. "I don't fear being watched, Mistress Ruskettle. As for trials—" Winterhart's eyes focused on something in the distance, and her voice trailed off as she spoke. "—I am quite used to trials," she said.

Olive watched the younger halfling's gaze as it followed the progress of the new croamarkh's carriage away from the Tower. "Some trials are more difficult to bear than others," Olive muttered, though she spoke not to Winterhart, but for her own benefit.

\* \* \* \* \*

"Blast them all to Baator!" Lord Victor thundered as he strode into the main hallway of Castle Dhostar. He threw his cloak at the footman. The butler appeared briefly, but upon seeing the look on his master's face, he retreated back into the servants' quarters, unwilling to deal with the young lord unless called upon to do so.

Victor stormed into the library, where Kimbel was calmly reviewing piles of Mintassan's books and scrolls. In the center of the table hovered a glowing sphere that the assassin had stolen from Blais House when he'd retrieved the swordswoman's armor.

"Difficult day running the city?" Kimbel queried as he rose and crossed to a sideboard. He poured a generous amount of Evermead into a glass and carried it to his master.

Victor had thrown himself in a chair and sat there brooding.

"I think this land was once completely forested," the croamarkh muttered. "Then the bureaucrats invented paperwork." He took the glass of Evermead, gulping it down like water. "There is a form for everything, sometimes two forms, on occasion, three. And gods forbid you sign anything without reading it, or else some clan might receive a windfall and the other clans will start screaming for your blood. And while you're reading every bloody piece of paper the city clerks put in front of you, the other clans are robbing you blind, since you haven't got the time to address your own business. Why can't they just learn to shut up and follow my orders? That's why they made me croamarkh, after all."

"Interim croamarkh," Kimbel corrected softly.

"Maybe I didn't kill enough of them," Victor mused. "Any charges we can trump up against one or two of them? Make an example of them to keep the others in line."

"Most unwise," Kimbel replied. "It would be bad for business, and the reaction of those remaining would be distrust rather than fear. These are not Night Masters, but nobles, and even the young and inexperienced ones have believed all their life that power is their right. Besides, you already eliminated the most likely candidates."

"The irony," Victor snarled, "is that I've kissed up to them for years to assure myself this rotten job, only to discover that I have to *keep* kissing up to them to keep it. We need a monarchy around here. I'm tired of all this open rebellion." He turned to Kimbel sharply and asked, "Did you recover my mask?"

Kimbel nodded. "Durgar stashed it in a desk drawer, no doubt unable to come to grips with having covered up Luer Dhostar's infamy. I replaced it with a stage prop of Jamal's, which I looted from Mintassan's lair. It may be some time before Durgar realizes it's not the genuine article. And, of course, I knew you'd appreciate the irony."

Victor allowed himself a smile. "Good old Durgar. There's some more irony. I think I impressed him, arguing that we should tell the 'truth.' about Father. But Durgar is so anxious to preserve the established order that he concealed all father's crimes." An unsettling thought occurred to the young lord. "You don't think he doubts that Father was the Faceless, do you?"

"He does not appear to be pursuing the matter," Kimbel replied, pulling a heavy tome from the pile and opening it to a page marked with a red ribbon. "Now, this is fascinating," the assassin said as he perused the page. "A fortuitous coincidence, no doubt, considering your interest in monarchy."

"What?" Victor said.

Kimbel motioned for the croamarkh to come and look.

With some annoyance, Victor rose from his lethargic sprawl. He leaned over the tome, which had of late belonged to the sage Mintassan. The book was quite old, its cover cracked and frayed, its binding nearly disintegrated, its pages loose, covered in ornate, sweeping script.

"The writing is Elvish and dates back to the last days of King Verovan." Kimbel explained, but Victor held up a hand to silence him.

"I can see that for myself," the noble snarled. "You know Father insisted I learn all the subhuman languages—the better to trade with them, he would say."

Victor frowned with concentration as he pored over the text. "This describes the procedures and protocols of King Verovan's court."

"I direct you to the fourth paragraph," Kimbel said, "on the right-hand page."

"Hmmm." Victor ran his finger along the script, mouthing the words silently, too self-conscious to translate aloud in front of the assassin. "It's about Verovan's treasure hoard!" he whispered excitedly. "It's under, no, tucked away in an interdimensional demiplane, guarded by a . . . portion of the king's own soul!"

"Planes and dimensions were a specialty of young Mintassan's," Kimbel remarked.

"At the top of Verovan's castle, there is a portal into this plane," Victor translated.

"Matches the common folklore," Kimbel said. "Verovan's castle—that would be Castle Vhammos now, wouldn't it? How terrible that the population of House Vhammos was decimated by the iron golems. The new lord of the castle is still, I believe, on business in Waterdeep, leaving the castle prey to all sorts of thieves. I presume the new croamarkh will want to step in and offer to protect this landmark until the new lord's return."

"The key to open the passage to the demiplane is described as a copper feather," Victor said. "The new croamarkh would need such a key before he tried anything so blatant. What's this scrawl in the margin?"

"I believe that is a notation of the late, unlamented Mintassan," Kimbel said dryly.

"But what does it say? 'Lily Netted'? Why do sages always have such awful handwriting?"

Kimbel bent over the book, peering at the notation. "I believe it says, 'Lady Nettel.'"

"The symbol of House Thalavar is a green feather, and the Thalavars are distant relatives of the Verovan line," Victor said excitedly. "Copper patina is green. Doesn't—didn't Lady Nettel always wear some kind of a garish green brooch? You don't suppose they buried it with her, do you?"

Kimbel shook his head. "I believe Lady Thistle is now in possession of it. She was wearing it at her grandmother's funeral."

"King's Verovan's treasure hoard." Victor laughed with fiendish glee. "The loot gathered from a lifetime of sucking Westgate dry. Why, the gold alone would be sufficient to build a small empire. And the key hangs on dear little Dervish's bosom—that sweet young girl who's been left all alone in the world." Victor chuckled nastily.

Kimbel raised an eyebrow. "House Thalavar remains one of the most powerful rival houses. Forging an alliance with Lady Thistle could prove most useful when the council of merchants elects the next croamarkh."

Victor snorted. "Croamarkh! Once I charm that key from little Dervish, I can be king, with or without her support. Although . . . she could prove very useful, as the swordswoman was useful. She's popular, lovely—can't swing a sword, but at least she's of the proper class. And she is young and impressionable. She could be easily swayed by the interests of a kind and dashing noble, eh?"

"Assuming that said noble wasn't still supposed to be mourning his last love," Kimbel noted with a chill tone.

"I should call on Lady Thistle. We can commiserate with one another over our losses. A girl like that will do wonders to help assuage the sorrow I feel over the death of dear Alias."

## Twenty-One
# New Contracts

Kimbel insisted it should not appear as if the new croamarkh was singling out Thistle for special attention. He arranged for Victor Dhostar to pay a courtesy call on each grieving noble family to express his sympathies. The calls took two full days. House Thalavar had been scheduled last, and Victor came to think of it as a reward for the ordeals he suffered at all the other houses. At each call, one of the ruling survivors button-holed him with some demand, request, or poorly veiled threat involving the family's continued support. Victor could only shake his head sadly at these people as if to reprimand them for sullying such a solemn occasion with common business.

He was received in the main hall of Castle Thalavar by Lady Thistle herself. The new head of House Thalavar was flanked by a pair of the ever-present halflings that plagued her particular household.

Victor recognized the halfling on Thistle's right as Alias's ally, Olive Ruskettle. The halfling's suspicious questions in the Faceless's lair remained ingrained in his memory. When he saw the icy look in her eyes, he wished he had thought to include her somehow in the party that had "disappeared" with Alias in the sewer. The furry-footed creature could have no proof of anything, but that might not keep her from spreading rumors. He reassured himself with the knowledge, delivered by Kimbel, that the halfling seemed to be handling her grief over the swordswoman's death by crawling into an ale keg.

The other halfling was a reed-thin, stiff-backed girl dressed in a black gown so austere that she reminded Victor of the deceased Lady Nettel. As if that weren't enough to make him uncomfortable, the halfling's bright green eyes seemed to pierce Victor to his soul, looking for any smudge of evil with the relentless nature of a paladin's gaze. The nobleman found himself unconsciously reaching to feel for his amulet of misdirection to be sure he was warded from her penetrating misglare.

If these two were Thistle's advisors, Victor knew he might have an uphill battle for the lady's affection. Lady Thistle, however, proved to be as charming as her bodyguards were sullen. She was dressed in mourning, but her golden hair shone in the afternoon light, and her face was flushed with excitement. She wore the green feather brooch that had once been her grandmother's.

Victor expected Thistle to try to show him how mature she was, and she did not disappoint him. Once she'd led the croamarkh out onto the veranda overlooking the city, she asked if he would prefer tea or wine. After the other three visits he'd made today, Victor really felt like wine, and he was really curious to see what effect it might have on Thistle, but the looks on the faces of the halfling bodyguards cooled his desires. He asked for tea. Thistle rang for a servant and ordered a tea tray, then motioned for Victor to take a chair opposite her. The servant who returned with the tea tray politely disappeared back into the castle, but Thistle's two bodyguards remained standing behind her, like attack dogs restrained only by their mistress's will.

The talk was irritatingly small, as it always was when dealing with other nobles. It started with stilted condolences on each other's losses and then shifted to the weather. They discussed in a guarded way their latest shipments in from Thay or caravans from Amn. They speculated on whether or not the Night Mask threat had abated or even disappeared entirely. Thistle expressed the opinion that if it were so, they owed it all to Alias. Victor agreed completely, giving him a chance to appear more aggrieved as he added that he wished the price had not been so high. In the end, to the apparent alarm of both halflings, Victor got what he'd really come for, a dinner date with Thistle for the next evening.

Victor rose to leave just as a message arrived for Thistle, so Olive was assigned the task of escorting the croamarkh from the castle. Victor paused at the door and turned to the halfling. "I know you're hurt by what happened to Alias," he began.

Olive scowled. "How nice of you to remember her."

Victor took a deep breath and pressed on, "She knew the risks, and all of Westgate is in her debt. I want to propose a statue in her honor. Would you like that?"

Olive was silent for a moment, then asked, "Lord Victor, have you mistaken me for a child?"

"I'm sorry. I'm afraid I missed something."

Olive sniffed. "Yes, you did," she agreed coolly, "and now I miss something as well. If you'll excuse me."

Victor bowed and stepped outside. Olive shut the door firmly behind him. He's sorry, he says, the halfling thought cynically. "If I find out he had anything to do with Alias's death, he'll be sorry, all right," she muttered as she stalked down the hall.

Even if he weren't involved in Alias's death, Victor Dhostar was a vain jackass. Statue, indeed! He may have deceived Alias, but he was not going to ensnare Thistle, Olive resolved. Not if she had anything to say about it.

Unfortunately, Thistle made Alias's impulsive nature seem positively reasonable. When Olive returned to the veranda, the young noblewoman was in a heated discussion with Miss Winterhart.

"I felt a little sorry for him," said Thistle. "He's like one of those tragic figures in a sad, romantic opera. He strives to break up the Night Masks, yet on the eve of his triumph, he loses both his father and his love."

"Triumph!" Winterhart laughed in an imperious tone that in any other household might have gotten her bounced down the front steps. "What triumph?"

"Why, over the Night Masks," Thistle responded, flustered by Winterhart's attitude. "Everyone agrees that since everything has quieted down so, the Faceless must be dead and the Night Masks in chaos."

"Really?" Winterhart exclaimed. "Did you think thieves observed a period of mourning?" She looked at Olive. "Is she old enough to hear about the Grayclaws?"

"She runs House Thalavar. I guess she must be. The Grayclaws," Olive began before Thistle could lose her patience, "is the name of the thieves guild in Tantras. Tantras is a dead magic zone, so murder is just a little more common there than in other cities. Should the Grayclaws' guildmaster meet an untimely demise, as happens every few years in that city, everyone knows about it—immediately. There's blood in the streets for weeks while various factions vie for control of the guild. The Tantrans call it a spell of red weather. I suppose there's a very slight possibility that it's different here in Westgate. It could be that the Faceless ran everything so tightly that his minions are afraid to make a move without him. It's much more probable, however—"

"—that the Faceless is still around," Winterhart concluded, "and his grip on the Night Masks is as tight as ever."

Thistle considered their assessment silently for several moments. "It would be awful if that were true," she said at last. "That would mean that Victor lost both love and father for nothing. That poor man."

Winterhart gave Olive a frustrated, angry look. The elder halfling shrugged, resigned to the battle to come. It was going to be a fight to keep Thistle away from Victor, but at least she seemed to have a reliably informed ally in the very proper Miss Winterhart.

\* \* \* \* \*

Victor noted that the door closed a trifle fast behind him—not enough to merit an insult, but enough to make the halfling's point. In a few weeks, he thought, it might be reasonable for the Night Masks to make a reprisal attack on the halfling who was the friend of the woman responsible for killing their leader.

Victor climbed into his carriage and set off for the Tower. He didn't know how much longer he could tolerate the interminable paperwork and meetings. He spotted Jamal's street troupe giving a performance, and, overcome by an urge to procrastinate, ordered the driver to stop.

The Faceless lived, at least on stage, though Jamal had replaced her stolen prop mask of coins with a veil of golden fabric. She was ordering her Night Masks about with a large wooden spoon, ordering them to "be still." The Night Masks would freeze in impossibly ridiculous positions under the Faceless's merciless eye. Jamal's Faceless would smack an offender for twitching or swaying, and he would go catapulting forward. One Night Mask tried to surreptitiously pick a fellow thief's pocket, but was spotted and received a smack for his action.

The audience, and it was a small one, appeared unimpressed as the Faceless put the collected Night Masks through a precision drill. They dropped to the floor as one and jumped around like frogs while Jamal sounded the beat with the pounding stick. Victor noted that the various puppets representing the noble families were not in use, and that there was nothing mentioning the new croamarkh, either good or ill. He wasn't sure whether to be pleased by that or not. Jamal might have complained about her eviction from Mintassan's, but she might also have at least given the new croamarkh credit for the relative peace in the city, even if she didn't seem to believe the Faceless was deceased.

Then up popped a figure wrapped completely in black bandages, save for its right arm, which was bare. The arm was marked with Alias's tattoo and wielded a wooden sword. Jamal's Faceless quailed in the presence of Alias's disembodied spirit and sent the Night Masks out to stop it. The thieves were quickly bested, one after another. Then the spirit chased the Faceless himself around the small stage until he tripped. As the villain lay on the ground, the arm pressed the sword into his breast. The shrouded figure cried out, "Heroes never truly die!"

and lunged forward. The Faceless shuddered and expired.

Scattered, bored clapping broke out in the crowd, but that did not prevent Jamal and her troupe from bouncing nimbly to their feet and bowing to the applause.

Victor grinned with delight. Most of the populace was sick of the Night Masks, bored with dead heroes, tired of Jamal's proselytizing theater. If something happened to Jamal, there would be fewer questions.

Of course, destroying potential threats took a low priority with all the other work to be done. With a sigh, Victor, signaled his driver to continue on to the Tower.

There, annoyed at being kept waiting by the croamarkh, a Thayan representative awaited, a female Red Wizard who really only wanted to be reassured that trade would continue as it had under Luer's administration. The Thayan was followed by a Sembian, various Dalesmen, and representatives of King Azoun's court. Each, in turn, was similarly reassured. One of the surviving old nobles, Maergyrm Thorsar, had scheduled an appointment to lecture the croamarkh on Waterdhavian moneylenders. Victor was afraid he'd fall asleep before he was able to show the old bore the door. After Thorsar came the widow of Ssentar Urdo, who was protesting a rumor she had heard that Alias would get a statue when none was being erected for the widow's dear, departed husband and sons. Then, when Victor thought his schedule was finally cleared, Durgar arrived with the arrest reports, which required the croamarkh's attention due to the delicate nature of some of the arrested persons.

As it was, Victor was drained, both mentally and physically, when he finally escaped back to his castle. Yet not even then could he rest. He stood wearily as Kimbel bedecked him in his heavy, dark robes, tied on the porcelain mask that protected him from magical discovery, and finally covered him with the coin mask, which transformed him into the Faceless.

With a sigh, Victor stepped up to and then through the mirror in his chambers. The reflective surface parted for him like a pool of still water and deposited him in his latest secret lair. This one lay in a rough-hewn sub-basement beneath the currently empty Vhammos Castle.

The Night Masters were as restless as halflings waiting for dinner. The irregularities of the days since the ball had strained their self-discipline to the limits. They spoke out of turn, often all at once, questioned his every command, and made demands of their own. They made the nobles in the surface world seem like reasonable, rational beings. For a moment, Victor considered turning his remaining golems loose among them, but only for a moment, for he still needed the Night Masters to keep the peace among the Night Masks. Later, he thought, when they've outlived their usefulness.

"When can we get back to business?" Harborside asked.

"Do you realize how much money I'm losing?" Thunnside whined.

"People are saying that witch Alias killed you. Why aren't you doing something about it?" Noble Relations clamored.

"How do we know you really are the Faceless? Can you give us proof?" Enforcement demanded.

Victor let his frustrations drain away as he embraced his Faceless persona. Once again he was demanding, powerful, and sure of himself. He turned his face toward Enforcement.

"Would you like the same demonstration I gave to Gateside?" the Faceless queried, a certain amount of amusement creeping into his magically disguised voice.

All voices were silenced immediately. The Faceless motioned for all to be seated.

"Alias is dead. Of that you had proof. Perhaps you would like me to leave her arm on this table as a centerpiece for a few weeks. Alias's allies and the croamarkh who hired her are also dead. It is hardly my fault that people are fools enough to believe she succeeded in destroying me. Nonetheless, for the moment it suits my plans for people to believe in my demise. The new croamarkh is far more pliable than his father was, and he will serve us well, but it is important that his power be more firmly established. Therefore we will let him take credit for my destruction, for the time being.

"As for how much money you are losing, Thunnside, I really don't care. You've earned more wealth in this position than a dragon could hoard in its lifetime. If you could contain your urge to gamble, you would still have all that wealth. And, last, but not least, Harborside. Your business at the moment is to contain your forces. This is essential to your continuing in your current position. I guarantee it will be worth your while."

Having poured oil on their turbulent waters, the Faceless pressed on. "As a direct result of our success against Alias and her allies, information has come into my hands regarding the treasure hoard of King Verovan."

There was a collective gasp, just barely audible, but unmistakable. The Faceless smiled. Now he had them by their pocketbooks. Verovan's legendary hoard was the secret fantasy of every thief in Westgate.

"The young fool Mintassan discovered the secret," the Night Masters' lord explained, "though the sage never investigated it. Just as legend has it, there is a magical gate from the battlements above. Unlike all who have tried before me to locate this gate, I have discovered the location of the key. Once I have that key, Verovan's hoard will be ours to pillage."

A murmur of approval rose from the nine surviving Night Masters, but the Faceless was not finished. He silenced them with a stroke of his hand. When they grew silent, their master continued. "I want you to call together your lieutenants, their assistants, and their assistants' minions, along with whatever fighters, priests, and wizards you trust and choose to reward. We will gather in the main hall of Castle Vhammos in three nights' time to loot Verovan's hoard. Then there will be no doubt that it is the Night Masks who truly rule Westgate!"

Harborside led a round of applause, which silenced any other questions or doubts. The Night Masters filed out, congratulating themselves on their good fortune.

Seated on his stone throne, Victor, the Faceless, cradled

a heavy head in his hand. It was exhausting managing a city, a family business, a criminal cartel, and a seduction all at once. When he finally had Verovan's treasure, he would turn loose his golems on this nest of thieves. Then there would be nothing standing between him and his eventual empire.

## Twenty-Two
# The Gathering Storm

Olive's attempts to steer Thistle away from Victor were thwarted by the hard-line attitude of her supposed ally, Miss Winterhart. The halfling newcomer, while capable, intelligent, and alert, had to be the most tactless halfling in Faerûn. Unfortunately, Olive did not discover this flaw until the morning after Thistle's dinner date with Victor Dhostar, and by then it was too late.

That morning Olive was headed toward the dining hall, her mind on mushroom-and-chicken omelets, when she heard Thistle, angry and strident, shout, "It is *none* of your business what Victor and I did last night."

All thoughts of breakfast took a back seat to whatever potential disaster was brewing with the mistress of the house. Olive veered in the direction of the shout. She spied Thistle seated on the veranda, cornered by an irate Winterhart.

"It is very much my business if it threatens you or your household," Miss Winterhart snapped back just as Olive stepped outside to join them.

"Something amiss?" Olive asked helpfully, hoping to instill some calm in the air before the other halflings in the household heard the argument and began gossiping about it.

"This new halfling of yours," said Thistle, her eyes squinting with annoyance, "is prying into my private affairs. Her manner has gone beyond mere halfling cheek, and verges on full-fledged impertinence." If Thistle had been standing, Olive was sure she would have stamped her dainty little foot, but she was not, and so Olive was spared that bit of theatrics.

"She sneaked out to dine with Victor Dhostar last night without a chaperon or a bodyguard," Winterhart explained to Olive, "and she did not return until well after the midnight bell."

"I am mistress of this house," Thistle retorted shrilly. "I will not be given a curfew."

"Of course not, Lady Thistle," Olive agreed. "Yet midnight is a little late for a dinner engagement to run, even in Westgate. Surely you can understand how Miss Winterhart must have worried for your safety."

"There was nothing to worry about," Thistle replied, her voice softening a little. "It was just a dinner aboard *The Gleason*, a farewell banquet for the captain and the officers. Afterward we climbed up the lighthouse, just for the view. That's all."

"A likely story," Winterhart exclaimed.

"I beg your pardon?" Thistle said with a shocked expression.

"You heard me," Winterhart replied. "He didn't take you up there for the view. He took you up there so he could give you his little speech about how he dreamed of finding Verovan's treasure so he could use it to make Westgate the greatest city in the Realms—greater than Waterdeep. How he'll make Westgate safe, fill it with scholars and musicians, irrigate the fields."

Thistle started at the mention of Verovan's treasure, but her tone was as cold as the Great Glacier when she answered. "I do not appreciate my own staff spying on me. How dare you follow us?"

"Did you believe him when he told you he felt he could conquer the world with you by his side? When he asked if he would have the support of a clever, beautiful lady, what did you tell him? Have you given him a token of your esteem?" Winterhart asked snidely.

The girl reached without thinking, to feel the feather brooch pinned to her gown. "I find this petty espionage most unappealing," she snapped back, but her face flushed scarlet as she spoke.

"How else can I be expected to protect you from such a devious scoundrel?" Winterhart demanded.

"Victor," Thistle replied icily, "is . . . not . . . a . . . scoundrel. Mistress Ruskettle, I think you should find some other duties for Miss Winterhart. I simply cannot tolerate her as a lady's maid." The girl rose and strode imperiously back into the castle.

Olive surveyed Thistle's untouched breakfast tray and plucked a piece of bacon from the plate. She crunched on it as she thoughtfully appraised Winterhart.

The younger halfling glared back at her. "How can she be such a fool to fall for that arrogant, conniving greengrocer?" Winterhart growled.

"She's a girl, Winterhart," Olive said, picking up a forkful of fried potatoes. "Remember when you were a girl? When you argued with your mother about the relative worth or worthlessness of some boy who took your fancy? When you were certain you could take care of yourself without anyone's help? When no one could reason with you?"

"I was never like that," Winterhart argued.

"Never? I'm beginning to wonder about you, Winterhart," Olive said and wolfed down the forkful of potatoes.

She motioned for the other halfling to follow her down to the lower courtyard, where Kretschmer, one of the few surviving members of Lady Nettel's guard, was drilling the new recruits Olive had hired. Olive pulled two wooden swords off the rack and tossed one to the prim halfling. Winterhart caught the practice weapon smoothly.

"It's time I assessed your reputed skill with a blade," Olive said.

"Is this another trial, Mistress Ruskettle?" Winterhart asked.

"No. Just a little exercise while we discuss tactics." Olive gave Winterhart's wooden blade a smack with her own. Winterhart responded by weaving her sword warily.

"I applaud your initiative following Lady Thistle last night," Olive said. "I can't, however, say I think much of the way you gave yourself away." She struck a blow aimed at Winterhart's thigh.

Winterhart parried the strike easily. "Does this mean you will try to convince Her Ladyship to keep me on as her personal maid?"

Olive shook her head, parrying a blow of Winterhart's aimed directly at her heart. "I can't afford to invite censure on myself. Someone's got to undo the damage you've done."

"Damage I've done?" Winterhart squeaked, lunging with her blade at Olive's shoulder. "Victor Dhostar is the one who'll being doing all the damage. That man is a menace," the younger halfling snarled.

"Agreed," Olive replied, leaping backward to avoid the lunge.

"If you know I'm right, you have to keep me close to Lady Thistle," Winterhart said, pressing her advantage, lunging again with her blade at Olive's shoulder. "Did you see how she blushed when I asked her if she'd given him a token? Did you notice she left the veranda instead of ordering me away? Even she knows I'm right."

"It doesn't matter who is right to a girl like Thistle," Olive said with a sigh, smacking the hilt of Winterhart's sword away from her body. "It matters who makes her feel good about herself. Dhostar makes her feel like a woman. You made her feel like a child. You've practically driven her into Dhostar's arms. I've got to try to make her feel like a lady before Dhostar makes her forget her position." She struck a blow against Winterhart's hip.

Winterhart's blade whipped back before Olive had a chance to parry. The tip of the younger halfling's weapon slid across Ruskettle's throat.

Olive stepped back and saluted with her practice weapon. "You have the drive and the skill and the reflexes," she told Winterhart, "but you still have to learn when to pull back. I'm assigning you to help Kretschmer drill the new recruits. That would be a better use of your skills, I think."

Winterhart glared at Olive.

More softly, Olive added, "Should you happen to show any more initiative and follow Lady Thistle about, without getting caught at it, or letting her know afterward, that would probably be the best use of your skills."

Winterhart smiled slyly and saluted Olive with her own wooden blade.

*   *   *   *   *

Kimbel stood in the center of the Faceless's new lair, turning slowly, surveying the contents of the room. From inside his shirt he pulled out a golden rod and began tapping it against all the magic in his sight, against the remaining iron golems, against the masks worn by the Night Masters, against the enchanted staves and weaponry hanging on the wall. A tiny spark jumped from the wand each time it touched a magic item.

A bell chimed, and Kimbel turned to face the magical portal mirror as a figure stepped through and entered the lair.

"You're late," the assassin noted calmly to the new arrival, a comely halfling dressed very primly.

"I've been reassigned," Winterhart explained. "Ruskettle's got me drilling the Thalavar castle guard. You've never seen a sorrier bunch of would-be warriors. I couldn't get away until lunchtime."

"You aren't eating with the others? Someone might suspect you're not a halfling," Kimbel said.

"It will be over before anyone guesses the truth," Winterhart replied.

"So you aren't Lady Thistle's maid anymore? Do you think you'll get a chance to snatch her brooch in your new position."

"No, but despite my warnings, Thistle is obviously crazy about your master. I'm sure he'll have no trouble sweet-talking her into handing it over to him. He'll probably enjoy that more than receiving it from one of us."

An evil chuckle drifted around the pair. "So true," a disembodied voice agreed.

Kimbel whirled about, the little golden wand in his hand held out at the ready, but Winterhart stayed his hand. "It's only the dragon skull," the halfling woman said. She turned to the corner of the room where the dragon's skull sat balanced on an iron tripod, its eyes glowing like hot coals. "Hail, Mistinarperadnacles Hai Draco," the halfling said coolly.

"Hail, servants of the Faceless," Mist replied and chuckled again.

"And what amuses you so?" Kimbel asked the creature.

"I have lost my life, my body, and my freedom, yet I still have my sight," Mist replied, "and a dragon's sight is not easily deceived by invisibility, illusion, or other magic."

"Prove it," Winterhart challenged. "Tell me what you know."

"Very well. You, Miss Winterhart, are no more a halfling than I, but I know what and who you are," Mist retorted. "As for Kimbel, I think the Faceless would be very interested to know the truth about his magically enslaved assassin. There is a way, however, to ensure my silence. You know what it is."

Winterhart nodded. "Once the Faceless has obtained Verovan's hoard for the Night Masks, I will grant you your boon."

\* \* \* \* \*

Victor Dhostar sat in his office in the Tower, listening to one of the city's accountants explain why the budget for the preceding month had been exceeded by twenty thousand gold pieces, but how the deficit for the current month would only be half that amount if the croamarkh passed the oar and sail tax. Fortunately, the croamarkh was delivered from having to deal immediately with the budget nightmare by a knock on the door.

"Come," the new croamarkh called out.

A guard entered the room. "Excuse me, Your Lordship. Lady Thistle Thalavar is here."

"Thank you. Please show her in," Victor said. To the accountant he explained, "I'm afraid my business with House Thalavar is more urgent than this problem. We will have to continue this discussion later. Make another appointment with my scribe."

"But, Your Lordship, we need—"

"Dismissed," Victor growled with an expression that would brook no argument.

The accountant gathered his books and pens and bowed. He bowed again to Lady Thistle as she entered the room. As the accountant exited, Victor smiled with delight. The croamarkh had no appointment with Thistle, but on the off-chance she would take it into her head to visit him here he had left instructions that she be shown up immediately. "What service can I do for Your Ladyship?" Lord Victor asked.

"I can wait if I'm interrupting your work," Thistle began.

"Lady Thistle, you are the head of one of the leading families of Westgate. I wouldn't dream of keeping you waiting."

As he rose from his desk and circled around to stand before the girl, Victor noted how his flattery caused her to straighten with pride. "Besides, if I kept you waiting and you left, I would be disappointed that I'd missed seeing you." He took up the girl's hand and brushed his lips along her fingertips.

"I've given a lot of thought to our conversation last night," Thistle said. "I'm feeling very unhappy that I would not—could not give you the token you asked for." She touched the feather brooch pinned to her gown. "After more careful consideration, I have decided to give you my wholehearted support, and you will have my token, tonight."

"Oh, Thistle, my darling," Lord Victor whispered. He swept the girl up in his arms and kissed her as if she were a woman.

"Lord Victor," Thistle remarked when the croamarkh finally released her, "I fear you've mistaken my meaning."

Victor stepped back and turned his head away as if to hide his disappointment. "Forgive me, Lady Thistle, I thought . . . I dared hope . . ."

"Oh, Victor," Thistle whispered, stepping forward and taking the croamarkh's hands. "It's not that I don't lo—

that I'm not honored by your declaration. It's only that I meant something different by offering my support."

Victor looked the girl in the eyes once more, confusion written on his face. "What did you mean, Thistle?"

"I meant I will deliver Verovan's hoard to you. So you can do all you said for Westgate. So you can make it the greatest city in all of Faerun."

A smile fluttered across the croamarkh's face. "Oh, Thistle. Sweet lady. All that talk of Verovan's treasure— that's just dreams, faerie tales. Someday, I will do all those things I spoke of, but when I asked for your support I was thinking more realistically—I was thinking of the kind of support a woman gives a man. Thistle, I love you. I want you to be my wife."

Thistle beamed with pleasure, but she was still determined to prove herself. "There is no position I'd like more," the girl replied, "but I will give you Verovan's hoard. It's not a myth. Meet me tonight at Castle Vhammos, and I will prove it."

Victor shook his head. "Darling, even for Verovan's hoard I cannot meet you tonight. I must be at the Temple of Gond for the ceremony to initiate apprentices. If I did not attend, it would offend every artisan in the city, not to mention the priests of Gond, and probably Gond himself."

Thistle laughed. "You are so dutiful. Meet me tomorrow night then. You shall have Verovan's treasure, and you shall have me."

"Very well," the croamarkh agreed. He leaned forward and whispered in the girl's ear, "Tomorrow night I'll let you prove whatever you like."

\* \* \* \* \*

The next morning, Thistle called Olive out to the veranda to join her for breakfast. The lady was watching Kretschmer and Winterhart drilling the castle guard. Marching in formation, the new recruits were beginning to look like a force to be reckoned with.

"Miss Winterhart is better suited to her new post, I

think," Thistle commented.

"Miss Winterhart tells me you visited Lord Dhostar yesterday afternoon, again without an escort," the halfling retorted.

"She followed me again? Of all the nerve! I want you to dismiss her at once."

"No, Lady, I will not," Olive replied. Before the girl could protest, the halfling pressed on with an explanation. "I authorized Miss Winterhart to follow you. I couldn't care less about your courtship of Victor Dhostar, but if you're attacked by Night Masks, there must be someone present to defend you. I'm sure Lord Victor would agree with me that your safety is more important than your privacy."

"Yes, he probably would," Thistle agreed, her tone softening at Olive's assessment of the croamarkh. "He cares about me. Oh, Olive, he's so wonderful. I wish grandmother were here. She would be so happy for me. I know she'd approve of my supporting him, don't you think?"

"That all depends," Olive replied. "Your grandmother was the most dignified lady I ever met. I think she hoped you would be like her. Are you offering this support in a dignified fashion or like a schoolgirl?"

Thistle straightened her back as if her grandmother had just chastised her for poor posture. "Of course I will offer my support in a dignified fashion," she insisted.

"Good," Olive replied, "because however wonderful he may be, Victor Dhostar is still the head of a rival house. What was that thing your grandmother used to say about marrying into rival houses?"

" 'You can marry into them, but don't offer to cover their losses,' " Thistle replied. "Olive, Lord Victor doesn't need my money, but if he did I would give it to him because I know he would use it for the good of all Westgate."

Olive *tch*ed just as Lady Nettel might have done.

"Don't you halflings have any sense of romance?" Thistle snapped with annoyance.

"Sense and romance," Olive sniffed. "Now there are two words that definitely don't go together."

Thistle harrumphed and stormed off the veranda, just as she had the day before, leaving Olive in complete possession of her breakfast.

* * * * *

After assigning duty rosters to the newly trained guards, Olive spent the rest of the day in her room, strumming nervously on her yarting. Try as she might, she could not shake off a sense of impending doom she had, not for herself but for Thistle Thalavar. The halfling was racking her brain trying to figure what Victor Dhostar's game was. Thistle was a good match for any noble in the city, but men like Dhostar didn't care about making a good match, Olive realized. They cared only about power.

Jamal came calling on Olive at Castle Thalavar shortly after sunset. "There's something very strange going on," the actress reported. "Kel says there are all sorts of Night Masks out tonight. He followed a pair of them down to Castle Vhammos. He says he thinks they're all holding some sort of war council."

Olive set down her yarting and began strapping on her scabbard. At that moment, Miss Winterhart burst into the room. The younger halfling was dressed all in leather and armed for combat with a human-sized sword strapped across her back in the fashion of warriors of the north.

"Lady Thistle has gone to Castle Vhammos," Winterhart reported, "but I didn't dare approach too closely. The guards are letting all sorts of unsavory types enter, but I do not think they will let a halfling pass. I know another way in. Follow me."

Winterhart turned about and strode off with Olive and Jamal dashing after her. The younger halfling led them to her quarters in the lower regions of the castle. Olive was just wondering if there was some secret passageway Lady Nettel had neglected to mention when Winterhart plunged, like a diver into a pond, into the mirror hanging on her wall.

Olive's startled reflection rippled for a moment and then was still. "I'm probably going to regret this," the older halfling whispered just before she stepped into the darkness of the mirror.

Jamal was left facing her own reflection. There was probably nothing she could do, she told herself. She wasn't much of a fighter, and she doubted very much there would be any call for an actress wherever the mirror took her. "Some cheap hero you are," she said, glaring at the aging face glaring back at her. Taking a deep breath, she leaped into the mirror, thinking, I *know* I'm going to regret this.

Darkness seemed to fill the other side of the mirror. After a few moments, however, Olive's eyes adjusted to the dim light cast by a brazier. She stood in the center of an underground cavern containing items removed from the lair of the Faceless—most notable were the remaining iron golems, the empty rack for the masks of the Night Masters, and the skull of the dragon Mist, with the red lights spinning in its eye sockets.

"Where are we?" Jamal whispered.

"The Faceless's newest lair, I'd guess," Olive replied. "Winterhart, how'd you get a magic portal mirror into here? What's going on, woman?"

Winterhart held up a finger to indicate Olive should wait for a moment. The younger halfling stood before Mist's skull, holding a small golden wand.

"Your associate is in the chamber above with the Night Masters and their followers," the dragon's skull was saying to Winterhart. "There are over two hundred Night Masks waiting for the Faceless to lead them to Verovan's hoard."

"Verovan's hoard!" Olive gasped in astonishment. "But where are Lady Thistle and Lord Victor?" she demanded.

"Lord Victor has taken Lady Thistle to the top of the southern tower," Mist reported. "With no idea that her lover is the Faceless, Lady Thistle is showing him how to open the portal to Verovan's treasury."

"Dhostar is the Faceless?" Jamal gasped.

"Of course," Olive said. "That explains how he managed

to make it look like his father was the Faceless."

Mist growled at Winterhart, "I've fulfilled all my promises to you, warrior. Free me now, as you promised," the dragon's spirit demanded.

Winterhart stepped forward and tapped the golden wand on Mist's disembodied skull. "Rest now, wyrm," the halfling said.

The light spinning about in the skull's eye sockets seemed to flow toward Winterhart's golden wand, then vanished. The bone of the skull crumbled into dust. An eldritch wind blew through the cavern, blowing the dust about in a cyclone. By the glow of the brazier the dust seemed to take on the shape of a red dragon.

"Farewell, you red-headed witch," Mist's voice whispered, "and farewell to you, Olive Ruskettle."

Then the wind increased, knocking Winterhart to one knee before carrying the dust away to some far plane.

Olive had her sword pointed at Winterhart before the other halfling could rise to her feet. "You've known all along that Victor Dhostar is the Faceless?"

"Of course," Winterhart replied. In the blink of an eye, the prim halfling had drawn her own sword and crossed the blade against Ruskettle's. "That is why I led you here, so you could witness his moment of triumph."

## Twenty-Three
# Battle With the Night Masks

With Winterhart on one knee, Olive pressed her advantage before the other halfling had a chance to demonstrate her superior skill with a blade. Olive circled to Winterhart's left side and lunged with her blade, but the younger halfling switched her sword to her left hand and parried her opponent neatly.

"Ruskettle, you're making a mistake," Winterhart declared. "I'm not working for the Faceless."

"Oh, no," Olive replied sarcastically. "You just have a secret entry to his lair so you can come for tea."

As the two halflings faced off against one another, Jamal looked around for something, anything she might use to help Olive fight Winterhart. A two-handed broadsword hung on a wall behind the iron golems. The actress grasped the weapon by its hilt and slid it from the hooks that held it in place. The sword was unbelievably heavy, and Jamal was unable to raise it without her arms shaking from the exertion.

"Perhaps you would care to try something smaller, Jamal," a man whispered behind her.

The actress swung around, trailing the broadsword with her, but unable to raise it to defend herself. Kimbel stood in a doorway, eyeing her with cruel amusement. She glared at the assassin who unfastened the scabbard about his waist and tossed it at her feet.

Distracted by the sound of Kimbel's voice, Olive retreated a step from her opponent, giving Winterhart a chance to get to her feet.

"Winterhart," Kimbel barked, "you haven't got time for

this. The Faceless is about to address his troops. You'll miss your cue." The assassin retreated through the doorway.

Winterhart dashed after him, calling out, "Come on, Ruskettle, Jamal. You don't want to miss the fun." She disappeared into the darkness beyond the door.

Olive exchanged a confused look with Jamal; then the halfling raced after Winterhart. Jamal dropped the ridiculously heavy broadsword. She considered for a moment the sword and scabbard Kimbel had given her. It could be a trick, but she needed a weapon. I really wish I'd read the script before I jumped into this play, she thought as she followed Olive.

On the other side of the doorway, hewn into the bedrock, was a stairway. There were more than a hundred steps, and Olive was breathless when she reached the top. The door was a pivoting section of wall, which someone had propped open with a spike driven into the floor. A tapestry hung over the door on the far side, concealing it from view. With her dagger, Olive poked a hole in a threadbare spot in the tapestry and pressed her eye up close.

She looked out on a dais and, beyond that, a cavernous chamber. Once, long ago, this had been the audience chamber of King Verovan, but when the castle had fallen into the hands of House Vhammos it had been converted to a dining hall, with feasting tables on the dais and in the hall below.

Now Night Masks packed the room, hundreds of them, dressed in costumes as varied as the citizenry of Westgate. There were merchants and priests, sailors and drovers, pickpockets and cutthroats, all wearing domino masks and all of them armed with deadly weapons. All had their attention focused on the dais. Ten figures wearing black robes and half masks of white porcelain stood on the stairs leading up the dais. Olive recognized one of them as Kimbel despite the mask he wore.

A man dressed in a blood-colored robe of velvet stood at the top of the dais. His face was a magical blur of colors. He stepped forward, and a buzzing sound spread through the room as hundreds of Night Masks realized he was their master.

"The Faceless," Jamal whispered behind Olive. The actress had poked her own eyehole farther up the tapestry.

Kimbel motioned for silence, and a hush fell over the room.

"You see, I live while those who oppose me have perished!" the Faceless thundered. The magical distortion of his voice, caused by the mask that obscured his features, sent a shiver down Jamal's spine. "The nobles opposed me, and they are no more. The croamarkh opposed me, and he is no more. The sell-sword Alias and her companions opposed me, and *they* are no more. This night I claim rulership of this city, and all of you who are loyal to me will be rewarded!"

A cheer went up from the crowd.

"Tonight begins a new era for Westgate," the Faceless continued. "The treasure of King Verovan is ours to take—"

At the mention of treasure another cheer rippled through the crowd. Gold always had a way of rallying the troops, the Faceless thought. He waited patiently for the din to die down.

"There will be danger," the Faceless warned matter-of-factly. "Verovan's treasure lies in another plane, and like most treasure hoards is guarded by creatures that dwell in that plane. Your lives will be at risk, yet your reward will be great. All of you who survive will receive a share of what is looted from the hoard. Once that share is yours, you will no longer be criminals, but the wealthiest men and women in Westgate."

There was another cheer, but the Faceless cut it off with a sharp motion of his hand. "I am the one who made the Night Masks the most powerful guild in the Heartlands. I am the one who destroyed your enemies. I am the one who will lay Verovan's treasure at your feet, but first you must pay my price." The Faceless paused.

The room went silent as each Night Mask worried what that price might be, and each considered what price would be too high.

"I demand your fealty," the Faceless announced in a

sepulchral tone, "not as a crime lord, but as your king! I will make Westgate the greatest empire in the Realms, and you shall all share in the riches of that empire! If you share in my vision, if you accept my terms, kneel now before me."

Like faithful worshipers, the Night Masks below the dais knelt as a body. The Night Masters on the steps did not seem certain whether or not they too were required to join in this physical display, but when Kimbel knelt, the others followed. If any one of them held a republican sentiment or inwardly questioned the wisdom of agreeing to so empower an anonymous crime lord, they did not share it with their fellows.

"All hail the Faceless," Kimbel cried, "King of Westgate!"

"The Faceless," the crowd shouted, "King of Westgate!"

The Faceless, surprised but very pleased by Kimbel's call for the crowd's allegiance, held up his arms and basked in the adulation of the thieves of Westgate. Unfortunately, his moment of glory was followed immediately by an uncomfortable silence as hundreds of Night Masks grew anxious for their reward and wondered if it was too soon to get off their knees.

"All hail the Faceless," a shrill but clear voice called out from the back of the dais. "Master of an honorless, greedy mob. Traitor to his duty and family. Murderer of his father and his lover." The speaker leaped up on the feasting table behind the Faceless so that all could see the red-haired halfling woman in leather armor—Winterhart. The sound of her sword slipping from its scabbard slithered through the length of the hall. She aimed the blade at the Faceless's neck.

"My gods," Olive gasped under her breath. "She's going to get herself killed.

"But if that isn't an entrance to die for," Jamal whispered, "I don't know what is."

The aura of puissance momentarily faded from the Faceless as he retreated from the point of the halfling's weapon and nearly took a tumble down the dais steps.

"Maybe we could grab her and escape down the stairs," Olive whispered. She began to pull back the tapestry, but

Jamal set a heavy hand on her shoulder and held her back.

"Wait," the actress whispered. "Heroes never truly die," she added with a delighted grin on her face.

She's as crazed as Winterhart, Olive thought.

The Night Masks held their breath, waiting to see what their master would do.

From behind his mask the Faceless glared with fury at the insolent halfling facing him. It would not look particularly valiant for him to skewer the vermin, but none of his Night Masters showed the least inclination to grab the creature and throw it at his feet. All were no doubt afraid of losing a hand to the steel weapon still pointed in their master's direction. Even more aggravating were the charges the halfling brought. How had she discovered his secrets?

He would have to make a joke of her. It was not the dignified beginning he imagined for his reign, but he had to keep her from making further accusations. "Did you intend to challenge me all by yourself?" the Faceless asked with a tone of amused derision.

Miss Winterhart smiled. "Well, to tell the truth, I did bring a few friends."

Olive's heart leaped to her throat. Surely this crazy halfling didn't expect the three of them to fight a horde of Night Masks! Did she expect Olive and Jamal to step out from behind the tapestry and make another dramatic speech?

Apparently Winterhart had not been counting just Olive and Jamal among her few friends. The halfling swordswoman gestured to the back of the hall just as platoons of the city watch marched toward the back ranks of Night Masks. The soldiers all wore leather armor and copper helmets and were armed with swords and crossbows. The room rang with the echoes of their boots stomping on the stone-paved floor.

Durgar the Just stood at the front of his troops in his silver plate armor, carrying his mace like a staff of power. "In the name of the watch," the priest bellowed, "I order you to lay down your weapons and surrender. Failure to obey will be met with lethal force. This is your only warning."

The Night Masks, who for years had considered the watch a joke, were not about to surrender to them when the largest treasure they'd ever looted was nearly theirs.

The thieves charged first, with their weapons drawn. The front ranks of the watch knelt in a precision maneuver, leaving the second rank clear to toss out great capture nets. The kneeling first rank let loose a volley of crossbow bolts. Night Masks at the battle's front who were not dragged down by the heavy, weighted nets, were felled by the shower of missiles.

The Night Masters and the Faceless began moving toward the door hidden behind the tapestry. Winterhart leaped down from the table in front of them, blocking their escape. The Faceless and four of the Night Masters drew swords.

"I guess this is what you call a cue, isn't it?" Olive asked the actress.

Jamal nodded grimly. She pulled back the tapestry, and, with swords drawn, the pair burst onto the dais to back up Winterhart.

In the back of the hall, swordsmen of the watch maneuvered right and left on the thieves, and soon steel clashed against steel. There was a burst of light as some thief, equipped with a powerful amulet, teleported from the hall. Three thieves standing behind their fellows aimed wands at the watch. Blasts of eldritch energy issued from the wands, and five swordsmen were knocked back by an invisible rain of blows. A moment later, however, all three wand-armed thieves became pincushions of crossbow bolts—a warning to any other Night Masks that those using magic would be favored targets.

On the dais, those Night Masters not armed with long blades shrank back from the naked steel presented by the two halflings and the actress. The remaining four flanked the Faceless.

Winterhart squared off against the Faceless and one Night Master, Jamal against a second Night Master, and Olive against the remaining two. Winterhart dealt the Faceless an immediate blow to his sword hand with the

flat of her blade, and her return sweep parried a blow
from the Night Master who stood beside him. Faceless
lost his grip on his weapon—the blade spun across the
dais. The leader of the Night Masks was forced to retreat
to retrieve his weapon.

Jamal remembered immediately why she'd given up
adventuring twenty years ago. The thought of a sharpened steel blade slicing through her skin, her flesh, and
her innards filled her with a nauseating fear. In his
scornful offering of a sword, Kimbel had challenged one
of her greatest fears. She wished desperately that she
was wearing some kind of armor or carrying a shield, but
she knew that in the shape she was in the weight of the
armor would be too great and she needed both hands to
keep the sword before her steady. The goddess of luck
must have been looking out for her, though. The Night
Master before her seemed to be neither an aggressive nor
skilled fighter. Perhaps he'd drawn a blade only to
impress the Faceless. Jamal held her own, parrying the
blows the Night Master delivered. She even managed to
draw first blood across his arm.

Olive was not feeling so fortunate. One of the two
humans attacking her was a burly man, quite skilled
with his weapon, while the other human was so tall that
she had trouble keeping her sword high enough to parry
his blows aimed at her head. She'd only just managed to
ward off a stroke that might have decapitated her, but
the cost was accepting a smack to the ribs. Her leather
jerkin kept the blade from cutting into her, but the force
of the blow knocked the air out of her and left her side
throbbing. As if that weren't enough, it appeared as if the
assassin Kimbel were about to join the two swordsmen in
their attacks on the older halfling.

Kimbel placed his hands on the head of the taller
Night Master facing Olive. An aura of ball lightning
erupted from the thief's head. His hair stood upright
from his scalp, and Olive could see the bolts of energy
crisscross the flesh left exposed by the mask. The Night
Master fell forward, steam pouring from his ears.

Olive gaped at Kimbel with astonishment. If she'd told

every halfling in Westgate that the Dhostar assassin had helped her, not one of them would believer her. She didn't believe it herself.

Kimbel blew on his hands. With a sly grin, he asked, "Haven't you ever seen a *shocking grasp* spell before, Mistress Ruskettle?"

The remaining Night Master engaging Olive was distracted just enough by the fall of his fellow for Olive to deal him a critical blow. Kimbel moved on to give another shocking grasp to the Night Master battling Jamal.

In the meantime, Winterhart dispatched the Night Master before her with professional precision just before the Faceless returned to the fray.

Olive turned to a corner where two Night Masters without swords cowered, waiting for the tide to carry them one way or the other. Olive barked an order for them to surrender or fight. To the halfling's delight, they surrendered.

Jamal and Kimbel bullied the remaining three Night Masters into lying with their hands over their heads.

Olive looked out across the hall.

The superior teamwork of the watch was delivering the victory to them. For years they had fought their enemy in the streets, where the thieves could too easily go to ground. Now, however, the watch's more conventional combat training had the Night Masks pinned, and the thieves were surrendering in droves. Some lay down or played dead with the plan of creeping off once the battle front crossed over them, but these were thwarted by the watch, who dropped heavy nets over them before moving forward. Durgar was in the middle of the room, charging the dais, his glowing mace administering his judgment against those who had disobeyed his command.

Kimbel, Olive, and Jamal stood back and watched as the Faceless attempted a powerful strike against Winterhart, which she parried with a strength beyond any Olive might have credited to a halfling. "Admit your guilt, Victor Dhostar," Winterhart demanded, "and surrender to the watch, or you will pay for your crimes with your life."

The Faceless snarled like a beast, but admitted nothing, and neither did he surrender. He and Winterhart battled on. It soon became apparent which combatant had more skill. Every stab the Faceless delivered to the halfling she matched and bettered.

Olive was just beginning to realize that there was something familiar about Winterhart's parries and attacks when the Faceless's blade caught on the fabric of the young halfling's sleeve and tore it away from her arm.

Olive gasped, and even the Faceless stepped back in surprise. Winterhart's right arm was marked by an azure brand, a tattoo of thorns and cresting waves, with a blue rose at her wrist.

"I knew she had to be a cheap hero," Jamal declared with a chuckle. Beside the actress, Kimbel muttered some unintelligible spell words.

A shimmer of light rippled across Winterhart's body and the halfling began to transform before their eyes. Her frame grew to human size, her muscles took on the definition of a warrior in training, and her plump cheeks and rounded chin grew more drawn and angular. She became the former defender of Westgate—Alias the Sell-Sword. With the *polymorph* magic dispelled, the chain-mail armor, boots, and cloak she'd worn upon her transformation into a halfling were now revealed. The scar from Victor's ring still blazed across her cheek.

Alias swung her weapon with an uncustomary fierceness and let out a blood-curdling battle cry as she dashed at the Faceless. Shocked, the Night Mask retreated three steps, stumbled on his long robes, and fell on his back. The swordswoman stepped up to her foe and set her booted foot down on his sword hand, keeping enough pressure on it to prevent him from raising it. With the tip of her blade she pried off the coin mask, which obscured his features.

Victor Dhostar's face appeared at her feet. "I should make you pay for your crimes now, with your blood," Alias said coolly, "but I will give you instead to Durgar for trial. The quick death of a warrior is too good for you."

"Alias, my darling, no!" Victor cried. "It wasn't me! It was Kimbel! He was never enchanted to serve my family. It happened the other way around. All those years ago, he put me under his spell so he could use my family and finally destroy them. I tried to resist, but he was too strong. All I have done has been at his command. He is the true Faceless."

"Why did he help us in combat then?" Olive demanded.

"And why," Durgar said, climbing the stairs to the dais, "did he turn over all the Night Masters' books to me and dispel all their magic yesterday?"

Victor glared up at the assassin standing beside Jamal. "You will pay for your treachery!" he screamed. Pointing a ringed finger at the assassin, he snarled, "*Kreggarish.*"

Kimbel grabbed the sides of his enchanted mask, screaming as Melman had when he had been branded.

"Enough," Alias commanded, smacking at the nobleman's hand with the tip of her blade, leaving a crimson streak across his fingers. Victor whimpered like a child, but a moment later he laughed at the assassin. "The brand is permanent Kimbel. You'll never be rid of it. You shall always feel the pain," the vanquished Faceless gloated.

Kimbel tossed aside the white mask with a hearty chuckle. His face was untouched. "Sorry, old boy," he said, "but not only do you have the wrong man—" Kimbel's figure began to glow and shimmer as Winterhart's had when she had transformed into Alias, and in a moment he reappeared as none other than Mintassan the Sage. "—but a magic ring like that hasn't held power over me for decades."

"If you're not Kimbel," Olive asked, "who is?"

"Why Kimbel is, of course," Mintassan replied. "Though at the moment he's chained in the dungeon of Castle Dhostar and looks like a feeble-minded sage named Mintassan."

"And where's Dragonbait?" Olive demanded.

Alias looked up at Mintassan. "Where is Dragonbait?" she asked.

In the swordswoman's moment of distraction, Victor Dhostar slid his wounded hand deep into the sleeve of his robe and pulled out a twisted glass vial. He smashed the vial against the floor.

Quicksilver dribbled from the broken glassware. The liquid metal glowed white-hot until it bathed Victor Dhostar in a glaring light. When the light faded a moment later, Victor Dhostar had vanished.

"What was that?" Jamal asked, blinking away the spots on her eyes.

"He's slid through a dimension door. He cannot have gotten far," Mintassan explained.

"Spread out," Durgar ordered a patrol of his men. "Search the entire castle."

"I'll check the lair, in case he tries to escape by one of the portal mirrors," Mintassan said. "Silver path, Faceless's lair," the sage murmured, then vanished.

"Thistle!" Olive cried. "He would go after Thistle and try to snatch something from Verovan's hoard. Mist said she's—"

"At the top of the south tower," Alias shouted. The swordswoman dashed from the hall with Olive and Jamal at her heels.

# Twenty-Four
# Verovan's Hoard

Thistle Thalavar paced anxiously on the roof of the southern tower of Castle Vhammos. Her heart was heavy, her mind uneasy. The evening was not turning out as she had imagined it would. In the daydreams she indulged in all day, Victor had been amazed when she proved she really did know how to reach Verovan's treasure. He had recognized how clever she was and had considered her his equal. He had made her his confidant on all matters of state. Once again he had declared his love. In her fantasy, they had spent the rest of the evening in one another's arms.

In reality, when Thistle had used her grandmother's feather brooch to open the magical portal into the treasure hoard, Victor, although pleased, had not seemed particularly amazed. He had accepted the feather brooch as her token with a warm kiss, but he had been unable to hide his annoyance when he discovered he himself could not use the token to open the hoard. When Thistle explained that only someone of Verovan's bloodline could use the brooch, the croamarkh had bristled.

Thistle realized with sickening dread that Victor was sensitive to the fact that she was descended of royalty and he was only a noble. Even worse, no matter how loyal and loving she was, the nobleman did not like having to rely on her to reach the treasure.

The final disappointment came when, instead of spending the rest of the evening alone with her, the croamarkh had asked her to wait on the tower while he assembled his forces to help clear out the treasure.

Now Thistle waited alone, trying to convince herself that Victor was still worthy of the treasure because he would use it to make Westgate a city of beauty and justice, admired by all. She suspected, however, that he was not the lover she had dreamed of.

The interdimensional portal to Verovan's treasure hung twenty feet from the edge of the tower. By stroking the spine of her feather brooch Thistle could cause the portal to open just a crack. First a section of the sky would ripple, causing the stars to shimmer. Then a searing white light would flash out from the eldritch rent in the planar fabric. As soon as the girl removed her hand from the brooch, the portal snapped shut, leaving her standing in the dark, beneath the starlit sky. If she held the pin long enough, the portal grew into an oval eight feet across by twelve feet high. Once the portal was completely opened, it sent out a dark, arcing bridge to the edge of the tower.

Thistle stroked the feather brooch, causing the sky to flash as if with heat lightning. Something hissed in the darkness behind her, and Thistle turned around slowly, more curious than startled.

Dragonbait stepped out of the shadow of the tower battlement. He had been hiding there since Thistle and Victor had arrived at the castle. He had seen how Victor had played on Thistle's affections and had watched as she had demonstrated how to use the feather brooch to reach Verovan's hold. Thistle had arrived with Victor giddy and carefree, but now she was solemn and melancholy. The saurial hoped that meant he could now convince her to come away from the tower—for he was growing nervous for her safety—for the safety of all of Westgate.

Each time Thistle stroked the feather brooch, cracking open the portal, the paladin's *shen* sight sensed a bolt of lightning and went momentarily blind, leaving him with a stabbing pain in the back of his head and a throbbing sensation in his teeth. His *shen* sight was being overloaded by some great evil that lay beyond the portal— within Verovan's hoard. Whatever it was, Dragonbait did not want to risk its release over the city.

The paladin motioned for Thistle to come away from the battlement and go with him down the tower stairs.

"I can't," Thistle replied. "I promised Victor that I would wait here for his return."

Dragonbait made the sign for danger in the thieves' hand cant.

"I know all about the dangers," the girl said. "Grandmother first told me the tale of Verovan's hoard when I was six, just in case she died suddenly and I became the keeper of the key."

Thistle turned away to look over the tower battlement as she explained the history of the key to the paladin. "King Verovan's greed is legend," she said. "He was so obsessed with hanging on to his treasure that he exchanged a piece of his soul with a lord of the Abyss to create a planar pocket to hold his treasure hoard. When Verovan died, the lord of the Abyss ordered his minions to loot the king's hoard. Their lord gave them the piece of Verovan's soul encased in amber so they could use it with the key to open the portal.

"My grandmother's grandfather, Gen, was the king's third cousin. Gen was an adventurer, a paladin, like you. Luckily, he was in Westgate when Verovan died. He sensed the evil things swarming to the royal castle and followed them. He waited until they had opened the portal and had rushed inside. The minions of the Abyss left the key and the piece of Verovan's soul on the battlement with a single guard, a true tanar'ri. Gen battled the tanar'ri and destroyed it. Then he smashed the amber, freeing the piece of his cousin Verovan's soul, but the piece of soul flew to what it loved most—the treasure. Once the soul was separated from the key, the portal closed. Gen fashioned the key into a brooch, hiding it in plain sight, making a green feather the trading badge of our family's house."

Dragonbait shook his head at the girl's foolishness. If her ancestor had seen fit to leave the portal closed, why couldn't she do likewise. A lifetime of city dwelling, even in so dangerous a city as Westgate, had left Thistle innocent of the greater powers of evil.

"Grandmother warned that the treasure might not be worth the price to be paid for opening the portal, but I believe Victor should have the treasure. He will do good things with it," Thistle insisted.

Dragonbait shook his head again and wished this girl understood Saurial, so that he could lecture her on Victor Dhostar. He considered dragging her from the tower, but with the battle raging downstairs, the noblewoman was probably safer up here.

Thistle stroked the feather brooch again, releasing a streak of light from the portal and delivering another momentarily blinding blow to the paladin's *shen* sight. The saurial snatched Thistle's hand and pulled it away from the brooch.

The girl looked puzzled. She hadn't a clue as to the source of the paladin's anxiety.

There was nothing left to do, Dragonbait realized, but guard Thistle until Alias came to the roof. The swordswoman could tell Thistle about Victor's crimes. He leaned back against the battlement and waited patiently.

The paladin was taken unawares by the sudden appearance of Victor Dhostar. The nobleman manifested on the roof with some magical spell. His robes were torn, and he was bruised and bleeding.

Catching sight of him, Thistle ran to his side before Dragonbait could hold her back. "Victor, you're hurt!" the girl exclaimed. "What happened?" she asked as she tenderly touched a bruise on his face.

"There's a battle going on downstairs," the nobleman explained. "Night Masks and Durgar's men. Kimbel has framed me. You must open the portal so I can hide from my enemies."

"Victor, you did not give me a chance to explain fully before. There are evil things trapped inside with Verovan's treasure."

"Thistle, there are evil things in the castle down below, coming after me. If you loved me, you would not argue. Now open the bloody portal!"

Dragonbait stepped forward and hissed, but Victor had grabbed Thistle by the waist and aimed a dagger at her belly. "Don't try anything foolish, lizardman," the noble-man said. "Open the portal, Thistle, quickly."

Thistle's face colored with anger, and for a moment Dragonbait thought she might argue with Victor. The moment passed. Thistle collected what was left of her dignity. Giving the nobleman a chill look of disdain, she touched her hand to her brooch. Light spilled out on the tower as the portal grew. A crystal bridge, as dark as the sky, arced over the battlement.

Victor clasped his hand about Thistle's so that she could not remove it from the brooch. "You first," the nobleman ordered Dragonbait.

The paladin looked aghast at the portal. The waves of evil spilling out sickened him, but now he sensed some-thing worse. Hunger. Something within Verovan's hoard was eager to devour whatever came its way.

"Move it!" Victor screamed, poking his dagger into Thistle's side until she whimpered. "I haven't got any-thing to lose by killing her," he snarled.

Dragonbait climbed up the bridge and made his way toward the portal. Victor followed, dragging Thistle after him. Just as he reached the other side of the bridge, the paladin drew his sword. He was not going to be devoured without a fight. Victor did not seem to object. The noble-man's eyes had the look of frightened prey, and his mind seemed to be occupied with other thoughts.

* * * * *

Alias dashed up the stairs three at a time and burst out on the roof of the tower just in time to see Victor pull Thistle into a magical portal hanging in the sky beside the tower. The swordswoman leaped up on the battle-ment and stepped onto the bridge leading to the portal. At that moment the bridge began to retract, knocking Alias from her feet. She grabbed hold of the end of the bridge and hung on for dear life, knowing better than to look at the ground hundreds of feet down.

When the end of the bridge came within a yard of the portal, Alias swung herself backward into the planar pocket with only moments to spare before the bridge vanished. The portal snapped shut behind her tumbling form.

The swordswoman gasped and choked as she breathed in the mists drifting along the floor. The vapors shone with a yellow radiance and smelled like sulfur. They swirled so thickly, they obscured the floor. Alias could see no walls, and overhead there was only darkness.

A few feet away, Dragonbait stood as alert as a hunting cat. The tip of his tail and the tip of his sword twitched in nervous apprehension. Alias noticed that the mists, which swirled about her legs, seemed to swerve away from the paladin.

Victor, clutching Thistle about the waist, stood off to one side of the portal. He tore the feather brooch from Thistle's gown and slid it into a pocket of his robe. Alias stumbled to her feet and moved toward the girl, but she halted when she saw the dagger Victor pointed at Thistle's throat.

"Where is the treasure?" the croamarkh demanded.

"What difference does it make, Victor?" Alias snapped. "You're never getting away with it."

Victor smiled slyly at the swordswoman. "No one knows where I am. No one saw us enter here. In a few hours they'll have given up the search, and I can leave with Thistle. "You and Dragonbait, though, will have to remain within. Might as well get used to it."

Alias glared at the nobleman, desiring vengeance more than ever. The man had tried to take her life only hours after proffering his love. If not for Mintassan, she and Dragonbait would both have been dead. Mintassan and Dragonbait had counseled her against killing the noble, and she had agreed to turn Victor over to Durgar. Now, however, seeing him threaten yet one more innocent, Alias wanted to tear the nobleman's heart out. Yet she realized she had to remain cool.

"Why don't you let Thistle go?" the swordswoman suggested. "You don't need a hostage now that you've escaped."

"But I need to keep you and your lizard friend in

check," he argued, pulling the girl closer to him.

Alias noted that at least now there was nothing in Thistle's eyes but contempt for the nobleman. The girl maintained a dignified silence.

Dragonbait began moving deeper into the planar pocket.

"Where are you going?" Alias asked.

"I sense evil everywhere," the paladin explained in Saurial, "but there is a stronger mass in this direction."

"Don't we want to stay away from anything like that?" Alias demanded.

"There is not much point to that now that we are in this place," the paladin replied solemnly. He continued onward.

Alias followed after the saurial. Behind her she heard Victor ask again, "Where is the treasure?"

"Maybe there isn't any, Victor," Alias taunted. "Perhaps the Thalavar clan frittered it away over the past century."

"No, Grandmother said no one had ever touched it," Thistle replied. "It must be here."

Alias rolled her eyes, wishing the girl had been savvy enough to agree, or at least say nothing. Then the swordswoman halted in her tracks. She had come upon an island in the sea of mists, a great glowing yellow sphere, larger than a man. Just beneath the surface of the sphere, misty shapes writhed and flowed. The swordswoman reached out and touched the sphere's surface. It was as smooth as glass and warm to the touch.

"It's a giant pearl," Thistle whispered.

Dragonbait stepped out from behind the sphere. He spoke to Alias in Saurial. "At its core I sense great greed."

"The piece of Verovan's soul?" Alias guessed.

"Probably," the paladin replied.

"What's surrounding it?" the swordswoman asked.

Dragonbait pointed to the mist on the floor. "A pearl might actually be a good analogy," he said. "The soul shard is like a piece of grit in an oyster. These creatures have coalesced around it to soothe the irritation it causes them," Dragonbait replied.

Alias looked down at the mist. "You mean this mist stuff is living creatures?"

"Unformed manes," the paladin whispered.

Alias swallowed hard. She would have leaped above the mist if there had been anywhere to leap to. "Manes? Are you sure?" she asked in Common.

Dragonbait gave her an aggrieved look. To remind her that he was an authority on evil would be to state the obvious.

"Manes?" Victor asked. "What's a mane?"

"They're what the lord of the Abyss sent to loot Verovan's treasure," Thistle explained.

"But what are they?" Victor growled.

"The form the dead take in the Abyss," Alias explained. "Dragonbait says the mist is unformed manes."

Victor whirled about, dragging Thistle with him, as if he could shake the mist away. Alias noted there was considerably more of it drifting about the nobleman than around herself.

"Why so uncomfortable, Victor? That's what you'll end up as when you die," Alias declared. Dragonbait made some comments in Saurial, and the swordswoman chuckled. "Pardon me, Victor," she said. "Dragonbait says you are not chaotic enough to end as a mane in the Abyss. More likely, you will be a lemure in Baator, though it is possible you will become a larva, since your selfishness is so great."

"Why are the manes unformed?" Thistle asked in an anxious whisper.

Alias listened to Dragonbait's reply in Saurial, then translated. "They have existed in this place for over a century with nothing but a bit of Verovan's soul to gnaw on. So they've gone misty to conserve their energy. As soon as they sense there's something here to devour, they'll begin to take shape."

"They'll eat us?" Thistle asked with a whine in her voice, her sophistication finally crumbling beneath the weight of her fear.

"Don't be ridiculous," Victor snapped. "She is making all this up. Trying to get me to leave so I can be captured.

I want to know what's happened to the treasure," he demanded.

The saurial tapped his sword on the floor.

"Dragonbait says we're standing on it," Alias explained. Curiously, she knelt beside the saurial, where the mists were thinner, and examined the floor. "He's right," she replied. With her dagger she pried up a brick of solid gold and held it out for the others to see. "The floor's paved with these, and there's another layer beneath this one. I wonder how many layers."

Victor motioned Alias and Dragonbait to move back. Dragging Thistle down with him, he knelt on the floor and investigated for himself. He pulled up a second brick of gold and stuffed it into a pocket of his robe. He smiled coldly as he stood up. Bits of mane mist clung to his back and swirled now as high as his hips, but the nobleman did not seem to notice.

Alias exchanged a look with the paladin. She was tempted to say nothing, but Thistle was still the nobleman's hostage, and what endangered him endangered her.

"Victor, are you going to wait for those things to draw first blood before you come to your senses?" the swordswoman asked, pointing to the mists swirling about the nobleman. "Let Thistle open the portal so we can get out of here before we're eaten alive."

"I am not some foolish peasant you can deceive with your adventurer faerie tales," Victor snapped. "It is just mist." A strand of mist swirled about the nobleman's head. Victor swatted at it irritably, then tried to back away from it. His eyes widened, and Alias saw fear in them. He seemed to be struggling to move.

It was Thistle who verbalized the problem. "My legs!" she shrieked. "Something's holding on to my legs!"

Victor let out a scream as though he'd been hurt. He released Thistle and slashed with his dagger at the mists about his legs.

Alias seized the opportunity. She threw herself at Thistle and managed to jerk the girl away from both Victor and whatever was holding her. The swordswoman and noblewoman tumbled backward on the floor. They came to their feet, choking on the mist, but free of Dhostar.

Dragonbait moved forward to help the nobleman, but Victor straightened, thrusting out his dagger to warn him back.

The paladin snarled and stepped back. The mist still seemed to be evading him, so Alias pushed Thistle in his direction. Then she turned to deal with Victor.

The nobleman backed away, apparently having stabbed to death whatever had hindered his movement. There was blood on his hands and dagger, but some of it, Alias suspected, was the nobleman's own. "Victor, we can't stay here any longer. Give Thistle the key," she ordered.

Victor smiled coldly. "Not a chance," he said.

"Victor, we could be swarming in manes any minute. We can't fight them all. We'll die. *You'll* die."

"You've destroyed everything I have worked years for. At least I'll have the satisfaction of knowing I had my vengeance on you, bitch."

Alias shook with fury. She drew her sword and took a step in his direction. "You can give me that key, or I can slice you in half and loot it from your body."

Victor pulled the feather brooch from the pocket of his robe and held it up. Alias reached her hand out. The nobleman laughed, and flung the brooch away. The piece of jewelry arced over Dragonbait and Thistle and disappeared into the mists. It made a tiny clatter when it hit the floor.

"You've gone mad," Alias growled. To Dragonbait and Thistle she said, "You'd better start looking for it. Hurry. I'll keep Dhostar still." She raised the tip of her sword to the nobleman's throat.

Dragonbait took Thistle's hand and led her in the direction Victor had thrown the brooch.

"Maybe you should give them a hand," Victor joked.

Alias kept her sword leveled at the villain's throat.

"Then again," the nobleman said with a smirk, "I don't suppose that will be necessary anymore."

Behind her Alias heard a hiss, then a growl. Alias

whirled around and backed up quickly so that Victor would be at her left hand instead of her back. Advancing toward her was a halfling-sized creature with pale white skin, a bloated torso, and razor-sharp claws and teeth. Pus dripped from its mindless white eyes.

Alias waited until the mane was just within reach of her sword. With a single stroke, she cleaved the Abyssal creature in two, and it dissipated back into a stinking mist. Alias gagged from the stench.

"My, how valorous," Victor taunted.

Alias did not reply. Her attention was focused on the hoard of creatures rising from the mists, all as disgusting as the first. Ten, twenty, thirty, she counted to herself, knowing there would be more.

"Too bad it's vaporized," the noble continued. "You could have had it mounted—show off your—" Victor went silent.

Alias sensed the nobleman backing away.

"Dhostar, stay at my back," she barked. "It's our only chance."

Whether Victor chose to abandon the swordswoman or simply panicked, Alias would never know. Whichever it was, the nobleman turned and ran. Alias glanced over her shoulder and saw him trip and fall into the mist.

More manes rose up, surrounding the downed noble, then leaped upon him, rending his flesh with their claws and teeth. Alias had turned away to keep her eyes on the larger hoard of manes approaching her, but Victor's screams filled the air all around the swordswoman. The nobleman's death gave her no satisfaction, but neither did she feel any regret.

With ice in her heart, she charged a flank of the manes, swinging her sword fast and hard, felling instantly each creature she struck. They were not tremendously powerful monsters, but Alias knew better than to be heartened by her victories. They could reform again within a day. The real strength of manes, however, lay in their numbers and their mindless compulsion to attack regardless of any danger to themselves. It was only a matter of time before enough manes formed to overwhelm her. She could choke on the poisonous vapors of their dissipating corpses, or slip on a patch of their slick blood and find herself beneath a mound of their bodies, or just grow exhausted and fall unconscious.

The longer she kept the monsters interested in herself, though, the longer Dragonbait and Thistle would have to find the feather brooch so they could escape.

As the manes closed in on her, Alias worked at felling their flanks so that she could not be surrounded. She was beginning to regret that they did not remain corporeal. She could have used their bodies to make a defensive wall.

In the nightmare of endless slaughter Alias began to lose track of time. A few of the beasts had managed to evade her sword long enough to slash at her back and arms or sink their teeth into her legs. The wounds were all minor, but they burned like fire. She tried not to think about how much she was bleeding.

Then came the moment she knew she was doomed. Her legs would not move—something held them frozen. She slashed downward with her sword, but the blade *thunked* against something hard at her hips. She looked down to find herself encased, just as the shard of Verovan's soul had been, by the mist of unformed manes, which had hardened into a pearl-like shell.

The swordswoman switched her weapon from hand to hand, trying to keep the manes from reaching either side of her body, but she was blind at her back. One of the monsters sunk its teeth into the back of her neck, and it took her several awkward stabs before she managed to dislodge it.

"Alias!" Dragonbait shouted.

Alias twisted her head, her heart pounding with hope at the sound of the paladin's call.

The paladin came rushing toward her, his sword blazing with fire, cutting down manes like a farmer scything hay. Once at her side, he wheeled to protect her back. "We found the key and opened the portal. I sent Thistle out. I think the sooner we leave, the better."

"I'm stuck," Alias explained, "like the piece of Verovan's

soul."

Dragonbait tapped on the casing about the swordswoman's legs.

"I didn't know manes could go hard like this," Alias said.

"The manes that make up this mist are not like ordinary manes. This planar pocket, or the years they spent trapped in here away from the Abyss, has altered them," Dragonbait said. He smashed his sword against the casing, without effect. The scent of violets wafted from the saurial's throat—the scent of his fear.

"Alias, listen carefully," the paladin ordered. "These manes are hungry for more than your flesh. They want to devour your essence—your spirit and your soul. But they can only do that if they can find a weakness—" The paladin paused to slash through another wave of manes, then continued. "They look for open wounds on your soul and spirit and drink from them like flies. You have to rid yourself of those things that make you bleed inside—"

"What's going on?" Mintassan's voice called out. The sage was drifting across the mists, flying just high enough to remain out of reach of the manes. "Lady Thistle's outside, holding the portal open. She said you might need some help."

"Can you teleport us out of here?" Alias asked.

"Afraid not—something in the makeup of this plane resists alteration magic," the sage explained. Upon spying the shell surrounding Alias's legs, he gave a low whistle. "That looks bad. Perhaps it can be dispelled," he suggested.

Dragonbait shook his head. "It's not magical. It would be more use if you could circle us with protection from evil," he said.

The sage must have already cast a spell to understand Saurial, for he immediately began circling the warriors, casting the protection spell Dragonbait had asked for. When he'd finished, the manes all began moving away. They lingered at the edge of Mintassan's magic boundary, waiting for it to dissipate. The mist, too, flowed out of the circle of protection. The shell about Alias's legs, however, remained.

Trying desperately to conceal his own anxiety, Dragonbait spoke as calmly as he could. "Concentrate on your feelings," he instructed Alias. "Clear your heart of everything that poisons it. Verovan's soul was cut by his greed, Victor's by his lust for power."

"Victor's dead," Alias said softly. "The manes got him."

"I know," the paladin replied. He did not mention that he could feel the man's evil spirit hovering nearby, no doubt waiting to witness the swordswoman's death. "You have to let go of your anger and hatred for Victor Dhostar."

Alias did not reply immediately. She didn't know how to tell the paladin that she didn't wish to do as he bid her. She cherished her anger and hatred of the nobleman. Victor had deceived her in the worst way. She had every right to be angry, to hate him.

The saurial sighed, realizing how hard it must be for Alias to give up the powerful emotions. They had fastened themselves so strongly to her essence that losing them would feel like losing herself. She could not accept that there was so much more to her being than these poisonous, wounding feelings. He ran his fingertips down the brand on her sword arm, trying to kindle a spark of the link that bound their souls together.

Alias shivered at the paladin's touch. She could sense his great serenity, his compassion, his tenderness and concern. She knew, though, that she was nothing like him, would never be, could never be as good. There were times she wished she were, but wishing did not make it so.

Dragonbait looked up suddenly at the manes massing behind Alias. He could feel their evil darkening, growing more powerful.

Alias struggled, but she remained trapped in the mist shell.

"Alias, please," the paladin begged. "Let it go. I know you can do it."

"I can't," the swordswoman snapped. "I've tried."

"You can!" Dragonbait snapped back.

"No, I can't!"

"She doesn't dare," Mintassan interjected. "It's her only protection."

"Protection?" Dragonbait growled. "It's trapped her in this evil place. How is that protection?"

"If she gives up her anger and hatred, there's nothing left but bitterness and despair," the sage pointed out. "Why would she want to feel them?"

The paladin nodded. Bitterness, the shadow of anger, and despair, the evil without a color. He wasn't very familiar with them, so he'd forgotten them both. Mintassan knew them though, intimately.

"Alias, what Mintassan says is true. You're holding onto the anger and hate because you're afraid of the bitterness and despair. You know they'll hurt you even more. But you can shed them, too. Trust me."

"I am not bitter and despairing!" Alias shouted. "I'm just stuck in a damned rock. Go get Durgar. Maybe he's got some priest prayer that can break this thing open."

Behind Alias the mist was taking on a serpent shape, and the serpent was rising up. "Alias, there isn't time," the paladin insisted. "Your life depends on it. Let them go."

"I have no reason to be bitter or despairing," Alias argued. "Victor was a monster, and I'm well rid of him. He wasn't worthy of my love. I know that."

"It's not the loss of that worthless man that brings you pain," Mintassan said. "It's the loss of the love you felt. *Your* love was good, and when it died, it left you empty."

The mist serpent began winding around the border of the spell of protection.

Alias glared at Mintassan. "I don't have time for stupid conversations with sages. What do you know about my love? You don't know anything except what you read in your dusty old tomes."

"Oh, don't I?" Mintassan replied, holding her eyes with his own. "Do you think it was easy for me watching someone I cared about fling herself at someone as unworthy as Victor Dhostar."

Alias felt as if the wind had been knocked out of her, as

if she'd run into a wall of understanding. When she'd first arrived, the sage had cared less about Westgate than she had, but for some reason he'd been there to save her life. Then he'd thrown himself into her quest for vengeance. Now he stood in this stinking, gods-forsaken, evil-ridden pit of a planar pocket arguing with her.

The swordswoman flushed with embarrassment. Why did he have to tell her this?

"So the question is," Mintassan said, "if the lowly sage survived his battle against bitterness and despair, why won't the great warrior woman risk battling them, too?"

Alias squeezed her eyes shut, trying to keep tears from falling out of them. Mintassan was right. She missed her love. It had made her feel warm and safe and happy.

But she could feel those things without it. She knew she could. Besides—she might even love again—maybe.

Dragonbait sighed with relief as the shell of mane mist began to melt from Alias's legs and drift away from the adventurers.

"What in Mystra's name is that?" Mintassan whispered, finally noticing the serpentlike evil wrapped about the circle of protection and hovering over them.

"The manes have found a focus," the paladin said, "a leader to organize their attack."

Alias spun around and looked up at the serpent of mist. She looked into its bright blue eyes. She gasped. "It's Victor!"

"Move toward the portal," the paladin instructed, taking Alias's arm. "The circle of protection should move with us."

As the three adventurers shifted their position, the serpent hissed with anger, but it uncoiled and let them pass, unable to withstand the magical constraints of Mintassan's spell. It followed them to the portal, devouring mist as it moved, growing larger and darker.

The portal loomed ahead like a hole of darkness. Dragonbait stepped out onto the bridge and held his hand to Alias.

As Alias stepped into the night sky over Westgate, she took a deep breath of the cool air and laughed. Mintassan flew out from the portal and swooped over the bridge.

Dragonbait gasped and spun about. His *shen* sight suddenly perceived a hundredfold increase in the evil emanating from the mane serpent. Mintassan's circle of protection had dissipated when he had flown through the portal. The serpent wavered over Alias's head and struck before the paladin could pull her out of danger.

From the top of the tower, Jamal, Olive, Thistle, and Durgar watched in horror as a huge, dark serpent swung down over Alias and coiled around her body. Dragonbait thrust his fiery blade into the creature, and Alias stabbed at it with her sword. Little bits of glowing mist seeped from the creature wherever it was hit, but the beast remained intact, healing over the cuts almost immediately with some otherworldly power. Mintassan hovered over the beast and sent five magic missiles shooting into the creature's hide, but they passed right through the monster and fell to the ground.

The serpent brought its head down to survey the warrior woman in its embrace. Noxious poison dripped from its fangs. It opened its jaw and brushed its tongue along her face. It was toying with her before it devoured her—lording its power over her, just as Victor had when he had embraced and kissed her poison-paralyzed body.

"Close the gate!" Olive shouted to Thistle.

"If I do that, the bridge will collapse. They'll fall to their deaths," the girl argued.

"Durgar, Lady Thistle said the place was full of manes. Aren't they some sort of undead?" Jamal asked. "Maybe this thing is, too. Use your power to turn it away."

Durgar looked exceedingly doubtful of the actress's suggestion, but he began a prayer, nonetheless, asking Tyr to compel the monster to flee.

"It's working!" Olive shouted.

The serpent began to turn translucent, all except the tongue, which took the shape of a man and fell from the monster's mouth to the ground far below. The body of the serpent began to turn to mist, which drifted quickly back through the portal.

Unfortunately, the part of the serpent that had been

coiled about Alias was no longer over the bridge. As the coils dissipated, the swordswoman fell with a shriek toward the ground—

To be caught by the arm by a flying sage.

Mintassan set the swordswoman down on the roof of the tower just as Dragonbait stepped off the bridge. They turned to watch the last of the mist escape through the portal, fleeing from the power of Durgar's god. Thistle flung the brooch across the bridge and into the portal. The bridge retreated and disappeared, then the portal snapped shut, leaving the top of the tower in darkness.

Olive leaned over the battlement and stared down at the ground. Members of the watch held torches aloft as they surveyed the dark shape that had fallen to the ground from the top of the tower.

"It's Lord Victor!" one of the watch shouted.

"He's dead! He just fell from the tower!" another guard cried out.

"No," Olive whispered to Jamal, "he fell a long time ago."

## Twenty-Five
# Curtain Call

The day after Lord Victor Dhostar, Croamarkh of Westgate, was found dead at the base of the southernmost tower of Castle Vhammos, Mintassan the Sage held a private tea party to celebrate with four close friends. The Faceless was dead; the Night Masters and many of the Night Masks had been killed or captured. The deadly magic once at their disposal had been destroyed. Citizens of Westgate were tossing the remaining bullies and thieves into the harbor. They had a lot to celebrate.

Mintassan sat at the head of the table in his workroom with Jamal the Thespian and Olive Ruskettle on his left and Alias the Sell-Sword and Dragonbait the Paladin on his right. The boy Kel had been banished to an upper room to work on learning his letters with his new tutor, Mercy. The former Night Mask had accepted his and the half-elven girl's banishment with such grace that it caused Olive to mutter, "Who's teaching whom, and what's being taught?"

After taking a sip from her mismatched mug of tea, sweetened with five sugar cubes, Olive returned to her interrogation of the conspirators, as she had come to call Alias, Dragonbait, and Mintassan. "So let's see if I have this straight finally," the halfling said. "After Kimbel shot Dragonbait and kidnapped him, Mintassan followed Kimbel and knocked Kimbel out. How'd you get the drop on an assassin as sharp as Kimbel?"

"My superior tactics and skill with weaponry," the sage said.

*He was invisible when he snuck up on Kimbel. He hit him on the head with a rock,* Dragonbait signed in the thieves' hand cant.

Jamal laughed. "Then you rescued Dragonbait, polymorphed Kimbel into yourself and yourself into Kimbel and feebleminded Kimbel, all so you could find out what Victor was up to."

Mintassan nodded. "Yes. Actually the double polymorph and feeblemind was Dragonbait's idea."

"Figures," Olive said. "Paladin's are a sneaky lot, and Dragonbait's the sneakiest of the sneaky."

"You stayed in character pretty well," Jamal noted as she poured a hefty dose of brandy into her tea. "Especially considering Dhostar brought you a dying Alias. You must have some acting blood in you after all."

"If I had known at the time that Dhostar was the Faceless, that he was upstairs poisoning Alias," the sage said softly, "I would have come up and stopped him without bothering to stay in character. Fortunately, knowing the Faceless had iron golems at his disposal, I had actually prepared a slow poison spell."

"Because iron golems sometimes breath poison gas," Alias explained.

"But the golems at the ball were the cheap Thayan kind, so they didn't," Olive noted. "Then you faked Alias's death with a phony tattooed arm. Where did you get the arm?" the halfling asked.

"Ham hock with a polymorph spell cast on it," Mintassan said. "Before that, though, came the hardest part of the plan."

"What?"

"Convincing Alias not to go storming up into Castle Dhostar and run Lord Victor through with a sword."

"But why did you turn her into a halfling?" Olive insisted.

"Because it fit in with our plan," Alias said. "When I recovered from the poison, I told Mintassan about all the things Victor had ever said to me. Learning of Victor's fascination with Verovan's hoard gave Mintassan an idea. He knew Lady Nettel's brooch was the key to the hoard—"

"You knew about Verovan's hoard?" Olive exclaimed.

"For about eight years," the sage answered.

"And you never did anything about it?"

Mintassan shrugged. "I don't need gold."

"Bite your tongue!" the halfling demanded. "Such blasphemy. As if it isn't bad enough that Thistle threw the key back into the portal so that no one can ever reach all that gold again."

"She was also making sure the manes didn't escape, Olive."

"To get back to your plan," Jamal insisted. "You knew Victor would go after Thistle, so you became a halfling to help protect her, since House Thalavar trusts halflings and hires them," Jamal guessed.

"Yes," Alias said. "Although I didn't do a very good job. Thistle fired me. I guess I didn't make a very good halfling."

"You weren't so bad," Olive critiqued. "A little too bossy and crabby."

"Well, I did use you for a model, Olive," Alias pointed out.

Olive did not comment on the swordswoman's claim. Instead she asked, "Why couldn't you tell me, though?"

"And me," Jamal seconded, glaring at Mintassan.

"I'm really sorry, Jamal," the sage apologized. "But at first we didn't realize how much Dhostar relied on Kimbel for all his information. If Dhostar had other spies watching the two of you, he might have learned you weren't really grieving. I made sure Blais House had room for you before I followed Dhostar's order to evict you from my house. As it turned out, Victor left everything to Kimbel. He trusted me alone in the Faceless's secret lair. I was able to use a wand of cancellation on all the Night Masks' magic. That's also how I managed to get so much damning evidence on Victor and the Night Masters. I needed it, too. Durgar was hard to convince. He insisted on interrogating Dragonbait, too, using another mage as a translator."

"But Durgar still isn't willing to admit Victor was the

Faceless," Jamal said with disgust.

"No. He admits Victor's guilt," Mintassan replied. "He just doesn't want the rest of Westgate to know. He's afraid it will cause unrest."

"Well, it certainly makes me unrestful," Jamal growled. "He put the fox in charge of the henhouse."

"So Durgar is going to stick to the story that Victor died trying to find Verovan's hoard in order to make Westgate a better city?" Alias asked. "Why is Thistle letting him do that?"

"Thistle has her own agenda," Olive said, "as does a certain actress who had agreed to go along with the tale."

Alias looked at Jamal in surprise.

"Thistle is going to get Durgar elected the interim croamarkh. Thistle and I like the idea of the interim croamarkh owing us a big favor," Jamal explained with a grin.

"Why?" Alias asked suspiciously.

"The noble houses are in disarray. This is the time to push for giving the people political power. Before the end of the year I intend to see that every man and woman in this city has a vote."

"Everyone? Halflings, too?" Olive asked.

"Oh, really! She's not that crazy," Mintassan said. He threw up his hands to ward off the looks he received from both the halfling and the actress. "Just kidding. Didn't mean it."

"Thistle has agreed to grant votes for other merchants and small shopkeepers and craftsmen, artisans and scholars," Jamal explained. "I'll talk her around to the rest. Back, though, to the conspirators," Jamal insisted. "Did you ever find out why Victor hired you to go after himself? Wasn't he taking an awful risk?"

Alias looked at Mintassan. The sage leaned back in his chair. "According to information Durgar gleaned from Kimbel, Victor was very concerned about rumors that the Harpers wanted to clean the Night Masks out of Westgate."

"Harpers?" Olive asked.

"Harpers," Mintassan explained. "They're this semisecret

organization who're supposed to work for good—"

"Yes. I know all that," Olive said. "What do they have to do with it?"

"Nothing, as far as I know," Mintassan replied. "But Victor learned that Alias had connections to them."

"The Nameless Bard was her father," Olive said.

"Yes, she told me," Jamal answered.

"But she's not really a Harper," Olive said.

"Well, when Alias started fighting with Night Masks her very first evening in Westgate, Victor thought she must be a Harper agent," the sage explained.

"But why hire her?"

"Because with the magical misdirection that's cast on her, Victor couldn't scry on her. If he hired her, she would report right to him. He was careful to make it look like Luer's idea."

"You still look puzzled, Olive," Alias noted.

"Well, I'm just wondering about the rumors Victor heard. It wasn't me the Harpers sent to Westgate. I came down here for some time away from them. I hadn't even heard they had any interest in the area. I wonder who else is down here."

"Why would the Harpers send someone to Westgate when they have a perfectly good agent here already?" Jamal asked. She flipped up her collar to reveal a silver moon-and-harp pin.

Olive's eyes widened, and she laughed. "So now that you've taken care of the Night Masks, where are the Harpers going to send you?" she asked.

"You misunderstand," Jamal said. "I've assigned myself to Westgate. My next assignment is making sure everyone in this city is given political power."

"Jamal is like you, Olive," Alias said. "Finder befriended her when he was in Westgate and pinned her before she knew what she was getting into. You aren't the only rogue Harper."

Olive laughed. "Finder always did have a soft spot for trouble-making redheads."

"I was actually hoping you might assign yourself here," Jamal said to Olive. "We can make our own little rogue contingent."

"Now that has possibilities," Olive said. "What about you, Alias? I know Dragonbait wants to get back to the Lost Vale, but your name will carry some weight in this town for years to come. Interested in politics?"

"Thank you, Olive, but no. I've had my fill of Westgate for a while," Alias said with a smile. "I'm heading north to the Lost Vale."

"Too bad. Well, we'll still have Mintassan. He can be our honorary advisor, like Elminster the Sage is for the big boys up north."

Mintassan coughed politely. "I'm afraid not, Mistress Ruskettle. I've got a few adventures planned away from the city."

"Where to this year?" Jamal asked. "Beastlands? Arcadia? Astral?"

"Lost Vale," the sage replied.

"Why?" Olive asked. "There's nothing there but saurials."

Dragonbait chuckled.

"Alias asked me to visit," the sage said.

"Dragonbait and I could use a mage when we travel," Alias explained. "And Mintassan wants to learn more about saurials."

In the alcove, Mintassan's tea kettle whistled.

"Be right back," the sage promised, heading toward the back of the workshop.

"Let me give you a hand," Alias offered, following him.

"She's taking away our honorary advisor," Olive pouted.

"Yes," Jamal said with a mock frown.

Dragonbait drained much of his tea and set it down on the table. He knocked for attention. *Haven't they both just taken care of the Night Masks for you Harpers?* he signed.

"Yes," both women agreed grudgingly.

*Shouldn't they both be rewarded?*

Jamal and Olive nodded.

"I move that Alias and Mintassan be allowed to adventure happily ever after," Jamal said.

"I second that motion," Olive agreed.

"All in favor?"

Two hands and a reptile claw went up.

"Any opposed? No. Motion carried," Jamal announced.

\* \* \* \* \*

In the alcove, Alias stirred tea into the pot as Mintassan poured the hot water.

The sage leaned forward; the swordswoman leaned forward; their lips hovered inches apart.

Unable to contain the giddy feeling inside her, Alias turned her head away and giggled.

Mintassan scowled. "Are you sure you want my company?" he asked, trying to hide his fear that she was laughing at him.

Alias looked back at the sage. Light danced in her eyes, and she smiled. "I'm sure," she said.

The sage grinned and leaned toward the swordswoman, and they began the dance again.